A CERTAIN SMILE

Also by Judith Michael

Acts of Love
A Tangled Web
Pot of Gold
Sleeping Beauty
A Ruling Passion
Inheritance
Private Affairs
Possessions
Deceptions

JUDITH MICHAEL

A Certain Smile

DOUBLEDAY DIRECT LARGE PRINT EDITION

Crown Publishers, Inc.

New York

This Large Print Edition, prepared especially for Doubleday Direct, Inc., contains the complete unabridged text of the original Publisher's Edition.

Published by Crown Publishers, 201 East 50th Street, New York, New York 10022. Member of the Crown Publishing Group.

Random House, Inc. New York, Toronto, London, Sydney, Auckland
www.randomhouse.com

CROWN is a trademark and C + SUN Design is a registered trademark of Random House, Inc.

Printed in the United States of America

ISBN 0-7394-0283-8

OO B644

In memory of
David N. Schramm

Because I could not stop for Death
He kindly stopped for me—
The Carriage held but just Ourselves—
And Immortality.

—EMILY DICKINSON
Time and Eternity

Acknowledgments

We are grateful to Xiangdong Shi, Liang Feng, Xiaochun Luo, and Yaping Chen for their generosity in helping us with our research on contemporary China. Special thanks go to Diane Perushek, scholar and friend, who was unstinting in her help with everything from information on the Chinese State Security Bureau to renovated courtyard houses to cursing in Mandarin. To them goes credit for the accuracy of details in this book; any errors are our own.

Finally, we want to express our thanks to Janet McDonald for her superb copyediting.

A CERTAIN SMILE

Chapter 1

Miranda Graham and Yuan Li met in the Beijing airport when he appeared out of nowhere to rescue her from the shoving, elbowing crowds buffeting her on all sides. She was stuck in the taxi line just outside the terminal, pinned there while others thrust in front of her, indifferently pushing and knocking against her as she struggled to stay close to her suitcase. Assaulted by the high-pitched, incessant din, she shrank from the press of strange bodies, feeling helpless and suddenly afraid.

This can't be happening; I'm in one of

the world's biggest airports; there's nothing to be afraid of; no one is going to hurt me.

But they don't like Americans and nobody smiles or gives me any space . . . they walk right into me, as if they want to knock me down . . .

She knew that was ridiculous, but she felt threatened and alone, and she had not moved an inch in ten minutes. I could be here all night, she thought, and never get to my hotel. I've got to do something; what do people do to get anywhere in this country?

And that was when Li appeared, standing out from the crowd, taller than those around him, coming close to put a hand on her shoulder. Alarmed, she jerked from his touch, but there was no place to move, and so she shrank into herself, tucking her head away from him.

"Please, let me help you," he said, and she was so astonished to hear English, clear and perfect, that she straightened up, staring at him. He was smiling. "At this rate, you'll be here all night, and never get to your hotel." Her eyes widened in surprise, but he did not notice; he had hung her garment bag over his arm and was bending to pick up her suitcase. Then, holding her arm and using his body like a wedge, he plowed through the crowd. As it melted before him, he grinned at her, like a small boy triumphant over obstructive adults. "You simply pretend they are not there. It is the only way to survive in China. And now," he said as they reached a taxi at the head of the line, "I will accompany you to the city, to make sure you reach your hotel."

"Oh, no. No." The thought of getting into a car with a foreigner was almost as terrifying as the crowds had been. "Thank you for helping me, you've been very kind, but I can manage; I have the name of my hotel written in Chinese . . . the driver can read it . . . I'll be just fine."

He nodded. "I will not push myself upon you if you insist, but I've found that it is always good to have help when you make a beginning in a strange place." The driver had stowed Miranda's suitcase and garment bag, and was gazing phlegmatically at the impatient customers waiting for the next taxi. "I am going into the city anyway," Li said. "It won't be off of my way to do this."

"Out of," she corrected automatically. "It won't be out of your way." Perhaps it was his small mistake in English that made her feel less intimidated, or perhaps the exhaustion of twenty-two hours of travel, but finally it just seemed simpler to give in and get in the taxi with him.

Sitting beside her, he took a tiny cellular phone from his pocket and spoke briefly into it in Chinese. Folding it with a sharp snap, he returned it to his pocket, and settled back beside Miranda.

Cringing again, she shrank into the corner of the back seat, pushing herself against the cracked leather, telling herself that she was a fool. She knew nothing about this man, not even his name. What if he and the taxi driver were a team? Maybe they did this all the time: kidnapped women traveling alone, and killed them if a ransom were not paid, or paid quickly enough. Probably he had just made arrangements on the telephone with some cohorts, lying in wait. Why hadn't she thought of that before?

"My name is Yuan Li," he said, and smiled, a warm, open smile that Miranda would swear had no ulterior motive. He held out his hand. "I'm pleased to meet you."

"Miranda Graham." She gave him a quick glance as her hand came up to meet his. He had a nice face, and his handshake was firm and brief. "Thank you again for rescuing me."

"I was pleased that I could help."

Involuntarily, her glance went to his pocket, where his cellular phone lay hidden.

"I called my driver," he said briefly, "to tell him to take my car home."

She nodded, embarrassed that she was so transparent, embarrassed that she felt so relieved, embarrassed at being so inexperienced.

But she was not a traveler. Until now, except for brief trips concentrating only on business, she had never turned a gaze of curiosity and adventure outward from her home: the leafy college town of Boulder, tucked into the Colorado foothills, where everything was familiar. Now, unbelievably, she was on the other side of the world, in a city where she knew no one, where she could not understand a word the people were saying. "Impossible," she murmured as the taxi passed an incomprehensible highway sign. "I won't be able to make sense of billboards or street names, stores, menus—"

"But in many places you can," Li said. "Hotel restaurants have menus in English. Street signs are spelled out in your alphabet, so you can find your way around with a map. And in areas popular with tourists, you will find store clerks and waiters who speak English, often quite well."

She flushed with shame. She was an American citizen on a business trip; she should never let anyone know that she felt helpless. "I'll be all right," she said coolly.

"I'm sure you will." His smile seemed tolerant of her inexperience, and in an instant she disliked him. He had seemed pleasant, but everyone knew that foreigners, especially Asians, were usually untrustworthy. I don't need him, she thought, or anybody else in China. I don't have time for friends, anyway; I only have eight days here. I'll be busy every minute, and then I'll be gone. She watched lighted windows flash past in block after block of identical five-story concrete apartment buildings.

Soon, the windows became larger, giving fleeting glimpses into apartments in newer buildings, until they gave way to skyscrapers, to a strange amalgam of modern office buildings towering over squat, darkened structures that looked liked relics of another time. And then, suddenly, in a narrow, crowded street, they stopped at her hotel.

It was named the Palace, hinting at fairytale romances and heroes and heroines, but in fact it was sleek, modern and anonymous, with a spacious lobby displaying the *Wall Street Journal* and the *International Herald Tribune* on tables and newspaper racks, a tuxedoed staff speaking impeccable English, a swimming pool and health club, two nightclubs and a restaurant. I could almost be in America, Miranda thought, and immediately felt better.

And better still when Li said goodbye in front of the hotel, and drove off in the taxi they had shared. He had been so casual that she had felt a moment of pique, but then she remembered that she was glad to be rid of him, and a moment later, dealing with the bellhop, and registering, and making sure her luggage got upstairs, she for-got him completely.

In her suite, she turned slowly in place, awed at its elegance. The draperies were of heavy silk doubly and triply embroidered in many-colored threads; the chairs and sofa in the sitting room were rosewood with silk cushions; a rosewood breakfront filled one wall, its shelves arranged with translucent porcelain vases and a celadon tea set. The wide bed was covered with a silk spread appliquéd with lotus flowers, and on the lower shelves of the rosewood nightstands were slippers with padded soles and a strip of beautiful woven paper across the instep. Porcelain table lamps cast soft light on the patterned carpet, and the bed had been turned down for the night. Miranda took it all in, then, light-headed from fatigue and new sensations, she pulled her nightgown from her suit-case and slipped into bed. It was eleven o'clock on a late September night in Bei-jing, China, and in five minutes she was asleep.

At eight o'clock the next morning, Yuan Li called. Miranda had been up since six-thirty; she had found the hotel swimming pool by using sign language to ask directions of maids, had found her way back to her room after a swim, and had showered and dressed. By the time the telephone rang she was feeling fairly triumphant. Still, there was a shock of pleasure and relief at hearing a familiar voice. "I thought there might be some way I could help you on your first day in Beijing," he said.

His voice was warm and easygoing, and she forgot her fears of the night before. It was odd to have him take an interest in her when so few men did, but in a place where everything was new she had no time to wonder about each strange thing that happened. "I was just going to find some breakfast," she said.

"I'll meet you downstairs."

He was waiting across the lobby when she stepped from the elevator, and for a moment she stayed out of sight, studying him. He was tall and very lean, his face dark, thin, somber, with sharp cheekbones, a thin nose, and heavy straight brows above narrow, almond-shaped eyes with the upper lids folded in. He wore a brown leather jacket over a white, open-necked shirt and dark corduroy pants, and his light brown hair was thick and unruly. That isn't Chinese hair, Miranda thought, comparing him to other men in the lobby, with their smooth, black hair, thin eyebrows, and smaller, almost snub, noses. And he's taller than they are. And more handsome.

He turned, and saw her, and smiled.

"You look rested," he said as they shook hands. "And less anxious."

"I swam this morning. That always helps. And the pool was empty. I like it when I'm alone."

They walked toward a restaurant off the lobby. "Do you swim every morning?"

"As often as I can."

"You said it always helps. What is it that it helps?"

"If I'm unhappy about something, or worried—" She bit her lip. *He's a stranger, for heaven's sake.* She looked through the double doors before them. "Is this an American restaurant?"

"Vaguely. And vaguely European."

Inside, Miranda gazed at the buffet that

stretched the length of the room. "So much food."

"We're just learning how to feed westerners. When one is not sure what to do, one does everything. Here is our waitress. Would you like coffee or tea?"

"Coffee, please. Black."

At the buffet she ignored the section with Chinese dishes, slowing to stroll past pancakes, waffles, omelets, oatmeal, a pyramid of cereal boxes, smoked salmon, platters of cheeses and cold meats, croissants, muffins and coffee cakes, and served herself fruit and a blueberry muffin. The large room, with tall windows looking onto a busy street, was filled with western and Chinese businessmen, almost all of them speaking English, none of them paying the slightest attention to her or looking surprised because she was having breakfast with a Chinese man. Her self-consciousness faded, and with it some of her stiffness.

"To the success of your trip," Li said, raising his cup of tea in a toast. "I hope you enjoy Beijing and make many excellent friendships."

How formal he was! One moment he was casual, the next he spoke like a guide or a politician. Miranda contemplated him. "Your hair isn't Chinese," she blurted, then put her hand to her mouth. "I'm sorry."

"It's all right; I'm used to hearing about it. You could call it American hair, from my father."

"Your father was American? You were born in America?"

"No, in China, in Chungdan. My father was an American soldier. There were thousands of them here, helping us build military bases when the Japanese invaded. When my father returned to America, he said he would send for my mother as soon as he finished his military service and got a job, but—" His hand lifted and fell.

"He left his wife and son—?"

"I was not born yet; my mother did not even know she was pregnant until a month after he left, and she had no address to write to him. It's an old story; there are probably thousands like it. I'm sure you've heard such things."

"Only in an opera. *Madama Butterfly*."

He shook his head. "Japanese, not Chinese. And a tale of weakness: she kills herself in the end. My mother was stronger. She endured."

"What did she do?"

"Moved in with her parents on a farm near Wuxi. She told everyone that my father had been killed fighting the Japanese. She worked on the farm and I grew up with her and my grandparents."

"And brothers and sisters? Your mother must have remarried."

"No. She already had a husband."

"But he was gone."

"Would that have been enough for you?"

"I have no idea," she said coldly.

"Well, it was not enough for my mother," he said quickly, as if apologizing for being too personal. "She never remarried."

"Where is she now?"

"She died some years ago."

"Oh. I'm sorry."

"Yes, it was very sad. She was still young, only in her sixties, but she was tired after so many years of turmoil. There were few people I admired as much, or liked as much. She was one of my closest friends."

"But you had friends in school."

"A few. We had many secrets, and a

clubhouse with a password, and even codes to talk in and write notes at school. We thought we were more clever than everyone, more . . . how do you say it? Cold?"

She smiled. "Cool."

"Yes, isn't that odd? To be cool is to be very good. So why would you not say that to be cold is to be the best? English is a curious language. Well, we built a clubhouse, and I discovered that I was good with my hands, and happiest building and repairing things. Perhaps I needed to build up, after so much around us had come crashing down: the Japanese invasion, my vanished father, the civil war . . ."

The civil war. Yes, she had read about that. Now here was someone who had lived through it, and through all the history she knew only from books. Miranda leaned forward, her chin on her hand. How different he was from the people she knew! How different his whole life was! How far she was from home! "Where were you during the civil war?"

"On the farm. I was a child when the communists took power, and we had to stay there. My mother knew that we would not be allowed to leave China, nor would my father be able to come to us. And so I never met him and have nothing of him except for my hair and eyebrows."

"And your height."

"Well, yes, but there are other tall Chinese. We're not all tiny."

She flushed. "I didn't mean—"

"I know; I'm sorry. How could you know all about us when you have never been here? Won't you take some more food? You've eaten very little."

"You had less. Only tea."

"I ate at home."

"What did you eat?"

"Rice and stir-fried greens. Dragon Well tea. And some bean paste dumplings left over from dinner."

Rice and fried vegetables for breakfast, Miranda thought. And bean paste dumplings, whatever those were. And Dragon Well tea, whatever *that* was. She felt like Alice in Wonderland: nothing was entirely strange, but nothing was really normal, either. She wanted to ask questions about everything, but instead she said, "Your wife must be a good cook."

"My wife is dead. I am the good cook."

"For you and your children?"

"For me alone. My son and daughter are grown and in their own homes."

"Oh. You don't look . . . How old are you?"

"Fifty-five. And now you must tell me about yourself. Why you are in China."

"Oh." Startled, she looked at her watch. "I'm here to work. I don't know how I could have forgotten—" She shoved back her chair. "I have to go; I have an appointment. Oh, now I'll be late; how could I have done this?"

"What time is your appointment?"

"Ten. But I have to get to the Haidian district and I don't know how long that will take."

"It's a large district. What is the address?"

Miranda took a letter from her purse. "The name at the top."

He read it aloud. "The Beijing Higher Fashion Garments Factory. I know that factory; it will take about forty minutes to get there. Traffic is always bad, and worst at this time of day. But that still leaves a little time for more coffee."

"No, I want to be early. I hate being late;

people get upset. Do you think this address is enough? Or should I tell the taxi driver something else?"

"It should be enough, but I'll write the cross street, and the name of the company, as well." Next to the English, he swiftly wrote a string of Chinese characters. "Where will you go after your meeting?"

"I have another meeting at three, but in between I'd like to see some shops. My guidebook says there are good ones in . . . Wangfujing?"

"It's pronounced Wong-fu-jing," he said. "Yes, there are many areas for shopping, but that is a good place to start, and it is right here; the Palace Hotel is in the center of it. But you should look at Xidan, too; slightly lower prices and larger stores." He wrote it in English and Chinese. "She-don. Whenever you see an X, that's how you pronounce it."

"How peculiar. Why not just write it that way?"

"Why don't you write 'thought' and 'rough' the way they sound?"

Startled, Miranda said, "I don't know. I never think about it."

"Well, we didn't invent this spelling; an Englishman did. And why he did it this way, perhaps the devil knows, but no one else, and we're stuck with it, or, rather, foreigners are. Come; let us find you a taxi."

The doorman hailed one, and when she stepped into the tiny car behind a driver locked inside his protective Plexiglas enclosure, Li bent to shake hands. "If you have no business or social plans for dinner, I would be pleased to take you to my favorite restaurant."

She met his eyes. Seemingly lidless, they were clear and direct, dark, liquid, beautiful, revealing nothing. *He's a stranger who picked me up at the airport. All I know about him is the little bit he's told me . . . if it's the truth. But he seems safe, and he's somebody to talk to.* She started to say yes, then tightened her lips. *This is crazy. I'd never go out with a stranger in America; why would I do it in China?*

"A restaurant," Li said quietly. "Very public. A place where people can talk, and perhaps become friends."

She flushed, feeling young and inexperienced. Maybe, if I checked on him, she thought. . . . "If you give me your number at work, I'll call you later, when I know my schedule."

"A good idea." He wrote it down. "Please leave a message with my secretary if I'm not in my office."

Secretary. Office. How respectable it sounded. But of course he had an office; he had told her last night that he was a construction engineer. She had been too tense to pay much attention, but it occurred to her now that that was yet another way they differed from each other. She designed cashmere sweaters: small, soft things that could be folded up and tucked away. He created buildings, huge, solid structures that thrust into the sky, visible from afar. Almost a parody of feminine and masculine stereotypes, she thought. Really, they had nothing in common: not their work or their cultures, not their history, not their ideas about the world and themselves, not even what they ate for breakfast.

But, in spite of all that, she liked him. She liked his quiet voice and the change in his face when he smiled, and the serious way he listened to her. And his English was so good it was almost like talking to an

American. And what could be more public, and safe, than a restaurant? And so she nodded. I should smile, she thought; I should look friendly. But her lips were stiff, as if caution could protect her from disaster, and she could not force them into relaxation. She wondered if Li were insulted that she was so cool. She could not tell; he gave nothing away. "I'll call later," she said, and met his eyes, and that was as close to warmth as she could get.

Her taxi careened through the streets of Beijing, swerving to dodge bicyclists who looked neither right nor left, and buses, trucks, vans, cars, and motorcycles that cut back and forth without wasting time on hand signals or glancing at rearview mirrors. Pedestrians crossed the streets at their own deliberate pace and, miraculously, drivers managed to avoid them. Horns blared, black fumes poured from exhaust pipes, policemen waved batons that were universally ignored. Miranda sat upright, rigid with the certainty of disaster, her eyes darting from one side of the road to the other. The lanes seemed reserved for different groups: the outside ones were the quietest, used by bicyclists and old men and women, mostly women, stooped low between the long poles of loaded handcarts they pulled behind them. In the two inner lanes crammed with motor vehicles, all—at least to Miranda—was chaos and terror.

"Ignore it," Li had said the night before, as the airport taxi plunged into the teeming streets of the city. "Most often, most of us get where we are going."

"And when you don't?" she asked.

He shrugged. "There are many accidents, but most of the fatalities are cyclists and pedestrians. In a car, you have a better chance."

She studied his face, but, in the darkness and the flickering lights from oncoming headlights, she could not be sure whether he was serious or not.

Now, alone in the taxi, she was repeating his words to herself—*in a car . . . a better chance*—when suddenly September sunlight broke through the clouds, and the sudden burst of brightness made everything seem less alarming. For the first time, she unclenched her fists and began to notice the tall sycamore trees lining the streets, the throngs on the sidewalks, the food vendors, the shops opening for the day. *Most often most of us get where we are going.* She gave a small laugh. *What a comfort.*

The taxi crossed Changping Road, familiar to her from studying her map, and she knew they were close to the Haidian industrial district. She ran a hand through her hair, and took a small mirror from her purse to examine her face.

She wished she were beautiful. But then, she never had been; she didn't know why she still worried about it. She had a pleasant, friendly face (she had told herself that over the years, never able to come up with a more exotic description); she knew many people called it a bright and open face, prettier when she smiled—but she could not see anything dramatic enough to attract a stranger in an airport. My eyes are good, she thought critically, widening them; they were large and long-lashed, changing from hazel to green to light gray, but her skin was pale and her blond hair was nothing like the golden blond of fairy tales and magazine models: it was too fair, almost white in the sunlight, and short and curling around her face, which was easy to take care of but hardly glamorous or memorable. But that's the point, she thought: nothing about me is memorable. I do have a good mouth, though. Women's mouths usually get smaller as they age, but thank goodness mine hasn't done that. And I'm not really so old. I mean, I don't feel old, and forty isn't exactly ancient.

Except that I don't feel young. It's been ten years since Jeff died, and even if I wanted to get married again I probably wouldn't be able to. Men want young girls, not ordinary-looking middle-aged women with two teenage kids and no money to sweeten the pot.

Her taxi came to an abrupt halt and she put out her arm to stop herself from being flung forward. She glanced at the building before her, assumed it was the right one, and counted yuan from her wallet. "Don't tip them," Li had said. "It's not done, and not expected." But she was an American; how could she not give a tip, even though the driver had terrified her for most of the drive? She added one coin, and waited, but no smile or "thank you" was forthcoming, and she turned away, faintly annoyed.

Even if tipping weren't done, *especially* if tipping weren't done, he could have had the grace to thank her for it.

Inside she was directed to a conference room, and when the door swung open, she saw fifteen men and women around an enormous table, all of them looking at her, all of them looking alike. She knew they didn't, really, but their faces seemed cut from a mold, and so did their eyes: dark, lidless, intense, never blinking or revealing their feelings. And their language slid up, down and sideways around sounds that had no resemblance to anything she recognized as words. It was the most foreign language she had ever heard.

Taking her place at the conference table, she felt isolated, almost a nonperson. She knew that partly that was because she had no experience with other cultures, and so the tiniest differences from American ways loomed huge and threatening. But maybe that will change, she thought. I haven't worked with them. Maybe they'll turn out to be the same as the people I know in Boulder.

"Miss Graham, we welcome you," said one of the men in clipped English. "May I present our executives and our manufacturing group. I am Wang Zedong, director of manufacture; this is our vice-president, Xie Peng; the general manager of the factory, Zhang Yinou . . ."

The names rolled past Miranda and she knew she would never remember them all. Wang Zedong, she thought, director of manufacture. Zhang Yinou, general manager of the factory. The ones I'll be working with. The ones I really have to remember. And Li told me the first name is their last name. Something else I have to get used to. "Thank you, Mr. Wang," she said when he ended his introductions. She opened her briefcase. "I hope you've had a chance to look at the designs we sent you two weeks ago."

"We have studied them carefully." Wang fanned Miranda's drawings in front of him. "There are some areas of difficulty we need to address, but we do have other designs and solutions at hand to help us solve these problems, if we all agree."

Difficulties. Problems. They wouldn't start that way at home, Miranda thought. They always found a few good things to say first, a scattering of praise for fine work, a smile, a nod, maybe a few jokes, questions about spouses or children . . . something personal. Not here, she thought. Nothing personal here.

She forced her trembling hands to stillness as she brought out her own drawings, and samples of cashmere knits and weaves, braids, buttons, toggles, and spools of thread. There was nothing complicated in what she was here for, she told herself; she had done it before, at home. She just had to stand firm and get good pricing and reasonable manufacturing schedules, repeat the whole process at two other garment companies, and then go home, maybe even before the eight days were up.

"Difficulties?" she asked.

"This knit suit." Wang drew out one of Miranda's watercolor sketches. "You specify four-ply cashmere and the suit has a shawl collar, which makes a very heavy jacket indeed—"

"I want it heavy," Miranda said, and heard a note of anxiety in her voice that she knew should not be there. "The suit is meant to be worn with a blouse or lace sweater; I've designed lighter knits that are two-piece outfits."

Wang waited patiently, then went on as if she had not interrupted him. "A heavy jacket that is nearer the category of coat than suit. That involves a different group of knitters and therefore the pricing is different as well."

"I don't understand. No one could confuse this jacket with a coat."

"Ah, but in manufacturing terms, the weight, the design. . . . I will ask Yun Chen to explain it."

Yun Chen held her own copy of Miranda's sketch. Like all the women there, she wore a severe dark suit, and no jewelry or makeup. She was older than Wang, Miranda thought, but you really couldn't tell how old Chinese people were: they were either smooth or incredibly wrinkled. This woman's English, too, was clear and clipped as she described the different knitting machines for heavier garments, the knitters who specialized in them, the inspectors who had separate checklists for them. "It is of course labor, as you know, Miss Graham; we do not stamp these out like automobile parts. We are known for our excellent products, for the skill of our labor, and we know how long each type of garment will require to be done perfectly, and therefore what will be the cost."

"And what *is* the cost?" Miranda asked.

Wang gave a figure and Miranda wrote it down, calculating the exchange rate and figuring what the stores would charge their customers. She shook her head. "The suit would cost over eight thousand dollars; we must keep it to five."

"Partly it is the tiger-eye buttons," said Yun Chen. "We could reduce the price by using another button."

Miranda looked at her in disbelief. "You think changing the buttons would cut the price almost in half?"

"Perhaps bone," offered one of the men.

"Or plastic," added another woman, this one with small wire-rimmed glasses. "We have one that looks like bone, very like, it is an excellent product."

"This is not serious," Miranda said in frustration.

"But if the suit is three-ply instead of four," said Wang, "we could use our standard knitting machines. We understand, Miss Graham, that one- or two-ply would not achieve the look you want, but surely three-ply would be satisfactory."

Someone spoke in Chinese and Yun Chen answered in Chinese and Wang translated, "Three-ply cashmere is accepted by most people; many find four-ply too heavy, certainly too heavy to wear indoors. Three-ply is certainly adequate."

Miranda felt as assaulted as she had in the airport. *I didn't come here to end up with an "adequate" line, and you're the ones who used the word "excellent" just a few minutes ago.* But she could not say that aloud; it sounded too critical, it might make them angry.

"Perhaps without the shawl collar," said another woman with a long braid down her back. "A smaller collar, notched, you know, would work with three-ply and be very smart. And the braid could be left off the collar and cuffs; it is not essential."

Miranda was sketching small alterations in the margins of her watercolor drawing as the voices swirled about her, picking away at her design. *Maybe it's not as good as I thought it was. As Talia thought it was. Maybe all my designs are just ordinary, like lawnmowers or bicycles, and the only important thing is how cheaply they can be made, for how much profit.* She did not really believe that, but at this moment, when she heard only criticism, with no smiles or jokes or small talk, and not a word about how interesting her ideas were, how cleverly she had devised sleeves or collars or buttons . . . or *anything complimentary,* it was not easy to believe in herself or to fight for her designs. "I'll think about it," she said at last.

"Yes, very good," said Wang, as if she were a student who had given a satisfactory answer. He brought out another sketch. "Now, this sweater, the V-neck, it has no difficulties; the cable stitch at the cuffs and the hem will take a little longer to set on the machines, but we are quite skilled in that." He named a price and Miranda wrote it down, and they discussed colors and scheduling and quantities. Miranda made notes, telling herself that she would go through them tonight, in her hotel, and if anything seemed questionable she would bring it up tomorrow, when she was fresh.

One by one, endlessly, it seemed, they went through the sketches. On one, Yun Chen suggested that the sleeves of a long cardigan sweater be turned into cuffs, and stitched in place, and Miranda agreed. On a cable-stitched sweater set, Wang said the cost could be reduced significantly over the entire production run by making the shell one inch shorter, and again Miranda agreed. "As long as the cardigan remains the same," she added, almost as if she were asking Wang to be kind and leave the cardigan alone. She bit her lip; she had to stop doing that, *they* work for *us,* she thought, not the other way around. But when Wang nodded graciously, she was as relieved as if she were indeed a supplicant and he a dispenser of largesse. *I don't know how I'll do it, but I have to learn how to stand up to them.*

And finally, after a tour of the garment factory, the meeting was over. In the taxi Wang had called for her, Miranda sat back with a sigh. Like getting out of school, she thought, and was able to smile at that. They didn't even let me have a recess. And lunch was awful; served right there at the conference table, and then I couldn't eat because—

"To where?" the taxi driver said, evidently exhausting his supply of English with those two words.

Miranda sat up. She had something to do. She took an envelope from her purse and held it so that the driver could read the address. When he nodded, she sat back again. She had no idea where the address was, or what she would find there, but this was something she had promised to do, on her last day in Boulder, when she was packing to leave. A favor.

Please, would you deliver a letter for me? It is to my parents and they have not heard from me in such a long time . . .

Sima Ting was a young woman from Beijing, thin, plain, dark hair swinging about her face, thin hands gesturing as she spoke, legs tucked under her on the couch in an apartment in Boulder. She had fled China after the tanks rolled through Tiananmen Square, scattering and crushing the thousands of young demonstrators who had set up camp there. For two weeks they had cooked their meals in the enormous plaza, sung, debated, danced to the music of portable radios, listened to newscasts, slept on concrete, and waited for the government to invite them to sit down and talk about democracy in China. And then, into the smoky flickering lights of torches and cooking fires, had come the hard beams of floodlights, and tanks and soldiers, and in one night the makeshift city had been swept away. All that had remained in the silent plaza was debris, skittering in the light wind across stones streaked with blood.

Sima Ting, nineteen years old, was arrested, along with her brother and many of her friends. It was a month before she learned that the young man she loved had died beneath the treads of a tank; another six months before she was put on trial, found guilty, and sentenced to five years in prison. The day after her release, she met with an underground group of six young men and women who liked to sit around a table and discuss political change, and who occasionally sent letters to newspapers suggesting legislation to protect civil rights. That meeting sent Ting back to prison, this time for a fifteen-year term.

"And she'd still be there, except that she was very sick," said the woman who had sponsored Ting's trip to America. Nancy

Magoon, one of Miranda's few close friends, was on the board of directors of a group that sponsored political refugees coming to America. When Ting was diagnosed with breast cancer, and told her choices were to remain in prison or leave China forever, it was Nancy who was called by people in Beijing who knew of her. And it was Nancy who welcomed Ting to Boulder, arranged for her medical treatment, and found her an apartment and a job at the library.

"You'd like her," Nancy told Miranda at lunch one day. "She's very quiet, but who wouldn't be, after what she's been through? She needs friends, and since you're going to China, I thought you'd like to meet her."

"I don't know if I'm going to China. I told Talia I wasn't sure."

"Of course you'll go! You can't pass this up, Miranda; once in a lifetime you get a chance like this."

Miranda gazed at her with a small smile, envying her lovely face, her smile that drew people to her, her sophistication, her perfect clothes, her energy. *Everything I'm not.* And yet, somehow, they were friends and loved each other. "How do you do that? There don't seem to be any obstacles in your world and there always are so many in mine."

"Because you keep thinking about them, so they swell up like pregnant cats. Ignore them; you'll be amazed how fast they shrivel away to nothing. You can be a very determined woman, you know; if you work on that, there's nothing you can't do."

"There's nothing *you* can't do. You're always helping one organization or another, getting people to do things they never thought they'd do, or said they definitely couldn't do; you and Bob go everywhere, you collect art, you go to parties, you *give* parties . . . you have time for everything and you never seem in doubt or worried or overwhelmed . . ."

"Of course I am, a lot of the time, good heavens, I'm not superhuman. Everybody gets tired, even overwhelmed sometimes, you know that; it's just that not all of us show it. I'm a lot like you, you know; how else could we be friends? Now, listen, I want you to go to China. I haven't been there in years and I want a complete report. Meet new people, eat everything, go everywhere, and then come back and tell me about it."

"I've never done anything like that. You know that."

"Well, it's high time," Nancy said lightly. "Look, take a first step. Come and meet Ting. She can tell you about China and give you courage. Come to dinner; she really does need friends, Miranda, and you have a way of making people comfortable."

"What way is that?"

"Oh, quiet, not jumping all over people to get them to do things or say things, not demanding."

"You mean passive."

"I mean listening. Waiting to hear what comes next. Waiting for something to happen."

Miranda frowned. *Waiting for something to happen.* She didn't know it was that obvious to others. *All my life I've been waiting for something to happen.*

And now many things were happening. How do we get to the places we find ourselves? she wondered. Here she was in a taxi in Beijing, at least partly because she had met Sima Ting.

Ting had talked all through dinner, about

China, about her trip to America, and about her hopes for going home.

"But you must like it here," Miranda said.

"I do, please do not think me ungrateful; I am happy to be here and Nancy has been amazing, wonderful, and everyone has been so kind; it is truly a lovely country. But it is not *my* country, you know."

"You'll make it yours. Look what your country has done to you and to your friends; they tried to destroy you; they did destroy many of you. You can't really want to go back there."

"My country has not tried to destroy me; a few men in the government did that." Ting paused. "I think you cannot understand the longing someone has for home, because you *are* home. I belong in China, you know, just as you belong here. My family is there, and my friends, and my work, and there are things we can do, there *must* be things we can do, to change the system there. Probably we moved too quickly, at Tiananmen; we must learn to be more gradual, more patient; these are things we must think about." She smiled. "You have a saying, that something is in your bones. My bones are Chinese, they hurt when they cannot touch the ground in China."

Miranda frowned. "Millions of people have come here and they become Americans and they forget their other homes."

"I think they never forget their other homes," said Ting gently. "But whether they do or not, I could not. And I could not truly become an American any more than you truly could become a Chinese. Miranda, I am not saying your country is not wonderful; I am saying that my country is mine, wonderful or not. And this is an important time in China. They call it the 'Beijing Autumn,' do you know why? Because the old men who run the country soon will die and fall, just like leaves from the trees in autumn, and then things will change."

They had dinner together one more time, talking about the China Miranda would see if she took a business trip there. "I think it would be good if you go there," Ting said. "It is always good to discover new places, and there are many wonders you will not find anywhere else. How do you know what will happen next year? Do things when you can; life changes too quickly to put them off."

Nancy, who had been listening quietly, nodded firmly. "What did I tell you? Go! A whole world is out there, and you haven't even scratched the surface. I have absolute faith in you; you'll learn things about yourself you never knew before."

Miranda did not tell her that she found that idea alarming. But also, in a strange, rippling way, exciting.

A week later, Miranda called Ting to tell her she was indeed going to China. Ting's voice was excited. "Would you do a favor for me?"

"A favor? In China?"

"A small one, of no great consequence, but I would so appreciate it. Please, would you deliver a letter for me? It is to my parents and they have not heard from me in such a long time. I write often and put the pages together, hoping to find someone to deliver it. If you could, I would be so grateful."

"Of course I will. I'm sure I'll have plenty of time to myself, and I'd like to meet your parents."

"Oh, you will not meet them; their home is too difficult to find. If you will take the letter to this small shop, the people there will deliver it to my parents. You will do this for me?"

"Of course," Miranda said again, and the next day Ting brought a bulging manila envelope to her. So, as she sat in the taxi in Beijing, rocking from side to side as the car took corners with screeching sharpness, she asked herself again, How do we get to the places we find ourselves? How can we ever predict, or even understand, all the forces that shape us and move us through our lives?

The address turned out to be a tiny food store, with bins on the sidewalk piled high with vegetables. Inside, the shelves were stacked with cans and jars covered with labels she could not read. A few things she did recognize. If I lived here, all we'd eat would be peanuts, eggs, noodles and dried mushrooms, she thought. At the back of the store, a man and woman stood behind a counter. "Please?" the man said.

Miranda held out the letter. "I was asked to deliver this."

The man made a small bow. "Thank you." He gestured to shelves in the store. "Please?"

"I don't understand," Miranda said.

The woman walked around the counter and selected a bag of dried mushrooms and two cans. She put them in a paper bag and handed it to Miranda.

I have to buy something, too? Miranda thought. But the man and woman were both making small bows; then the man held out his hand and when Miranda put hers in it, he shook it vigorously. "Good-bye," he said. "Thank you. Thank you."

My reward, Miranda thought, amused, and made her own goodbyes before returning to the taxi. She showed the driver a letterhead from the Palace Hotel and he nodded. Done, she thought, settling back as they merged into a busier street. Such a simple thing; it will make Ting's parents happy. She imagined not seeing Adam and Lisa for five years, hearing from them only intermittently, if at all. She wouldn't be able to bear it. These people must be very strong.

I'll ask Li about that, she thought. How many people go through this, how many went to prison. . . . Then she changed her mind. She didn't really want to tell him about Ting. She liked the idea of having her own errand, going about Beijing alone, on business that had nothing to do with Talia or Li.

And so, instead, in the restaurant that night, she told him about tipping the taxi driver that morning. "He didn't thank me."

"How do you know?" Li asked. "You don't speak Chinese."

"He didn't say anything. He didn't even smile. But, then, I didn't see very many smiles today."

"People were unpleasant to you?"

"Oh, no, they were incredibly polite. And they did smile, but they weren't real smiles. I mean, they were like handshakes: something you do in business. They weren't warm."

"The people or the smiles?"

"Neither."

"Perhaps they save their warmth for people they know."

"I'm not asking them to love me," she snapped. "I just think they might be more friendly."

"Well. Friendly." He made a small gesture. "That is often a problem for foreigners in China." He refilled their glasses of Yanjing beer and settled back in his chair. "Let me tell you an ancient fable. One day a poor man met an old friend who had become an immortal. As the poor man complained of his poverty, the immortal pointed his finger at a brick by the road-side, which immediately turned into a gold ingot. 'This is for you,' he said. When the man was not satisfied with this, the immortal pointed his finger at a pile of stones, turning them into gold coins. But the man still was not happy. 'What more do you want?' asked the immortal, and his friend replied, 'I want your finger.' "

Miranda laughed. "I like that. And the moral is, everybody will always want more, but nobody is willing to give everything, so at some point we ought to be satisfied with what we have."

"Exactly. That fable is from the fourth century B.C. Nothing changes, you know, across the centuries, or across borders. Now tell me about the rest of your day. Was it a good one for business?"

"No. Well, maybe it was; I'm not sure. No one asked for my finger, but they did demand things that I didn't want to give. . . . Oh, I don't know; I have to sort it all out. There was so much going on it felt like three or four days, at least. I'd rather be here, at this lovely restaurant. Fangshan? Is that how you say it?"

"Fong-shon. An imperial restaurant, which means the chefs have revived the cuisine once served to emperors. An elegant cuisine. It suits you."

She frowned. "Why do you say that?"

"You think it is not true?"

"I know it's not." She looked away, shutting out his gaze. The room he had chosen was the smallest in the restaurant, with only six tables, each beneath a red, fringed paper lantern. A large window overlooked Beihai Lake, pale silver in the fading light, with dark trees massed along the shore, their overhanging branches trailing in the water. The restaurant was on an island in the lake, suspended between shimmering water reflecting the rising moon, and filmy clouds moving across an opal sky. It was a dreamlike oasis in the frenetic city, shielded from automobile horns, the acrid fumes of buses, and neon lights flashing in staccato bursts. "This must be the only peaceful place in Beijing," Miranda said.

"On the contrary, we have many, each

different from the others. If you will allow me, I will show them to you."

Again, she frowned. "I don't under-stand—"

Two waitresses, theatrically made up and wearing identical silk gowns slit to the thigh, arranged four serving dishes on their table. "I ordered for both of us," said Li. "I thought that would be easiest."

"Yes, of course. I wouldn't know where to start."

"We start with cold dishes . . ." He spooned a portion onto Miranda's saucer-sized plate, and then onto his own. "Spiced beef. The others are shredded chicken, duck's tongue, and fried eel. Eat only what you like."

I'll eat it all. If he thinks he can scare me off with things like duck's tongue and eel . . . well, he could, but I wouldn't let him know it. She reached for her fork, then realized there was no fork. Two ivory chopsticks lay against a small porcelain rest, gleaming malevolently. Her face flooded with embarrassment. She had not eaten lunch because she had been ashamed to admit she did not know what to do, and she had assumed Li would take her to a place that had knives and forks, like the hotel restaurant where they had had breakfast.

Desperately, she glanced around to see what others were doing, but the others were all Chinese, perfectly at home, no help at all. I hate this, she thought angrily. I hate being in a strange place. I hate Li for bringing me here.

She picked up the chopsticks and tried to hold them as she saw others doing. It looked simple, but no matter how she wound her fingers around them, she could not make them move separately.

"Like this," Li said gently. Covering her hand with his, he guided her thumb and fingers to hold the two ivory sticks, smooth and cool, tapered slightly, with red Chinese characters etched along their sides. "The bottom one stays still; the top one moves up and down, like a pincer. Put your thumb across both, right here, to stabilize them. Now we will bring the tips together, like this, and pick up a piece of beef. Perfect. Now, again. You see? Now you try it." He took his hand away and watched Miranda practice. "Ah, very good. Now another. Good, good. You're very quick. You never used chopsticks in America?"

"The restaurants always had forks on the table. I never thought it was necessary."

Or intriguing. Why wasn't I more curious to try them, even once?

The beef was delicious, spicy hot and sweet, and when she looked up and met Li's waiting look, she said, "It's wonderful. And now that you've taught me how to get it into my mouth, I think you should eat and not worry about me."

"I want you to be pleased."

"I am," she said, and it was true. She felt happy. After a day of being intimidated and insecure among foreigners who knew everything while she knew nothing, isolated every time they spoke Chinese, nervous about the responsibility of negotiating for her company with strangers so totally different from her . . . now, for the first time, she could relax.

She liked the hushed room with its crisp white tablecloths and translucent paper lanterns, the red and gold porcelain lamp on their table, the small white plates that held one serving at a time of the foods parading before them. She liked the muted colors of the carpet, the dark silk drapes at the window looped back with gold cords and medallions, the strange music wafting in a minor key from hidden speakers. She liked the intimacy of their table, a small island of English in an incomprehensible sea of rapid-fire Chinese. Without Li, she would have felt she was drowning; with him, she felt adventurous, able to think about dinner.

She took a long drink, to cool her mouth from the spicy beef. The Chinese beer was soft and mellow, but with a distinctive bite, and it was served like water, the waitresses keeping their glasses filled just as waiters filled water glasses at home. Miranda had always thought beer was common and cheap, compared to wine, but it was just right with these dishes, and even if it had not been, she would never call attention to herself by asking for wine or anything else that would make her stand out as even more different from everyone else. She disliked being the center of attention, and that was even more true in China. Anyway, she liked the beer and it was new, which made her feel still more adventurous. A wave of gratitude filled her and, abruptly, out of context, she said, "Thank you," to Li, and he said, very simply, "I'm glad you're pleased."

When her plate was empty, he refilled it from the bowl of shredded chicken. "Now," he said, serving himself. "I still want to hear about what you did today. And what you thought and felt."

Miranda took a thin strip of chicken between her chopsticks and carried it smoothly to her mouth. How about that, she thought exultantly. One lesson and I'm eating like a local. She felt a rush of confidence, and from that came honesty. "Mostly I kept wishing that I'd done more and seen more in my life."

"Like learning to use chopsticks?"

"Learning everything. If I'd traveled more, if I knew more about the world, I would have handled things better today. I wasn't aggressive enough; I didn't make it absolutely clear that my company expects certain things done in a certain way."

"Are you ever aggressive?"

"What?"

"I'm sorry; that was rude. Perhaps when I know you better I will ask such a question. Or by then I will not need to."

Deliberately, Miranda laid her chopsticks on their porcelain rest. "What is this all about?"

"This? You mean my rudeness? My apology?"

"You know what I mean."

"Well." He nodded. "You mean the two of us sharing breakfast and dinner and perhaps someday knowing each other well enough for me to discover whether or not you are aggressive. May I answer you later? I promise I will answer you, but for now would you accept it if I say simply that I enjoy your company and find it pleasant to dine with you, and that I would like to help you have a pleasant evening, and a more pleasant stay in Beijing?"

No, she thought, but she did not say it. Just as she avoided calling attention to herself, she always tried to avoid making a fuss. It was best to keep everything smooth by going along with people as much as possible. Besides, it really was a pleasant evening: far better than eating alone in her hotel room.

"Yes, all right," she said.

"Thank you. Did you like the chicken?"

"It had an odd flavor. I almost liked it."

He chuckled. "Next time perhaps you will like it better. This is the fried eel." He spooned a portion onto her plate. "A bit slippery, for chopsticks, but I'm sure you can manage it; you are doing so well. Whom did you meet today?"

"The vice president, the manager of production, the general manager of the factory, the people in charge of production, and some others I never did figure out. The factory is enormous; have you ever been there?"

"My company built the number two building."

Her eyes widened. "That was a huge project. It's much larger than the number one building."

"And better built. They should have called us first, but they were trying to save money."

"Who was? Your government?"

"No, the Japanese. That company is a joint venture, funded mostly by a Japanese investment firm. Chinese investors own a small part of it, and of course the management is Chinese, though they brought in a group of Japanese advisors. It is an excellent company; you'll find them good to work with."

"I think they find Americans demanding and arrogant."

"Americans are demanding and arrogant. It comes from being the most powerful nation in the world." He refilled her plate. "I see that you like the eel."

"Yes, very much." She frowned. "I don't think I'm demanding, and I'm certainly not arrogant. I don't feel more powerful than anybody. Mostly I'm ashamed because I'm so ignorant about things. I didn't know your government let foreigners own companies; I thought communism meant the government owns everything."

"That is no longer true. Did they give you a tour of the factory? What did you think of it?"

"It was very impressive."

"Tell me about it. I haven't been there since we finished work on it."

Miranda described the air-conditioned, brightly lit workshops, more than a city block long, each with long rows of individual worktables where women sat bent over their sewing machines. Pieces of brightly colored fabrics were piled beside them, looking like sleeping birds, wings folded, voices still. In fact, there were no voices at all: no one gossiped or laughed or described ailments or bragged about children or grandchildren, or hummed a tune. The only sound was the whirr of sewing machines, the only movement the controlled motions of swiftly stitching hands . . . though every one of the women did look up to make a piercing survey of Miranda as she walked past, from her hair to her shoes.

"What were you wearing?" Li asked.

"A suit." She flushed. "I only brought suits. I didn't think about going out at night."

"The one you're wearing is fine for going out. It's very beautiful. You look excellent."

He had no idea how fine the suit was, Miranda reflected, remembering its price tag, and the price of her other new suit. My first foreign trip, she had thought defensively; I'll have so much to be nervous about, I don't want to have to worry about how I look.

"Chanel, isn't it?" Li asked casually.

She looked at him in astonishment. "How would you know that?"

"CNN has programs on fashion and Hollywood, and it covers the designer shows in New York and Paris and Milan. And I am interested in all Western things, not just some of them."

"Because they're your heritage."

"That is one of the reasons. In fact—" He hesitated, then smiled, a small inward smile, as if amused at himself for what he was about to say. "I think it is because I've still not outgrown the hope that my father will come back. It is embarrassing, but, you know, I can't stop it: at odd times the idea suddenly springs up that *today* he will appear on my doorstep and embrace me and say, 'Well, it took a long time, but I found you and now we can become friends.' It is an absurd fantasy, a child's fantasy, but still it springs to life, as it has since the moment my mother told me about him. That was when I decided to learn about his country, so that when he came back he would be impressed with me. Later, of course, it was obvious that he was truly gone, but even though the dream faded, it did not disappear, and neither did my studies of America." Ruefully, he shook his head. "I am too old for such fantasies, don't you think?"

Pitying him, Miranda said, "It's been

very hard for you. Not knowing, always wondering . . ."

"Yes, exactly. Much harder even than not having a father. Well, and what about your parents?"

"They live two blocks from me. And right now they're living in my house, staying with my children."

"So you have children. How many?"

"Two. Lisa is fourteen and Adam is thirteen."

"And they are of course wonderful."

She laughed. "Of course. Smart and curious and fun."

"You must miss them very much."

She was silent. She had been so busy, and overwhelmed with strangeness, that she had barely thought of home. But at his simple words, her eyes filled with tears. "Right now, this time of night, we'd be in one of their bedrooms, talking about whatever had happened that day to make it special. We do that every night before they go to sleep."

"And is there always something special?"

"Always. Sometimes it's very small and

we have to hunt for it, but we always come up with something."

"How lucky you are."

"Yes. I always have been."

"But what of your husband? He is not staying with your children while you are in China?"

"My husband died many years ago."

"That does not sound lucky to me."

"Oh. Well, no." He waited, and she said, "I've been lucky in other ways."

"But you do not talk about your marriage."

Not to you. Why should I?

"Not to me," he said. "And indeed why should you?" He saw her startled look. "Have I said something wrong again?"

"No, it's just that— No."

"Well, then, tell me about Adam and Lisa. And your parents. Have you always lived so close to them?"

"All my life. I grew up in the house they're in now, and when Jeff and I married, we bought a house just down the street."

"And you are very close?"

"Yes, very. And Adam and Lisa love

them; I couldn't have come on this trip otherwise."

"So they move into your house for all your long trips?"

"I don't take long trips. This is my first."

His eyebrows rose. "Americans are the world's greatest travelers."

"Well, I'm not. I've been busy with my children and my work, and I'm very happy where I live. I do go to Denver a lot."

"How far is that?"

"About twenty miles. I've never felt the need to go any farther; there didn't seem to be any reason for it."

He contemplated her. "Is that true?"

She began to reply, then hesitated. "I'm not really sure," she said after a moment. "Mostly, I guess. It isn't that I'm not curious; I do think about going to other countries, seeing great museums and monuments, festivals, markets, all the different ways people live . . ."

"Well, then?"

"Nothing. It's just . . ." She looked up and met his close look. Prying, she thought, but, still, she felt oddly at ease. "Actually, I've been afraid of going any place where I don't know the language or understand the culture. And I don't like to travel alone."

"But you must have friends who could go with you."

"My friends are women like me; we haven't traveled and we don't speak any foreign languages, and we're afraid of finding ourselves in places where people could take advantage of us."

"I'm sorry," he said softly.

"You don't have to be sorry for me," she said coldly. "How much have *you* traveled? Your government won't let you go anywhere, even around your own country."

"I have been to all parts of China, and to Tibet and Mongolia. It is no longer true that we cannot travel as we wish, even outside the country. Many people do; it is not difficult."

"You can go where you want?"

"We can travel within China and Hong Kong as easily as you travel in America. And anyone who has the money can go abroad if other countries will give them visas. It is not so easy to get a visa from the United States."

"Why not?"

"Well, perhaps you should ask your government that question."

She was silent. She did not want to debate governments and politics; she knew almost nothing about them and he seemed to know a great deal. Whatever they talked about, she thought, they come back to the differences between them.

The waitresses brought the hot appetizers, and refilled their beer glasses. Once again Li served their portions. Miranda looked at her plate, and met the beady black eyes of a bright red shrimp. Its long feelers seemed to wave at her; its coral shell glistened with sauce. Oh, God, she thought, I can't do this. I cannot eat something that is staring at me.

Li picked up a shrimp with his fingers, twisted off the head, and sucked the meat from the shell. "It isn't really looking at you," he said conversationally.

He had not sounded condescending, but she was sure he would if she gave up now. She picked up a shrimp, slippery with sauce, averted her eyes, and twisted off its head. Without the eyes, things were easier, and the spicy meat was unlike any shrimp she had ever eaten. She looked at Li. He seemed engrossed in his own shrimp. Well, I don't need his approval, Miranda thought, and realized that she had been looking for it. *For eating a shrimp? How absurd can you get?*

Night had turned the window black and it reflected the small lamp on their table and the flashes of their ivory chopsticks. As they tasted the fourth appetizer, Li said, "Do you like them?"

"I like them all."

"Even the shrimp?"

"Especially the shrimp. Everything is wonderful. Much better than the Chinese food I've eaten at home."

"I would hope so," he said, smiling. "Do Adam and Lisa like Chinese food?"

"They like everything. In great quantities."

"Yes, I remember how teenagers never seem to fill up. And you had no one to help you, help earn a living. Have you always designed clothing?"

"No, I started out as a secretary at the University of Colorado, in Boulder. Jeff taught engineering there. I wanted to quit when Adam was born, but we needed the money and then Jeff died, very suddenly, when Adam was a year old and Lisa was two, and I had no choice but to keep working."

"He was in an accident?"

"No. He just came home one day from playing tennis and didn't feel well and lay down and when I went to find him for dinner, he was dead."

"How terrible. You went to wake him—perhaps you shook him and spoke his name—and he did not respond."

Miranda watched him curiously. "Exactly. Is that what happened with your wife?"

"No, no, we had been separated for years when she died. I was just trying to imagine what it must have been like for you. You had no warning; you expected a normal evening, and when you went to find him you were thinking about something quite ordinary, probably the dinner you were cooking, perhaps whether you had turned off a burner—"

"Yes," Miranda said sharply. It was as if he were sliding inside her, taking over her experiences.

"Well, so your husband died. And you stayed on as a secretary?"

"Yes, but at another place, a company that imported sweaters and knit suits and sold them under its own label. I started sketching for fun, mostly on my lunch hour, and a friend of mine showed a few of them to the president of the company and they sent me to school for a year, and I became one of their designers. There are only three of us, and it's not all that glamorous, you know: we don't go to fashion shows; our own names aren't on the label; usually we don't even work with models."

"But you like it."

"Yes, because I like creating things. It's the best way to feel you're in control; there's a beginning and a middle and an end, and you make it happen."

"And it brought you to China."

"Yes."

The main courses were served, platters of beef with oyster sauce, chicken curry with noodles, and Beijing duck.

"Wrap the pieces of duck in one of these pancakes," Li said, taking up a paper-thin pancake and sprinkling shredded green onion over it.

"It's like a crepe," Miranda said.

"Exactly. In fact, food is so much the

same everywhere. Here is our pancake and the French crepe—"

"And in Mexico a tortilla."

"And in Russia a *blini.*"

"And in Israel a *blintz.*"

"And in Italy a crespelle."

"And in Africa . . ." She laughed. "I'll have to look it up."

"But you see how alike we are: everyone, everywhere, eating pancakes. One can learn a great deal about people through their food. You should visit some of our markets while you are here; you would enjoy them."

A large bowl of bean curd soup was set in the center of the table. Miranda gazed at it in despair. She could not eat another mouthful, and, anyway, whoever heard of soup coming at the end of a meal?

"It clears the palate," Li said. "Try just a mouthful."

In fact, it was light, fragrant, and delicious and they both had second helpings.

"The markets," Li said. "Lively and colorful, something like country fairs I have read about in America. And there is food up the harmonica."

Miranda stared at him. "Up the what?"

"Is that wrong? I read it in a magazine and looked it up. A toy musical instrument—"

She burst out laughing. "A kazoo. Food up the kazoo." She could not stop laughing. "I'm sorry, I'm not making fun of you, it's just that it's mostly kids who say it, and it has nothing to do with music—" She began laughing again. "Please, I'm sorry, I'm being rude."

"No, it's all right, I only wish I understood the joke. Ah, here is our dessert. Let me serve you."

He was in charge again. Thank God, Miranda thought, and realized how awful she had felt, seeing Li at a disadvantage, in fact, putting him there, embarrassing him, perhaps even hurting him.

She watched him cut the fresh fruit into neat wedges. With dread, she waited for the rest of dessert to be served, knowing she could not eat it, whatever it was, but soon it was clear that the fruit was it. Thank God, she thought again, and reflected on the strangeness of an evening when the things that made her grateful were a man taking charge with dessert and there being no real dessert.

Li poured pale green tea through a silver strainer into their cups. "We can go to one of the markets tomorrow," he said casually. "You must tell me your schedule so that we can set a time. I have a meeting at ten, but it is best to go early in any case, say seven o'clock, when the foods are freshest and the tourists have not come. We could get breakfast there, too, on the street."

"On the street?"

"The vendors make excellent food. I will show you."

On the street. Totally unsanitary. How many inspectors check to see what's going on? None. I know it. But Li wouldn't take me anywhere that's really awful, a place that would make me sick—would he?

Putting off her answer, she nibbled on persimmon and pineapple and drank the steaming tea, its flavor subtle and smoky. What an extraordinary evening it had been. Strange and exotic. She and Li were alone now, and, in the silence, their voices had dropped to a murmur even more intimate than their earlier conversation when they had leaned toward each other beneath the surrounding chatter. They had found so much to talk about, skipping from one subject to another, making small discoveries. But they had barely begun: most of their lives still lay untouched. She remembered the feel of his hand on hers as he taught her to use chopsticks. A hard hand, the skin taut over thin bones, but also warm and gentle. And protective.

Her fingers curved around the warm skin of the persimmon. "I'd like to see the markets. At seven o'clock? I'll be ready."

Chapter 2

Li saw Miranda look for him as she stepped from the elevator, and he moved forward, his hand raised in greeting. From the quick glances of other men in the lobby, he knew his smile revealed how glad he was to see her, and he smoothed his features to neutrality and waited where he was, instead of meeting her halfway. She wore a different suit from that of the night before; this one was gray silk, and she wore it with a white silk blouse tied in a bow at the neck. How pale she is, Li thought. Her skin was clear and translucent, her blond eyebrows like fragile wings, her ash-blond hair a shimmering cloud that made her hazel eyes seem larger and darker, almost startling, when she widened them to look around. There was something ethereal about her, Li thought, especially surrounded as she was by Chinese, with their slightly sallow skin, black hair and eyes, and solid, purposeful bodies. Among them, Miranda seemed to float. Fragile, Li mused. I think. I have no idea how much of her is real and how much illusion.

He watched her make her way through the crowded lobby, slipping sideways between men standing in tight groups and bellboys maneuvering around them with rolling carts teetering with luggage. She stood straighter than she had the night before, more curious about her surroundings, as she surveyed the bustling lobby thronged with sleek businessmen and groups of camera-laden tourists clustered around guides holding aloft colorful banners with the names of universities and museums. Miranda's gaze settled on the tourists, on their cameras and name tags and trusting gazes as they followed their guides, and when she frowned Li knew that she was feeling separate from them. She is here to work, he thought, and she has met me, so she is not exactly a visiting stranger, but neither is she one of us. She is in between: sometimes a difficult place to be.

He felt himself reach out to her, to gather her in and protect her. That was what had happened at the airport. He had just seen a friend off to Hong Kong, and had been walking back toward the garage, when a gap had opened in the milling crowd and he had seen Miranda's face, pale and cringing above shoulders hunched defensively against the indifference of Chinese throngs. Then the gap had closed, swallowing her up. Li had pushed forward, to find her. Around him had been the blank faces of Chinese in public places: focused straight ahead, allowing nothing to invade the inviolate few inches of space they wrapped around themselves as they plowed toward their destinations. Li had forced his way through them, barely aware of being jabbed by elbows, knees and buttocks, determined to reach her, thinking that someone should bring a smile to her face and brightness to her eyes and take away that awful look of fear and helplessness.

Of course there had been more to his impulse than that. She was American. And she reminded him of—

"Good morning." She had made her way across the lobby and was holding out her hand to him.

Aware of the scrutiny of the men close by, Li took her hand in a businesslike clasp, then stepped back to let her walk ahead of him. "I have a car waiting."

At the corner, a small black car protruded into the intersection, the driver, absorbed in his newspaper, serenely unimpressed by the furious chorus of horns and shouts from other drivers forced to edge around him. "At home, this would be illegal," Miranda said. "Parking in an intersection."

Li smiled as he sat beside her in the back seat. "If the car had a bumper sticker attacking the government, *that* would be illegal."

"Would it? A bumper sticker?"

"If it were considered subversive."

He watched her digest that and then, it seemed, brush it aside. He wondered why. Didn't all Americans like to discuss politics? Perhaps not this American, because she was talking again about automobiles. "But you must have traffic laws," she said.

"A great many. But some things are more illegal than others, and traffic laws are rather far down the list." He leaned forward to speak to the driver, then sat back. "I promise we won't run anyone down today; even the Chinese consider that significant."

She shook her head. "I can't tell when you're being serious."

"I'll give you fair warning."

Her face changed and he gave a small sigh of impatience. Why couldn't she relax and stop worrying about comments that might seem too personal for her taste? "Well, let me tell you about the market. Not one of our largest, but it's my favorite because it hasn't grown as commercial as the ones that attract tourists. Oh, wait," he said suddenly, and told the driver to slow down. "This is one of our projects," he said to Miranda. "An office tower, most of it already leased by General Motors and IBM."

Miranda gazed at the concrete shell

thrusting skyward. But it was the scaffolding that held her attention. "It's very strange; what is it made of?"

"Bamboo. Lashed with plastic straps at the joints. Extremely strong, and light enough to move easily from job to job."

She studied it from top to bottom, where the poles were planted on the sidewalk without anchors. "It looks as if one gust of wind could bring the whole thing down."

"Oh, I imagine it would take three or four gusts, at least."

She shot him a look. "I wasn't making fun of it. Can we get out for a minute?"

"Of course." They stood on the sidewalk, looking up at the building, and Miranda laid her hand along the scaffolding. "It's just that I'm so used to steel—"

"Father!" Li turned and saw his son striding toward him. "You told me you wouldn't be here until later."

"We just stopped by for a minute," Li said in Chinese, then, in English, he introduced him to Miranda, "My son, Yuan Sheng. Miranda Graham." The two of them shook hands, Miranda smiling tentatively, Sheng stone-faced, and Li knew that Sheng was waiting for an explanation. "Excuse me," he said to Miranda, then spoke in Chinese to Sheng. "We're on our way to the market; would you care to join us?"

"No. Who is she?"

"A designer from New York." That was not exactly true, but it was simpler than trying to explain Boulder Colorado. "She's working with some garment manufacturers and I'm showing her Beijing; it's her first visit here. Why don't you join us?"

"I have too much work to do to loll about markets in the middle of the day. Is she the reason you're being followed?"

Li stared at him. "What?"

"Yes, I thought you hadn't noticed. Usually you can spot them as well as any of us; why haven't you seen it?" He looked challengingly at Li, as if accusing him of getting soft . . . or, perhaps, too absorbed in a woman to see what was happening to him. But why should I be alert? Li wondered. I have not been followed in years. Why would I be now? Unless, Miranda is the one who— No, there is nothing in her that would interest the government.

"How do you know she's really a designer?" Sheng demanded. "What *do* you know about her?"

"Enough to believe she is a designer. I don't believe anyone is following either one of us. You're probably mistaken."

"I know what I saw."

"Then it's someone else's mistake," Li said impatiently. "I'll find out. Probably some minor bureaucrat got me mixed up with someone else."

"How will you find out?"

"I'll find out; I know some people—" He stopped. "Why don't *you* find out? Your friend Pan Chao works at the State Security Bureau; why don't you ask him?"

"I never ask him about his work. Where is she staying?"

"At the Palace. Why?"

"I just wondered. Stay away from her, father; no one was following you before she came along." He turned to Miranda. "Enjoy your visit," he said curtly, in English, and strode off.

Li gave a small shrug, annoyed by his son's shortness. But he was more shaken than he had revealed to Sheng. Why would he be under surveillance? If he really was. . . . He scanned the opposite side of the street but saw no one unusual. That meant nothing; skillful operatives blended in with any crowd; they could blend into an empty room, if they really were good.

But, Sheng could be wrong. Moody, unpredictable, prone to tantrums even as a grown man, he exaggerated dangers, partly because he liked the thrill of living with them. Li knew his son was involved in illegal businesses and he knew what some of them were. If Sheng thought his father was being followed, perhaps he was imagining it from the fear that someone might be watching Li to find out more about Sheng. Convoluted, Li thought, but in China, we live with such complicated thinking.

But I'm sure it's his imagination. It is not a particularly odd fantasy, in China, where such things go on all the time.

But still, I'll keep an eye out.

"I apologize for my son's rudeness," he said to Miranda, "and for my own, in leaving you out of the conversation. He had something to say to me—"

"It's all right," Miranda said. "He's in his own country; he can speak his own language."

Li watched her consider questions about Sheng, then put them aside. She has better manners than my son, he thought. But then Sheng's voice echoed in his memory. *How do you know she's really a designer? No one was following you before she came along.*

And how much do I really know about her? Li thought. She talked about her children, her husband, a little bit about her work. Not so much, really. If even that much was true.

In the car, he said, "I don't think you told me the name of the company you work for."

She was surprised at the change in subject, but once again she was too polite—or too clever?—to say anything. "Talia," she said. "It's a small house, but we're growing very fast. Talia Greenhouse is the owner, and her husband is the treasurer. If you watch fashion shows on CNN, you'd know Talia. Of course we've only been part of group shows of small companies, but—"

"I do know it. The suit you're wearing is a Talia."

"Was that a lucky guess?"

"It was the cut of the jacket."

Miranda contemplated him. "Do you always notice details like that?"

"Construction engineers always notice

details," he said, making light of it. "And you've worked for Talia . . . how long?"

"Almost ten years."

"But not as a designer the whole time?"

"No. Didn't I tell you this? I was a secretary first, and then they sent me to school for a year." She looked at him closely. "Is something wrong?"

"No." He said it swiftly. Because nothing was. Why would he doubt her? She was open and honest; there was nothing devious in her face or her voice. He was beginning to think like Sheng and it made him ashamed. "My son asked about you," he said, "and I realized I didn't know your company."

She let it go even though Li could see that she was still puzzled. "Tell me about your son."

"Sheng and I are not close, but we work together and I hope someday he will run the company himself."

"Doesn't he want to?"

"Very much, but it will take time for him to learn everything, especially how to behave with clients and foreign investors. He's not ready for the responsibility that goes with someone being—how do you say it?—groomed for the job. Right now, he and two friends—or perhaps accomplices—have their fingers in too many pots for him to give our company his full attention. The three of them own two nightclubs, and some other businesses. So I have no idea if he ever will settle down in my company, but right now he does his work adequately and it keeps us close—in proximity, that is—and that should help us if he decides he would like to be my friend."

"Is he married?"

"Yes, and he has a son. His wife is the daughter of a government official and she and her father are part-owners of a company that makes copies of Benetton clothing. I do not think Sheng is involved in that."

"That's illegal. A company's line of clothing is copyrighted. And China has signed the International Copyright Agreement."

"But as it happens, illegality is a loose term in China."

"I don't understand. If your government signed the agreement, either it's illegal or it isn't."

He shrugged. "It is illegal except when it makes money. Benetton is only one of hundreds. Tearing off is a thriving business in China."

"Ripping off. Why doesn't the government stop it?"

"Because the government is involved in it; because people in the government, like others outside the government, make money at it. Those of us who don't like it look the other way."

"That's crazy. The *government* owns businesses that are illegal?"

"Not exactly the government. People in it. Mostly the sons and daughters of high government officials. That will change someday; already they are stopping the military from owning factories and smuggling goods." He saw her look and sighed. "It is a long story."

There was a pause. "You said you had two children. A son and daughter."

"Yes, I have a daughter, Shuiying. Her life is not like mine, but still, we are better friends than Sheng and I. Sheng has much growing up to do. We would have to work at becoming friends and it is not clear that he wants that."

"Perhaps he doesn't know how."

"And you think I can teach him?"

"I think we never stop teaching our children; we just teach them different things in different ways as they grow up, try to make suggestions without their realizing we're doing it. My friends talk about how much easier life will be when their children leave home, but from what I can tell children never leave home. I mean, they're always inside us and I can't imagine ever not worrying about Adam and Lisa being well and happy and not in danger, or thinking they need my advice."

There was a silence. "Yes, you are very wise," Li murmured. "However much we would like to peel them off from us, we cannot do it. Well, now let us pay attention to where we are. You should be seeing the city and I should be telling you about it."

Together they watched Beijing unfold as they drove down wide avenues and narrow alleys, turning corners from commercial streets to residential ones, then to chaotic jumbles of both. Twice Li looked through the rear window of the car, but he could not pick out anyone in the dense traffic who might be following them. No one, he thought. There's no one. Sheng was imagining it. I already decided that.

He saw Miranda looking to right and left and knew that what caught her attention was something he took for granted these days: everywhere, up and down the streets and alleys, dozens of yellow construction cranes stood out against the sky, swinging about like prehistoric monsters shining through the haze of polluted air. "As if a whole new city is going up," Miranda said wonderingly. "But what was there before the skyscrapers? They must be tearing down whole blocks of . . . what?"

"*Hutongs.* Streets—more like alleys, really—lined with small shops and huts where the poor lived for centuries. Now there is no place for them."

"The *hutongs* or the poor?"

"Both. The *hutongs* are demolished and the poor are pushed back, to the edges of the city. Exactly as it is in America." He saw Miranda begin to say something, then stop. "What?" he asked.

She gave a small laugh. "I was about to defend America. But the poor aren't welcome anywhere, I guess; we'd rather make them invisible and go on believing that we're prosperous and successful."

"But you are, you and your family: prosperous and successful."

"Oh, no, we've never been prosperous."

"No? What have you been, then?"

"Oh, sort of on the edge of being poor. Not starving, but always having to watch every penny."

"And you call that being poor."

"Compared to—" She stopped. "Why are you smiling?"

"Because only a spoiled child defines poor as something compared to something else. People who are truly poor know that it is an absolute. You are starving, and you have no pennies to watch."

"*Spoiled child?*"

"No, no, I did not mean that you are one. America is the spoiled child. Too much money, too much wealth, too many *things.* Americans have no idea what true poverty is." He waited, but she said nothing. "It has nothing to do with you. I did not mean to insult you."

"There's no superiority in being poor," she said coldly. "You're not better than we are, *less spoiled, more grown up,* just because you've known worse poverty. We may define it differently, but that doesn't mean we don't have problems, too."

"You're right. I apologize. Tell me what it means to you to be on the edge of being poor." She was silent. "Please. I want to understand."

"It means you don't have any savings," she said flatly, "and you worry about what would happen if you got sick and couldn't work. It means you can buy necessities, but all around you, on television and in stores, are gadgets and art and jewelry and designer clothes and expensive cars, and they could all be on the moon as far as you're concerned. We have one car with about eighty thousand miles on it and our house is small and needs a new roof—why do you keep looking out the back window?"

He swung around. "I'm sorry. I was looking for something, but it is not there. Please forgive me. Will you tell me about your house?"

"It's really very ordinary. It's made of cedar siding that's weathered to gray, and everything is on one floor: one big living and dining room, three small bedrooms, a family room, a sunroom that Jeff and my father built, a two-car garage with a work-shop at the back and Adam's basketball net—"

"Your son."

"Yes."

"Thirteen years old."

"Yes, what a good memory you have. His basketball net is over the garage door. We have a front porch with a swing that needs painting and wicker chairs and tables, and they need painting, too. The front yard is all wild grasses and flowers and huge old trees, with a stream running through it and an old bridge that you cross to get from the street to the brick front walk that goes up to the house. We have a real yard in back, where Lisa and I—"

"Your daughter."

"Yes, fourteen years old. Lisa and I grow flowers and vegetables along the fence, and their friends come over for croquet and badminton and lemonade. And there's a small kiln in the garage for Lisa's ceram-ics; she's very good; she's won national prizes for two of her pieces."

"And where do you work?"

"In the sunroom. I put my computer in

one corner, and a copier and a couch and my files, and a—"

"What is in the files?"

"Sketches, yarn and fabric samples, buttons, trimmings, magazine clippings, photos from designers' shows. I put cork squares on the wall so I can pin up the sketches I'm working on."

"And a drawing table?"

"No, I like to curl up on the couch when I'm sketching. I scan the sketches into my computer to finish them. And I have a sewing table; I make a lot of our clothes."

"It sounds like a very nice house," Li said, after a moment. "Not what I would call ordinary."

"Oh, it is. There are millions like it, all over America." There was a pause. "It's hardly a mansion," she flung at him. There was another pause, and then their eyes met and they laughed, and Li felt a rush of affection because her laugh showed that she understood that, to most people in the world, her house *would* be a mansion, and not ordinary at all, although, until now, she probably had never thought of it that way.

"Where do you live?" Miranda asked.

"In an old courtyard house from the last

century. I will show you; we can go there—"
Her face changed, as it had before, surprise verging on suspicion, and, as before,
Li backed off. "We're almost at the market;
just a few minutes."

"Can we walk?" she asked. "I can see
more that way."

"A good idea." He spoke to the driver,
and when he and Miranda stood on the
sidewalk, he bent to tie his shoe, making a
quick survey of the street as he did so. Half
a block away, a car stopped and a man got
out and turned in their direction. Li noted
his dark suit and blue shirt with a red and
blue tie, then stood up and turned to
Miranda. "I told the driver to pick us up in
an hour and a half, which should get you to
your meeting in good time. Is that all
right?"

"Yes. Thank you." She looked in the
direction he had looked, and in a moment
turned back, to observe the street before
them. They were on a narrow, crumbling
sidewalk running along a solid wall of identical five-story apartment buildings that
stretched block after block into the distant
haze, each apartment with an open bal-
cony piled high with green vegetables. On

their other side was a busy four-lane street. In the curbside lane, old men and women pulling loaded handcarts looked up to observe Miranda, their gaze lingering as they moved past. Li saw her face tense, then relax as she recognized that there was no animosity in their eyes, only curiosity, and soon she was returning their looks steadily, even smiling, and once, when she said a clear *"Ni hao"*—"Good day"—she was given a smile in return.

"It's a few blocks this way," he said, and they began to walk.

In spite of the worry he could not banish, he was happy, feeling like an explorer in his own city. But soon he became uncomfortable, aware of the filthy, littered sidewalks, the choking exhaust fumes and strident din of traffic, the dingy buildings, the shabbiness of the old people and their dragging steps.

He wanted Miranda not to see all of that; he wanted her to feel the vitality of Beijing, the surging energy evidenced by construction cranes and young people in jeans and Nike running shoes; professionals in sleek Italian business suits carrying cellular phones and shiny leather briefcases filled

with the commerce of the world; sophisticated department stores and international
boutiques. Instead she was eyeing the
garbage along the curbing. He tightened
inside. "This is an old part of town. You've
seen how different things are in the modern neighbor—"

"Oh, look," Miranda said. They had come
to a tiny clearing between apartment buildings. In the hard-packed dirt, old men in
baggy trousers and faded jackets were
hanging covered birdcages on wire hooks
dangling from the branches of scrawny
trees. When the men pulled off the covers,
the birds, tiny canaries and parakeets,
began to sing. They sang and sang, joyful
with the freedom of sunlight, hopping from
perch to floor to swinging perch while the
old men sat on worn tree stumps, gossiping.

Li smiled. "They do this every day. Their
apartments are cramped and dark, and
they bring their birds here for fresh air.
Sometimes they swing the cages in wide
circles; they call that exercising the birds.
But the main thing is to be in the fresh air."

"How lovely. They all get to escape."

"Not the birds," Li said, amused.

"Oh, but they do; they escape the bigger cages, the ones the men live in. Look at them, how happy they are, the men and the birds, all sharing their freedom. Don't you think so? I mean, we all have more than one cage, don't we, and if we can escape from one . . ." Her voice faltered beneath his intense gaze. "Of course I don't know anything about it, not in China, anyway."

"What are your cages?" Li asked.

"Oh, it was just an idea, very foolish, I'm afraid. These are the first pets I've seen; where are the dogs and cats?"

"The cats remain inside, and there are no dogs. Or very few. The fee for a license is too high for most people."

"Why? What's wrong with dogs?"

"They're messy; people don't clean up after them, they take needed resources. . . . The city is really better off without them."

She stared at him. "Your government decides it doesn't like dogs messing up the sidewalk, so it makes it impossible for people to own them?"

"Yes. Is this an important issue?"

"It's an issue of freedom."

"To have a dog."

"To have anything you want."

"How often in life can you have anything you want?"

"Oh—!" Frustrated, she paused, then she said, "Did you say the owners bring their birds here for *fresh* air?"

"Well, not as fresh as it might be," he acknowledged, and smiled, trying to make the discussion light again. "But better than inside an apartment."

"Is it?" she asked. "It's so hard to breathe."

"You get used to it." He was annoyed again, and did not care if she saw it. "Some countries don't have the luxury of spending money on clean air and water. That will come later, when we are as rich as you are." He met her frown. "It isn't easy to defend all of these things, but we had to decide where to put our energy and money, and we chose new offices and factories—"

"But some things are basic," she said. "Air. Water. Yours is so bad you have to use bottled water."

"Someday that will change." He turned to walk on and she hurried to catch up to him. The old men and their singing birds were left behind; nothing interrupted the solid gray wall of concrete apartment buildings. Then, in the next block, they were stopped by hundreds of bicycles, locked and leaning against each other in a tilting, tangled mass, all of them old, rusting, utilitarian, without gears or hand brakes. Most had dented baskets clamped to the handlebars or to the rear fender.

"Commuters," Li said. "They park here and take the subway to work." As they turned to walk on, out of the corner of his eye he caught a glimpse of a blue shirt and a red and blue tie. Silently, he cursed. It could be a coincidence. Or Sheng was right. If he was, it was obviously a mistake made by some stupid clerk who got Li's name mixed up with someone else's, but to cut through the bureaucracy to correct these things took time and he resented having to do it.

Unless they're following Miranda.

No. He did not believe that. The more he knew her the less he could believe it.

But whatever the truth, it seemed that there would be surveillance, but no arrest, at least not yet. So he would not let it ruin the morning. *Let them follow us; all they will learn is that two people enjoyed the market.*

"Breakfast," he said firmly, to himself as much as to Miranda, and walked a short distance to a woman and two men standing in a cloud of steam. "These are friends of mine; their food is excellent."

Warily, Miranda surveyed the small butcher-block table, scored and darkened with use, the battered oil drum with a hole in the side revealing a raging fire, and a wok perched on top bubbling with peanut oil. The woman, small and plump, swathed in an apron that hinted at once having been white, stood at the butcher-block table, kneading an enormous ball of soft dough. Li knew exactly what Miranda was thinking: Beijing's water was not drinkable; the woman's apron was not clean; and who knew when she had last washed her hands or the table top or the utensils she and the men were using, or where their ingredients came from, or how safe any food could be, prepared in the open on a dusty street, in city air acrid with exhaust fumes and residue from burning coal.

"Shall we eat?" Li asked. He knew he

was making it a test, but if she wanted to understand Beijing, she had to accept the city for what it was. *If she wants to understand me, she has to accept me for what I am.*

"Yes." Miranda exhaled a long breath, her face tight with determination. "I'd love some breakfast. I don't know how I can be hungry after last night's dinner, but I am."

Again Li felt a rush of affection, and admiration. It was harder for her to take this step than for someone who was casual about new adventures. *I wonder how many adventures she has in America. Not many, I'll bet. But, then, how many do I have in China?*

He introduced his friends to Miranda. "They play in a jazz band at night, but every day they are here. They make the best *youtiao* in Beijing. That means fried breadstick. And these are chive pancakes. You wrap a pancake around a breadstick and eat them together. It requires a wide mouth, but it is worth it." He grinned as Miranda managed to take a bite of the end of the long, thin breadstick and the oversize crepe-like pancake she had rolled around it.

She looked at him in surprise. "It's wonderful."

"One of my favorites," he said, and saw the rigid determination on her face relax as she chewed and watched the man turn another batch of breadsticks in the bubbling oil. "Would you like another?"

"Yes. Thank you."

They strolled on, eating, becoming part of the life of the street. Li casually sidestepped the chickens and roosters at his feet, but Miranda was fascinated and stared at them as they pecked at the ground around old tires, abandoned furniture and piles of garbage. But soon her attention was caught by shopkeepers unlocking their doors to reveal minuscule spaces where the entire stock could be seen from the sidewalk, goods crammed onto shelves, hanging from the ceiling, piled on the floor and, once the doors were open, helter-skelter on the sidewalk.

While Miranda was absorbed, Li looked past her. He thought he caught a glimpse of the man in the blue shirt and red and blue tie, but he was not sure, and he dismissed him once again, and studied the neighborhood. This part of town was so far from the commercial centers that it was as if they had stepped back in time, and he felt a tug of nostalgia for a simpler, slower-paced city, without massive westernization. Of course that was foolish. No one could go backward, especially Yuan Li, engineer and contractor, whose work depended on China becoming westernized: more commercial, more efficient, bigger, faster, smarter, more capitalist. This kind of neighborhood would soon be barely a memory.

Even now, it seemed strange to him, but then he realized that the strangeness was Miranda, quiet, slender, foreign. She was like a shaft of light in the drab streets, her silver-gray suit, the halo of her light hair, the creamy paleness of her skin. Li felt her beside him as if they were touching. Their steps matched, and he felt he was on a journey: this morning, he, too, was a foreigner in Beijing.

"Look," said Miranda. "Chestnuts."

Hundreds of them were lined up on a long wooden table in rows as precise as a military formation, mesh bags bulging with hundreds more on the sidewalk below. "This is where the market begins," Li said, pointing up the narrow street to their left, lined on both sides with tables and booths stretching as far as they could see.

Miranda's face was bright with discovery. "How beautiful it is."

Beneath the slanting rays of early-morning sunlight, the market was a tapestry of colors: deep brown chestnuts, pale speckled eggs, yellow-brown strands of lily buds, light brown gingerroot, glossy purple eggplant, bright red peppers and reddish-brown star anise, loops of ivory *lo mein,* skinny, yard-long green beans, deep orange carrots, pale green *bok choy,* yellow-green cucumbers shaped like scimitars, and fat, fifteen-inch-long crinkly green Chinese cabbages, the same vegetable they had seen on apartment balconies, here stacked ten feet high against walls and fences. "A favorite food," Li said wryly as Miranda stared at them. "And it stays fresh for months."

In wooden lean-tos, ducks and chickens hung upside down above blood-stained wooden counters where vendors used huge cleavers to whack them into pieces. In the middle of the street, a man in shorts and an undershirt squatted beside a wooden block, using a small knife to scrape a few last hairs from a goat's thigh. As the customer watched, he took his cleaver and hacked the leg into stew-size pieces. Scooping them up, he set them on a saucer at one end of a hand-held scale, and adjusted the weight at the other end. When the customer nodded and took coins from a purse, the butcher tilted the meat into a plastic bag, wiped his hands on a damp, blood-stained cloth, gave the wooden block a quick wipe with the same cloth, and turned to the next customer.

Farther along, fish leaped and splashed in plastic trays. When a customer chose one, the vendor killed it by slamming its head with a two-by-four, slit it open to remove the entrails, made a pass at scaling it with a few quick swipes of a blunt knife, and weighed it on a hand-held scale. Next to the fish, a table was piled high with eels no thicker than a pencil. A woman behind the table picked up an eel, slit it precisely down the center, cleaned it out with one swift movement of her finger, and flipped it to a pile ready for purchase. It was done so quickly and economically that it seemed to be one graceful movement, and even Li, who had seen it hundreds of times, paused to watch and admire.

Across the street a young girl was pressing bean curd and cutting it into neat squares, and in a booth beyond hers men with muslin caps covering their hair were making dumplings, their hands a blur as they brought up the edges of thinly rolled dough around a filling, then pinched the dough closed so that it resembled a small purse with a drawstring top.

Miranda sighed. "There's too much to see. It's like a circus, only better. So much color. Except for the people."

Li felt defensive again, even though he had had the same thought a few minutes earlier. The people wore dark blue, dark brown, black, gray, like somber splotches in the vivid oil painting of the market. "It's like the air and the water," he said as they turned to walk on. "We'll get around to brightness when we have time and money."

"And when you feel better about yourselves? More hopeful?"

He gave her a sharp look. "Why do you say that?"

"Because everyone looks so grim. Oh, not everyone—you don't—but your son did, and so many people do, as if they can't imagine having anything to smile about. Maybe they can't, maybe life really is terribly hard and they just don't feel happy. But when things get easier, when they're more hopeful, they'll wear hopeful colors, bright ones."

"Like Americans."

"Well, yes. Why not? It's good to be hopeful."

"But Americans are more than hopeful. They *expect* life to be good."

She looked at him. "Don't you?"

"No one in China expects life to be anything but hard. As it always has been. Except that we're beginning to be more like Americans; we're learning to hope. And I suppose, after that, we'll begin to expect things. Maybe even demand them. Like Americans. Always demanding."

"Oh, that's ridiculous. You said that before. You keep making such absolute statements about Americans. How do you know anything about us?"

"I read. I watch—"

"CNN. Yes, you told me. What a peculiar way to learn about a country. Why don't you talk to Americans?"

"Isn't that what I'm doing right now?"

She stopped walking and stared at him, then gave a small laugh. "Well, I knew there had to be a reason for all this attention. You want to hear about America."

"That is not the reason. Shall we have tea? We had none with our breakfast."

Just ahead of them, two women kept kettles boiling on a grate over an oil drum fire. Li and Miranda sat on a bench and watched the women put a pinch of tea in each of two mugs and pour boiling water almost to the top. "Hold it like this," said Li. He wrapped his burning-hot mug with a large paper napkin, and Miranda did the same, and they drank the fragrant tea, watching others watching them. Suddenly a woman pointed at Miranda, talking to her friend, then another did the same, pointing at her hair, her shoes, and then at Li.

"What's wrong with them?" she asked. "They're *pointing* at me. And staring. It's so rude. . . . Why are they doing it? What's wrong with me?"

"Nothing. They're admiring you. They say

your hair is like silk and your shoes are well made. They point and stare because in China that is not considered rude; it is the way people are, on the street. When life is crowded and poor, the street becomes a theater, a pageant, everyone's daily entertainment, free to all. And so they point and stare and make comments, just as you would in America, watching a show."

"We never point or stare."

"Well, here you may do it, and no one will think badly of you. Perhaps it will give you a new way of looking at the world."

Their tea was cooling and they drank it easily. The sun rose higher, growing warmer. Miranda and Li let the sounds of the market lull them. Li felt content just to sit. He thought of the man who was most likely following them. He thought of his son—hostile, contemptuous of Miranda, involved in illegal activities that might eventually threaten the company, and himself— and he knew he would have to deal with all of these things soon. But for now he simply absorbed the warmth of the day, and Miranda beside him.

"It must be time to go," Miranda said, her voice soft, almost drowsy.

"Soon."

A group of schoolboys appeared, dressed identically in shiny blue running suits with small red scarves, and backpacks bulging with books. They bought sections of grapefruit-like pomelos from a man who squatted at a low table peeling off the bitter skin and separating the large triangular segments of fruit. Juice ran down the boys' fingers and they flicked drops at each other, laughing, dodging back and forth.

Miranda sat straighter. "How lovely they are. So full of life. Like Adam and Lisa."

Li felt an odd stab of jealousy, seeing her withdraw to thoughts of her daughter and son and a life on the other side of the world, with nothing at all to do with him.

"Isn't it strange," she said. "I've been so busy, but then something reminds me of them and I remember how incredibly far away they are and I feel . . . oh, helpless, I guess; not part of their lives, with no way to be close to them. At home, you know, I hardly think about them during the day; I'm working, they're at school, we're where we belong. And I guess I miss that as much as I miss them: all of us where we belong, in our proper places. There's something so comfortable about that." She was still looking at the schoolboys. "Those red scarves . . . don't they mean they're Young Pioneers? Sort of a children's Communist Party?"

"If they want to join when they're older," Li said indifferently. "They don't have to. Many of them do, because it helps in business. It's an easy way to achieve *guanxi*. Connections."

Miranda smiled. "In America it would be called clout."

"The same thing."

The boys ran off, still in a group. Miranda watched until they were gone.

"Why did you come to China?" Li asked.

She looked at him in surprise. "I told you. I'm working with—"

"I understand that. I meant, why did you accept this assignment? You said you don't travel much, you don't like to leave home, you miss your children and the comfort of everything in its proper place."

"Yes, but—" She hesitated and Li could almost hear her debating with herself about how much to say. Was she afraid of getting too personal, or was she making sure her story was believable? Why can't I stop being suspicious of her? he thought angrily. Everything is so good, we are becoming friends. But I want to know her. Not from suspicion. Just because I want to understand who she is.

"You said you were born in Boulder Colorado," he said, "in the house where your parents still live. And you have always lived there?"

"Yes."

"And you like it very much."

"Of course."

"Even when you went to college?"

She gave him a quick look of surprise. "It seemed strange when I went to college."

"Where did you go?"

"The University of Colorado."

"In Boulder Colorado?"

She smiled. "Yes. But I met people from all over the world, and I realized that I was the only one who hadn't been anywhere, except Denver, and that was less than an hour from my front door."

"Is that what seemed strange?"

"Yes."

"Why?"

"Because I'd always thought I was the same as other people, but then I heard conversations about places I'd never even heard of. . . . No, it wasn't the places so much as the way they talked about going to them, so smooth and easy. . . . They *knew* so much, it was all part of their lives, and I didn't know anything."

"And it made you unhappy?"

"I suppose it did. But mostly just . . . envious, I guess. But then they'd talk about tetanus shots, and gamma globulin injections, and malaria pills, and buying insect repellant and Imodium and those little rolls of toilet paper for places that don't have any—maybe not even toilets—and fending off beggars and not drinking the water, and everything sounded uncomfortable and dangerous and I'd think that even if they did know more than I did, I couldn't imagine going through all that. Besides not knowing languages or how I'd get around. . . . And then I married Jeff and we never had much money."

"So you've still never been farther than Denver."

"Of course I have. I go to New York two

or three times a year to meet with Talia and other designers, and some of our customers."

"So you know New York."

"A little. I go there to work; I don't have time to be a tourist."

"But you could make the time?"

"I suppose so. I'm always anxious to get home."

"Because your children need you?"

"Because that's where I like to be," she snapped. After a moment, she added, "It would be different if I were with someone. I do go to museums and art galleries sometimes, but I hate eating alone in a restaurant, so I eat in my hotel room, and once I went alone to the opera, and I hated that, too. Everyone was part of a couple and at intermission they were all drinking champagne, talking, laughing, and I wandered around thinking they were all wondering what was wrong with me that I didn't have anyone—"

Li's eyebrows rose in shock, and she said quickly, "I *know* they weren't really wondering that—I know that no one was paying any attention to me at all—but that's how I felt, I felt *different,* and I can't stand that, so I just went back to my seat and stayed there."

"The same as eating dinner in your hotel room," Li said.

"What's so terrible about that?" she shot back.

"Only that you miss many things. And it can be fine to be alone with one's own thoughts and feelings; often one's own company is the best."

"What do you know about it? You live in a country where there are always crowds."

"You just told me you can be very much alone in a crowd. And I am, often, very much alone."

"Why?"

"Well, we can talk about me later. Right now, we are talking about you, and I am wondering why you are in China."

"Because Talia asked me to come."

He heard more in her voice. "And?"

"I thought it might be interesting." She gazed across the road, watching the vendor slit open another pomelo and strip off its thick skin. "A lot has changed in my life in the past couple of years, so much that sometimes I can't seem to get a handle on it—" She saw his look of puzzlement, and said, "Understand it. I can't seem to understand what I'll be, *who* I'll be, when the pattern of my life changes. I thought it was fixed, like a painting, you know, with everything permanently in place, so it never occurred to me to wonder who I really was and who I want to—" She stopped. "I don't know why I'm telling you this."

"Because I am interested. Because it is often easiest to talk to someone you do not know well. Because when we are far from our familiar world we see ourselves in new ways. Because the sun is shining. Because you are comfortable with me."

She was smiling. "Probably."

"Then tell me. A lot has changed in your life."

"Yes, just in the past couple of years. Adam and Lisa grew up so fast—they took a huge leap when they went into junior high school—and they're thinking about themselves and their world in new ways, and most of the time they don't want me to be involved. I'm not complaining—I know they love me and they like knowing I'm around—but what they really need is to be with their friends, and by themselves, too, and they don't want me hanging over them, telling them what to do or how to solve their problems, worrying about them . . . well, they know I can't stop worrying; what they really don't want is to worry about me worrying about them. They want the freedom of not feeling guilty about me, and I understand that, but it's hard to deal with."

"And it's hard not to feel hurt when they shut you out," Li said. "So you said, 'The hell with it, I'll go to China.' I'll bet they were surprised."

She laughed. "They were. You would have thought I was abandoning them."

"But they got over it."

"Right away," she said, her voice faintly wistful. "Nothing really changed in their lives, you know. In fact, the day I left, Adam had a soccer game after school and Lisa was going to meet with her ceramics class to get ready for their first show of the school year, so we said goodbye at breakfast and they went off to school and my parents took me to the airport."

"And have you talked to them since you've been here?"

"No, I'm going to call at noon today. That's nine o'clock last night in Boulder. I think. Is that right? It makes me feel even farther from them, not even sharing the same day, much less the same time. Oh, time." She looked at her watch. "I really must go."

"Yes," he said, and stood up. He felt a little dizzy and thought he must have moved too quickly, or perhaps it was the sunlight, or sitting too long. But as Miranda stood with him, he knew it was for none of those reasons; it was a sudden rush of desire, almost overpowering, the kind he had not known for years. And from the abrupt way she turned from him, he knew she had seen it in his eyes. "My driver will be waiting at the corner, near the chestnut stand, and he is always on time." He was talking rapidly, to cover the pounding of his heart. "You will not be late, I promise, even with the traffic; we took account of that, and there are many routes we can take. You need not worry; you will be on time."

Miranda was looking at the market, as if absorbed in the vendors and their wares, but it was clear to Li that her thoughts were elsewhere. They walked in silence, pushing through the crowds that had increased since their arrival. Li was amused to see that Miranda did not cringe when others shoved her; she still had difficulty making progress because she had not learned to shove back, but she had made a beginning. He lost sight of her as shoppers thrust between them, and even though he saw the man following them suddenly come very close, he could not think about him; almost frantically he searched for Miranda amid the throngs until, in a few seconds that felt like an hour, he saw her slim, pale figure, that shaft of light amidst the dark, and caught up to her. "Stay with me," he said, keeping his voice light. "If we lose each other you'll be late for your meeting." And so they moved forward, pressed together in the crowd.

His car was waiting and when they sat in the back seat and closed the doors it was as if they had entered a cave, hushed and dim behind the tinted windows. Li looked at his watch. "My driver will take you to the garment factory, but I must get to my office for a meeting. If you do not mind, we will go there first and discard me—"

"Drop you off."

"Yes, that sounds better, thank you. Drop me off. You will still be on time. When you are finished, would you like me to send

him back for you? He can take you wherever you want to go."

"No, thank you, you've been a wonderful
guide but you have other things to think
about; you can't be worrying about me. I
have so much to do; I'll be busy all day."

"And for dinner?" he asked.

She let out her breath in a long sigh. "I
could pretend that I'm busy, but . . . no, I
have no plans for dinner. Except—" She
looked at her hands, then looked up at
him. "I probably ought to stay in my room. I
have work to do, writing up today's meetings and getting ready for tomorrow."

"Another dinner alone in a hotel room?"
She flushed, and he said, "I'm sorry; I don't
mean to criticize you. I would very much
like to have dinner with you, and if we
begin a little earlier than last night, there
still would be time for you to do your work."

Her eyes searched his face. "There is
nothing sinister in this," he said quietly.
"Just more time to be together."

"So you can learn more about America."

"That is not what I'm thinking about right
now."

"What are you thinking about?"

"You. How to be with you. Nothing more."

She flushed again, a rush of color suffusing her face. Her eyes were still on his, and Li felt the air charged between them. They sat in opposite corners of the plush seat, but they were being drawn together, and he knew Miranda felt it, too.

The car pulled up at a modern office building. Li took his briefcase and held out his hand and they shook hands formally. "Thank you for a wonderful morning," she said. "I enjoyed it so much."

"And so did I." He waited, still holding her hand.

"Six-thirty," Miranda said. "If that's all right."

Relief swept through him. "Yes."

"If you can't come, you can leave a message at my hotel."

He shook his head and smiled, exultant because, whatever else this day held, he could look ahead, toward their evening. "I'll call you from your lobby at six-thirty. And everything will be excellent."

He walked across the small plaza to the double doors of his office building. Glancing around, he saw the car with the man following him parked across the street as his own driver edged away from the curb.

Miranda was looking back. He held up his hand in farewell and hers came up in just the same way, and then the car plunged into the stream of traffic and was gone. He paused for another moment, still feeling her palm against his when they shook hands, seeing her eyes, direct and searching, hearing her voice, a little wavering on, "Six-thirty," firmer and settled on, "If that's all right."

Oh, yes, he thought, it is very much all right. Once in the lobby of his building, he gave a moment's serious consideration to what would be the perfect restaurant for dinner. Then, reaching the elevator, he thought of what he had to do: first a meeting to put together a bid on a new project, and then the complicated process of finding out why he was being followed, and whom he could get to quickly, to end it— someone high enough in the bureaucracy to change an order with one phone call.

He was angry at being forced to do all this. They had left him alone for so many years; he had created a life that was quiet and orderly and unthreatened, and it was infuriating to face once again this fear that grew from the seeds of intimidation, and to be distracted from his time with Miranda, the first woman in a long time to—

How do you know she's really a designer? What do you know about her?

Enough, Li thought. Well, perhaps not yet enough. But I'll learn more about her; I'll find out everything. I just need some time, and I'll find out all I need to know, about everything.

Chapter 3

Miranda and Yun Chen bent over the table, so engrossed they had forgotten there were others in the conference room. This was Miranda's second day at the factory and she had arrived prepared to do battle. Instead, the men had remained silent while Yun Chen opened the meeting, and then the two women had gone to work. All morning, they had worked on designs that had caused problems earlier, and, to her surprise, Miranda was having a good time. And as they arranged and rearranged various parts of suits and sweaters, she had discovered, with even greater surprise, that they shared the same goal, of achieving the best designs at good prices, not exorbitant ones, for both Talia and the Beijing Higher Fashion Garments Factory.

"Perhaps a cape," Yun Chen said.

Miranda shook her head. "I tried that." She took a sketch from her folder. "It doesn't work with the short skirt. It will, when we get to the long skirts . . ." She paused, contemplating the sketch in her hand. "A shawl, though . . ."

The suit was cashmere and wool; the sweater cashmere and silk, with a silk scarf. It was a simple, elegant design, but just before Miranda arrived in China, Yun Chen had seen the Dolce & Gabbana spring catalogue, with a suit so close in design that Miranda knew she would have to drop hers or change it.

"A shawl," Yun Chen repeated. She watched Miranda make quick strokes on the sketch, adding a lightweight shawl, the silk scarf a colorful splash in the soft folds at the neck. "Yes, very good, Miranda. This is a good idea. And a shawl is lower cost to make than a jacket."

"Double-faced cashmere," Miranda said. "Washed for softness."

"Yes, absolutely. And perhaps a trim—"

"A fringe. Very fine threads of silk, multi-colored, to match the scarf."

"Oh, I like this very much. Better than Dolce and Gabbana. You have a good eye. You see the whole picture. That is an excellent talent."

"And so do you," Miranda said.

"No, alas, I do not. I am very good at catching ideas and perhaps modifying them and thinking how to manufacture them at a good cost to us, but the original design . . . I do not have that talent. I stare at my piece of paper for hours and nothing comes to me."

Miranda smiled. "That happens to me, too. I think anyone who creates goes through that: when it seems there's absolutely nothing in your mind to fill the paper."

"But then you think of something. I do not."

"Well, it's my job," Miranda said simply, ending the discussion. They were being ridiculously kind to each other. But, when had she had *that* complaint since coming to China?

"It is almost noon," Yun Chen said. "You said this was the time you wished to make a telephone call?"

Miranda looked at her watch. How quickly the morning had passed! "Yes, thank you. Is there an empty office I can use?"

The men at the table stood up and Wang Zedong, the director of manufacture, bowed and said, "I will take you to my office. You may use it for as long as you wish."

"And we will continue after lunch," said Yun Chen. "It is going so well."

Very well, Miranda thought as Wang shut the door of his office, leaving her alone. Better than before. And that meant she could call home without defeat resonating in her voice.

She gave the operator her telephone number in Boulder, and sat back, looking around the room: a steel desk, three straight-backed chairs, two steel filing cabinets. A vinyl floor; no window. The office would have been completely anonymous were it not for a photograph on the bare desktop, showing a woman smiling shyly at the camera, a young boy grinning on her lap.

She wondered what Li's office looked like. Whose pictures were on his desk?

The telephone rang. "I have your party," the operator said in careful English.

"Mom!" Adam yelled. "Can you hear me?"

Miranda laughed. "As if you're just around the corner. You don't have to shout, sweetheart."

"Say something in Chinese." His voice was barely a notch lower.

"*Ni hao. Zai-jiang.*"

"Really weird. What does it mean?"

"Good morning, or How are you? And goodbye."

"Yech, boring. Say something else."

"That's for next time. Now tell me what you've been doing."

"Nothing."

"What does that mean?"

"You know, the usual."

"Mom, hi, we miss you," Lisa said on another telephone.

"Hey," Adam protested, "we said we'd talk one at a time."

"I couldn't wait. Mom, say something in Chinese."

"She already did that."

"Not to me."

"Well, she was talking to me! It's my turn!"

"It's both our turn!"

"I see everything's absolutely normal," Miranda said, strangely delighted with their squabbling. "Okay, one of you tell me what you've been doing. And don't say 'nothing.' I've been gone three days; you must have been doing something."

In a rush, before she could be interrupted, Lisa said, "I sold one of my teapots at the ceramics show."

"Oh, Lisa, how wonderful. Your first sale. Oh, I wish I'd been—"

"We beat Longmont in soccer," Adam yelled, "if you really want something *exciting!*"

"Very exciting." She settled back and listened as her children described their triumphs. As their voices overlapped, her thoughts wandered to the Chinese students she had seen that morning. They had been just as lively as children everywhere, but somehow less aggressive, more orderly in their play than most American boys, with not even a hint of rowdiness. *Li must have been like that: a serious, quiet little boy wishing for a father.*

She listened to her children's bubbling enthusiasm, and closed her eyes, picturing her house: golden sunlight pouring in through big square windows along the back, the front porch shaded by towering trees. When she opened them, and saw the stark walls and gray furniture of a Chinese office, she thought what an odd place this was for her to be. I belong in Boulder Colorado USA, she thought, hearing Li's voice saying it that way, like one word, and I'm going to finish here as soon as I can. Six days left; that's not so many.

"What about homework?" she asked as her children's stories wound down.

"Oh, right," Adam said. "Tons. Bye, Mom." And as abruptly as his conversation had begun, it was over. In a minute, Lisa followed, and then Miranda's parents were there. "I apologize for my grandchildren," her father said. "They didn't ask one question about you."

Miranda laughed. "At thirteen and fourteen? The only thing kids that age find fascinating is themselves. Anyway, even if you could civilize them, you haven't been there long enough."

"They're lovely children; I'm not complaining—"

"What *are* you doing?" her mother asked. "Is everything going all right?"

"Today it did. Everything is so different, I can't always tell, but today I worked with a woman in manufacturing and we liked each other, so it was fun. I'm learning a lot, and seeing a lot, and I've made a friend—"

She stopped. She had not meant to say that. But when the words kept coming, she knew how much she wanted to talk about Li, and had no one to talk to, except her parents. "He's an engineer, his company builds office buildings and apartments— you wouldn't believe the amount of building going on here—and he's been so helpful, explaining things and showing me the city—"

"How did you meet him?" her father asked.

He picked me up at the airport.

That won't do, she thought in amusement. Think of something else. But she was not good at lying, so she evaded it. "It was just chance. His company built the factory where I had my first meeting, and since then we've gone to dinner and this morning to a local market—"

"Who introduced you?"

"No one, we just started talking. His father was an American soldier, helping the Chinese build airfields—"

"No way did we help any communists build airfields," her father declared.

"It wasn't the communists then; it was just the Chinese and they were being invaded by the Japanese—" She sighed. It seemed far too complicated and perhaps unbelievable. Told by Li, the story had been simple and moving, but with her parents it became a tangled web that she could not weave into a smooth tale. And so, as much as she wanted to talk about him, she could not. "Let me tell you about the market this morning; both of you would love it."

But she had barely begun to describe it when her mother said, "But what about your work?"

"I told you," she said, almost impatiently. "It's fine."

"You said today was all right. What about before that?"

"It was different; I told you, everything is different. And it takes a while to learn how to get along in—"

"Are they trying to take advantage of you?" her father demanded.

"I suppose so. Well, I mean, we expect that, don't we? We all do that in business."

"What are you talking about? Americans play fair. Tough but fair. You can't let those people get away with anything, Miranda; you have to keep your guard up."

"I am, but that isn't the problem."

"Well, what is?"

"I am. I'm not pushing hard enough. Li says that all Americans—"

"Who?"

"My friend, the one I told you about. Yuan Li. He says Americans are aggressive and demanding, and I suppose a lot of us are, but I'm not."

"You shouldn't put yourself down," her mother said. "Talia wouldn't have sent you to China if she weren't sure you could handle it. Are you saying they don't like your designs? I can't believe that."

"I have no idea whether they do or not."

"They didn't say? But that's very rude."

"They're never rude; they're painfully polite."

"What does that mean?"

Miranda sighed. "Mother, rudeness isn't an issue. Whether they like the designs or not, they'll make them, because it's their job. They don't have to like something to make it to our specifications."

"Well, but they could admire your designs. It would make for more pleasant relations between you."

"They're not looking for pleasant relations; they're trying to make a profit. And they never seem to get tired; they're ready to talk forever, wearing everyone down, to make a point or get a concession."

"Well, they won't wear you down," her father said flatly. "It's just a matter of being more strong-willed than they are. Don't tell us you aren't aggressive, because you can be if you have to be. When you don't like what they're saying, just tell them it's not acceptable. Tell them you're going home. I'll bet their tongues are hanging out for this deal and if you started for the airport they'd chase you and beg you to come back."

Miranda tried to envision the Chinese officials she had dealt with chasing her with their tongues hanging out, and she burst out laughing.

"What?" her father demanded.

"They would never be seen with their tongues hanging out," she said. "They're very uptight."

"You mean they're proper?"

"Very."

"And respectful?"

"Very."

"But not pleasant."

"Not especially. They're controlled and tenacious and determined to make the biggest profit they can."

"They sound like capitalists," her mother said.

"They're communists!" her father exclaimed.

"They're not communists or capitalists," Miranda said. "They're businessmen."

And with that, she knew she had taken the first step in understanding China. Li would be impressed, she thought.

And when she told him that night, he

was. "An excellent observation," he said, opening a bottle of red wine. They had arrived at the restaurant a few minutes earlier and he had led her through the noisy, cavernous room, crammed with round tables for twelve, to a row of doors in the far wall. Opening one of them, he let Miranda go ahead, into a small private room. In the center a round table was set for two; in a corner stood two deep armchairs, with a small cinnabar table between them. The walls were of red damask hung with Chinese landscapes, and light came from lanterns and two flickering candles on the table.

Miranda stood just inside the door, alarmed by the intimacy of the room. *A bordello.* What did he think—?

"Pleasant, isn't it?" Li said. "My partners and I thought Beijing needed something like this."

"Your partners?" Her voice was tight, but he seemed not to notice it.

"Four of us own the restaurant."

She thought of asking him how people could own private businesses in China, but she was too upset. *I should tell him to take me back to the hotel.* But the words would not come. All day she had looked forward to the evening, storing up things to tell him, taking pleasure in the idea of sharing her day with him, and even in her anger she could not end it before it had even begun. *I could tell him I want to sit out there, in the big room.*

"What is it?" he asked. "You're angry."

She had been looking around the room; now she found herself staring at the table, perfectly set for two people. Li's eyes narrowed, as he understood. "That is an insult to me."

"That's too bad," she said, finally regaining her voice. "*You've* insulted *me.*"

"*Lao tian,*" he said in exasperation. "Why are you such a child? I brought you to one of the finest restaurants in Beijing, I offered you a room with more beauty and comfort than the main room, and privacy and quiet if you want them. I did not say that we had to close the door. I would never say that to you."

Miranda's face grew hot. *Damn him. He's so superior—that damned Asian superciliousness—I'm getting so tired of it . . .*

But he's right. I decided, much too fast. . . . Why was I in such a hurry?

"You're right," she said. "I'm sorry, I really am sorry. I was wrong. It's just that . . . it's a lovely room, but, you know, it does look like a . . . at least what I *think* a. . . . It does have an illicit look."

He smiled easily, the storm passed. "Private is the word. Privacy is much harder to find in Beijing than sex. By the way, the table can be expanded to seat ten, so these rooms are used mainly for business." He gazed at her for a moment, as if waiting, but she did not move from the doorway, and so he did. Casually, he sat in one of the armchairs, legs crossed, at ease. "We're famous for our dumplings, and once again I've taken the liberty of ordering for us. I also brought this wine, in case you're getting tired of beer."

"French estate wine," Miranda said, making out the label from where she stood. "In Beijing."

"One can get anything in Beijing. And right now wine and liqueurs show up everywhere. Another symbol of growing wealth. Which means westernization." He

took up the wine opener. "Will you not sit
with me?"

Still standing near the door, she said,
"I'm sorry my father can't see this room,
and your restaurant. I told him today the
people I'm working with aren't communists
or capitalists, but businessmen."

He laughed. "An excellent observation.
There are no serious political systems
anymore. Just business. And connections.
And money. Which, when you think about
it, are all the same thing."

He was concentrating on the wine bottle. Miranda watched him, then glanced at
the crowded restaurant, and finally took a
deep breath. "It's so noisy out there. Could
we close the door?"

"Of course," he said easily, and she
closed it quickly, quietly, and went to the
other armchair. She could feel her heartbeat, and knew that it was because of the
room. She had apologized for thinking of it
as illicit, but she could not banish its intimacy, and as she was engulfed by red
damask walls and flickering candlelight,
she felt she had stepped out of something,
as one would a costume or a pair of heavy

boots, leaving behind much of whatever had made her the person she had been, living the life she had known.

It was no longer a frightening feeling; actually, she felt quite well. After a long day, she was grateful for the hushed room: a place apart from the teeming crush of the city and the fray of negotiations, apart from the world. Privacy, she thought. Silence.

Li filled their wine glasses. "To privacy and silence."

Startled, she paused, then raised her glass. "Thank you for both of them. Beijing certainly needs them, but so did I."

"Was it not a good day?"

"It was better than yesterday. And the afternoon was better yet."

"After you explained Chinese business-men to your father? Neither communists nor capitalists?"

"Yes. Everyone began to seem almost ordinary."

"And were you more aggressive then?"

She tasted the wine. "Oh, this is very good. May I see the label?"

He gave her the bottle. "Are you familiar with burgundy wines?"

"I'm not familiar with any wines. I just like to know what I'm drinking."

"Very wise." He waited while she read the label. "So you were not more aggressive, even when you knew how ordinary we all are."

She set down the bottle. "You're not."

"Thank you. I hope not, because I think by ordinary you mean dull and predictable. But it is difficult to know who is ordinary today, and who is different. In fact, there is more difference between generations in China right now than between Chinese and foreigners."

"That can't be true."

"Oh, it most certainly is. Our young people have become like Americans: they don't care about politics; they only want to make money and pile up possessions and live the good life: restaurants and nightclubs, designer clothes, fast cars, travel abroad."

She felt herself tighten up again. "That's how you define Americans?"

"There are many ways to define a people. I should have said most Americans, not all. And most French and Germans and Russians and Egyptians and everybody else."

"But not you?"

"I have a comfortable life, but it is not my only goal."

"What is?"

He smiled. "That is a long story. Are you ready for dinner?"

"Yes."

At the table, he held her chair for her, then pushed a button in the wall. Almost immediately a waitress appeared carrying a steamer basket of woven bamboo. She set it in the center of the table, lifted off the lid to reveal four tiny dumplings, and left, closing the door behind her.

"Shrimp," Li said and used his chopsticks to set two dumplings on Miranda's plate, and two on his own. He pulled a shallow, divided serving dish close to them. "These are for dipping. Be careful of this one; the chilies are quite hot."

Miranda gazed at the white pouches on her plate, no more than an inch across, their tops pinched together, their surfaces glistening. They looked slippery. And she had nothing to use but her chopsticks. *Finger food. It must be finger food. And is this all there is for dinner? These tiny things?*

"We will have fourteen baskets," Li said, neatly picking up a dumpling with his chopsticks, "each with a different kind of dumpling. If that is too much for you, we can stop any time."

Twenty-eight dumplings? How do these people stay so thin?

"Absolutely not," she said. "I don't want to miss one of the fourteen; I might miss the best." She clamped her chopsticks around a dumpling, and lifted them. The dumpling fell to the plate, bouncing once. She tried again, and then, grimly, again. When, yet again, it fell, she began to see the humor in it. "I don't know how the Chinese stay thin, but I know how tourists do it; they don't eat. Can I stab it?"

He laughed. "Anything you want."

"No, I'll do it right." She tried again and by the fifth try figured out how to wedge the dumpling securely. Timidly, she dipped it in the red mixture and ate the whole thing at once. "Oh, how wonderful," she murmured, and was more reckless with the second, swirling it in the red dip before popping it into her mouth. Tears sprang to her eyes; she gasped for breath.

"A little too much," Li said with a smile.

"The other dip is soy sauce; you might want to try it."

Miranda drank her wine, and slowly her breathing returned to normal and she could feel her tongue again. The waitress returned, deftly replacing the empty steamer basket with a new one. "Pork," said Li, and once again placed two tiny dumplings on Miranda's plate. This time she picked one up with ease, and smiled at Li. "It's like passing a test."

He raised his glass. "To passing all the tests that stand in our way."

They touched their glasses. And then the waitress was back. Li spoke a few words to her and she turned red. She set down the new steamer basket and left. "What did you say to her?" Miranda asked.

"I told her she should not rush us; that we prefer pauses between the servings. I had told her that this afternoon, but she is new and she forgot."

"But it seems that food always comes quickly here, at least wherever I've been, so far."

"You're right; China hasn't learned the art of leisurely dining. For centuries people were on the edge of starvation so they grabbed and gobbled whatever they could. Now, everyone is too busy making money to relax at a dinner table. But in some places, that is changing. A few more years, a few more lessons about the way the rich behave in western countries, and we too will have three-hour dinners." He put two more dumplings on Miranda's plate. "Sweet bean paste. These you do not dip in the sauces."

"Sweet? But . . . this can't be the end of dinner."

"No, no, we have eleven baskets to go. In China, sweets are served alternately with other dishes; it creates balance and harmony."

"Goodness. I'll have to tell Lisa and Adam; anything that moves dessert forward they'd like."

"They must have been happy to talk to you today."

"They were. In fact, they told me more about themselves, even what they were thinking, than when I'm with them. Usually they come home from school and can't wait to go off with their friends."

"And at night?"

"They have homework, they talk to their

friends on the phone, they read in their rooms. But it's not that they're so busy; I told you, I'm not the one they want to confide in. They don't think I understand them or sympathize with them the way their friends do, or even care about them in the same way."

"Does that bother you?"

"Of course. Except, they're right, you know."

"You mean, you seem ancient to them."

"That's part of it. And I really don't see the world as they do. I love them and they know that, but their tragedies just aren't as tragic to me as they are to them, their agonies aren't as agonizing . . . even their triumphs seem more fantastically triumphant to them than to me. I just can't get inside their feelings."

"No parent can do that."

"Maybe not, but I'd like to."

"No, no, it would not work. Young people need their own dreams. Parents should not try to influence their visions any more than they should try to force love."

"Did you try to influence your children's visions?"

"Once. A long time ago. I have not tried

since then, and now I do not want to share their vision; it is a warped one."

"Warped? What does that mean?"

He refilled their wine glasses. "Have you heard of the Cultural Revolution?"

"Yes, of course. It was a very bad time."

"It was a terrible time. It showed us that decency defines a loser; that what wins is indifference, callousness, cruelty, brutality. That was the lesson of the Cultural Revolution."

"You don't believe that."

"That indifference and cruelty win? Of course I do."

"But you're not . . ."

"No, I am not indifferent. Nor callous, nor brutal, nor cruel. And so I am not a winner."

"But you are. You have a good life. You own this restaurant. You have your own company. You said it was a good life."

"And it can be taken from me in a minute. The ones who have that power are the winners. That is the history of China, and the Cultural Revolution showed us that nothing had changed. A whole generation of us grew up in the early years of the communists; we believed absolutely in the Party; we were convinced that we were building a new world. And we were kicked in the teeth by the Cultural Revolution."

"Why?" Miranda asked. "Why would anyone let something like that happen?"

"Because winners want to stay on top; it is no more complicated than that. What terrifies winners most is the danger of sinking into the mass of losers. And so, in 1965, when there was a power struggle in the government, some leaders solidified their power by tearing the country apart. They gave young people, teenagers, mostly, a glorious vision of paradise, a lying vision, and told them to build it by destroying the society we had. The young people worshiped those leaders, partly for that vision, but mostly for the freedom the leaders gave them. They were told to defy their parents and teachers, and to denounce them to Party officials for any suspicious behavior, such as criticizing the government, admiring western culture, praising classical education or freedom of the press or democracy . . . the list was very long."

"And your children were involved in that?"

"At first they were too young, but growing up in such a time set them against me. I was not with them the whole time, but I knew from neighbors that they were—what do you call it? Dangling? Dangling out with—"

"Hanging out?"

"Yes, hanging out with the Red Guards and speaking against me."

He turned his wine glass within his fingers. "For us, those years were anarchy; for children they were a ten-year holiday. The government ordered free travel for them on trains throughout the country, and free food wherever and whenever they asked for it. The leaders told them to smash anything that was intellectual or part of the past. So these children roamed China like packs of wild dogs, egged on by the government to destroy in the name of creating a better tomorrow.

"But they created nothing. They shut down the schools, so no one was educated. They smashed hundreds of our greatest temples and art works. They burned entire libraries. They ruined hundreds of thousands of lives by false accusations and drove many to their death. And at the same time the government sent millions of professors, writers, doctors, and business professionals into far-off rural areas to work as laborers. They said we had become elitist and needed to be close to the common people. What they really wanted was to destroy the will of anyone who might have an independent thought."

"You were sent away?" Miranda asked. "Was that because of your American father? Did anyone know you had an American father?"

"Everyone knew it. All those informers, you know." The door opened and the waitress peered in. Miranda looked startled. "No, she is not one," Li said, smiling. He beckoned to the waitress, and watched her exchange steamer baskets and set two sauce dishes on the table. "Duck," he said. "With plum sauce."

Miranda looked at the smooth pouches in the steamer. "How do you know what's inside them? They're all identical."

"I know what I ordered."

"You remember all fourteen, in sequence?"

"I have an excellent memory. It is a

blessing and a curse." He served their dumplings. "Yes, my American father was a mark against me, and against my mother, too. She was sent to a village near Tibet; she was already sick and could not take the cold and the meager portions of food and working fourteen hours a day in the fields. She died within a year. I was sent to make bricks for kilns—"

"Bricks? Where?"

"A village named Mianning, not far from my mother, as it happened, but we were deep in the Himalayas and there was no road between her village and mine. I never saw her again after we were forced to leave the farm."

"And your wife? Where was she?"

"Well, that is a different story." His face was impassive. "She thrived during the Cultural Revolution; she became an informer, denouncing many of our friends as subversives, especially writers and college teachers. Eleven of them committed suicide; most of the others died in prison while she rose in Party ranks, rewarded for her patriotic fervor. She also knew whose bed to sleep in. When I returned from

Mianning, she had moved to Shanghai and I did not try to find her."

"And she died?"

"She was beaten to death in her apartment. The killer was never found. It could have been someone she denounced; it could have been a quarrel with a lover. But I think she fell from favor with the Party and they got rid of her, because there was no public announcement or investigation of her death. It was a long time ago; she has been forgotten."

"Not by you, with your excellent memory."

"What I remember most is the pain she caused, the ugliness of her betrayal of our friends, my own discovery of the kind of person I had married—how blind I had been, so anxious to marry and have a home, to be a father, as if to replace my own. And that was when I gave up the idea of passion. It was not something I did deliberately, but I realized, over time, that I had rejected it; what I wanted was to pick my way through the minefields that China had become, and survive in my own way, without turmoil. And that is what I have done."

The waitress returned. When she left, Li chuckled softly. "This is not the kind of dinner one chooses for uninterrupted conversations."

"But most of the time it's very private," Miranda said, wanting to reassure him that he had chosen well. "This wonderful room, and wonderful food."

"Thank you. And thank you for listening so well. It is very comfortable, talking to you."

He served the dumplings—"Lotus seed; another sweet"—and poured the last of the wine. With the door shut, silence wrapped them again. Miranda looked for something to say. "When we met your son yesterday, he seemed angry. Was it because of me?"

"No. Of course not."

She smiled faintly. "You said that too quickly. But perhaps he thought you should not be seen with an American woman."

"It had nothing to do with you. Sheng is often unhappy; his life is filled with problems. I told you, he has so many ways of making money. I have done a little investigating, and I think one of them may be involved with pirates, which is a dangerous business."

Miranda smiled uncertainly, thinking she should get the joke. "Pirates? You mean unscrupulous businessmen?"

"No, I mean real pirates. Bands of them roam the South China Sea, ambushing cargo ships. They take them to Beihai, a small town on the coast, and unload them."

"But they'd be seen. I mean, even at night . . ."

"They do it in daylight, and indeed they are seen, but it does not matter because the police and city government work with them."

"*The police? The government?* But . . . why?"

"Because they are paid to do it. It is always the same story, is it not?"

"Who pays them?"

"Sheng, if he is indeed in this business, and his partners, and all those who deal in this. They pay the pirates, as well. It is a large payroll."

"They *hire* pirates? And pay them salaries? That is so bizarre. But if they're ambushing ships, other companies, other governments must be involved. At some point they'll be stopped, won't they?"

"Most likely, and that is probably Sheng's biggest worry, whether it is this pirate business or some other. But he is not a child; he will fend for himself. Do you like the lotus-seed dumpling?"

Miranda wondered how much of his nonchalance about Sheng was an act. But she could not ask that, and in any event, he had changed the subject.

"Yes," she said, "very much." She ate slowly, aware that she was handling chopsticks and dumplings quite expertly, but mostly thinking of Li's story. She could not imagine a life of such turmoil.

"What are you thinking?" he asked.

"That I've never known such pain as you've known."

"Your husband died."

"I'm not saying that wasn't hard. It was a shock, suddenly not being a wife; it was as if I didn't know who I was. I felt unmoored—"

She saw his puzzled look, and said, "When a boat isn't tied to a dock, when anything is cut loose and is drifting, it's unmoored. It was almost as if I had no purpose in life. Of course Lisa and Adam were there, but then I worried about bringing them up alone . . ."

"So you did have pain."

"Not like yours. You lost years of your life, and love and trust and hope. When Jeff died, my life barely changed." She looked up sharply, stunned by her words. They were astonishingly revealing. How could she have said them to this man, whom she barely knew?

But I do know him. I already know more about him than I do about a lot of people I've known for years.

So what? All my life I've known you can't trust foreigners; you have to be on your guard against people who are really different, because you can't believe anything they—

"That's totally ridiculous," she burst out.

Li's eyebrows rose. "That your life barely changed?"

"No. I'm sorry, I was thinking about something else."

"And it was ridiculous?"

"Yes."

Because I do know him. And I trust him.

"Do you want to tell me what it was?" he asked.

"No. I'm sorry, but—"

"Of course, your thoughts are your own. You were telling me about your life after your husband died."

"Yes. It hardly changed, and that was almost sadder than his death. I lived in the same house and slept in the same bed and my days were the same. I made the same food and moved around the kitchen in the same ways, and stood in the same place in front of the stove where I'd stood for years. . . . And when Lisa and Adam went to school, I worked in the sunroom, just as I always had. And my parents or friends would come to dinner, or we'd go there, so I was cooking just about as much as I always had. And at night I read in the living room or in bed, just as I always had."

"But you had lost a husband."

"I'd lost a friend, and I missed him, but I had other friends, and my parents, and I didn't have to be alone or go anywhere alone if I didn't want to."

"A friend," Li said.

"Yes." Her gaze turned inward and after a moment, she said, "We used to go for long walks after dinner. Our street makes a gradual descent into town; there are wonderful old trees on each side and on a parkway that runs down the center, and moonlight flickers through the leaves when the summer breeze comes down from the mountains, and the air is soft and it smells of cut grass and roses, and there's a kind of murmur coming from front porches where people are sitting and talking—you can hear the clink of ice in their glasses and sometimes the squeak of a swing or rocking chair—and we would walk for hours, not talking, just being part of our town."

"Not talking," Li echoed again.

"Not much. The last few years, we didn't have a lot to talk about, except for the children and the house. Jeff was so sweet, he was such a good person, but he wasn't happy, and he couldn't seem to get interested in things, not even his work. Nothing seemed to satisfy him."

"What did he look like?"

"Tall, handsome, blue eyes, sandy hair getting thin on top which drove him crazy, a little overweight—he kept trying new diets, and he jogged every day and lifted weights, but he always stayed about the same—and he liked action movies with lots of blood, which I didn't, and he read mysteries and science fiction."

"Which you didn't?"

"No, I like novels and poetry and history. And travel books and magazines—" She saw Li's eyebrows shoot up and she gave a small laugh. "Well, I do read about other places even if I don't go there; I always have."

"So you've wanted to travel, but didn't?"

She looked away, briefly embarrassed. "I told you: it seemed so daunting. But I like travel books, and when I read them, late at night, when everything is quiet, I can almost see myself in another country; it really is something like being there. I know it's not the same, but it's what I've—" *Settled for,* she thought, but did not say it. "It's what I've chosen."

After a pause, Li asked, "Did your husband read travel books, too?"

"No, he said they were dull. Like politics and history; he said they didn't have any plot."

"So you are interested in more things than he was."

She gave a small laugh. "I hope so. It

wasn't that he didn't care about things; he cared about doing a good job and being a good father and a good husband. But everything was so hard for him. He'd wake up each morning dreading the effort of getting through the day, coping with the demands of work, acquaintances, family, parents . . . all of us who expected things of him. He tried, though: he worked hard at doing the things he was supposed to do, and he did most of them well, but he never . . ."

"Caught fire," Li said when her voice trailed away.

"Yes."

"Not even about you."

She shook her head. "What Jeff wanted most was security and quiet. He was terrified of uncertainty or ambiguity or conflict. He wanted a family of friends who would keep him safe. If he'd ever felt passion, he would have run from it, because it's messy and unpredictable and it might have made his heart beat faster."

At her sarcasm, Li looked at her sharply, but she was absorbed in her memories.

"After a while, I felt I was smothering. Whenever I was happy or excited, or wanted to try something new, I couldn't talk about it, because he'd change the subject or leave the house, actually run away, and that would spoil everything. So I kept it all to myself." She paused. "Those long walks into town . . . I loved them. I felt Boulder wrap itself around me, and I was part of it, and part of the mountains and the prairie, and all the lighted windows were guiding us, and on the way home the moon would light our way, and the air was fragrant and silent, even the birds had gone to sleep, and I felt so full of joy and love . . . and there was nothing I could do with it." She laughed lightly. "I gave it to my children, so most of the time I only felt partly smothered."

"And then he died."

She nodded. "We'd been married ten years."

"And it was harder for you, knowing that you had not loved him."

"I loved him once. I think. I may have been looking for security just as much as he was."

There was a silence. Miranda looked up to find Li contemplating her. "But since then, you have loved, have you not?" he asked. "In all the years since he died, someone must have come into your heart."

She hesitated. A lie might deflect further questions, might protect her defenses, but at that moment she could not imagine lying to him. "Not that way."

"But by then you knew what you longed for, what you had missed. You must have searched for it."

She shook her head. "There are so many women searching. I was afraid of being one of them, single women with hungry eyes, looking for a man. I wasn't unhappy, I had my children, my work, a good life . . ." She shook her head. "I didn't search."

"Or want?"

"Oh, want . . . Of course I wanted. I wanted a lover and a companion; a voice late at night in my silent house; conversations full of ideas and curiosities and new ways to make sense of the world. I wanted to reach out and find a hand to hold, steps to match mine, someone protecting me while I was protecting him. I wanted to share all the things that are pleasant when we're alone but wonderful when they're shared. I never pretended I didn't want all that; I just couldn't go out looking for it. I couldn't imagine *dating,* like a teenager, starting from scratch—"

"Scratch?"

"The beginning. Getting to know someone from the beginning, over and over again, probing, revealing . . ."

"Like traveling to a foreign country," Li said. "All the effort, all the unknowns. All the fears. But did no one appear, without all those things from scratch? Did no one come on his own, to stand at your side, and give you a chance to love?"

She met his eyes, warm, questioning, accepting, and knew her own were filled with the surprise of discovery, that she felt safe enough to talk of these things to this man, without fear or defensiveness. "I met a lot of men. My parents wanted so badly to see me settled, and my friends had a fine time being matchmakers, so there were dinner parties and theater parties, Christmas caroling, hiking, skiing . . . and I was always paired up with someone."

She was looking inward again, remembering. "It was a little like a drug, you know; I didn't know how to stop it, even when I wasn't having a good time. Usually it was better to have a partner than to be the single person tagging along with couples, so I kept doing it, saying yes to meeting someone new, saying yes to seeing him again, saying yes to—" She stopped.

"But did none of them come into your heart?" Li asked, pressing her, and she knew he was not interested in whether she had slept with men, but in whether one of them had consumed her.

"No," she said, then smiled faintly. "I might not have recognized it, though; I didn't know what it felt like."

Li reached for her. It happened so quickly that his hand was on hers, curving around it as if to shield it from harm, before either of them realized that he had moved. And then it was over: he pulled away and tried to cover the moment by reaching for the second bottle of wine and opening it, fumbling slightly in his confusion. "Please forgive me. I had no right."

"You felt sorry for me," Miranda said.

"I felt sad for you." He filled her glass. "Did you not even pretend?"

Her eyes widened. "Yes; how would you know that? I did try. I thought there was something wrong with me, that I couldn't fall in love even when everyone was telling me how fine these men were, how good for me. . . . Once I did think I'd found someone, a man I'd known a long time, who'd moved away but came back to Boulder after his wife died. I liked him, and for a while it was so comfortable letting him take charge of everything, but that wasn't what I wanted, you know: to have my life organized by someone else. I'd always dreamed—"

"Yes?" he asked when she fell silent. He sat back, as if to give her more space. "What did you dream?"

"That I might love and be loved without defining the boundaries or compartments of our love. That there would be a flow of giving and receiving, of understanding, of laughing and crying together, of being awed by the wonders of the world and held close against its dangers. I know it's a fairy tale, the kind of thing people look for in novels because they don't expect to find it in life, but when Jeff died and I realized how lonely I'd been, even in marriage, I knew it was what I wanted, and I've clung to it ever since." She smiled at Li. "Like your clinging to the dream of your father coming back. Maybe there are some things we just can't outgrow."

Li's eyes were brooding, fixed on her face.

"You're feeling sorry for me again," she said.

He shook his head. "I am admiring you. Because you dream of an encompassing love, and you hold your dream close. Too often our dreams are knocked away from us."

His gaze moved past her, to some memory she could not imagine. "Sometimes we are afraid to try," he murmured, "because the pain of loss is so great. So many of us, in so many ways, snagged by fear."

Miranda was about to ask him what he feared, whom he had lost, when he shook his head a little, as if shaking something off, and turned to their dinner. Briskly, he opened the new steamer basket on the table. "Vegetable," he said. "And two dipping sauces; this one is hot. You know, when I was a boy, we had mostly vegetables to eat. No one could afford meat."

He described the farm where he had grown up, and his grandparents, to whom he had been so close in the years when his mother was deeply depressed. "Eventually she recovered, but she never got over my father; she was betrayed and lonely, but she could not lose that destructive hope that keeps real life at bay." He talked about his friends and their clubhouse, his school, the hours in his room when he dreamed of a father and of America. The waitress came and went, steamer baskets appeared and were taken away, the wine level fell in its bottle, all in a dreamlike rhythm.

And then the waitress brought in a large tureen and placed it on the table. Miranda, startled, looked at Li. "I thought there would just be baskets, one after another, forever and ever . . ."

He laughed. "This is our soup."

"Then dinner is over." She felt a deep sadness.

"Not until we eat our soup."

She shook her head. "I can't. All those dumplings. . . . I really don't have room for any more."

"Try a little. It is very good. And it helps create—"

"Balance and harmony." They exchanged a smile. Once again, to her amazement, Miranda finished hers. She sat back with a sigh as Li poured the last of the wine. "What an extraordinary dinner. I'm having such a good time."

"I hoped you would. There is another very fine dumpling restaurant, Defachang, in Xi'an. If you like, we could fly there tomorrow evening and try it out. That would also give you a chance to see the terracotta warriors."

Miranda set down her wine glass. The dreamlike rhythm had shattered. "I want you to explain all this to me."

After a moment, he nodded. "I will—"

The waitress brought in a blue and gold teapot, filled two small handleless cups, set their lids upon them, and looked at Li. He said a few words and then she was gone.

"What did you tell her?" Miranda asked.

"That we have everything we need. Now we will be completely private." He leaned back, stretching out his legs, and contemplated her. "Would it satisfy you if I told you I was attracted to you the moment I saw you, and I want to be with you, and that is all there is to it?"

"No."

"Why not?"

"Because I'm not beautiful, I'm not witty or brilliant or mesmerizing. There has to be another reason for you to—"

"What?" he prompted.

"Pursue me."

He smiled. "One of the reasons I have pursued you is what you just said."

"*Because* I'm not beautiful—?"

"Because you insist you are not. This is nonsense. What does it say about me? That I am stupid? Or blind? That I have no high standards or aspirations?"

"It has nothing to do with you."

"I know that. I know you do not think me stupid or blind; this is about how you see yourself. So. I will tell you how it comes about that I pursue you. When I was sent to Mianning to make bricks, I had not had a real marriage for almost a year; my wife and I were living separate lives. I was criticizing her activities in the Party and finally she had me sent away; I found out much later that that was her doing. So I was already lonely before I was expelled from Beijing, and of course it was far worse in Mianning, where I knew no one and found no one who shared my interests. They were poor people, you understand, with no education and no time or energy to wonder what was beyond their village: they lived in dirt-floored hovels; they were diseased and starving, freezing in winter, faint with heat in the summer; without hope. They had no idea why I was there and I could not make them understand; they thought it was a big joke. And then I met someone."

Miranda's eyes widened. "And I remind you of her."

"Well, that is getting ahead of my story, but, yes, in some important ways you remind me of her. Do you want to hear about her?"

"Yes."

"Her name was Fu Wei. She was young, about seventeen, she thought, but she was not sure. They did not record women's births in those days; sons were all that mattered. She had never been outside Mianning. She was small and very thin— there was never enough to eat, and during the time I was there the crops failed and no help came from outside—and I thought she was frail, one of those whom poverty quickly destroys. But she was quite tough in her optimism and resilience, and she smiled and laughed more than I thought anyone could, in such a place at such a time."

He removed the lid from his cup, then sat staring into space. "Wei could not read or write and knew nothing of my world, but she had fresh thoughts about people, and she longed for learning and adventures. She did not know that: only in our conversations did she realize how much she yearned to see more of life, though even then she said she could not ever leave home because she did not know how to behave anywhere else. She had a quick, curious mind, and much instinctive understanding, but she believed that she had no intelligence, no cleverness, and of course, no beauty."

Abruptly, Miranda stood and walked across the small room, then back again. She stopped at a scroll painting and pretended to examine it. "You're accusing me of being as ignorant as that peasant girl."

"I never mentioned ignorance and I made no accusations. And I said that you reminded me of her, not that you are like her."

"But you think I am. Frail and delicate; that seems to attract you."

"Fragility does not attract me; I do not admire or like it. When I first saw you in the airport you had a look in your eyes that reminded me of Wei: alert, wary, fearful, but trying to think of a way to deal with strangeness. I did admire that and it drew me to you."

Miranda turned from the painting. "What happened to her?"

"We were together for a year. We were all sick and on the edge of starvation, people were collapsing in the brickworks and in the fields, but Wei and I were very close. We were together as much as possible, and in all the rain and mud, and the terrible winds, and the freezing cold and crushing heat, with nothing but rags to wear, somehow we were happy." He looked at his hands, opening and closing them. "I was teaching her to read. She was so excited about that. And then she died."

"Oh. . . . How?"

"She was injured in an accident in the brickworks and she got an infection.

There were no medicines. I got word to a friend in Chongking, asking him to help us leave so I could take her to a hospital. He tried to get an order to have us transferred, but everything took so long; weeks went by while papers were shuffled and sent on to one desk after another. And so Wei died. I held her for a day and a night. She was burning with fever, but she knew I was with her, and she was crying—the tears dried so quickly on her hot face—and saying that now she would never learn to read, and I would never be able to show her the ocean, and we would never make love in warm and beautiful places . . . and then she breathed a long sigh, of great sorrow, and died. Four months later, the order came through and I left that place. And since then I have been alone."

Miranda went to him and, tentatively, touched his hair, then rested her hand on his shoulder. He covered her hand with his, and in a moment rose and took both her hands in his. "You are stronger than you believe. You have talent and intelligence and a will that you have not yet recognized.

You are honest and open to change. And you have your own beauty, which no one else has. Like Wei."

They looked at each other, their hands clasped. For the first time in many years, Miranda wanted to kiss and be kissed, to embrace and be embraced. But she knew it was not time; there was still too much she had to understand. She studied Li's almond-shaped eyes, the hard lines of his face, the prominent cheekbones and long, thin nose, the strong chin and heavy brows, the brown, unruly hair. It seemed she could not look at his face enough. And then a shadow crossed her thoughts: a young woman, barely visible. She frowned. "If you're trying somehow to recapture a lost love . . ."

"No." He smiled. "I do know the difference between fantasy and reality. You are very real, Miranda Graham, and very much your own person, and the more I know you the more distinctly you are different from Wei, and from everyone else. But the best that was in her is in you, and much more, waiting to be discovered. China is a good place for discoveries, and I believe we could have a wonderful time if you would allow me to share them with you."

She looked and looked at him. It occurred to her that this could be the real beginning of her journey, even more than the flight from Denver to Beijing. But, this time, what was her destination?

She shrank from the thought. If she did not know where she was going, she should not start the journey. But the neat categories that until now had so precisely organized her life, providing an abundance of "shoulds" and "oughts," and "can'ts," suddenly seemed fuzzy. What was far more clear was that she knew Li was right: they could have a wonderful time if she would allow it.

"So you will come with me to Xi'an?" he asked, as naturally as if he were talking of a stroll around the corner.

Still she hesitated. And then, at last, she thought, Well, why not? Xi'an and . . . whatever else we can do. It's only for six more days. Not enough to do any damage, but enough to learn something new about the world and about myself. So, why not?

She gave a small, almost imperceptible nod. As if she were standing across the room observing the two of them, she saw herself rest her hand along Li's face. "I'm glad to be compared to Wei. And I think the best discoveries are the ones that are shared."

Chapter 4

Yuan Sheng sat at a corner table with a good view of the room and the jazz band on a raised platform beside a small dance floor. "They're very good," Wu Yi said, and he nodded, preoccupied with checking the crowd, peering through dense swirls of cigarette smoke to make sure every chair at every table was filled. Of course he knew they were—he had made a swift survey as he and Wu Yi arrived—but he always made a more thorough one when he was seated, drink in hand, beginning to relax enough to think about his investment in this club without a tight clutching of fear at his stomach.

He had put too much money into it; his father had told him at the beginning that he should look for a fourth partner. But whenever Li gave him advice, especially good advice, Sheng's mind shut down in that direction, and went its own way. So, with only two partners, he had opened the Du Fu Club just six months earlier, their second club in a year, and even though his partners' connections with government kept them from being taxed too highly, and prevented police raids, still, they had not yet begun to make a profit.

"A good crowd," Wu Yi said, and again Sheng nodded. He knew she was trying to make him feel good, but he resented it because that meant he must look as if he needed stroking, which meant he must look vulnerable . . . and she had no right to put him in that position. He was not vulnerable. He stayed close to the line, cut corners, took risks, backed and filled and lied and maneuvered, but that was what competition meant, and only those who were willing to play by the new rules could hope to triumph in today's China.

His father, for example, would fail.

"I'd like another martini," Wu Yi said.

There was an edge to her voice and Sheng swiveled his attention to her. He ordered martinis, and dinner, then sat back and took her hand. "That's your new dress? I like it."

"Not new; just one you haven't seen."

"I gave you money for a new dress."

"Yes, but this was what I wanted." She held out her arm, displaying a gold bracelet. "Thank you, Sheng; such a lovely gift."

Their eyes met, hers challenging, a little mocking, and Sheng's face grew hot. He would have dropped her hand, but that would have given away his anger, and he knew that those who revealed nothing always had the advantage over others. "Enjoy it," he said amiably. "It becomes you."

He was rewarded with a smile, and then their martinis arrived, and a platter of lobster in black bean sauce, and the difficult moment was over. She could have her pick of men, and she often infuriated him, but his hunger for her gnawed day and night, and losing her was inconceivable. Besides, she did not want to marry, and that suited him perfectly, since he had no intention of divorcing his wife. That was his first condition: he needed women who could handle an affair without making impossible demands. He needed Wu Yi.

He took a piece of lobster in his chopsticks, coral and white in a glistening sauce. Coral was the color of Wu Yi's silk dress, coral her lipstick against creamy skin, and coral the filigreed comb in her glossy black hair pulled tightly from the perfection of her face and twisted into an elaborate knot. She was a film actress becoming popular throughout China, and Sheng knew that her presence here attested as much as anything to his bright future. He watched her chew a piece of lobster. "Perfect," she said. "You did well in choosing your chef. And the martini is excellent. Very American."

"I hope better than that." He smiled so that she would not think he was correcting her, even though he was. "Americans are heavy-handed with their drinks, as with everything else; it will not be long before we surpass them everywhere, as we did long ago in the beauty of our women."

She laughed, and Sheng felt a rising

satisfaction. It was going to be a successful evening.

Everything was successful these days.
Sheng prided himself on being the modern
Chinese man. He wore designer suits,
drank Louis XIII Rémy Martin Cognac
which, someone had told him, cost the
equivalent of a thousand American dollars
a bottle, and he subscribed to *Trends Gen-
tleman,* the blindingly glossy magazine
filled with valuable tips on clothes, food
and drink, home buying, real estate investment, skiing and snorkeling, buying cars,
finding the right gift for a woman. The magazine's credo had become Sheng's: con-
sumption is good, as long as one
consumes wisely. Since that was directly
opposite to communist doctrine, Sheng
was profoundly pleased that he had
become a businessman at this time in his
country's history. Politics bored him, and
so did people who were interested in it, but
he was aware of what was going on, and
he knew that the Chinese government,
whatever it still called itself, had traveled a
long way from communism.

Instead, they had something called

market socialism. No one knew what it meant, but they all swore by it, because it had turned China into a gold mine, at least for Sheng's generation. Opportunities for getting rich were around every corner, and no one stood in their way. The police in China, understaffed and underpaid, were always grateful for extra money, so Sheng's generation formed partnerships with policemen and police chiefs to buy and run hotels, restaurants, karaoke bars, saunas, nightclubs, and dance halls. They also owned brothels in partnership with the vice squads in a number of cities. There were always plenty of girls for the dance halls and brothels, plucked from the hundreds of thousands of teenagers wandering the country in search of a better life.

But it wasn't easy, climbing to the top. Sheng knew that he could not do it without his friendships with the sons and daughters of government officials and military officers: the powerful, protected, ruthlessly ambitious young men and women who were the key to the future. Two of them, Pan Chao and Meng Enli, were his partners in the nightclubs and, because of them, Sheng would soon be a shining star in the firmament of China's new elite.

Once his father had asked him about his increasingly lavish life style, and Sheng had replied with vague talk of profits from his nightclubs. His father had not asked again; it was as if he did not want to be lied to. Their conversations now were mostly about All-China Construction, the company his father had begun that would someday be Sheng's.

Many times, Sheng would have liked to talk to Li: odd times when he found himself about to ask his father for advice, or for help in understanding something, but then he would catch himself. His father could never understand his life. Yuan Li was mired in outdated ideas of loyalty and responsibility and working for a better life for everyone, even those who didn't have the brains or the willpower to scramble up from the bottom. The Americans had a good saying for that: the poor should pull themselves up by their bootstraps. Well, why shouldn't they? Sheng had done it. The opportunities were there: if others did not grab them, they had no one to blame but themselves. Sheng thought about them only when he climbed over them on his journey to the top.

Dahu—big money bugs—that was what people called him and those of his generation who were getting rich. But what did he care? He paid attention only to each day, and how smoothly and profitably it could be made to slide into the next day, and the one after that. That was all he cared about.

Except for women. Especially, except for Wu Yi. And this night, at his club, his successful evening with her unrolled through the hours as they ate and talked and danced; as Wu Yi took her time drinking her French cognac; as she leaned forward for Sheng to light her cigarette, putting off, deliberately, it seemed, the moment when they would go to her apartment, to her bed. Sheng, weak with wanting her, grunted with the effort of sitting still. "In time," Wu Yi said smoothly, letting him know that no one hurried her or ruled her schedule. And it was at that moment that the manager came to their table with a portable telephone and told Sheng that he was wanted.

He could not ignore it; only a few people knew where to find him, and they would call only in an emergency. He excused himself to Wu Yi and leaned back in his chair. "Well?"

Meng Enli's voice was abrupt. "We need you. Now. At the office."

Sheng's struggle was brief. Every nerve within him quivered to be in Wu Yi's bed, but a call at this time of night meant there was a crisis that took precedence over everything. Business, Sheng thought, the true center of his life. He began calculating the best way to end this part of the evening. Planning, complex and devious, was what he loved best.

"I am deeply unhappy," he said to Wu Yi, "but I must see to a crisis in my business." Her face hardened, but Sheng, perched on the edge of his chair, was barely aware of it; already she had dimmed in importance. "Nothing else would take me away; you know what you mean to me. Dear Wu Yi, so much is changing around us, none of us can shut our eyes for a minute or we could lose everything. Believe me, I have no choice but to go. Tomorrow will be better; we will have all the time we wish. Tomorrow night?"

He had not meant to ask; he had meant

to state it with absolute certainty. But, on its own, his voice slid into a question and he saw Wu Yi recognize his weakness and harden further. "Not tomorrow night, certainly not, I need time to myself. I'll let you know how soon you may call again."

"The next night," Sheng said, adopting the boldness he had failed to find the first time. "I'll call you then."

"I may not be at home."

"That would be very sad." He was so anxious to be gone that he was behaving almost carelessly, and he saw Wu Yi's eyes widen. With admiration? With annoyance? He could not take the time to find out. He stood up. "I'll take you home."

She walked ahead of him, ignoring him. She ignored him in his car and ignored him when she went into her apartment building. At any other time, Sheng would have been in despair. But by now he was tight with apprehension, and he had stopped thinking of Wu Yi even before he turned the corner and headed toward the northeast. He was recalling Enli's voice, hard with anger.

The office he shared with Chao and Enli was in a nondescript building near the airport: three rooms at the rear of the first floor, with no name on the door, and no secretary. When Sheng parked and got out of the car, he saw Enli waiting at the door.

"They panicked," he said, his words cold and measured. "Your crew—the one you hired last month—you said they knew what they were doing."

"Crew? You mean something happened to the sugar shipment?"

"Get in the office."

Sheng followed Enli inside, his heart pounding. *They panicked.* How? When he hired the pirates they had told him they knew all about this business; that they would have no trouble boarding the Vietnamese ship and sailing it to Beihai where it would be unloaded and the sugar transported by truck to customers in two cities. Not even complicated enough to work up a sweat. "What happened?" Sheng asked.

Enli shut the door. "They beat the crew, pistol-whipped and beat them—"

"They couldn't! They said—"

"Shut up and listen. They pistol-whipped and beat the crew, tied them up and threw them overboard. Twelve men dead."

"No! They said it wasn't complicated . . .

they said . . . wait a minute." Sheng bent his head and breathed in and out to slow down his heart. He had given strict orders: no one was to be killed. Their business was piracy, not murder; a simple business of transferring cargo from one place to another and selling it for a good profit. Piracy was lucrative and relatively easy; it harmed no one except a few wealthy manufacturers and shippers in other countries, and why should Chinese entrepreneurs care about them? Piracy was an enterprise with guaranteed results, as long as the rules were followed.

Someone had ignored that. Had ignored Sheng. After all he had done to gain the confidence of Enli and Chao, to be considered a full partner in their businesses, if not yet a friend, someone had ignored him and now his life was far more difficult than it had seemed just an hour ago.

Enli's voice rolled over his bent head. "Of course it could not be kept secret; everyone in Beihai knows about it."

Sheng forced himself upright: he was a man, not a child to be scolded. He would find his way out of this setback and not only would he survive, he would triumph.

That much, at least, his father had taught him: that it was possible to rise again, and again and again, even after terrible times.

"But the murders are not the problem," Enli said. "It is a nuisance that they happened—"

"Twelve men are dead!" Sheng exclaimed before he could stop himself.

"A nuisance," Enli said as if Sheng had not spoken, "but not serious. What is serious is that the police were at the harbor not ten minutes after the boat came in, and they are holding the ship."

"But the police are on our payroll."

"Not this time. They're under orders from the International Maritime Bureau."

"The International. . . . How did they . . . ?" But Sheng understood. Someone had tipped off the Maritime Bureau. Which meant that, aside from the murders, which made him queasy, he also had to face the fact that he no longer knew whom to trust in Beihai. Yesterday he had been sure that the mayor and the chief of police, handsomely paid, would provide help in unloading pirated ships in the harbor, and space in a shed on the beach where the ships could be repainted and sold for a profit.

Now he could not be sure who was making the highest payoffs to whom. "And our men?" he asked.

"You mean the amateur pirates you hired? Still on board. The police won't let them off."

"And the sugar?"

"There was no time to unload it."

Sheng let out his breath, almost gasping. Terrible. Terrible. Worse than anything he had imagined. Murder was bad enough, but on top of it the partnership had lost two million dollars' worth of sugar. They had already paid the pirates half their fee for ambushing the *Ana Lia* as soon as she was in international waters, safely away from the plantation in Vietnam; they had paid the Beihai mayor and police chief their monthly fee; they had buyers waiting.

Meng Enli's beeper went off. "A call from Pan Chao," he said. "I'll be in my office. When I come back you will have thought of a plan, which means, I would think, that you go to Beihai and settle things so this does not happen again."

Alone, Sheng closed the door and switched on his desk lamp. He turned on the CD player on a shelf behind the desk and inserted a disc. He loved American jazz and country and western; they helped him relax more than anything else, including sex, since sex, like business, was a barometer of performance and endurance, and he could never let his mind wander from either one.

Listening to Loretta Lynn's seductive twang, he sat upright, hands folded on the edge of the desk, eyes closed. A plan. But what plan could get around the International Maritime Bureau? What plan could reinstate him in the esteem of his partners? Meng Enli was the son of a director in the Department of International Trade, and, through his father, had a job in the department, shuffling papers in the import/export division; Pan Chao was the son of a high-ranking military officer posted to the State Security Bureau, and he, too, had a job, basically a flunky with a desk and a title, through his father's influence. They were powerful men because their fathers were powerful, and Sheng needed their confidence, even their admiration, if he expected to triumph rather than merely survive, like his father and so many others.

Well, then, a plan. Find someone to

blame. Obviously, the people who were supposed to be working for them: the mayor of Beihai, the head of security, the Party member who was supposed to keep Sheng informed. And Fang Youcai, the chief of police. A stupid man and the greediest, thought Sheng. And as he thought that, he was sure that Youcai was the one.

So here was his plan. Find the person who had betrayed them, probably Youcai, who had found someone to pay him even more than Sheng. Stupid, Sheng thought; did Youcai really believe that a policeman from a fishing village on the south coast of China could get away with betraying three sophisticated businessmen in Beijing? "*Za zhong. Gou zai zi,*" he muttered. "Bastards. Mutts. They had a business arrangement with me. We knew where we stood. They have no honor."

Well, he would take care of that. He would find Youcai and have him call the partners and confess. Then bribe the police to let them transfer the sugar from the boat to trucks, for shipment to the buyers waiting for it. If that did not work, the sugar probably was lost, but there were three more piracies planned for the next six weeks, and, with Youcai and everyone else cooperating, they would all be money-makers, and the partners would be on track again.

I'll have to hire more pirates, Sheng thought, and his heart sank at the thought of what a failure his first hiring experience had been. Well, not again. He would screen them more carefully, have some-one keep their relatives as hostages, if necessary: whatever it took, he would not fail again. And with a new group of pirates, and his plan in place, his partners would once again see him as an equal.

But . . . go to Beihai! What a punish-ment, to have to go to that godforsaken place. A mudhole, a fishing village with no fine restaurants, no clubs or karaoke bars or cappuccino cafes, no women, not even a decent hotel. Sheng would have to stay in the mayor's house, suffer his company, sleep alone. But he had to go. His partners expected it.

But he could not leave without telling his father. He was working with construction supervisors on buildings in Beijing and Shanghai, and they were about to break ground on a hotel in Hangzhou. He would have to tell his father he would be gone, and for how long. Which meant he had to find a reason.

He riffled through file drawers and cartons, making notes on parcels of land in Guangdong Province that might be worth buying for later development. He would make this a legitimate business trip. His father would be proud of him.

He was absorbed in writing when Meng Enli returned, opening the door without knocking. Sheng looked up, frowning, then thought better of it. "This morning I am going to Beihai," he said, forestalling questions, "and take care of everything. I am sure—" He stopped. "What is it?"

Enli was leaning against the doorjamb. "Why is your father under surveillance?"

Sheng stared at him. "Surveillance?"

"For two days. You know nothing about this?"

"Why would I know anything about it?"

"You were talking to him yesterday, in front of one of your buildings; he was with an American woman. While you were talking, he became alert, as if you had warned him; since then he has looked to see who might be watching him."

"I saw that he was being followed," Sheng said after a moment. "I don't know why. I suppose Pan Chao told you this? His department . . . the State Security Bureau . . . does everyone there know about it?"

"Who is the American woman?"

"She's here on business. He was showing her the city."

"He said."

"She's a designer, working with garment manufacturers."

"He said."

"He doesn't lie!" Why am I defending him? Sheng wondered. But it's true: he doesn't lie. I have never known him to tell anything but the truth.

"Where is she staying?"

"The Palace."

Enli nodded, and Sheng realized that he had known that, obviously from Pan Chao at State Security. It had been a trap, then, to see if he were telling Enli the truth. Which meant whatever his father had done, or was suspected of doing, was already spilling over to

Sheng. "Why is my father under surveillance?" he blurted out.

"Why don't you ask him?"

"He doesn't know! Ask Pan Chao!"

Enli contemplated Sheng for a long moment. "They'll be calling him in, you know, to interrogate him. Now perhaps you will ask him why he is under surveillance."

"I have. He doesn't know. Ask Pan Chao."

As they were at a dead end, silence fell. Enli returned to his contemplation of Sheng. "Perhaps it is time for you to think about taking over the company," he said at last. "Your father is getting old; All-China Construction should be yours."

Sheng's eyes widened. The words hummed in his ears.

"We talked about this last year. Your father did well in beginning the company but now it needs young, dynamic leadership, which you could provide if you were independent of him. He keeps too close an eye on you. He does not treat you like a man. And now it seems he is in trouble, which places a new burden on the company, and who will end up bearing it? You, the new president, unless he leaves before his taint can spread."

In the silence, with Enli's words humming and strumming into his very being, Sheng was startled by the double beep of his watch and Enli's. "Two o'clock," said Enli. "I'll be going. When will you be back from Beihai?"

Sheng shifted his thoughts: the ship, sugar, the crew, murder. "I don't know. Two days, probably."

"We'll wait for your call." And he was gone.

Sheng sat very still. His hands were folded on the desk and he saw the tremor that ran through them, a trembling just beneath the skin. He clenched them. Even alone, he would not let any weakness show.

And it was weakness: to respond to a few words so strongly that his heart pounded and his hands trembled. *Young, dynamic, independent, a man.*

Enli knew what to say; he knew the vital words.

He keeps too close an eye on you.

He did not say too much, or too little; he knew when to start and when to stop. He knew when to leave.

You, the new president.

But the beeping of his watch had, in a

sense, awakened Sheng, and he understood just how carefully those words had
been chosen, how shrewd was Enli's timing, how cunning the modulation of his
voice: intimate, approving, helpful, conspir-
atorial.

He knows me, Sheng thought. He
knows how to . . . what is it the Americans
say? Push my buttons.

As if I am his mechanical toy.

No, he admires me. Respects me. He
and Chao often tell me how quick I am,
how clever, how sly. How well I know how
to navigate in this new China.

He swiveled his chair and put a new CD
on the player, the volume turned low. Was
it too late to call Wu Yi? He looked at his
watch. Two-fifteen in the morning. She
would not be amused. Well, then, he
would think about business. He had plenty
of problems to think about, to fill the time
until he could call Li, and then leave for
Beihai.

He and Chao and Enli had been
together for one year under the company
name Dung Chan, making big plans. First
had been the piracy, a great success, then
the two nightclubs, soon to be successful,

they were sure. And there were other plans: a factory to make Cuban cigars for young Chinese entrepreneurs who were always hungry for something new, a way to cut in on the McDonald's hamburger franchises springing up all over China, a scheme to provide protection for small businesses wanting to evade high taxes.

But problems with the piracy sprang up. They needed a reliable place to store the pirated goods, and a way to transport them, in secret, to their customers. Chao thought of a way.

"So simple," he said. "We'll use All-China Construction. Your father buys building materials from overseas and from all over China; often he returns or exchanges some of them; he even sells his own surplus to other companies. All these things are so legitimate they are boring, so we use your warehouse to receive the materials from the pirates and do the paperwork on them, then ship them out in All-China's trucks. Those trucks are back and forth all the time; it's no problem at all."

But it was a problem, for Sheng. To his own surprise, he balked. "I don't think that will work."

"Not work?" Chao echoed. "What does that mean?"

"It would jeopardize the company."

Enli's eyes narrowed. "You're worrying about your father."

"No." But he knew that he was. He could not do this to Li. Why not? Since when was he worried about his father's feelings, or reputation, or even his safety?

He did not know. He only knew that he would not endanger his father, not even to please Chao and Enli.

"Well, give it some thought," Chao said at last.

And there they had left it. But Sheng knew that his partners were no longer sure that he was the one they wanted, as the partnership went into new businesses.

He knew he had to come up with something to restore their confidence in him, and he brought them a complete plan. "We'll contract with factories to manufacture copies of American and European building components—windows, frames, doors, flooring, carpeting, plumbing fixtures, electrical parts—and sell them to contractors instead of the genuine ones."

It was all displayed in graphs and

charts. "Architects always specify high-quality, expensive building parts. At least foreign and joint-venture architects do, but they never check the deliveries. And what gets delivered will be our building components made in our own factory, with American and European labels on them. And we pocket the difference."

His partners approved; they complimented him. "And what is best," Sheng went on happily, "is that all this hurts no one; not one building will collapse because of it; no one will die. Our products will wear out faster than the American or European ones would: carpeting will fray sooner, doors probably won't fit as well; windows won't close or open as securely. But none of this is dangerous. It is, however, very profitable."

It was a moment of triumph, and it brought a smile to Sheng's face as he sat in his office, listening to the soothing sounds of Dolly Parton, and contemplating his future. Chao and Enli had congratulated him on his presentation and the three of them had gone to work arranging with other sons and daughters of military and government officials who owned small

manufacturing plants to make the components. They detailed pricing; hired a printer
for spec sheets, instructions, and brand-
name labels; and found a manufacturer of
cardboard cartons to copy those used for
the American and European products.

It was the kind of detail work that Sheng
loved best, and it made him feel even
closer to Chao and Enli. They were so different from his father! Men of action: ruth-
less, cunning, determined men who would
exploit every opportunity to climb higher
and higher: ultimately to rule China. There
would be only two groups of people in
China—in the whole world, Sheng con-
cluded—those who held power and made
things happen, and the powerless who,
without even being aware of it, lived lives
that were shaped and ordained by the
leaders.

There was no third group, no middle
ground. So how could there be any doubt
which he would choose?

Sheng felt better now; everything was
clear and simple; everything would be all
right. He would handle Beihai and the
pirates and the sugar. Wu Yi would greet

him warmly when he returned. He would be president of All-China Construction.

No, not yet; I don't know how to manage every—

He crushed the thought. He could learn. He was smart and quick. He was his father's son.

He tilted his chair and gazed at the ceiling, his thoughts drifting, waiting until it was time to call Li, to tell him he was going out of town. And precisely at seven-thirty in the morning, he sat up and dialed the number at the office. He would catch him just as he arrived. Unless he was wandering around someplace with that woman again. Taking risks. Putting all of them at risk.

She's the reason he's being followed.

Of course. What else could it be? Enli practically said as much, doubting everything about her.

She'll get him into trouble.

Didn't Li know that? What was wrong with him? Where was his sense of responsibility?

Of course he knows it. So of course he's not with her. Too many risks, and, anyway, he knows I don't like her. And he knows he's being watched. He wouldn't dare see her again. He wouldn't dare—

His rage building, he listened to the telephone ring in his father's office.

"Yuan Li's office," his secretary said.

"Where is he?"

"Who is this please?"

"I expected him to be there!"

"Oh, is this Yuan Sheng? I'm sorry, sir; I didn't recognize your voice."

Any secretary I hired would be a lot quicker, Sheng thought, or out she'd go. "I need to speak to Yuan Li. Immediately."

"I'm sorry, sir, he isn't here. I expect him—"

"*Where is he?*"

"He hasn't come in yet. I expect him any minute. But he has a meeting on the bid for the new office complex, and after that—"

"I can't wait that long; I have to go out of town. Tell him—" Sheng went through the story he had concocted; in fact, it was better than having to lie directly to his father. "And tell him I'll call tomorrow morning, just to check in."

"Oh, I'm sorry, sir, he won't be here."

"Again?" Sheng exploded. "I need to talk to him!"

"He leaves tonight for Xi'an; he'll be there all day tomorrow. I don't expect him in the office until Monday. You can call him after ten o'clock tonight at the Xi'an Garden Hotel; the number is . . ."

Sheng wrote it down, scowling. They had no projects in Xi'an. They had plans for an apartment complex not far from the museum of the terra-cotta warriors, but for now they were too stretched to move into another city. Perhaps his father had pushed that project forward. Or he was exploring another one before presenting it to their board of directors. But he would have told me, Sheng thought. He values my opinion.

Suddenly he thought of the woman, and his father's face, looking at her just before Sheng came up to them. Different, somehow. Softer? More absorbed? Something like that. Something that made Sheng nervous.

He's taking her to Xi'an.

What the devil was he up to? What was he plotting?

It could be business: maybe she wanted to invest in All-China Construction, or start a joint venture with Yuan Li, or—

The hell it's business. He hadn't looked at her like a business associate.

He'd chosen sides. Chosen his American side, and he was using the woman to go to America, to defect. Leaving China. Leaving the company.

Leaving me.

He wouldn't dare, Sheng fumed. Wouldn't dare leave.

But isn't that what Enli was hinting? That my father should go away and leave the company to me?

"But I'd have to prepare for it," he muttered aloud. "And I'd be suspect, as the son of a defector. I'll bet he never thought of that. And why hasn't he told me his plans? *Gao shi.* Shit. The bastard doesn't tell me anything."

It seemed to him that he had been angry at his father ever since the Cultural Revolution, when Li had been sent to Mianning like a common criminal. Sheng knew it wasn't Li's fault, but he felt abandoned, and thought that if Li had been more clever he could have stayed home and been a real father. From then on, even after Li returned, gaunt and frighteningly quiet, things had been harsh between them.

And now, Sheng reflected, growing angrier, now that I'm becoming rich and important, he's messing me up again. Like a crazy man. Well, maybe he is.

Unbidden, the image of the woman came to him again, looking straight at him with that silly American smile that pretended to be friendly, then looking away as he and his father talked and she was left out, since, of course, she could not understand a word they were saying. Stupid woman; why hadn't she learned Chinese before coming to China?

Nothing, she's a nothing, he told himself: not beautiful, not interesting. Yuan Li isn't interested in her and he's not leaving China; it would never occur to him; he's too stodgy for anything like that, and, besides, there's no way he would walk out on me. He's going to Xi'an for something else; it's obvious.

Do I want to be rid of him, or not?

He shook his head angrily. He did not have to answer that question now. First he had to find out why his father was going to

Xi'an, and then, why he was under surveillance. *They'll be calling him in, you know,
to interrogate him.* Sheng trembled, suddenly afraid.

He would talk to Pan Chao. Chao would
know whoever would be tailing Li in Xi'an;
he always managed to ferret out the dirt
the State Security Bureau had on people.
He would tell Sheng why his father was
under surveillance, and what he was doing
in Xi'an. Then, Sheng would know enough
to plan his next move. He would make no
decisions until he knew what the government had on Li, what they expected to get,
and what they were going to do about it.

*And, most important, how it will affect
me.*

Chapter 5

Li saw the men before they saw him. He was entering his office, thinking about the meeting to bid on a new office complex, about flying with Miranda to Xi'an, about the man who was following him—when he saw two men lounging in armchairs near his secretary's desk. And with that one glance, he knew who they were.

He could have turned around and ridden the elevator back to the lobby, left the building through a back door, taken a taxi instead of his own car. He could have avoided them for most of the day. But then there would be tonight, when he would be with Miranda, and he did not want to be taken away in front of her. And so he walked through his office door.

They stood up, as if jerked to their feet. "*Anquan Ju.* State Security Bureau," said one of them, flashing a small card so that Li could read it. "The director wants to see you." Flanking him, they began to move him toward the door.

"Just a minute." His voice surprised him: how calm it was! He turned to his secretary. "I won't be able to attend the meeting on the construction bid or the one on window hardware; please call the supplier and reschedule it for Monday at 7:30. Leave a note on my desk if he confirms that, then cancel my other meetings for today. I don't know when I'll be back."

She nodded, her face carefully blank. "There was a call from Yuan Sheng." She held out a piece of paper. "I wrote down his message."

Li skimmed it. A rambling statement about a business trip, very sudden, very vague. Odd, Li thought, but there was no time to think further; the men were moving him to the elevator, standing silent and watchful on each side of him until they reached the lobby, and then, outside, a waiting car just behind his own. His eyes met those of his driver, who frowned, knowing he could do nothing, while the men propelled Li forward, so smoothly that passersby barely noticed, and those who did knew enough to look the other way, because they had seen it before.

Li shut down all thoughts except this one: what did they want? It could be about Sheng; was that why Sheng had left town? But this was not the police; this was State Security, dealing with matters more serious than piracy. No, this had to do with Li, and it baffled him. For twenty years he had shown that he was not interested in politics, that he cared only about constructing buildings stronger and more interesting than the shoddy stuff being thrown together by most contractors in China, that he might criticize government policies but never name names, that he was so neutral he could be overlooked, like a perfectly camouflaged caterpillar on an autumn leaf. And so everyone from local police to the military had left him alone. Often he was disgusted with himself for his tameness, but he had had enough of chaos, and his reward was that he was making a great deal of money, avoiding turmoil, and was reasonably content.

Had been reasonably content. Until he met Miranda and other kinds of longings had come to life.

How do you know she's really a designer?

I will not start that again, he told himself. I know her. This has nothing to do with her.

They drove in silence to an anonymous building on Chang An Jie East, and in silence walked through doorways and down corridors to a corner office, the heavy draperies closed against the brightness of the day, a man in a dark business suit barricaded behind a broad desk.

"Sit down," he said to Li. "A cigarette? No, you don't smoke. Nor drink, beyond wine and beer with meals. An abstemious man. Careful and cautious. Not one to make trouble or get into trouble."

The room was heavily hushed, the director's voice almost swallowed up by the dark carpet and darker drapes.

He read from an open folder Li's address and home and office telephone numbers, his cell phone number, the license plate of his car, the name of his driver. "You lead an exemplary life," he said, looking up. "All-China Construction is a major force in the modernization of Beijing; you build good buildings; you have good workers." He glanced at the folder. "Your wife is dead. Your son, Yuan Sheng, works in your company; has gone into partnership in two nightclubs with Meng Enli and Pan Chao. Ambitious, no doubt greedy. But that describes all our sons, does it not? Daughter, Yuan Shuiying, lives in Beijing, computer programmer, husband Chen Zemin, minor bureaucrat, also ambitious. You have a cook and housekeeper who live in your home." He looked up again. "Have I left anything out?"

"No," Li said. "You're very thorough."

"It would be good for you, and for us, if you were as thorough in checking the people you entertain at night, and drive in your car around Beijing, and guide through our markets."

Li's hands clenched, the only sign of his shock. "Mrs. Graham is a designer of cashmere clothing; she is here to work with our garment manufacturers." *I do believe this.*

She has not lied to me. "She has had two meetings with the Beijing Higher Fashion Garments Factory in the Haidian . . . but of course you know that."

"Of course. And what did she do after her first meeting there, day before yesterday?"

"I assume she returned to her hotel. We met later for dinner. As you know."

"She delivered a letter." The director named the district and address. "A neighborhood food shop. You are familiar with it?"

"I know nothing about it. Mrs. Graham went there?"

"She *delivered a letter.* You heard me say that."

"From whom? I don't understand. She told me she knew no one in Beijing when she arrived. She was feeling overwhelmed, afraid of the crowds—"

"And you were there to meet her."

"To meet her? No, I had seen a friend off, on a trip to Hong Kong. I met Mrs. Graham by accident. I don't understand what you are implying."

But of course he did understand. The director was saying that he had gone to the airport to meet Miranda's plane, to join with her in planning . . . in planning what?

Nothing. There were no plans.

But she had delivered a letter. To whom? From whom?

The director was reading from his folder. "Mrs. Graham is an intimate friend of Sima Ting, who served a prison sentence for attempting to overthrow the government of China. She was granted a humanitarian release two years ago for reasons of health, and now lives in Boulder, Colorado, in the United States of America."

Stunned, Li was silent.

"Of course we keep an eye on all dissidents, wherever they are," the director went on. "The letter delivered by your friend Mrs. Graham was ostensibly to Sima Ting's parents, through the contacts at the food shop, but of course it would have been widely distributed to other dissidents if we had not intercepted it."

They were waiting for her at the airport, Li thought, alerted by whoever was watching Sima Ting in Boulder. And they saw me speak to her, lead her to the head of the taxi line, go with her into the city. As if that was our arrangement.

And at that point, they began to follow both of us.

The chill that numbed him was so familiar it dragged him backward in time, to his marriage, to his wife's political alliances, to the weeks when he was interrogated over and over again, then told he was a regressive influence in the China of Mao's Cultural Revolution, and was being sent to Mianning, for reeducation. Now, older, wiser, a solid citizen, owner of one of Beijing's most prominent companies, he sat in the office of the director of the State Security Bureau, and felt the fear of a small cog in the machinery of society, easily flicked aside by a government whose goal was to preserve itself through total control of that machinery and all its parts.

So it is that all repressive regimes, all tyrannies, keep their people quiet, acquiescent, and in check.

"Well, then, let us review this." The director leaned back, lit another cigarette, thoughtfully watched the smoke curl to the ceiling. "How did you get the information about her arrival so that you could meet Mrs. Graham's plane?"

"I did not meet her plane. I knew nothing about her. I was at the airport to say good-bye to a friend who was flying to Hong Kong."

"And what do you know about her?"

"She is a designer of cashmere clothing; she works for a New York company called Talia, with an office in Boulder Colorado. The company sent her here to negotiate with three of our garment companies to manufacture Talia designs. She lives in Boulder Colorado and is a widow with two children."

"How much does she earn?"

"I have no idea."

"Without a husband, probably very little. So she would be amenable to earning extra money."

It took Li a moment. "You mean as a spy? She would never do that. Besides, what information could she gather?"

"That is one of the things you will help us discover."

Li stared at him. "You want me to spy on her to find out if she is a spy?"

"Let us return to our conversation. How many times did you communicate with Mrs. Graham before she came to China?"

"I never communicated with her. I did not know her until she came to Beijing."

"Letters? Telephone calls? Telegrams? Faxes? E-mail?"

"No."

"No to which of those?"

"No to all of them."

"Yet you knew what time to meet her plane."

"I did not meet her plane. I was at the airport for other reasons. As I was leaving, I saw that she seemed to be in difficulty, frightened of the crowds, unable to get a taxi, and I helped her."

"You already knew her."

"No."

"You knew who she was."

"No."

"But you left your car at the airport and went into the city with her, in a taxi."

"She seemed to need help."

"The next morning you had breakfast with her and, that night, dinner at Fangshan."

"Yes."

"Why?"

"I found her interesting."

The director's lips twitched. "Interesting.

And still interesting on the following day. A trip to the market; another dinner, this time in a private room in a restaurant of which you are part-owner. The door was closed."

"The noise bothered her."

"Whom does she expect to see while she is in China?"

"The executives and staffs of three garment manufacturers."

"Who else?"

"No one."

"You know that for a fact?"

"She told me she knows no one in China."

"But she delivered a letter, presumably to people she did not know. She could meet with other people she does not know."

"I think that is not part of her plans."

"But she may not have told you all her plans when you went to the airport to meet her plane."

"I did not go to the airport to meet her plane. I was at the airport seeing a friend off to Hong Kong. I saw her from a distance and she seemed to need help."

"Why are you spending time with her?"

"I find her interesting."

"And an American. Your father was American."

"Yes."

"And you tried to correspond with him when he returned to America."

"I was not born when he returned to America. When I was older, a student, I tried to locate him."

The director turned pages in the folder. "That was when you were editor of the student newspaper."

Inwardly, Li shrugged. In China, the past never became the past; it clung to the present, each moment of today and tomorrow and next year as *they* became the present, losing nothing with the passage of time, if anything gaining strength simply by virtue of enduring. And so his American father, his student days, his outspokenness about his wife—

"You did not approve of your wife's activities," the director said. "In arguing against them you used phrases you had written in your student newspaper. Personal honor, personal integrity, personal responsibility . . . always the personal over the communal, the personal over society, the personal over communism. You think too highly of the individual."

Li was silent. It was the truth.

"Also, you had a friend, a professor. He dedicated one of his books to you."

More of the past, Li thought. With the present so filled with change, how do they have time to wallow in the past? "Yes," he said briefly.

"Professor Ye. He died in 1971."

He did not "die." He committed suicide. Hounded to death by the Red Guards, his wife in a prison camp, his children fled to Hong Kong, his library burned, his home smashed. And so he killed himself, like so many others in the Cultural Revolution.

"His widow is still your friend."

"Yes."

There was a silence. The director lit a cigarette. "When you met Mrs. Graham's plane and discussed the letter she was to deliver—"

"I did not meet her plane." That was a mistake, Li thought. No government official liked to be interrupted. But the director went on, and so did Li, repeating the response he had given every time he was asked about meeting Miranda's plane. He used it again and again in the next two hours, as the questions were rephrased, information demanded in different forms, small traps set that kept him alert, even as his annoyance and impatience grew. At last, he came to the conclusion that nothing was going to come of this, at least not today: he was not going to be arrested or charged with some offense or other; he was going to be given a warning. It was done often; often enough to keep people on a path of caution and fear.

So, having decided that, he dared to look at his watch and frown deeply. "I have missed four meetings," he said, looking sternly at the director. "We must conclude this so that I do not lose the whole day. We are bidding on a new government office building; it may even have a suite for you and your staff."

Again the director's lips twitched. "We would not want to put obstacles in the way of better working conditions for our officials." He closed the folder and lit another cigarette. "You understand, Yuan Li, that we will continue to watch your activities. You are a productive citizen of China; you have a large house, a car and driver, a successful construction company, but even the most outstanding citizens can take a wrong turn and destroy a lifetime of work and comfortable living. That is something for you to remember."

Li bowed his head, like a student who had received a warning. He waited for the final order: *Do not see this woman again.*

"If any suspicious activity on your part is reported, we will ask you to return to us to explain it, perhaps with Mrs. Graham, who likes closed doors because noise bothers her." He smiled at his own sarcasm.

There was no order, Li realized, nor would there be. They wanted him to stay close to her, to lead them to the dissidents they were sure she would meet.

They don't need me for that, he thought. They could simply follow Miranda and discover that she knows no one. Or that she does. Why do they want me to be with her?

They think I am her guide, her translator, her confidant. They think she will be more daring with me than without me. And if I fall because of her, that makes no difference to them. In a country of more than a billion people, with absolute power at stake, what is one construction engineer more or less?

There was nothing more to say. In silence, he left the room. They did not shake hands.

On the street, he was breathing hard, and he walked slowly, sorting things out. They would follow Miranda whether he were with her or not. They would not find anything (he was sure they would not find anything) but that would not stop them from staying with her until she flew back to America. So it would not help her if he stayed away from her. Still, any suspicion, even if not one fact was behind it, cast a cloud that could darken one's life for years, perhaps forever, passed on to children and grandchildren, to friends, to coworkers. So it would be better for Li, and for everyone he knew, if he called Miranda and canceled their trip to Xi'an, canceled all their plans, canceled the pleasure he found with her, the aliveness she had awakened in him, the desire . . .

I can't do that. I won't do that.

They had nothing with which to charge him; his life was exemplary. The most radical thing he did was watch CNN. There was nothing in his life to interest them, or to give them cause to charge him.

And they had nothing with which to charge Miranda except the delivery of a letter. *(Why did she do it? And why didn't she tell me?)* With nothing beyond it, no secret meetings, no other contacts, they would not endanger relations with the United States by charging her; it would simply be a small curiosity in a straightforward business trip.

There was no reason for him to stop seeing Miranda, because there was nothing sinister in her activities, or his, and therefore there was no danger.

But they would be followed. Well, that could be endured. What would be far worse would be to cut her out of his life. He could not do that. He would not do that.

Unless there is more that she has not told me, plans, arrangements . . .

He did not really believe that.

In a taxi, on his way back to the office, he called his secretary. "I'm going home. Were there any calls?" He made notes on a small pad of paper, and dictated answers. "I won't be in the office until Monday morning; I'm leaving this evening for Xi'an, as planned."

He called Miranda at the garments factory, and left a discreet message with the receptionist that their plans for the evening were confirmed. There was no need to do that after their arrangements at dinner the night before, but the two telephone calls confirmed his decision to stay with her.

And if it did become dangerous . . .

Then he would rethink it. But not now. Now he was going on.

At home, he showered, trying to wash away the hours spent at the State Security Bureau, then spent an hour planning the meeting he would have on Monday morning, to bid on the new building. At first he had trouble focusing on it, but the process of putting together a proposal like a jigsaw puzzle finally absorbed him and the time sped by. The interrogation stayed with him like a bad taste, but he ignored it. One learned to do that, in China. It would fade. It always did.

But, still, he had to put it to rest with Miranda, and so that night, on the plane to Xi'an, as soon as their tea was served, he bent his head to her and, beneath the tumultuous noise of the cabin, said, "I want to ask you something."

Her eyes widened, and he knew she had heard the tension in his voice. "What is it?"

"I found out today that you delivered a letter from a Chinese woman in America to a—"

"How could you possibly know about that?" A shiver ran across Miranda's skin. What a strange and terrible feeling to know that ordinary things you did were known by others, and talked about.

"Chinese dissidents are watched, wherever they are, in China or abroad. The young woman—"

"You spy on people in America?"

"I do not. My government does."

"They can't do that."

"Well." Li shrugged slightly. "They do it. Americans do it, too, you know; your CIA has spies in most countries. It is part of the world now; it is the way things are. My government does not lose interest in people just because they have left China. So the young woman, Sima Ting, has been watched since she arrived in Boulder Colorado, which means that you were seen with her—after all, you are her intimate friend—and you also—"

"Intimate? What are you talking about? I saw her twice, at a friend's apartment. I've never even been alone with her."

Li frowned. "Twice. At a friend's apartment. Yet she asked you to become her courier?"

"I don't know what that means. She asked me to take a letter to her parents, so of course I said I would. Why wouldn't I?"

"But you did not deliver it to her parents."

"She said their home was hard to find, and to leave it at a small shop, a food shop. The people were very nice; they barely spoke English, but they insisted that I take a few things from the store, as a gift. I suppose because I'd done a favor for Ting."

"To make it look as if you were there to shop. A vain hope: tourists do not find their way to that neighborhood. But they did their best to cover up the reason for your visit for anyone who might be watching."

Miranda stared at him, because then she understood. *"Someone is following me?"* Involuntarily she looked behind her at the crowded plane. No one seemed the slightest bit interested in her. "This is crazy. I don't know anything about China; I came here not knowing one single person. Why would your government care about me?"

"You are a friend of Sima Ting."

"I told you I only saw her— Oh. That doesn't matter, does it? One meeting or twenty, just the fact that I talked to her."

"Yes."

"And other people know I delivered her letter. And the people in the shop knew, or thought, I might have been followed there. Does everybody know everything in this country?"

Li smiled. "In fact, we know almost nothing. You know more about your government in five minutes than we know in a year." He looked at his cup. "We have not touched our tea and it has grown cold. We will get fresh cups. Now that this has been straightened out, we will forget this subject and drink our tea and talk of other things."

"No, we can't." She was contemplating him with a small frown. "How did you know that I delivered the letter?"

He sighed. "Someone told me."

"Who told you? The people who followed me? The police?"

"The State Security Bureau. Like your FBI."

"They're the ones who followed me? And then they called you up and said I'd delivered a letter?" She looked at him more closely. "Is that what happened?"

Again he sighed, and shook his head. "They brought me in for questioning. They wanted to know about you, when we met, why we have dinner together. They were. . . . You have a way of saying this in English. Hunting. They don't have any information, but they are . . . hunting?"

"Fishing. A fishing expedition. What did you tell them about me?"

"That you are a designer here on business. Of course I did not know about the letter, so I could not respond to their questions about it."

"Why did they say Ting and I were intimate friends?"

"To trap me. It is an old trick; I should have seen it immediately."

"And now that I've delivered the letter, they aren't following me anymore?"

"They will follow you until you leave China, but it does not mean anything. It keeps people employed, you see, and that helps the economy."

"I don't think it's anything to joke about." She frowned again. "What could they do to me? Could they make me leave?"

"You mean revoke your visa? Yes, but they have no reason to do that. You are not meeting any dissidents, and, even more important, your president is coming to Beijing in a few weeks and they would not provoke an incident with an American citizen just before his arrival. Some of our dissidents might be arrested to prevent their trying to talk to your president or get messages to him, but Americans are safe."

Miranda shook her head. "How can you be so calm about this?"

"We are calm about what we cannot change until the time comes that we can change it."

"But they must be watching you, too. You're with me, and if they think I'm suspicious, they must think you are, too."

He looked at her broodingly. "How quickly you learn. I wish that you did not have to learn these things."

"You said it was part of the world now. So I should learn it."

"Not your world."

"Yours. And I want to understand it."

Li put out his hand as if to touch her, then drew it back. "Yes, I am being watched. But now I know that they are wrong about you and there is nothing to worry about. It is annoying, but not dangerous, because there is nothing for them to find. They will follow us, some distance away, and after a while we will forget they are there."

"I could never forget it."

"Then you will live with it and soon it will be like the weather. 'Oh, so it is raining today. Well, that does not affect my plans.' You see?"

"You make it sound so ordinary."

"And in China it is. You understand, it is not as bad as it used to be; we have many freedoms now that we never had. This is a remnant of the past and someday it will disappear. It is difficult for any government to throw out its old habits, you know, but eventually our government will have to; it is being pulled and pushed by the world of trade and money and the Internet that walls and guns cannot stop. But still, it takes time. And now we will concentrate on our tea and our visit to Xi'an, and talk of other things. Will you try to do that?"

"I think you're minimizing it for my sake, to make me less worried."

"I do want you to be less worried. But I am not minimizing it for that reason. There is no danger here."

"For me or you?"

"For both of us. Now, will you help me talk of other things?"

She hesitated, then nodded. She did not believe that there was no danger for Li, but she would pretend that everything was normal, if that was what he wanted.

And what is normal in China? I have no idea. How do people live with this uncertainty? I never could.

But the amazing thing was that they did talk of other things and for the rest of the flight, she did not think about the fact that some nameless, faceless, shadowy form —man or woman?—was on the plane with them, or waiting in Xi'an, ready to follow them wherever they went.

She did not see anything unusual in the Xi'an airport, and she saw no one outside the hotel. It was possible, she thought, that Li was wrong. But she did not really think he was. And she did not suggest that to him before they went to their separate rooms, or the next morning, when they met in the lobby after her swim. By then she was nervous for other reasons.

The minute they sat down to a breakfast of tea and rice and steamed buns, Miranda opened her guidebook and began talking about museums and tombs and warriors. Twice, she dropped her napkin, and each time a waiter appeared with a fresh one. Every few minutes she looked up to survey the room, then looked at her plate or her book, as if ordering herself to be casual.

"It does not help to look," Li said gently.

"I know, but it isn't only that. It's . . ." She smiled ruefully. "It's like the private room in your restaurant, only more so. Even eating breakfast feels illicit."

"Ah. Men and women do not travel together for sightseeing in your country?"

She smiled again. "They might call it that."

He chuckled. "Well, we will call it sightseeing, because that is what it is. And a chance to be together, away from work. Shall we go to the museum?"

"Yes."

The museum was a concrete enclosure as long as three football fields. Li and Miranda entered at one end, and stood on a railed walkway, looking down at six thousand terra-cotta warriors, larger than life-size, standing at attention in battle array. Over two thousand years old, they stood as they had when the emperor Qin Shi-haung-di commanded their placement to guard his nearby tomb: row on row of men in full battle gear, the generals wearing bronze swords still keenly sharp, the foot soldiers holding ghostly weapons of wood long since rotted away. All six thousand stared straight ahead, each face unique, modeled after living warriors of that distant time. Their ranks faded into the dim shadows of the concrete structure that had been built to protect them, with workers at the far end restoring warriors being pried every day from the hardened clay in which hundreds more still lay buried.

It was a magnificent sight, no matter how many times Li viewed it, but today his thoughts kept sliding away, to the woman beside him. He wanted to touch her. He wanted to touch her hair, to trace the pure outline of her face, to embrace her. Especially in Xi'an, where he was as much a visitor as she, he felt a new closeness and he was sure she must feel it, too.

In this he knew he was different from most Chinese, who kept aloof from strangers and frowned on openness outside their family and close friends. His mother had tried to raise him as his father might have, and Li's bedtime stories had been tales of his father's easygoing familiarity, his open gestures of affection, his laughter, even, sometimes, at himself. Li knew he had never mastered that—only Americans truly could, he thought—but he knew that he was more open than most Chinese, more willing to offer something of himself if his attention were caught.

He glanced at Miranda as she frowned in concentration at the warriors below. She was dressed as she had been when he first saw her at the airport, in a severe blue suit, her white blouse buttoned to the throat, her square leather purse hanging from her left shoulder, and she stood out among the casually dressed tourists crowding behind them. Why had she not brought informal clothes from America, Li wondered; had she not expected even a few hours of relaxation? Probably not. She had come here to work and to deal with the hazards of travel and a country where so much was foreign.

He felt a rush of tenderness toward her, for daring to try so much in so few days. And he wanted to touch her.

Not now. Not yet. He turned to the scene below: the standing warriors and kneeling archers, the wild-eyed horses pawing the ground, the standing archers facing outward, alert to approaching enemies. *Everyone is on guard,* he thought. *Especially Miranda. But perhaps, when she feels more at ease; when she feels, as I do, the pleasure of being together . . . .*

"Did he really think they would protect him?" Miranda asked.

Li brought his thoughts back to the warriors, and to the man who had them created. "He was the first emperor of China, the man who united all the warring provinces. I imagine he thought whatever he decreed would come to pass."

"He must have been terrified of death, to require an army to go with him."

"He expected the next world to be a replica of this one, and he was determined to be prepared for it. It's amazing how completely we fool ourselves into believing we can cope with whatever lies ahead."

Looking at the warriors below, he was aware of Miranda's quick look, and her small frown as she tried to understand him. And before he could stop himself, he said, "I love your frown. It's as if you're trying to bring the whole world to its knees, to capture it and make it yours."

Her eyes widened. Li met them, and was flooded with desire. He grabbed the railing in front of him, pressing the cold steel into his palms. "In some people a frown would be a door closing," he said, forcing back his desire with inanity, "but in you it is a greeting." He took a breath and turned to walk on, following a group of tourists. "I apologize. I should not have said that."

"No," she agreed, walking beside him. Her purse slid to the ground and she gave an exclamation of annoyance. Li picked it up and, as if to deflect attention from her nervousness, she said, "You said people fool themselves, thinking they can cope with the future. Do you?"

"Oh, certainly, in many ways. I believed I

could save Wei. I believed I could raise my children by myself, better than others, because I thought love could overcome all obstacles. I believed—"

"And it may not be able to."

His eyebrows rose. "I thought Americans believe that it can."

"Oh? Why would they?"

"Because Americans are romantics."

"Another one of your infallible pronouncements."

"But surely Americans believe in happy endings and that the way to them is through love."

"Some Americans. But a lot of Americans would say that money is the way to a happy ending. And people everywhere— you, too, I'll bet—accuse us of loving money more than anything."

He nodded. "I have said that about Americans, as others have, probably because we're all jealous of America, and jealousy breeds illogic. But sometimes I think that Americans believe the power of love is greater than the power of money, indeed, greater than anything."

"And you don't agree with that."

"No. Do you?"

"I'd like to." She paused. "I know that love may not always be enough, but I'd like to believe that most people would put it ahead of money and power and possessions. Anyone who has loved, even once, could never find money and power attractive enough to risk losing it."

"That is what I meant by romantic," Li said quietly.

"Well. Maybe."

But he wanted her to understand, and, to his surprise, because he had never admitted this to anyone, he said, "You see, I envy romanticism, that wonderful belief in love and magic and goodness triumphant. Once, when I was young, I believed in angels; kind forces in the universe that bring safety where there is danger, joy where there is despair, love where there is hatred. But too many of my dreams shattered for me to believe in angels; my solid world crumbled too often. I would like to believe in goodness, but even that is difficult in China these days. In fact—" He met Miranda's eyes and saw in them a warmth that stunned him, stopping his words.

"In fact?" she asked.

He let out his breath. "In fact, it seems

impossible that any of us, living in a culture that springs from warlords, emperors, nationalists, and communists, could truly believe in the power of anything except . . . power."

"What a terrible thing to say. Everything must seem so bleak to you . . . as if you're lost in a cave and your lamp has failed and you don't know the way out and you never will. Why don't you just lie down and die?"

"Because people don't do that. We always go on. That's hard to fathom, if you look at the world's history, but something compels us to go on, even in the midst of unimaginable horrors. Maybe we keep looking for another lamp. Or a way out, because we refuse to believe there cannot be one. Or perhaps romanticism. Although I would not let myself be fooled by beautiful dreams."

"Why don't you just believe in them? Sometimes they come true."

"Not often. Or not often enough."

She studied his face. "You gave up all your dreams?"

He shrugged slightly. "It was not a question of giving them up. I rejected them because they did not apply to me. In a way, you did the same, I think: you had your dream of love flowing between two people, but you put it aside for a calm life with your children and your work."

She turned from him. Li would have pursued it, but there was already too much tension between them. Tension, and something else, he thought: feelings that drew them together even as they seemed to draw apart in disagreement.

He saw her take a final glance at the archers, shoulder to shoulder, facing outward to scan the horizon for dangers, then turn away. "This way," he said, and led her to the exit.

Outside, they blinked in the brilliant sunlight. They took out their dark glasses and Miranda put on her hat, black straw with a wide grosgrain ribbon. They were on a concrete walk bordered with large chrysanthemums, and the spicy autumn scent followed them as they walked. "Are you ready for lunch?" he asked.

She nodded and they walked back to his rented car. As he drove, he saw by her face that she thought he was going too fast, like all Chinese drivers, with barely a glance at cyclists and pedestrians. Well, she's right, he thought, but I probably am too old to change my driving habits. And how brave or polite of her not to scold me, or even ask me to slow down.

In a narrow street, they went into a tiny restaurant tucked between two crumbling buildings. "Soon these will be gone," Li said. "Too old and too small to be renovated. I suppose the city will try to keep one or two, as a museum. The rest will be anonymous highrises."

"That should please you. All that work for your company."

They sat at a small table set with china, chopsticks and a steaming teapot. Li filled their cups. "It pleases the part of me that likes making a good living, but there is also the part of me that does not want to lose all of the past."

"But you didn't like the past."

"Much of it."

"What is it you want to keep?"

"A belief in art and poetry: glories that have nothing to do with money or muscle. A belief that we're not responsible for what our country was in the past, and not completely to blame for what it is becoming today."

"That's very bitter."

"Oh, I do not mean to whine. It is just that I am not . . . how is it you say it in America? Politically correct. And sometimes that makes life difficult. Shall I order for us?"

"Yes. Could we have *lazi jiding* and *mogu dufu?*"

He smiled broadly. "Anything you can pronounce, we can eat." He felt her studying him as he ordered, and he said, "What is it?"

"You haven't been looking behind us today. Is that because you think there's no one there?"

"I thought we were not going to talk about that."

"But I can't help thinking about it. How such a tiny thing, delivering a letter, can spread out and put people in danger . . ."

"This sounds like a James Bond movie," Li said lightly.

"It was real enough in Beijing to worry you."

"Did I seem worried?"

"Yes. Even though you were trying not to."

"Ah, already you know me too well," he

said, and smiled, making it a jest. "Well, it is real but not dangerous. It is what I told you: an annoyance."

"Sheng thinks it's serious, doesn't he? You started looking behind us after we met him. So he must have warned you."

"He did," Li said, surprised that she had made that connection.

"And he thought you'd be harmed, and he would, too, and maybe your company? All because you're with me." She pushed away her plate. "We have to go back to Beijing. I can't put you at risk; it isn't fair. I'll go home to America but you'll be stuck here."

"No one can judge that better than I. I told you: with your president coming here, they will do no more than keep track of you. Miranda, this is my home; I know its safe places and its treacherous ones. You must let me judge whether I am in danger or not."

She met his eyes, and Li knew from the racing of his heart how passionate his voice had been, perhaps desperate. He would not let her go. And now she knew it.

After a moment, she said, "I don't really want to go back to Beijing right away. But the minute you think there is danger . . ."

"I will tell you. I promise that. And now we will not talk about it anymore. I should not burden you with problems when you have your own work to think about. Tell me about it; what did you do yesterday?"

"It doesn't feel like a burden. It feels like trust."

He was taken aback and, strangely, filled with sadness. What is this, he thought, why do I feel this? To cover his silence, he reached out to serve them, but Miranda was ahead of him. For the first time she was the one to spoon portions onto their plates, and to Li's sadness was added a deep pleasure at the natural way she did it.

"You look very sad," she said, and Li realized that after years of schooling himself to turn a bland and noncommittal face to the world, suddenly he was becoming open again, his face and voice betraying his emotions, shattering his protective shell. *But there is a freedom in it that I have not felt for a long time. As long as it is only with Miranda . . .*

"I did feel sadness," he said, "because I suddenly realized how few people could say, as you just did, that they have my trust."

"You don't trust people?"

"I do not allow myself to trust them."

Miranda shook her head as if she could not, ever, understand that. The waitress filled their glasses with beer and they ate in silence until Miranda said, "Where did you learn English?"

"In school. The authorities assigned different languages to different classes and mine was given English."

"You didn't choose it?"

"In those days we were not allowed to choose anything. That is all changing now."

"How old were you when you began?"

"Seven. A good time to begin, when our memories are sponges. And when I was ten I discovered the wonders of western literature; from that time on, I fell in love with Shakespeare and Euripides, with Trollope and Dickens, Cervantes, Eliot, Rousseau, Swift—"

"You could get all those books?"

"They were my father's. He left four boxes of books when he returned to America. All of them had his name written inside, sometimes in his handwriting and sometimes in others.' 'Merry Christmas, dearest John, from Mother and Dad.'

Things like that. My favorite is from Aunt Mildred; it says, 'This is for the times you want to spit at the world, John; there's nothing like a few Shakespearean murders and betrayals to make you feel better about your own life.' I would have liked to know Aunt Mildred."

"So would I," Miranda said, smiling. "Do your children speak English?"

"Yes, very well. English is the only truly world language and young people, if they are ambitious, know they must learn it. Now tell me about your work. I asked you about it, remember?"

"Yes, but there's so much to talk about . . ."

And that was the wonder of it, Li thought as Miranda described her collaboration the day before with Yun Chen and a late-afternoon meeting at the Baoxiang Woolen Mills. They had so much to talk about, so much to learn and share and build upon.

To what end?

It doesn't matter, he thought. Or, at least, it is too early to matter.

". . . goats," Miranda was saying. "You have the best in the world, near the Gobi Desert."

"You've studied goats?" Li asked, diverted

and amused. "Of course I know that's where cashmere yarn comes from, but why do you study them?"

"To learn everything about the yarn so I'll know what it can and can't do in a design."

"Strange," Li mused. "I like cashmere sweaters; you'd think I would have asked a few questions about how they're made. Well, tell me about goats."

They ate slowly and Li listened to Miranda, taking pleasure in the sound of her voice and the eagerness in her face as she saw his interest. She described the combing of goats in the spring, the washing of the fleece, the dying and spinning, the knitting, mostly on machines, the fraudulent practice of mixing coarse hairs with fine underbelly ones to make cheaper, inferior products.

"The most expensive pieces are made only from the underbelly hairs, and by hand, on knitting frames, and monitors check them all the time, the tension of the yarn, the shape, the size, the evenness of the stitches, the tightness of buttonholes, everything at once. And the monitors at Baoxiang are the best I've seen. They know that without them the whole process could fall apart, and they think it's terrific that they're so important."

Surprised, Li said, "Did they tell you that?"

"Of course not. When would a Chinese man or woman say anything personal to me? I saw it in their faces and the way they worked and the way they talked about their work. They're proud of themselves."

"And you liked that."

"It made them seem human."

"Do you have many friends?" he asked abruptly.

Her eyes widened. "Of course."

"Many?"

"As many as I need. We're lucky to have any friends, I think; we're all so busy and wrapped up in our own lives. There are a lot of people I see now and then . . . . not good friends, but good enough. And I'm with my parents two or three times a week; it's good for the children to be close to them."

He heard the thread of defensiveness in her voice, and would have liked to ask her about it—*good enough for what?*—but he let it go. "I have two close friends," he said musingly, "a man I've known since university, and a woman my mother's age, who is very wise and dear to me. Of course I know dozens of other people, acquaintances, a few closer than the rest."

"Why are there only two really close ones?" Miranda asked.

"Because it is easier to be alone than to try to make oneself understood."

"Oh, how snobbish that sounds."

"You mean elitist. Well, if I am, is that so bad?"

"It is if you're lonely."

And then he understood her. *Good enough to stave off loneliness, to share a meal, to test an idea, to fill the silent hours of the night.* Their eyes met and he made a movement to touch her arm, but stopped himself before it was more than a rippling of the muscle. Even if they had been ready for it, it was not proper. Not in public. Not in China.

The waitress brought the soup, but neither of them reached for it; they sat quietly, looking through the window at the ebb and flow of the busy street. In a few moments the waitress reappeared with a fresh pot of tea, and took away the soup. The restaurant emptied. Li roused himself. "We've sat here so long. . . . I had hoped to take you to some other sights, but perhaps you would like to relax instead."

"Yes, thank you for saying that. It's been such a full day, I'd just like to be—I'd just like to think about it for a while."

I'd just like to be alone. That was what she had almost said. And she was right, Li thought; they needed to be apart for a little while, to take a breather from the nervousness they had felt all day. His had been below the surface, making him keenly aware of her every movement, and of the two of them together, bending toward each other, then away, like dancers who almost but never quite touch. And Miranda had dropped napkins and her purse, shifted in her chair, rolled chopsticks between her fingers, run her hand through her hair . . . in a dozen jittery ways she had shown how conscious she was of traveling with him and how, imperceptibly, they both had moved from friendship to desire.

"We'll go back to the hotel," he said when they were in the car. "And perhaps a drink before dinner? There is a pleasant bar off the lobby."

"Yes. Thank you, Li; this has been a wonderful day."

As she said his name, her voice tightened and she coughed, and Li realized how seldom she used it. Almost never, in fact. As if, he thought with sadness, saying his name reminded her of his foreignness.

In the hotel lobby, she turned to him. "Will they stop following you when I'm gone? When I go home?"

"I don't know. They have to keep all those surveillance people occupied, you know."

"What will you do, then? When I'm gone?"

"I do not think about that. All I am thinking about is having a drink with you, and then dinner."

She smiled faintly, and turned to go. Li waited until the elevator doors had slid shut behind her, then casually sat in an armchair, waiting. *Why? What does it matter whether or not I see whoever is following us?* There was no answer to that. He just wanted to know.

He sat quietly. After almost an hour, he was sure he had picked out two men in business suits who could be the ones following them. There have to be two, he reflected, in case we go to different places. He watched the men skim magazines through smoke rising from cigarettes dangling from their lips, watched them put down the magazines, light new cigarettes from the stubs of the old, pick up newspapers, turn pages. Now and then they looked up casually, making a languid survey of the lobby, their glances passing over Li without expression. But he knew they were the ones.

But knowing which ones they were was useless. He could not stop them; he could not avoid them. They were part of the landscape and there was not one thing he could do about it.

The hell with it. He stood up. He had a friend to visit and then he would go to his room. *Miranda and I have tonight ahead of us, and next to that, nothing matters. We will block out tomorrow and think of nothing but that: the two of us, together, tonight.*

Chapter 6

Miranda locked the door to her hotel room, kicked off her shoes and took a long breath, glad to be alone. Dropping her clothes on the floor, she put on the terrycloth robe she found hanging in the closet, and sat at a carved table in the window. She wanted to call her family; she needed to hear their voices and be pulled into their lives: out of this one, into theirs. But as she began to dial the hotel operator, she stopped. What was she thinking of? Five o'clock in the afternoon in Xi'an—the same time as Beijing, since, peculiarly, all of China set its clocks to Beijing time—was two o'clock in the morning in Boulder. Her parents, her children, the dog and the cat all would be asleep, and scared to death if the telephone startled them awake. Her parents would spring from their bed. *Miranda . . . drugged by Chinese bandits . . . kidnapped . . . imprisoned by communists . . . run over by bicycles . . . lost forever.* Her children would think . . . well, what would her children think? Nothing. They would sleep right through it.

She smiled, picturing them sprawled tangled in their sheets, oblivious to her late-night kiss on forehead and cheek. But even as she smiled, she had a feeling of loss and disconnectedness, as if, far from the orbit of their lives, she was no longer sure who she was.

Everything is so different, so incredible . . . I want to tell you about—

No, that wasn't really what she had wanted to say when she rushed to the telephone. The truth was, she had wanted to talk about Li.

It did not matter that she could anticipate her parents' scowls, and hear their warnings; she still wanted to talk about him. She wanted to hear herself say his name; she wanted to test her feelings by describing him. She wanted to make him seem more a part of her life by bringing him into a conversation with home.

But there was no way she could do it. Not tonight, anyway. And maybe not at all. When it came down to it, she really wasn't sure she wanted to wade through their hostility just to be able to talk about Li.

"Li," she said aloud, and it was as if she could taste his name on her tongue.

But that made her jittery, and she began to pace. Her corner room was divided in two by a long mahogany desk with a television set at one end that swiveled to face the bedroom or the sitting room. Miranda flicked on the set and watched a newscast on CNN about upcoming Congressional elections in the United States, then went back to her pacing, circling the two silk couches, the heavily carved cocktail table, the single lamp with a bulb too dim for reading. She stopped at the window on one wall. The hotel was four-sided, built around a lake, but her room faced the front, looking down on a sinuous stream bordered with boulders and animal sculptures nestled in low evergreens. A small bridge spanned the stream, and bright carp darted just below the surface like ghostly orange streamers. It was so perfect, so gentle and harmonious, that she wished Li were with her, to share it.

But she had just been feeling glad to be alone.

At the lighted shelf unit across the room, she poured tea from a heavy steel thermos into a porcelain cup painted with gold-rimmed lilies. Carrying the cup, she wandered back to the bedroom and stood looking down at the blouse folded on top of her open suitcase. How could it be so wrinkled, when she had packed so carefully? She picked it up, shook it out, gazed at it critically. Nothing about it pleased her. Even if she ironed it, its everyday utilitarianism would be unchanged. It was a blouse for the office: respectable, neat, relentlessly dull. It spoke volumes about duty and repression, and said not one word about a pleasant evening on the town.

Li would be hurt if she wore it. He would think that she did not care enough about him, or his efforts to make the trip pleasant, to pay any special attention to her appearance.

Well, that's too bad. As my mother says, All you really need is a clean face.

Anyway, it was all she had. Everything else was in her hotel room in Beijing.

She found an ironing board in the closet and set it up. She spread the blouse out, pulled it taut, and positioned the iron above a sleeve. And then stood there. *I can't wear it. I really can't. I don't want him to be hurt. And I want to feel special.*

She tossed the blouse back onto the suitcase. Somehow, she had to find something else.

On her way to breakfast that morning, she had paused at the window display of a women's boutique in the lobby. There had been a blouse with bright flowers, and a dress—some kind of blue—almost iridescent; she had not paid much attention. But the blouse and dress were still in the window when she went downstairs, the shop was still open, and the woman behind the counter, wearing a perfectly cut black dress, said, in perfect English, "Welcome. What may I show you?"

She looked incredibly old. Her face was

a web of fine wrinkles narrowly framed by pure white hair pulled back and twisted into a bun fastened with an ivory comb; her hands were almost translucent, with raised blue veins curving and intersecting like Chinese writing. She came only to Miranda's shoulder, but she stood as erect as a young woman, her face alert, her eyes dark and lively. Miranda liked her. "I'd like to try on that blouse," she said, "and the dress."

The woman gazed at her. "The blouse I think is not for you. The flowers are too large for your delicate face. I will show you some that would suit you better. The dress would be perfect, though I have others that you might also wish to consider. Please . . ." She pulled back a heavy gold curtain so that Miranda could walk into the dressing room. "One moment." She let the curtain fall as she left.

The dressing room was large and square, deeply carpeted and furnished with two damask-covered chairs and an antique floor vase filled with huge burnt-orange and gold chrysanthemums. The walls and ceiling were draped in fabric; on one wall gold light sconces flanked a tall mirror in a frame of carved peacocks and bamboo. Miranda looked into it, wondering what she was doing there. She did not need new clothes. And even if she did, from the look of the dressing room, there was nothing here she could afford.

Behind her reflection, the saleswoman edged through the curtain, her arm draped with a rainbow of silks. "Shall we begin with the dresses?" She hung them on a brass rod along one wall. "Would you choose which you would like to try first?"

The colors were vivid and Miranda narrowed her eyes to dim their brightness. "Don't you have anything softer? Something quieter."

"I do have ivory and pale yellow, but . . . are those truly what you came looking for?"

Miranda gave her a quick look. "No," she said after a moment. "I was thinking of . . ." She stretched out her hand and brushed her palm across the dresses. Her fingers paused at a cherry red one, but there was no way she could imagine herself in that, so, lingeringly, she moved on to a jade green and past that to the blue dress she had seen in the window, peacock blue, with a long, slitted skirt, a wide silver belt, and a sleeveless top with a deep notched collar. "If you have this in my size . . ."

"This is a U.S. four. Your size, I believe."

Miranda nodded. She should have known. She was in the hands of an expert. She watched herself in the mirror as the saleswoman slipped the dress over her head and zipped up the back.

The small room seemed to flare with light, as if someone had thrown a switch: suddenly everything was brighter, more positive, more exciting. The dress was a perfect fit, shaping itself to Miranda's slender form, the neckline plunging (what had happened to the demure collar that had seemed, on a hanger, fit for a schoolgirl?), the skirt, reaching to her ankles, slit thigh-high. Her bare arms seemed smoother and longer than usual, and her neck rose from the V of the collar with a grace she had not imagined it had.

"Ah, my dear," the saleswoman sighed.

Miranda met her eyes in the mirror and felt a surge of affection. It was as if she had slipped back in time and once again was with her mother, shopping for school clothes in the long hot days that signaled the end of summer. "Do I look all right?" she asked.

The woman smiled. "You look lovely. And happy."

Miranda frowned. She took a step back and shifted uncomfortably within the fine silk. She felt exposed and vulnerable. The fabric was so light it was as if she were clothed in air, with no comforting weight of wool or barrier of starched cotton to shield her. And her figure—surely taller and straighter than normal?—was so definitively blue: vibrantly, unmistakably, conclusively blue.

No one could hide in such a dress, or shrink away, or assume anonymity.

"It's not me," Miranda murmured.

"Or it truly is," said the saleswoman gently.

Miranda spread her hands beneath her chin, fingertips together, gazing at her face.

"Yes, you see," said the saleswoman. "It is the same. No more beautiful than before, not even prettier. But now people will look at you. And more than that: they will see you."

Miranda's eyes widened in surprise. How had this woman known that that was how she always felt: that people looked through her, not at her? In fact, that was usually what she wanted: to blend in, to find a niche where there were no surprises, no crises; a place where she belonged and knew exactly what was expected of her. A place where she could be calm and unpressured. Invisible.

Don't make waves. Her parents had taught her that. *Life is hard; don't overreach, don't get involved in other people's affairs. They'll sap your energy with their neediness and you won't have any left for yourself.*

Jeff had believed that, too. It was as much as he could do to cope with what was close to him, and familiar.

Miranda frowned at her reflection. *All my life I've been surrounded by fearful people.*

But now, strikingly blue, her hair a light-glinted halo above the vivid silk, it occurred to her that all the possibilities she had ruled out years earlier need not be scorned indefinitely. Perhaps they deserved a second look. Would it really be such a bad thing to step away from the crowd . . . and be visible?

Or—as they said in the fashion world—to make a statement?

What kind of a statement?

Oh, I have no idea, she thought crossly.

"Perhaps you would like to try the other dresses," the saleswoman said.

Miranda looked at the woman, who was gazing at her so warmly. "What is your name?" she asked.

"Ye Meiyun." Her body bent slightly; it was almost a bow. "And yours is Miranda Graham."

Miranda stared at her.

"I saw you this morning, coming from the elevator and going to breakfast, and I asked the concierge who you were. You must forgive me, but I was curious."

"Because of the friend who was with me."

"Yes, with Yuan Li."

"You *know* him?"

"I have known him for a very long time. Before I came to Xi'an, my husband was a professor in Beijing; he and Yuan Li were dear friends. When my husband died, Li and I became close, as survivors often do. He helped me start my business and he suggested I come to Xi'an; he knew a few shopkeepers here who could help me and be my friends, and he thought it would be easier for me in a small town."

"It has three million people!"

"That is small, for China. And shopkeepers form their own small community within a city. Even in New York they do that, as everywhere in the world. People with common interests and passions and backgrounds."

"You've been in New York? When?"

"Most recently, last year. And Chicago as well."

"And you still came back to China?"

"Of course. It is my home."

"But . . ."

"But you think that I should want to stay in America because everything is better there. And indeed many things are. But what I said about shopkeepers is true of everyone else, too. Common interests, passions, backgrounds . . . do you not think those are of the greatest importance in life?"

"Not more than freedom."

"Ah, well. That sounds to me like something one of your presidential candidates would say. There are many kinds of freedom, my dear, and there is the work to do to make freedom grow, and to protect it."

"Are you talking about America?"

"Both America and China."

"I don't understand that." She frowned. "There are so many things I don't understand."

"It is good to say that. No one except a fool would say the opposite."

Miranda laughed. "Thank you."

"Well, now, let us have tea." Meiyun clapped her hands, and a young woman came in and placed a tray on the table between the damask chairs. "I will pour," Meiyun said, "while you try on another dress. You should look at three, at the very least. It is always best to make a decision from comparisons. Try the gold."

Miranda put on the antique gold dress, close-fitting, with short sleeves and a high collar. She turned to let Meiyun zip up the back and then turned back and gazed at her reflection. "It's a little dull," she said at last.

Their eyes met in the mirror and they burst out laughing.

"It takes but a small shift in the prevailing winds," said Meiyun, "and the entire world looks different. Sit down, my dear, and have some tea. Then perhaps you will try another one. Perhaps the red."

Miranda shook her head. "The winds haven't shifted that much." She sipped the hot tea, then picked up the blue dress and turned it around and around in her hands. Suddenly she burst out, "But what do you *think* about this? You haven't said a word about my being here, in Xi'an, with—" She could not bring herself to say his name.

"With Yuan Li. But, my dear, it is not for me to comment, is it?"

"It's your country and I've barged in from somewhere else and taken . . ."

"One of our men?" She looked amused. "I do not truly think you have *taken* anything. In any event, we have an abundance of men in China, although, as everywhere in the world, there are too few wonderful ones."

Surprised, Miranda said, "Do you really think that?"

"Doesn't every woman think that?"

"Yes, but . . ."

"Ah, you are surprised that women are the same everywhere."

"We're not. We have different ideas,

depending on our countries, our governments, our schools, the way we live."

"Yet we all feel hunger and eat, we grow
tired and sleep, we ovulate and menstru-
ate and nurse our children, many of us get
cancer or other diseases, we find careers,
we fall in love and marry and worry about
our children crossing the street or getting
involved with the wrong friends—"

"That isn't what I meant. We think about
the world differently, about freedom and
civil rights, and freedom of the press . . .
all of that."

"Different governments handle these differently," Meiyun said gently. "And nothing
remains the same forever, in your country
or in ours. It is what I was saying before."

Miranda was silent, trying to deal with
ideas that contradicted everything she
had been taught. I'll do it later, she
thought, I can't handle every new idea at
once. "You haven't told me what you think,"
she said.

"About you and Yuan Li?"

"Yes."

"I do not think. I only observe."

"That's not true. You have opinions on
everything."

"Well . . ." She spread her hands. "In fact, that is true."

"And I want to know your opinion about my being with . . . Li."

Meiyun sighed. "I think it is a mistake."

Miranda's eyes widened. "For him or for me?"

"For both of you."

"For us to be friends?"

"No, no. Friendship is always to be nurtured and cherished. But surely what I hear in your voice tells me that you are leaning beyond friendship; that events are swift, but you are swifter."

"If that's true," Miranda said after a moment, "*if* it's true, why would it be so bad?"

Meiyun refilled their teacups. Sitting erect in her chair, she waited as the leaves swirled and slowly sank to the bottom of her cup. She took a long swallow and set down the cup. "I did not say it would be bad. It might well be exquisite. I said it would be a mistake."

"Why?"

"I think you know the answer to that. The impediments of two different cultures—"

"You just told me how much alike we all are."

"People are. But too often, in a complicated world, it is not enough. My dear, if you glimpse ahead of you even the chance of pain, it is wise to change direction."

Miranda looked at her over the rim of her teacup. "You sound like my parents."

Meiyun's eyebrows lifted. "And that is not good?"

"I don't think so. I mean I'm not sure." Feeling once again mired in unfamiliar territory, she looked at her watch. "Oh, how late it is. I haven't even showered yet. I really must go."

"With the blue dress?"

She hesitated. "Yes."

"And one of these blouses? For tomorrow, you know. Not the one with large flowers, but . . . let me see . . . ah, this one." She took from the rod a wine-red blouse with pearl buttons and sleeves that fastened at the wrists with tiny gold monkeys. "Will you try it on?"

"I don't have time. Could I take it with me, to try on in my room?"

"Of course. How very sensible. And, perhaps a jacket? September nights grow chilly in Beijing, and perhaps also back home?"

"Yes, very chilly."

The jacket was long, intricately cut from heavy black silk, with black embroidery on the collar and pockets and turned-back cuffs. It was Asian but not Asian, Western but not Western. "Cross-cultural," said Meiyun, and their eyes met and they smiled. "Take all three," she added, "and come back tomorrow to tell me what you are keeping."

"You'll be here tomorrow?"

"I am always here."

Miranda turned the jacket in her hands, luxuriating in the warm texture of the silk, almost alive beneath her fingertips. She glimpsed the label inside the collar, and looked at it more closely. "This is your name. You designed this?"

Meiyun bowed her head. "Everything in the shop is my own design."

"All of them," Miranda murmured, making a swift inventory of the garments hanging on the long rod. "Every one different. Double and triple stitching, bias cuts and straight, welting, and all the trims . . ." She looked up. "Is that why you go to New York? To sell your designs?"

"To make agreements, yes, with the stores that carry my dresses."

"Which stores?"

"Bergdorf Goodman and Saks Fifth Avenue, and Ultimo in Chicago."

"But, those are the most expensive. . . . You're very successful, then."

"I am happy to be doing well. I can help my daughter, who is weak in business and cannot weather bad times. And I can be generous with my grandchildren and great-grandchildren, and with my son, who has a taste for travel and not the skills to earn the money to pay for it. But how is it that you know so much about the design of clothes?"

"I design cashmere knitwear; I came to China to work with companies that will manufacture my company's designs." She looked around again. "You have no cashmere?"

"To my regret, no. It is a different kind of designing and I must study it first."

Miranda grew thoughtful, circling the room, fingering the garments. "Sweaters, jackets, cuffs and collars," she murmured.

"That design I did last month, at home. . . . Oh, what an idea!" She turned to Meiyun. "I have some designs that would fit so well with yours. Would you be willing to look at them? There are things my company hasn't wanted to do that I could design for you; I think they wouldn't mind. I've never really thought about it, I've been too busy, but your things are so beautiful and some of the designs I've been experimenting with would go so well with them. Would that interest you?"

"It is a possibility." Meiyun rested her hand on Miranda's arm. It was a light touch, but firm: a mother's restraining hand. "We will think about it, and talk again. It is such a brightness to contemplate new directions. But right now, my dear, you must go. You do not want to be late."

"Even if it's a mistake to be with him, and I should be changing direction?"

"That is not for me to say. I gave my opinion, which my children say I do too often. Beyond that, I must not go." She gazed at Miranda with a small smile. "You are a grown woman, my dear; no one can tell you what to do."

Miranda smiled ruefully. "I'm not sure I've ever really grown up. You seem like my mother, as if I need one, even here. Maybe especially here."

"Ah, it is not a mother that you need; it is a friend. And I will be that for you. And I think you are growing up very quickly. New places often do that."

"It's so strange. I think I like it, but I don't want to lose what I was and where I came from. Like *Alice in Wonderland,* you know: when Alice grew so fast she couldn't see her feet."

"I do not know *Alice in Wonderland.*"

"Oh. I'll send you a copy when I get home." She paused. "Will they let me?"

"They?"

"Your government."

"I am sure there will be no problem. Now, let me hang these clothes for you." She reached for a garment bag. "The dress, the blouse, the jacket."

"Wait. I can't take them; I can't afford them."

"Do you know the prices?"

"Bergdorf's prices."

"In China it is far less. And in any event, I will make you a special price for all three."

"Why?"

"Because we had a good talk and are more alike than you thought when you arrived. Because I like you. And because you like me, and that is pleasing to an old woman."

Miranda put her arms around Meiyun and kissed her cheek.

"You see," said Meiyun, smiling. "A fortunate meeting, for both of us. Come back tomorrow and see me. Save some time for tea and conversation."

"Oh, I can't. I just remembered. Our plane is at seven."

"Then call me when you are back in Beijing. And I will tell you then what you owe me and you can send it. I think we will have much to talk about."

Miranda kissed her again. "Very much to talk about."

Crossing the lobby, her feet skimmed the marble floor; she felt carried forward by possibilities. Suddenly she was no longer an outsider. The elevator was familiar, the corridor on her floor was familiar, and when she shut the door to her room and looked at her things scattered about, and at the carp swimming in the stream below, dimly seen in the fading evening light, it was like coming home. Even China, imagined in its immensity beyond her window, seemed less awesome, a land of ancient myths and modern factories and people like Meiyun.

And Li.

She showered quickly, and, while drying her hair, turned on CNN for the hourly newscast. A strike by miners in England. Scattered shooting in Bosnia. A volcanic eruption in Iceland. Forest fires in California. Demonstrations in Israel. A bombing in Afghanistan. A hot new British musical opening on Broadway.

How remote it all seemed. And how indifferent to it all, how enclosed and preoccupied, did China seem, minding its own bustling business, creating itself anew on layers and layers of history. One could get swallowed up here, Miranda thought, and find the rest of the world amazingly unreal.

And would that be a bad thing, she thought, to live here long enough to really understand it? What if I decided to stay for a while? I could bring Adam and Lisa here and they could learn more about China and Asia in a few months than in five years at home. And I could work with Meiyun, get something started with her that could continue wherever I am in the future. Make new friends. Spend time with Li.

Oh, what a fantasy. How ridiculous.

With the newscaster's voice in the background, she reached for the blue dress and let it slip over her head and settle around her body. The silk was cool and clinging, like a new skin. She fastened the belt below the deep open V of the collar, stepped into her black shoes—*they should be dark blue, but I will not go hunting for new shoes*—and stood before the mirror.

Oh, my dear. That was Meiyun's voice, sighing with pleasure. And she was right, Miranda thought. I look fine. *And happy.* Yes, that, too.

Her purse was on the carved table at the window and she reached for it, then paused. There was no way she could carry a purse that looked like a briefcase with this dress. But she had no evening purse. Well, the black silk jacket had large pockets; she could put a comb and lipstick and her room key in one of them. That was all she needed. Anything more would make the jacket bulge and sag.

Never, never go anywhere without money. It leaves you at the mercy of other people. That was her mother's voice. So. A few paper yuan in the other pocket, and she would have bulgeless, sagless insurance.

She was removing her wallet when she glanced out the window and saw a man standing beside one of the sculpted bushes below, looking at her window. She could have sworn their eyes met, but she knew that was impossible: with the light behind her, he could not even see her face. And how did she know he was looking at her window? He could have been looking at any of the windows to the right and left of hers, or above or below. Or he was just scanning the front of the hotel, idly, the way people do when they are waiting.

And he might be waiting. He might be the man who was watching her, waiting for her to come out.

She was shaken. Maybe we should get out of here, she thought. Leave the back way, go to the airport, return to Beijing.

This sounds like a James Bond movie.

Well, it was beginning to feel like one, and she didn't much like it.

It was ten minutes before the time Li had set for meeting in the bar, but she did not want to be alone, imagining vague possibilities; it would be better to be with people. Carrying her jacket, she locked the door behind her and took the elevator to the lobby.

Meiyun's shop was closed, but the high-ceilinged lobby was alive with people: groups waiting in line at the large, chandeliered dining room; men in business suits standing in clusters that looked identical to the ones Miranda had passed that morning; tourists lined up at the registration desk; men and women cramming the bar and spilling out through the doorway. We'll never find a place to sit, Miranda thought, but made her way there, to wait at the entrance.

"Miranda." Li was standing at the side of the doorway. His eyebrows shot up when he saw her, and a slow smile filled his face. "How wonderful you look. You must tell me. . . . Come, we have a table." He took her hand and led her inside.

It was like entering a dark cavern and hitting a wall of loud voices and swirling smoke. Miranda shrank from it, but Li was moving forward, and she followed him to a small table at the far wall, with a hand-lettered *Reserved* sign propped in the center. "They do it for special people," he said, "which means anyone who offers a significant tip. I'm afraid I can't offer you wine; they have none worth drinking. Would you like beer?"

"Yes, thank you." She coughed. "I'm sorry; the smoke . . ."

"I know. It's bad but one can't escape it. Museums, of course, but we can't spend our lives there. The government is just beginning to urge people not to smoke, but, as you know, governments move slowly."

"But they could just order it."

He chuckled and Miranda flushed deeply. "Why is that amusing?" she asked. "It's a dictatorship; they can order whatever they want. Even how many children people can have. One to a family. That is their policy; everyone knows it."

"Yes, but it is broken all the time." His voice was stiff. "Why do you always try to simplify China, to paint it in black and white? You'd be angry, rightfully so, if I did that about America. We do have a policy of fining people who have more than one child, because we were growing too fast to feed everyone, much less give them better lives. But people are making more money now, so if they want another child they simply pay the fine."

"But the *idea* of a government *ordering . . .*" She gestured in frustration. "It's just so wrong. And they control prices, too. So if they really thought people shouldn't smoke, they could just make the price of cigarettes so high no one could afford them."

"The market controls the price, just as in America, unless the government subsidizes tobacco farmers . . . which, I understand, your government does. One moment; I'll get our beer." He vanished into the dark-suited phalanx that surrounded their table: men—mostly men—drinking, gesturing, talking rapidly in high-pitched voices that never seemed to pause for a period or a new paragraph. "I know it seems overwhelming," Li said, materializing beside the table with glasses and two bottles of dark beer. "Another new experience."

His voice was as casual as if they had

had no disagreement, and Miranda, too, let it go. "American bars are as loud as this. And I'll bet they're talking about the same things Americans talk about: families, jobs, sports. Oh, and new cars."

"Money," Li said. "These days Chinese people talk only about money." He filled their glasses with beer. "The dress is wonderful; perfect for you."

"Thank you. I bought it here. At the shop in the lobby."

"Meiyun's shop. Yes, it looks like hers."

"Oh. Of course, you'd know that, wouldn't you? Have you talked to her?"

"I stopped in for a while after you left. We're old friends, you know."

"She told me."

"And I was glad to hear that you had found her. She does excellent work and she needs customers."

"But I thought . . . isn't she successful?"

"Very successful. More than most. But she has two no-good children who always have their hands outstretched."

"She talked about them. She said her daughter is weak in business and can't weather bad times, and her son . . . something about travel . . . she said her son likes to travel but doesn't have the skills to earn the money for it."

"She told you all that?"

"We talked about a lot of things."

"And did Meiyun select the dress?"

"She suggested it. This jacket was her idea, too, and a blouse. I seem to have made a substantial contribution to her taking care of her daughter's problems and her son's goofing off."

" 'Goofing off'? "

"Playing when he should be working. They shouldn't take advantage of her. She works hard."

"Mothers often let that happen. Soft-headed."

"I think you mean soft-hearted. Fathers probably do, too."

"Yes, too often."

Miranda watched him refill their glasses. "I saw a man from my room. Watching my window."

He looked up sharply. "How do you know?"

"Well, I don't, not absolutely. He seemed to be looking at my window, and he seemed . . . sinister."

"Because we have talked of this."

"Oh, I know that; I know I wouldn't have thought twice about someone just standing outside the hotel, if we hadn't talked about it. But someone *is* following me, following us. And it could have been that man. Or another one. We know it's happening."

"But we did not think about it all day."

"I did. Now and then."

"And tomorrow you will think of it less often. I promise you, that is the way it happens."

There was a pause. "It may happen that way tomorrow," Miranda said at last, "but that isn't how I feel tonight. And I really don't want to go out there."

"No one will hurt us. No one will even come close to us."

"It's just so unpleasant. And I'm not used to it."

"I understand that. And you are serious that you would rather eat here than go out?"

"Yes. Unless it's important to you; then I'd go with you."

"No restaurant is important enough to make you uncomfortable. We will eat here, in the hotel restaurant. The food is good. In about half an hour?"

"Yes. Thank you, Li."

"Well, then, we will have another beer, and I would like to know how you felt about Meiyun."

"I liked her very much. She said you and she are good friends, and that you were close to her husband before he died."

"Before he committed suicide. They were the people I loved best in the world. Does Meiyun remind you of your mother? In many ways she is like mine."

"I don't think she's at all like my mother. How is she like yours?"

"She keeps her husband's memory fresh, she loves deeply without talking about it, she sets high standards for herself before expecting them from others, she is fiercely critical and just as fiercely protective."

"Your mother criticized you?"

"Frequently."

"And protected you."

"Always."

"From what?"

"From those who believed, when I was growing up, that I could not be a good Chinese because I had an American father."

"You mean at school. They made fun of

you for having an American father. But you said you had friends."

"A few, but we do not need many in life, you know. Two or three is a miracle. So is love, even once." He tilted his glass, contemplating the thin layer of foam. "You have not had many friends, either."

Miranda's eyebrows rose. "I never told you that."

"When we talked about this before, I believe you said you had as many as you need. I take that to mean very few."

"Why?"

"Because you have not been adventurous."

Miranda stared at him. Then she looked away, at her glass, at the polished surface of the table with overlapping rings from the cold bottles of beer, and then the rest of the room. For the first time she became aware that the customers were leaving for dinner. She saw how they skirted the table where she and Li sat; she saw the glancing looks that slid over their faces, like a stream washing over boulders, and she felt their isolation, as if their table were a little island in the midst of a river rushing to the sea.

This is how he felt as a child, when they made fun of him for having an American father. This is how I felt as a child when my parents first made me afraid.

"When I was very young," she said, turning back to him, "I had asthma. It never was life-threatening, but my parents were terrified that I was going to die. They thought life was a quicksand of dangers, anyway, and my illness confirmed that. They truly believed my only safety was in staying close to home and close to the ground. My classmates climbed trees and crossed logs over streams; they bicycled in the mountains and scaled cliffs and explored caves and learned to ski . . . but if I tried anything like that my parents locked me in the house.

"I stayed home, and read and wrote stories and designed clothes, and I was the top student in my school, but none of that was enough to give me the kind of self-confidence that kids have when their body is as responsive as their mind. When I was thirteen, my asthma disappeared—no one knew why, and it's never come back—but by then I was as timid and terrified as my family, and when I married, I married a timid, terrified man."

"And Adam and Lisa?" Li asked. "Are they terrified, too?"

"No. But I had to fight with Jeff, and myself, to let them try everything."

"How could you do that, if you were so frightened?"

"I don't know. I just knew I had to. When Lisa and Adam were little, I'd see their faces when Jeff forbade them to do things, and as they grew up I'd hear their friends make fun of them for holding back, so I forced myself to tell them to go ahead and climb or run or whatever it was, and I'd look the other way because I was sick with fear. One day Jeff and I had a fight about it and I said that it would be better for them to have a broken arm than to have a broken spirit. I think . . ." There was a long silence. "I think, if Jeff hadn't died, I might have found the courage to leave him. Or maybe not. You're right. I've never been courageous."

"I said adventurous," Li said quietly. "I think you've been wonderfully courageous all your life." They were alone now; they could hear the clinking of glasses as the bartender cleaned up. "Frightened and alone, with your parents' warnings roaring in your ears, yet you never quit; you made a full life, with work and love—"

"Most people do that, one way or another. That isn't courageous."

"It can be, depending on what you struggle against. And now you're in China, being adventurous and courageous both. Looking so different from when I first saw you, sitting straighter, your head higher, wearing this most wonderful dress. How did you do that? Did Meiyun convince you, or were you determined?"

"I did it for you," she said.

Stunned, he gazed at her. Their eyes held, and suddenly Miranda felt light and buoyant, as if the weight of her childhood, and all that she had carried forward from it, had lifted with each moment she had talked about it, until it was gone. Li was so close to her that his skin and features and hair were the only things she saw, and he was China and adventure and all the world that had been beyond her vision for so long, a world she knew now that she hungered for, and always had.

And she knew that not often in a lifetime was a new world held out for the taking: a universe of sights and sounds and feelings, waiting to be seized. This was her chance. And she would not let it escape.

She took a deep breath. "I'd rather not eat in the hotel restaurant; it's so huge and glaring and noisy. I think . . . I think we should have dinner sent up to my room. Unless you truly want to . . ."

"No." His face was somber, but his eyes smiled at her. "I think that is a most excellent idea."

Chapter 7

Li went to the window as Miranda closed the door behind them. Without glancing at the gardens below, he unfastened the cord looping the drapery to one side and with a soft whoosh the heavy silk fell straight, covering the window. Instantly the room felt cave-like, muffled, the light softer and more golden. He saw Miranda gazing fixedly at the draperies. "Yes, someone is there," he said. "There is nothing we can do about it. This room is ours and what we do here is between us, and what is beyond the window does not matter."

"For now."

"Now is all that is important."

"It's like a ghost, hovering. Invisible but always there." She laughed slightly, embarrassed by dramatics.

But Li nodded. "That is exactly how it feels." He had felt it before: it was familiar. But this time it had a different cast. This time, it brought him and Miranda closer. *Alone together, with enemies outside.* Now I am the one being dramatic, he thought. "But we will not let it poison this night. This is our night; we will make it ours."

He waited a long moment, so aware of their closeness in this small muffled space that he did not know how she could withstand it. And then, at last, she turned her gaze from the window and looked at him. "Yes," she said.

He stood between her and the closed draperies, waiting another moment, letting the world slide away. "I have wanted to touch you, but the time was never right. You knew that."

"No one in China . . ." she began, trying for lightness, but her voice caught.

"Not in public." He held her face between his hands. Her skin was pale ivory, faintly flushed, and in the shadows her eyes were green and still. But, as they met his, he could almost see her thoughts come and go as her eyes grew wide and bright with alarm, then quickly changed again, darkening, and her shoulders straightened: determined, fixed in their resolve.

He stepped back. "Dear Miranda, this is not a test. I'll do whatever you want, whenever you want it. In fact"—he perched casually on the arm of a chair—"if you would like to order dinner, the restaurant has a few specialties you might like."

Miranda burst out laughing. She pulled him to his feet, and put her arms around him. "I don't want dinner, and neither do you. We've both been waiting for this."

He felt the same quick surprise, pleasurable and unsettling, that he had felt when she said she had bought her new dress for him. Chinese women were usually warier, less innocent; he was accustomed to things unsaid. But tonight he and Miranda were both moving in new directions, and he held her, and when they kissed it was not clear who had moved first. Their lips clung, their mouths opened. And then, just as he had seen her eyes widen with alarm, Li felt a sharp withdrawal in her body arching backward, an instinctive apprehension in the defensive curve of her tongue away from his, but again it was so brief he barely registered it before once again she pressed against him, almost burrowing into him, and his arms tightened around her, his head bending to hers, their mouths locked together, tongues exploring, until finally they broke apart, gasping and laughing a little, as if they needed to find a way to counter their fierceness.

Miranda's face was deeply flushed. "It's been so long . . . I haven't . . ."

He touched her lips and noted, almost abstractedly, that his fingers were trembling. "When something is good, we should not try to explain it; we should rejoice."

"Oh." She smiled. "I feel like rejoicing."

"And you will. We will." Hand in hand, they walked to the wide bed with its flower-embroidered blue spread. Li was so aware of her body moving in step with his that everything else receded into darkness, as if they were framed in a narrow spotlight with room for nothing else. The hotel room, China, the world past and present, were compressed into the woman beside him and the small, bright space they shared.

He unfastened Miranda's silver belt and bent to put his mouth at the deep V of the demure-seeming-but-quite-wicked collar that had been distracting him all evening. Her skin was warm, flushed, trembling, and he slid his hands around her to open her dress and let it fall to the floor.

Swiftly they undressed each other and then embraced, skin melting into skin, and Li felt a shock that made him feel like the boy of eighteen he had been when he discovered for the first time the pulsing life of a woman's body against his. Desire almost transformed him: he wanted all of Miranda, all at once, and he moved his hands roughly over her, molding, probing, learning the sharpness of her shoulder blades, the distinct ribs, the yielding hollows at her waist, the small, round buttocks. She was so slim beside his leanness that an image came to him of two blades of grass in a field threatened by storms and assailants—

And why do I think of that when I am so filled with joy?

—but the image vanished as Miranda's lips moved beneath his and she murmured, "If I don't lie down I'll collapse," and they laughed and lay together on the bed.

Lying beside her, Li looked at her body against the dark blue spread, her skin pale and smooth, with shadows of a summer tan on her arms and legs. She lay in an embroidered garden: pink, yellow, white flowers in profusion across the bed, their petals half-opened or wide and pouting, glistening with tiny drops of dew, their long, narrow leaves tangling in green embrace. Among them, Miranda was slim-hipped, with long thighs and small breasts; her close-cut hair a blond halo framing the delicate bones of her face. In all ways, she seemed smaller and more vulnerable than when she walked beside him on city streets or dined at restaurants, and Li felt obscurely ashamed, as if, somehow, he were taking advantage of her. He tensed, as if poised to move away. It was almost imperceptible but Miranda must have felt it, and even understood, because she reached up and brought him down to her.

Her breasts were flattened beneath his chest, his legs stretched along hers. Her arms held him with a strength he had not guessed at; her body moved powerfully beneath his. She did not seem small now; had he been able to put anything into words at that moment, he would have said that he and she were the same, driven by the same urgencies, and if one were vulnerable, so, equally, was the other.

But he could not hold onto thought. Everything scattered, borne away by the gale of his desire. He moved against her, pulling her to him, breathing her in. She smelled of coolness: plants and open meadows, hillsides lush with falling water and green-carpeted woods, an American coolness of savvy and ownership, and then, as she spread her legs and he settled between them, everything became heat: noon and shimmering air and molten sun. Their bodies nestled, parted, came together again; they breathed in quick bursts and long sighs. Then he was inside her, and a triumphant joy flared within him, so great he thought he would explode, that nothing could contain such exultation, and Miranda's eyes met his, wide with wonder, and their mouths met. Their bodies found a rhythm furious and exhilarating, and the fragmentary thought, *As if we've always known...*, broke to the surface of Li's consciousness before being swept into the vortex of desire and need and gratitude, and he moved inside her, pulled deeper and deeper, until he felt he had become Miranda, and she him, and there was no way, in their flaring passion, that mind or feeling could tell them apart.

When they lay still, clasping each other, his cheek against damp tendrils of her hair, her skin cooling beneath his chest, Miranda let out a long, slow breath. "As if we've always known each other."

He raised his head. "You thought that?"

"I felt it." She gazed at him. "So did you."

He nodded.

"Nice," she said. Her voice was languorous, as slow as his, her eyelids heavy. But then, watching him, she began to smile. "You don't like it that someone knows what you're thinking."

"You're not 'someone.' "

"And so . . . ?"

"It's surprisingly pleasant. I think I could get used to it. I could even come to rely on it."

She laughed. "Different indeed," she murmured mischievously, mimicking his words in the bar.

He laid his hand along her face. "How lovely you are. Beautiful and open and free."

"No, not—"

"Yes, you are. Do you know, when we first lay together, it seemed to me you smelled of meadows and mountains and coolness, of everything fresh, like the earth, open to spring, and to all that is new."

"I like that. I'd like to be like that."

"And so you are, with me."

"But we can't be sure of anything, can we? Everything is different, because . . ." Her gaze slid to the draperies. "Whatever is out there is waiting for us, and we don't really forget it, ever, and maybe that's why we're so close. Danger out there and the two of us, besieged in here."

He kissed her, denying what he himself had thought earlier. "I do not need danger to feel joyful with you."

"But it's there. It's part of everything we do."

"It is part of the other world we inhabit, and we will face it when we return there. But we all live in more than one world, and you and I are creating a world of our own.

No one else is part of it. No one can alter it."

She shook her head. "You know better than I how others can smash what people try to create."

"Yes, but they cannot alter how we feel, or what we give to each other and gain from each other. That comes from within us. What is outside is background, no more."

"You really believe that," she said wonderingly.

"And so will you. Because two people who have found each other are more powerful than governments and armies and all the dangers that fortune can hurl at them."

To end a conversation he was not sure he really believed, he kissed Miranda again, a lingering kiss, and in a moment her arms embraced him and brought him to her. They made love slowly this time, holding back, discovering their bodies' smallest curves and hollows and angles, the taste and feel of each other, what pleased the most. Li moved his lips and tongue over Miranda's body, holding her, turning her, tasting her, lying back so that she could move over him, taking him in her mouth and pulling him deeply into her throat, licking, drinking, offering herself, joining with him, and he with her, first one way and then another until they became one long sinuous form, finding a cadence, in that muffled room without clocks or seasons, as primitive as the earth, as old as time.

When they lay still again, Li's thoughts slowly stirred. *Miranda. A name of promise and magic.* And then, *Journeys end in lovers meeting.*

Startled, he raised his head.

"What is it?" Miranda asked.

"I thought of something. A line from a poem, I think. It surprised me. And I thought of your name. Something about magic." He held her hand, running his fingers over hers; their voices drifted lazily in the hushed room. "Does Miranda mean magic? Where did it come from?"

"Shakespeare. *The Tempest.*"

"I had forgotten that. Miranda is the heroine of *The Tempest?*"

"Yes."

"And why did your parents choose it?"

"My mother did. In the play, Miranda lives on an enchanted island, and my mother hoped that someday I'd find my

own enchanted place and live there forever. You were right about the magic;
Miranda's father, Prospero, is a magician,
and magic is behind most of the story. My
father scoffs at magic; he only believes in
things he can weigh and measure, so he
wanted to give me a down-to-earth name
like Susan or Joan. But my mother was
feeling romantic and hopeful when I was
born, so she insisted."

Li laced her fingers through his. "Is she
no longer romantic and hopeful?"

"Oh, I think romance disappeared a long
time ago. She's still hopeful, but mainly
that no disaster will befall any of us. Jeff's
death was awful for her. It was more than
being fond of him; she was comfortable
knowing that I had someone to take care of
me. Now she keeps imagining all the terrible things that can happen to a woman
alone, and she asks who will watch over
me when she and my father die. I say I'll
watch over myself, but that doesn't make
her feel better."

"She has so little confidence in you?"

"Apparently."

"But surely that reflects on the way she
raised you?"

Miranda laughed. "Yes, but I can't imagine myself telling her that."

"Why not?"

"Because it would only hurt her."

"But it is the truth."

"What good would it do? I'm all grown up, Li, there's nothing she can do with me anymore. Why tell her now about mistakes she's made over the last forty years?"

"It might make her stop telling you how worried she is."

"You think she can change her ways after a lifetime? It would be like expecting her to shed an arm. Anyway . . ." She frowned, the small frown that Li loved and always wanted to kiss away, but not until he found out what it was that had caught her imagination. "Maybe I don't want her to stop. Maybe it's nice, knowing someone cares enough to be worried."

He was silent. "You're right," he said at last. "I sometimes make a god of the truth. And gods are not always our best guides."

She gave a small smile. "Wasn't your mother very much like mine?"

"You mean, did romance disappear for her? Oh, yes, when she finally admitted that my father was truly gone. And was she hopeful? About him in a dreamlike way, but about other things more concretely. She held onto more hopes than most Chinese during the Cultural Revolution. She was stubborn, my mother, but she was also a dreamer and the Communist Party really . . . oh, what is it the Americans say about this? Convincing her of something even when there is no reason, and that damages her—"

"They did a number on her."

"Yes, yes, isn't that wonderful? What a crazy way to say it! It makes no sense but it makes you sit up and take notice. I love English when it has these crazinesses."

"But what about your mother?"

"Oh, she truly believed we would come out of that destructive time and find a communist paradise. She was easy to convince, because in spite of everything she still believed that destruction can be reversed, that unhappiness is not permanent, that we always recover and live lives that are better than before."

"I like your mother. I'm sorry I never met her."

"You would have been friends, both believing in love even in its absence. She would have asked you a million questions about America, to picture some places my father might be living." He kissed Miranda's fingertips. "Did Shakespeare's Miranda find love on her enchanted island?"

"Yes, with Ferdinand, the son of a king who had been her father's enemy. It takes a while, but eventually everyone reconciles and her father and the king bless their marriage."

"And they live happily ever after?"

"Shakespeare doesn't say. I'd like to believe it."

"It is a fine thing to believe." He kissed her and ran his palm slowly from her shoulder to her hip and down her thigh. He loved the feel of her, silken and fragile . . . no, not fragile; he knew by now how much strength there was in her slender form. Miranda Graham, about five feet four inches, and perhaps one hundred and ten pounds, with strong bones and well-defined muscles that moved with supple grace beneath a clear, unblemished skin. It was a body that had had time and attention, an exercised body, well fed, well kept, well rested. An American body.

And she was, to him, America, with all

its beckoning light and promise and wealth.

No. Never.

Roughly, he brought her to him, pushing away his thoughts as their bodies flowed together until they were perfectly meshed halves with no gap to define them separately, and no sound but their breathing and the whisper of flesh on flesh. They clung, lips and arms and legs, sinking into one small point of pure feeling, and from those depths, Li's thoughts broke free.

Not a country, not a system, not a prize. A wonderful, wondrous woman.

Whom I love.

But when they lay back, hands clasped, Miranda's head on his shoulder, he did not say that aloud. It was not time. It was not appropriate. And if anyone might find it peculiar to speak of appropriateness almost in the same breath as love, he could not help it: he knew what was right for him. And so they lay together, wrapped in the stillness of the room.

"I like the feel of you inside me," Miranda said, her eyes closed, and Li had to clutch at the vows he had just made, almost choking on the words he would not let himself say. "And I like to talk to you, and walk through cities with you and eat dumplings and sit in crowded bars, even smoky ones . . ."

He stirred, his resolve weakened by her openness. And then Miranda sat up, leaning back against the carved headboard, the silk spread pulled around her like a strapless gown. "What was the line from a poem you thought of earlier?"

"It wasn't a poem," he lied casually, sitting beside her. "I was mistaken. It was from a Chinese play about a man who makes love to a young girl and says he feels like the old world taking advantage of the new, the corrupt taking advantage of the innocent. I felt like that with you."

Smiling, she shook her head. "You made that up."

"That play is in Beijing right now; I can take you to—"

"Oh, I believe you about the play; it sounds very Chinese, pushing that tired old idea of gullible and unsophisticated Americans just because our country is so much younger than yours. I just don't believe for one minute that that's what came to you while we were making love."

Li chuckled ruefully. "It seems I'm not very good at lying. Well, I can't remember where I read it, but what I thought was, *Journeys end in lovers meeting*."

"Oh. Shakespeare again. It's from *Twelfth Night*."

"Have you seen it?"

"Many times; it's one of my favorites."

"How does it go, the rest of the line?"

"It's a song; I don't know the melody, but I think I remember the words." She closed her eyes and thought for a moment.

"O, mistress mine, where are you roaming?
O, stay and hear; your true love's coming.
That can sing both high and low:
Trip no further, pretty sweeting;
Journeys end in lovers meeting,
Every wise man's son doth know."

Li was thoughtful. "'Every wise man,'" he repeated. "Unless they are Chinese. We have poems like that, but most of them end unhappily."

"There are no happy journeys in Chinese poetry?"

"Some, but mostly they end in melancholy, gazing at a solitary reflection in a lake or greeting a peony. There may be some about true lovers coming and singing both high and low, but I have not found them. I wish I could see *Twelfth Night.* I have all of Shakespeare's plays and sonnets; they were in my father's collection. But I have never seen any of them. Are they performed often, in America?"

"Yes. And in Europe."

So they skated smoothly away from talk of lovers. The languor was gone from their voices; they talked of theater and American musicals, and Li described Chinese opera, even mimicking the traditional high-pitched singing that sounded to foreigners like the wailing of deranged hyenas, until Miranda's laughter stopped him.

"Of course I'm not a professional," he said modestly, "but that gives you the idea."

"I've seen Chinese opera on television," Miranda said. "It sounds very different when it's sung by a naked man in bed with me."

"And looks even more different, since the costumes are magnificent."

They laughed, and Li reflected on the wonder of laughter. The best of all the joy and magic of what we are discovering, is laughter. Talk and laughter. He kissed Miranda's palm, her wrist, her arm, her lips. *There are no differences that talk and laughter cannot bridge.*

Later, Miranda said, "Somehow we missed dinner. Do you think it's too late for room service?"

"No, it's open all night. What a good idea. Do they have robes here?" He went to the closet. "Two robes. Excellent. And a menu?" He went to the table in the window. "Of course. Everything we need. What shall we order?"

Sitting on the edge of the bed, they launched into one of their serious discussions of food. In the middle of it, as they pondered chicken curry and duck with fried noodles, Miranda suddenly said, "But when they deliver it, you can't let them see you."

His eyebrows rose. "You're ashamed to have me here?"

"No; you know that's not what I meant. We're already being watched; it would make it worse if they knew you were in my room . . . in a bathrobe . . ."

"What do you think they are assuming already?"

"But they don't know for sure."

"We have been seen in restaurants. And flying here together."

"It's not the same. That could be business."

"So you are saying my government is concerned with what I do in private?"

"Of course. Aren't they?"

"Sometimes. If you and I were organizing a demonstration or starting our own newspaper, or planning a new political party, they would be. Or they would be if I had state secrets that I might blurt out in a moment of passion. But since we are not organizing anything, and I have no state secrets, they would not pay any attention to something as uninteresting as sex."

"Uninteresting."

"In this context. To government bureaucrats."

"But they're interested in *us*."

"Only because someone thinks you will meet with dissidents, and that you will do it more carelessly because I am with you, as guide and translator, perhaps as lover. When it does not happen, they will lose interest and turn their attention to more promising targets."

"But they might think we fooled them."

"They would never think that. They would rather believe that we are in fact doing business. Your company could be looking for office space for a branch in China. Perhaps Talia wants to build her own building here, or invest in a Chinese construction company. Perhaps she wishes to start a joint venture company with one of our garment companies wishing to expand. Any of these are possible, and since our State Security Bureau cannot afford to believe it makes mistakes, someone will find a reason for everything, and that will be the end of it."

His thoughts moved beyond Miranda to Beijing, to tomorrow, when he would plunge back into a cauldron where thousands of small, vicious whirlpools of greed and competitiveness, of backbiting and suspicion and gossip, could threaten the stability and success it had taken him years to build. He had not thought he was taking a chance when he first approached Miranda; who would have thought that a timid American woman on a business trip could be a political liability? But in the bizarre nexus of people and places in a shrinking world, one could not rely on what seemed to be obvious. Miranda had met Sima Ting in Boulder Colorado—would anyone have imagined a Chinese dissident in *Boulder Colorado?*—and so, on the other side of the world, Yuan Li was once again under surveillance.

Preposterous. But this was a preposterous world. And in the midst of it, he had found Miranda Graham, and never would he regret that.

"Are you thinking about going back to Beijing?" Miranda asked.

No longer surprised by how clearly she understood him, he nodded. "There are things I have to deal with there."

"Are you afraid the Security Bureau will call you in again?"

"No. I think they will wait, to see what we do."

"Then you're thinking of Sheng?"

"That's a big part of it. I have to learn how to talk to him. After all these years, I still am looking for a way to connect with him. It hangs over me . . . you know, something above me, about to crush me . . . what is the word?"

"Looms."

"Yes, that's it. Loooooms. So descriptive, as if the word itself is falling over. It looms over me, like a weak structure that needs to be shored up. He and his generation, all of them, as foreign as if they lived in a different part of the galaxy. Oh, I would like to leave it all behind, shed everything and begin again somewhere where everything is completely new. But that would be running away," he said quickly. "And I have never done that." He picked up the menu. "We were talking about food. I know . . . we will have mooncakes. Shall we?"

"I don't know anything about them."

"They celebrate the Mid-Autumn festival, something like your Thanksgiving, which is a time of fruitfulness and hope for the future, and they symbolize the full moon, which is the symbol of unity and immortality. So we will celebrate harmony and hope and long life with mooncakes, filled with . . ." He scanned the menu, murmuring, "Orange peel, date paste, melon seeds, cassia bloom. . . . Date paste," he said firmly, "since you enjoyed the date filling in the steamed buns our first day in Beijing, and also cassia bloom, because you should have something new to try." He looked up and saw her watching him with a smile of such openness and tenderness that he was undone. His hand shook slightly and he dropped the menu. "I love you," he said, and it did not matter that he had sworn he would not say it, on this night, or perhaps on any night.

He took her hands in his. "I love you." And there was a freedom in saying it that filled him with exultation. He felt young and free and powerful, open to discovery, to certainty, to hope.

"Yes," Miranda said. She brought his face to hers. "A celebration. Long life, and hope, and harmony, and love."

Chapter 8

Wu Yi flung the dress to the floor. "It is not what I want. It is not right for me. Not *one* of these is right for me. Take them away!"

The saleswoman bit her lip as she knelt and gathered together the dresses tumbled on the carpet. The apartment was densely furnished in brocades and velvets and mahogany furniture piled with cushions embroidered with flowers and birds in bright coral, Wu Yi's favorite color. The saleswoman, eyes lowered, crouched to reach under a chair for a shoe that had been kicked there.

"You needn't put on that wretched look," Wu Yi stormed. "You knew I wouldn't like them, but you brought them anyway."

"They were the closest I had to what you said you wanted."

"Something different, I said! Dramatic! Special!"

The saleswoman slipped the dresses into their garment bags. "I don't know any-one else in Beijing. There is a shop in Shanghai, and one in Xi'an, but of course you want something closer."

"Which is the best?"

"Oh, Xi'an, by far, it is an extraordinary collection, but Xi'an is—"

"Call them! I want to talk to someone there!"

"It is almost five o'clock; the shop is probably closed."

"Call them!"

Wu Yi waited for the saleswoman to tell her she could make her own call with her own telephone in her own apartment, but after only a brief hesitation the woman went to the telephone and dialed. Being a famous actress is a good thing, Wu Yi exulted silently. People do your bidding.

Except for Sheng. A frown brought two

deep lines to her perfect forehead. Quickly, before any damage was done, she smoothed it out. Still, she was angry. He had not called; it was the longest silence since they had begun seeing each other. He had said something about going to Beihai, but that was no reason not to call her. It would be better if I did not find him attractive, Wu Yi thought, but the truth is, he is a handsome man who learns quickly what I like in bed, and sometimes he is like a sweet little boy, and he has a wife, which means he is not slathering to get married.

And he has good connections and soon will be rich.

She glared at the saleswoman, sitting at the telephone. Hurry up, she thought. I want the line clear for when Sheng calls.

The saleswoman held out the telephone. "The lady's name is Ye Meiyun. I told her you had definite ideas about what you want."

"Yes, yes." She waved toward the door. "I won't need you anymore today." She turned her back. "I am looking for unusual dresses," she said into the telephone. "I do not want to see others wearing my clothes when I walk down the street or go to restaurants, and especially not when I am on television next month to receive the Magnolia award." She waited for the woman to exclaim over the award, but the woman said nothing. "Tell me what you have," Wu Yi said after a moment, a faint thread of annoyance in her voice.

"It would be best if you came here, or, failing that, I could send you photographs." The woman's voice was cool. Impertinent, Wu Yi thought. Saleswomen do not speak that way to me.

"Describe to me what you have. If you will not, I will speak to the owner of your shop."

"I am the owner and the designer. The lady who called said you are Wu Yi, the actress. Is that correct?"

"Of course it is!" She should have recognized my voice, Wu Yi thought.

"Well, since this sounds like a matter of some urgency, I will tell you about a few of my dresses, but it would be best if you came to Xi'an."

"Tell me what you have!" Again, the woman said nothing, and Wu Yi remembered that she was the owner. She softened her voice. "If you would tell me what you have . . ."

The woman described a number of evening dresses, daytime suits, and blouses, and as she spoke, Wu Yi sat straighter, her eyes brightening. Clothes were what she thought of most of the time, so she was as knowledgeable as a designer, and she could picture clearly the fabrics the woman was describing, the cut of the skirts and tops and jackets, the look of the buttons and braid trims. Yes! she thought. Yes, yes, yes!

But her voice was casual as she said, "These sound promising. Bring all of them that you have described to Beijing so that I may try them on and choose. I may want them all."

There was a pause. "Ordinarily I would not do this," the woman said.

But you will, Wu Yi thought, because I am a good client to have.

"But there is someone in Beijing I wish to talk to. So this once I will come to you." She listed the dresses she was bringing.

"And a cape," Wu Yi said. "To wear with an evening dress, perhaps the gold one. It is cool now in the evenings."

"I have no capes, but—" Again there was a pause. "I could have one made. For the gold dress. Black cashmere with gold silk flowers, perhaps magnolias, since that is the award you are getting."

"Yes!" Wu Yi cried before she remembered to be casual. "Have it made and bring it—" She caught herself. "What would it cost?"

"I do not know. I would think two to three thousand yuan."

Wu Yi pictured herself on stage, making an acceptance speech after receiving the Magnolia award for best actress in a television film, seen by everyone in China in a gold gown with a black cashmere cape scattered with gold silk magnolias. She could not resist it. "If it is no more than three thousand, I want it. How soon can it be made?"

"I think . . . it could be rushed through in three days."

"Then bring it with the dresses."

There was no response. Wu Yi heard the echo of her voice, and once again reminded herself that this woman—she had forgotten her name—was the owner of the shop, and the designer, as well. "Please," she said, forcing the unfamiliar word through her lips. "Please bring it when you come. I think I may be buying many things from you and it would be good for us to meet."

"Yes," Meiyun said, still cool and distant. "I will see you in four days. Your address, please?"

Their goodbyes were formal, and when she hung up, Wu Yi felt as if she had been the supplicant, and this woman—Ye Meiyun; that was her name—graciously dispensing favors. She did not like it. But she could ignore that when it was a question of new clothes.

She gazed at the telephone. Where was he? She was supposed to meet friends for dinner but that could easily be canceled if he called. *Ring,* she said to the telephone. *Ring.* Half an hour later, it did.

She pounced on it. "I have thought of nothing but you," said Sheng's smooth deep voice.

Wu Yi smiled, but once again kept her voice casual, almost indifferent. Not for nothing was she an actress. "But you had many things to think about, many activities to fill your days."

"Annoyances that took my thoughts from you," he said.

"Yes? And are the annoyances gone?"

"I left them in Beihai."

"And you do not have to return?"

"No. At least, not for a while. I solved some problems"—Wu Yi heard satisfaction swell in his voice—"got rid of someone who was trying to blackmail us into paying extortionate fees, and signed someone new to watch out for our interests."

"It sounds quite successful. You must tell me all about it."

When he was silent, Wu Yi smiled again, imagining his brief confusion. It was seldom that she gave him such an opening, a virtual invitation. "Yes," he said. "Yes, I would like to. I was going to suggest dinner."

"Tonight?" Her voice rose in incredulity.

"Of course you are busy, I know how busy you are, but I cut short my trip because I could not wait to see—"

"I think I can have dinner with you tonight," Wu Yi said smoothly. "It is possible that I can change my schedule." She paused, letting him absorb this great news. How like a little boy he was! It was one of his charms: the little boy seeking reassurance, inside the shrewd businessman.

Both sides drew her to him. "Shall we say seven o'clock? I would like to try the new restaurant, Lao San Jie."

"Oh." He was disappointed; she could tell. He always liked to go to one of his own clubs, where he could count how many tables were filled, and feel like a boss. But not tonight, Wu Yi thought; he must be punished for going away from me. "Fine," he said. "I will come for you at seven o'clock."

The walls of Lao San Jie were covered with photographs from rural China, and magazines and newsletters from the years of the Cultural Revolution. In a spirit of nostalgia for a time none of them would want repeated, the kitchen served country food, beginning with tea poured by a waitress from three feet away, the hot liquid arching the distance from a long snout to a small teacup filled with dried leaves and fruits.

"I like this place," said Wu Yi. "Different."

Sheng was contemplating the photographs on the walls. He shifted uncomfortably in his chair. "My father was in one of those places." He lifted his chin toward a picture of huts huddled at the base of jagged mountains. "He said it was a hell hole. A death trap."

Wu Yi glanced at the photo. "It was a long time ago."

"I didn't believe him," said Sheng, his eyes still on the bleak village, and the gaunt men squatting in a doorway, staring at the camera. One of the men held a carving knife and a wooden figure. "I told him he didn't care about me, he hadn't even tried to take me with him. He was so quiet—he looked like those men in the picture—and he made wood carvings, too, when he was there; he still has one, of a woman looking at the sky. I was terrified of his silence, and the way he looked, like a skeleton, and so *desolate,* and that made me angrier and I would not talk to him." He looked at his hands. "That was when we stopped being friends."

Wu Yi felt a strange pang, almost like pity. It startled her and made her nervous. Sheng was supposed to be strong. It was what she demanded: that she feel admiration for a man, not pity.

"He's in Xi'an," Sheng added, a statement that made no sense to Wu Yi.

Why does he keep talking about it? she thought. I came from one of those places, poor and filthy and miserable, and my father and mother both starved to death, but it was a long time ago. We turn our backs on the bad times; we look at what we can grab now. That is how we climb out of the past and soar far above the little people who are trapped in memories of their own weaknesses. I will not have anything to do with any of them.

The waitress served a platter of pork with sweet potato noodles, and a large bowl of beef and potato chunks in a sauce pungent with soy. Sheng roused himself and tasted them. "Good. Very good."

"I ordered one other dish," said Wu Yi, just as the waitress brought a large platter with roasted kebabs of lamb rolled in spices. "I had heard of this," she said, tasting a tiny piece of lamb. It was tender and sweet and when the owner came to their table, asking if they were pleased, she smiled her approval. "Very good, excellent."

"I am grateful that you have honored us with your presence," he said, his eyes admiring her.

Wu Yi breathed deeply. How wonderful it was to be beautiful! And famous! People sought your approval and did your bidding and smoothed away obstacles. What a good time this was to be young in China!

They ate and talked of small things. Sheng, relaxed now, told amusing tales of his trip, as if it had been simply a small jaunt to straighten out some minor snags. He made Wu Yi laugh with his descriptions of Beihai's provincial ways; he made her eyes sparkle with his oblique references to important business deals; he took her hand at the end of the meal and told her how much he had missed her, with such sweetness that Wu Yi completely forgot that she had been worried about pitying him.

"I have a gift for you," he said. "But it requires privacy."

Wu Yi smiled broadly. By now she wanted him as much as he wanted her. But, as always, the timing had to be hers. "May we stop at your club for a drink first? I always enjoy that."

What fun it was to force him into a dilemma. He wanted to check on his club; he wanted to be in her bed. But in fact he had no choice. Simply by stating a prefer- ence, Wu Yi had decreed what they would do. Sheng could have both, as long as he was patient.

This time they went to his second club, a long, narrow, smoke-filled room with tables on raised platforms along the walls, giving the patrons a good view of the rock group and the dance floor. Automatically, Sheng looked for empty tables. Finding only two, he ordered drinks and turned his attention to Wu Yi. And as she felt the heat of his body close to hers, she knew that he was more interested in her than in his club, that focusing on her brought his desire to a boil again, and her own, in response, rose to a pitch that pleased her. How wonderful to enjoy sex! How excellent that they lived in a morally flexible time!

"In a moment," she murmured, and touched his hand and smiled at him with promise. And then she looked up and saw Pan Chao and Meng Enli approaching their table. "*Lao tian ye,*" she hissed through her teeth. "Oh God." She had been sure they stayed at the other club. Now she would have to get rid of them, unless Sheng was so hot for her that he did it himself.

"What a good surprise," said Pan Chao. Uninvited, he and Enli sat down. "We were not sure you were back from Beihai."

"Late afternoon," Sheng said. "I was able to finish and leave early."

"Congratulations. Did you—? No, we should not talk business and bore Wu Yi. Tomorrow we will discuss it. Three o'clock?"

"Five. I have work to do, to catch up, since I was gone for two days."

"Five o'clock then."

Meng Enli leaned forward and spoke to Wu Yi. "Sheng is an extraordinary businessman, in All-China Construction as well as in our partnership. We rely on him greatly."

"He brings expertise and wisdom to our dealings," added Pan Chao, also leaning forward.

Wu Yi nodded. She did not have to be told how fine Sheng was; she could make up her own mind.

But Sheng was beaming, she saw, in the bright light of his partners' praise.

"He will be president of All-China Construction soon," Enli said confidentially to Wu Yi. "He is too modest to tell you that, but it is true. No one is better qualified to build the company to a major force in the years to come."

"It is not clear," Sheng protested. "My father is very active in our company and he is still a young man; it is too soon to talk about—"

"No, no, that is your modesty speaking," said Enli. "Your father did well in beginning the company but now it needs new leadership, young, dynamic leadership which you could provide if you were independent of him."

The words came so easily that Wu Yi wondered if they had been spoken before. And in fact everything Pan Chao and Meng Enli were saying had an odd air of having been rehearsed. Not for nothing am I an actress, Wu Yi thought. I can tell a script from a conversation. And as they continued to talk, it became clear to her that they wanted something from Sheng, and it sounded as if they could only get it if he were president of his father's company.

So they are using him, she thought. And they know how to get to him.

She remembered feeling pity for Sheng. Now she felt the first stirrings of scorn. He should not be so weak as to let men use him. He should not be so weak as to inspire pity.

She picked up her beaded purse. "If you will excuse me . . ."

The men stood and she felt them watching her as she crossed the room and walked around the bandstand to the restrooms.

Sitting at the mirrored dressing table, she rested her head on her hand, carefully, so as not to upset her hair, and thought about what to do. She could write a note, say she was ill, and leave through the kitchen. She could tell Sheng to take her home because she was ill, and he would have to leave her at her door. She could simply vanish. But that would shame him before his partners and she would not do that to him.

That was the trouble: she liked him. And she liked being in bed with him.

And she was not positively sure what was going on with these two partners. She could be wrong. I do not think I am, she mused, but there is a small chance.

And all evening she had thought about his making love to her.

Well, then, it was time for that. And everything else could be thought about tomorrow. If he truly was weak, she would not see him again. If he was as strong as she had thought . . . well, that would be excellent.

She put on lipstick and powder, added a touch of mascara and eyeliner, ran her palms delicately over her hair. And then she returned to the table, making her way along the edge of the dance floor where young people were flinging themselves about to the pounding of rock music and the wailing of the singer.

"I must ask you to take me home," she said to Sheng without ceremony. "For me, the hour is late."

Sheng leaped to his feet. "I'm sorry . . . I should have thought . . . yes, we will go right away." His partners were already standing, and there was much handshaking and smiling, and then Pan Chao and Meng Enli left.

"I took you from them," Wu Yi said.

"No, no, this is fine. I wanted to take you home, you knew—" His eyes locked on hers. "You knew that."

"And that is where we will go."

The next day, when Sheng thought about that strange night, what he remembered first of all was that Wu Yi had been more passionate than ever before, and that afterward, when he was dressing to leave, she had seemed to withdraw from him even before he had his shoes on. It bothered him all morning, at his desk, so that he had trouble concentrating. His father had returned from Xi'an and Sheng knew he would have to talk to him as soon as he came out of his meeting, but the more he thought about it, the more reluctant he became. What he really wanted was to go back to Wu Yi's apartment and make sure that everything was all right. What he really wanted was to hear from her that he was the perfect lover and that what he had seen in her as he was getting dressed was exhaustion from the vigor of their lovemaking, and nothing else.

But he could not go back. She would probably be asleep. Even if she were up, she did not like visitors in the daytime; she did not like to be surprised. It would make things worse, if he went to see her.

He looked at his watch. This afternoon

he would call her. First he had to talk to his father, and then—

His telephone rang. "What happened in Beihai?" Meng Enli said.

"Youcai is gone; he was greedy and not to be trusted. The mayor has sent him to Shanghai, on some kind of assignment, and hired a new police chief, someone who is older, not in a hurry; he just wants security, and an easy time."

"His name?"

"Feng Zhiwen. Born in Beihai, married, with grown sons, one in Macao, one in Hong Kong, both in trade. He lives in the apartment he has lived in for thirty-five years."

"His wife?"

"She cooked dinner."

They laughed together, and Sheng relaxed with the gratification of two men understanding each other in a world where, even after decades of communist preaching on equality, women truly did not count.

"And the sugar," he went on. "I got it off the ship. It will be shipped this afternoon when the trucks arrive and Feng Zhiwen writes the permit for them to leave. Then, of course, I will hire a new crew for the raids scheduled this month. Feng said he could find fifteen or twenty good men, but I will not rely on him; I will go back and examine them myself."

"This was a costly venture," said Enli.

"Not as bad as if we had lost the sugar." Sheng gave the figures for bribing the police guarding the ship, and the amount he had committed to pay Feng for the first year.

"Expensive, but better than losing the sugar," Enli pronounced, and Sheng did not point out that he himself had said that a moment earlier. "This was well done, Sheng; a good recovery. I knew you would handle it well."

Sheng nodded. Of course he had handled it well; he may have stumbled this time, but he knew what he was doing; he was shrewd and aggressive. That was why he would prosper.

Unless his father ruined things for him.

He had meant to ask Enli why his father was being followed, and what he had done in Xi'an, and with whom. But he had not been able to do it. It was difficult for him to beg for information about his father, who was under suspicion.

He looked at his watch. Eleven o'clock. The meeting with the supplier should be over; why had his father not come to greet him, and tell him about his trip to Xi'an, and why he was under surveillance? For surely, by now, after Sheng had told him about it, he would have thought long and hard and come up with some reason for the government's interest in him.

He waited another ten minutes, then jumped up and left his office. He has no right to keep me waiting, he stormed silently, and flung open the door to his father's offices. "Where is he?" he demanded of Li's secretary.

"He just returned from his meeting; if you—"

Sheng barged past her and opened the door to the inner office. His father was talking on the telephone. He looked up, startled, then beckoned to Sheng to come in. Sheng stood beside an armchair facing the desk and his father finished his conversation quickly, then, to Sheng's utter shock, walked around the desk and greeted his son with a hug.

"I'm glad to see you. You've been away; your message was unclear, but I hope it was a successful trip. Do you want to tell me about it?"

Sheng, still in shock, stared at his father for seconds that seemed like minutes before he said, "It was something to do with the partnership; I took care of it. I'm sorry I had to leave, but I don't think it caused problems here."

"It did not," Li agreed. He went back to his chair and Sheng realized he should have hugged his father in return, instead of standing like a rag doll, his arms at his side, his body lax with surprise. But his father never hugged him; how was he supposed to know how to react?

"I need to talk to you, father," he said.

"Yes, we have things to discuss." Li went to the lacquered tea cart in the corner and poured two cups of green tea, setting one on the table beside Sheng's chair. "My secretary tells me you seemed displeased that I went to Xi'an."

"We miss you in the office." Li's eyebrows rose, and Sheng added quickly, "Not that we cannot manage, but we value your leadership. And of course there are decisions we cannot make without you."

"For those decisions, I can always be

found. And since you were gone at the same time I was, it is hard to see how you missed me."

"I meant . . ." Sheng struggled for a moment. "It's not just Xi'an. You seem distracted, thinking of other things, not thinking first of us. And you could have told me you were going to Xi'an. Not a word, you never said a word to me, I had to find out from your secretary!"

He sounded like a little boy left out of the grown-up world. He cursed himself. Why did he do that with his father? He did not talk to anyone else that way.

"I left a note on your desk," said Li, "and a message on your answering machine at home."

"Only that you were going out of town overnight. Not where you were going. Not why you were going. Not who would be with you!"

Li's eyebrows rose again. "Who *was* with me?" he asked with interest.

Sheng clenched his fist. He never made slips of the tongue with other people. "A friend in Xi'an called me and said he saw you going into the Xi'an Garden Hotel." He hesitated, but there was no time to debate it, and so he gambled that his suspicions were right. "My friend said you were with an American woman, and it sounded like the woman I met when you were going to the market."

He could tell from his father's face that he knew he was lying, but Li made no accusations. "What I do outside our company is no concern of yours," he said. "As I do not ask about your friends and business acquaintances, you have no reason to ask about mine."

"I do if they affect our company, our security. My security. You can do business with Americans, but to travel with one—" He bit off the words, cursing himself again. Li had not admitted anything. And anyway, that was not what he should be talking about. "Have you thought about why you are being followed? About what I said?"

Li was making little drawings and Sheng leaned forward to see what they were. Circles, triangles, squares scattered across the paper, none of them touching. Unconnected, Sheng thought. Does he feel that way about the two of us, or about himself and everyone else? "I know why I am being watched," Li said, "and it has nothing to do with you, or with All-China Construction. You need not worry about our security."

"But *why* are they watching you?" Sheng burst out.

"I will not discuss that. It does not concern you."

"It does! The American president is coming to see our president. They will be arresting anyone who seems suspicious. If they are already following you—"

"They will not arrest me. In fact, it is better that the American president will soon be here; the security people may pull in the most active dissidents for questioning, but they will not risk arresting prominent citizens; it would not be good public relations."

"You don't know that."

"I am sure of it. They watch me for their own reasons, but they will do nothing, and as I said it does not concern you."

"Anything that threatens the company concerns me!"

"I have just told you that it does not threaten the company."

"I have a right to know!"

"You have a right to be concerned about my welfare, as I am about yours. But you must accept my word when I tell you that I am in no danger. Will you tell me the same about yourself?"

"Danger? Of course I am not in danger! Why would I be?"

"I have no idea. Or, rather, I have many, but since I do not know for certain exactly what you are involved in, or how deeply, I cannot be specific."

"I'm involved in business!" There was a silence. Sheng's foot began to do a litttle dance against the chair leg. "Why are you talking about danger?"

"I have just told you. I think you and your partners, who do not impress me as excellent friends, are involved in illegal activities—"

"Nothing is really—"

"You may say that nothing in China is really illegal these days, but you know that is not true. We do have laws, and just because many are broken with impunity today does not mean that will be the case tomorrow. And when you cannot be sure of tomorrow, you are at risk." He paused. "Many will grow wealthy in this uncertain society, but many will fall and be left with nothing. Because without a structure that is honored by all, with laws and a system of justice that is consistent and stable, no one is safe or secure in his home or family or work."

"Structure," Sheng said sarcastically. "We had plenty of that before the government eased up."

Li shook his head. "I am not talking about a communist government relaxing the reins when it feels like it. I am talking about a democratic government giving its citizens a framework within which to prosper."

Sheng reared back in his chair. This could not be his father talking. No, no, Yuan Li would never speak such subversive nonsense. Unless he had lost his senses.

Crazy, he thought, as he had once before. My father has gone crazy.

Or . . .

The image of the woman came to him again, on the street in front of their building. Colorless, uninteresting. A pale shadow compared to Wu Yi's vivid beauty. But she was American, and his father had looked at her as if she absorbed his vision, and now he was talking about a democratic government.

And he had taken her to Xi'an; of that Sheng was absolutely sure. He had evaded Sheng's question; that gave him away.

"Are you going to America?" Sheng burst out.

Li's eyes met his for a long moment. It seemed to Sheng that his father was not surprised by the question; almost, that he had been expecting it. But all Li said was, "I have no plans to go anywhere. Why do you think I might do that?"

Don't lie to me! Sheng thought angrily. I need you to tell me the truth! It did not matter that he lied to his father all the time; he expected his father to be different. "*Were* you with her in Xi'an?" he asked.

Li sighed. "If you mean Miranda Graham, I went with her to Xi'an. Do you think that means I am going to America?"

"You've changed," Sheng said accusingly. 'You leave the office without warning; you travel with an American woman; you talk about democratic government—what does that have to do with China, and us, and how we live?—and you don't seem to care that you're under surveillance. It's as if you've already left. Left China, left the company. Left me."

He heard those last two words with dismay; what a weakness they showed in him!

"You don't want me to leave China?" Li asked. "I thought you could not wait to be rid of me."

Nothing in the conversation was going as Sheng wanted. Why did he always feel so mixed up with his father? "*Are* you leaving China?" he demanded. "Is that why you are being watched—because the authorities know it? Did you think about what that means to me? To my future? You said you worry about me, but if you really did, you wouldn't put me in a difficult position; you would protect me."

"I would like to protect you," Li said quietly. "But the danger for you comes from the paths you are taking, not from anything I do. I cannot protect you, Sheng; I am not in the military or the government, as your partners' fathers are."

"I don't need—"

"I think you might."

"Then how can you leave China?"

"I am not leaving China."

"But you might. You might change your mind."

Li smiled faintly. "If I do, I will tell you before anyone else. So that you can prepare to move into this office."

Sheng glared at his father. "Who told you that?"

Again, Li sighed. "Sheng, you must learn to think before you speak. Now you have given away that you have talked to others about this. Do you want so badly to be president of our company?"

Sheng was silent.

"Or have your partners decided you should?" Li's voice sharpened. "They must admire you very much. Or"—there was the briefest pause—"need you very much."

Sheng did not like the way that sounded. "They admire me, but we have not talked about All-China Construction; why would we?" No, no, no, he thought, do not open the door to that subject; my father is too smart. Quickly, he said, "You did not tell me why you think you are being followed."

Li gave him a long look. "It is a mistake. Someone thinks Miranda is in touch with dissidents in Beijing. She is not, but once they think that, they cling to it. And so they follow her, and they follow me because I am with her occasionally."

"More than occasionally," Sheng said bitterly.

Li nodded. "More than occasionally. I intend to see her as often as I wish, as often as she wishes, while she is in Beijing. If that distresses you, I regret it, but it does not change anything. By the way, I am told that you are seen, more than occasionally, with Wu Yi. This must be difficult for your wife to understand."

A silence settled between them. Damn him, Sheng thought. Fathers should not go on the offensive with their sons. Their time is past; they should defer to their sons, not attack them with personal matters they do not understand, and never will, because they are not modern.

"She and I have an understanding," he said at last. "We live our own lives."

"And your son? Rongji?"

"He is a fine boy. He will be seven next month, you know. You should spend more time with him."

"When? I have asked to see him many times, but you always say he is busy. Or it is not a good time for you. Or he is visiting friends."

"We can change that," said Sheng weakly. It was true: he had never wanted his father around very much, so, even when Li offered to take Rongji on an excursion for the day, or to take him home for an overnight stay, Sheng always found reasons to say no. "If you are really interested . . ."

"I am always interested in spending time with my grandson. Perhaps, in a week or two, I will take him to Xi'an. It is a good place to take friends and family, to see the terra-cotta warriors."

Sheng found that confusing, so he said simply, "Call whenever you wish. We will arrange for you to be with him. He is smart, you know. He learns quickly."

"I'm glad you are proud of him. And Wu Yi?"

"A friend."

"More than that, surely."

Sheng had wanted to say the same about the American woman, but the words stuck in his throat. He wished he could be flip and scornful with his father, as many of his friends said the new Chinese man should be, but he could not do it. Li might be old-fashioned, foolishly honest and boring, but somehow, inexplicably, Sheng still found himself longing now and then for a camaraderie with his father, shared laughter and shared problems, even, unlikely as it seemed, a chance to learn from him.

"She is more than a friend," Li repeated, pressing.

And Sheng opened up. "I am mad for her. She is spoiled and arrogant and willful and demanding and I know she is not an important person, not as important as business or—"

"Or family," Li prompted.

"—or family, but she has gotten inside me and I cannot dig her out. I do not want to dig her out. She is too exciting."

"Like fireworks."

"Yes, yes, she is all sparks and crackles and fire. We do not talk very much, you know; I can get that at home. It is not what I want from her."

"And will it last, do you think?"

Sheng's stomach clutched at the thought of his dependence. "As long as she wants me."

"And how long will that be?"

"Until she gets bored. Not long. Not long enough. She is not a person of deep feeling, or understanding, or constancy."

"You may tire of that before she tires of you. She may just fizzle, like fireworks." They smiled together and Sheng's heart swelled with sudden and dismaying love for his father.

Li stood up. "We have work to do. I'd like you to sit in on a labor meeting in an hour; the large construction companies are having problems with workers and you may have some good ideas."

"Problems?"

"There is talk of calling a strike for better housing. I sympathize with them—their housing is wretched—but I will not negotiate with them alone. If we have the cooperation of companies in our major cities, we can work out a way to solve this. I think it will be difficult, and I want you at my side on this, Sheng."

"Yes," Sheng said, pleased but distracted. If there were a strike, which men would go? He and his partners relied on warehouse workers in the largest construction companies to stock and inventory pirated goods. If the key people went on strike, they could be stuck with truckloads of merchandise and nowhere to put it. I'll talk to Chao and Enli about it, at our meeting this afternoon, Sheng thought. If we can't find a way to stop these revolutionaries from striking—"

"You look troubled," said Li.

"Yes, a strike could hurt us. I'm worried about the company."

He felt Li's arm around the shoulders—when had his father done that, in recent memory?—as they walked to the door. "I'm glad you're concerned," Li said. "We'll see what we can do at the meeting. Two-thirty in the conference room. And, Sheng, I will call about seeing Rongji. Perhaps, if I take him to Xi'an, you will join us. And your wife. It will be a family time, all of us together. I'll call as soon as I get my schedule in order."

As soon as you figure out which days you can spare from that woman, Sheng thought, the pleasure of these past minutes wiped out. It was amazing how quickly he could become angry with his father. Still, the idea of the family going to Xi'an was surprisingly pleasant. I'll think about it, he decided. I can't handle all these feelings at once. He nodded abruptly, and left Li's office, striding to his own, at the other end of the corridor.

On impulse, he called Wu Yi. "I was missing you. May we have dinner tonight?"

"No, impossible." Caressed by Sheng's deep voice, Wu Yi looked in the mirror. She had a dinner engagement that night with a lawyer whose wife was divorcing him; he had money and prestige, but none of Sheng's little-boy sweetness, and certainly not that deep, smooth voice. But Wu Yi was worried about Sheng: all her doubts of the night before had become magnified the minute they finished making love. She had been satisfied—oh, powerfully satisfied—and thoroughly worn out, but still the doubts had returned. She would not see Sheng again until she had resolved them. "I have engagements for the next few days, and then a dressmaker from Xi'an is bringing me samples of her work—"

"Xi'an?"

"Yes, why?"

"I don't know. Xi'an seems to be everywhere these days."

Yes, she remembered he had brought it up in the restaurant the night before, quite out of nowhere. "This woman owns a shop there and she is anxious for me to become a client so she begged me to let her come to Beijing to try on some of her designs."

"What is her name?" Sheng asked, an odd question, Wu Yi thought, but his mind seemed to be fixed on Xi'an.

"Ye Meiyun," she said, recalling the name more easily this time.

"I know that name. When I was young, my father knew her husband. He killed himself."

"What an interesting coincidence." Wu Yi found the conversation quite boring. "And after she is here, I go to Shanghai for my Magnolia award. You do remember that I am receiving one."

"Yes," Sheng said, but he sounded a little distant to her.

"Sheng? The award for best actress in a television movie! You could not have forgotten!"

"No, no, of course not. Why don't I come with you to Shanghai? It would be a holiday for us."

She hesitated. It would be good to have Sheng's adoring eyes in the audience when she gave her acceptance speech. On the other hand, he could be an impediment. Her career would not be helped by being linked to a failure. "Perhaps," she said. "I will see how I feel."

And he had to be satisfied with that. She hung up, still gazing at her reflection in the mirror. How beautiful she was, even in the morning, even without makeup. She picked up the jeweled comb Sheng had given her the night before, and used it to pull her hair from one side of her face and wedge it in place. Very nice. He had good taste in such things.

I will see him again, she thought. Or, I may not. There is no hurry to decide. He will wait forever, that sweet boy, for me to make up my mind.

Chapter 9

Miranda stayed behind when the meeting adjourned for tea, taking out her sketch pad to design a cashmere cape, black, with gold silk magnolias. There had been a message at the Palace Hotel when she returned from Xi'an, saying that Meiyun needed a cape to go with an evening gown, and describing it in general terms. "As soon as you can design it, please call me," Meiyun had said, and Miranda had barely been able to wait until this pause in the meeting. My first commission in China, she thought, and her pencil strokes were bold and sweeping.

But even working on her own private commission, she was having trouble sitting still. The sun had been shining when she had walked into the Baoxiang International Garments Center, and she had not seen it since. A bird had soared high above as she had paused in the doorway, a young girl on a bicycle had smiled at her, a soft breeze had touched her hair, and she had thought of Li's fingers, thin, elegant fingers lightly lifting her hair and letting it fall as they lay together in the Xi'an Garden Hotel, his lips on her forehead, her cheek, her mouth.

I have to get out of here, she thought. I have to move.

They had flown back from Xi'an at seven o'clock that morning, and whenever her thoughts turned inward, blocking out the meeting around her, she could hear again the roar of the plane's engines, the sound-track of the movie, blaring throughout the cabin since there were no headphones, the stomping of stewardesses dashing up and down the aisles to serve everyone before the short flight ended, and the shouted conversations among passengers trying to make themselves heard. Up front, in seats labeled first class because they were two inches wider than the hundreds stretching behind, she and Li sat within a small bubble of privacy. They looked at each other, then away, then back again, wanting to touch and be touched. Miranda's skin was electric with his closeness: his hand, arm, shoulder, thigh a fraction of an inch from pressing against hers, merging with hers as they had done all night in the deep silence of her hotel room so that nothing, not the thinnest ray of light, could find a way between them. Beneath the noise of the plane, now and then Li bent down to shift his overnight bag or tie his shoelace, and his shoulder touched Miranda's leg, his hand brushed her ankle: the briefest of contacts that left them short of breath, desperate for more. By the time they landed in Beijing, they were exhausted.

Now they were both at work and, while the executives of the Baoxiang International Garments Center drank their tea, Miranda could close her eyes and picture a map of Beijing, with Li at one end, sitting at his desk, talking to his son, and herself at the other end, drawing in her sketchbook. Grids of streets separated them, skyscrapers and *hutongs,* shops and apartments, teeming crowds. I'd rather we were in bed, she reflected, and felt again the hard smoothness of his skin beneath her lips and tongue, his swelling beneath her touch.

I have to get out of here, she thought. I have to move.

"Mrs. Graham," a secretary said, in the doorway. "There is a telephone call for you."

Li, she thought. No one else knows I'm here.

"I had to hear your voice," he said the minute she picked up the telephone in a nearby office.

"Oh." Her legs were weak and she sat down. "Yes. I've been sitting there, trapped by all those people and all I wanted was to be in bed with you."

"Why not, then? Can you leave?"

"No. And neither can you. How did it go, with Sheng?"

"Unsettling. In some ways better than I expected, but sad, too. I'll tell you tonight. How is your meeting?"

"Endless."

"I know. I kept thinking about you, all the

time I was talking to Sheng. I drew little shapes that did not touch each other, all unconnected, but then I said your name to myself and felt close to you. Miranda. And then I wondered where it came from, what it means."

"Latin. It means 'she who is to be wondered at.' "

"Ah, perfect. Wondered at. Admired. An admirable woman. I like your mother for choosing it. I have an idea for tonight; I would like to cook dinner for you. Shall we do that?"

"Yes, if I can help in the— No, wait, I can't. Can I? I mean, it's even worse than going to Xi'an together, isn't it? That could possibly have been a business trip, but no one would think I'm in your house on business. They'd see me going into your home—an American who had contact with dissidents—and that would be dangerous for you. Wouldn't it?"

"So many questions," he said gently. "You must not be afraid, Miranda."

"I'm not afraid for myself."

"Oh, my dear one. Thank you. But, you know, I am not foolhardy. Occasionally foolish, but not foolhardy. It will be all right."

"You keep saying that. Have they stopped following us?"

"No, but it does not matter. By now they must know that you are here only for business, but no one has gotten around to writing the order to stop the surveillance. There is so much inertia in bureaucracies that change takes a long time, even when everyone knows something is wrong. Besides, everyone is preparing to welcome your president; until then, the government will show its best face. You and I will do as we like, Miranda. No one will be hurt. I promise you that."

How much can promises mean in a country where the rules change at the whim of the government?

But I don't want to stop seeing him. So I'll convince myself that he's right. And he may be. It's his country.

"I want you in my house," Li said as she was silent. "In my kitchen, at my table, in my bed. Tell me that you will let me cook for you tonight."

She gave a small sigh. "Yes."

"Good. We will have such a fine time. I will pick you up—"

"But only if I can help in the kitchen."

She could hear the smile in his voice as he said, "Can you wield a cleaver?"

"No. But it can't be much different from chopsticks."

They were laughing when she heard a rustle at the door and knew she was expected back at the meeting. "I must go."

"I will be at your hotel at six."

Miranda followed the secretary back to the meeting, and as soon as she sat down the assistant production manager said, "This sweater." His finger tapped one of Miranda's watercolor drawings. "The two colors, it is more expensive, another step in the process."

"Of course." Miranda took out her original sketch of the sweater. "But less yarn, since it is sleeveless."

"But a turtleneck. I have calculated it at twelve hundred yuan."

Silently, Miranda converted it. One hundred twenty-five dollars. They would sell the sweaters to stores for two hundred fifty. The stores would price them at five hundred. A little higher than she had hoped, but about what their customers would expect to pay for a fine two-ply cashmere sweater, intricately seamed, in heather-like combinations of blue-gray, silver-black, green-blue, or gold-black, with a deep turtleneck ending in a long fringe pulled from the yarns themselves. It was one of her best designs, at once elegant and casual. She knew it would sell.

"The two colors must be perfectly consistent," she said, ignoring the price for the moment because it was never wise to agree to any figure immediately. "In the blue-gray combination, for example, there must be no variations such as two or three shades of blue, or blue and buff, or, worse, blue and white."

"Of course, of course, we will come as close—"

"No. I said exactly the same. We must be confident that the entire run will have this look of heather. Not tweed or anything like it. The two colors must blend perfectly into their own third color."

"Then I fear that the cost will increase, both for control of the yarn and the production time. The only way we can guarantee the price and time schedule I have given is to manufacture the sweaters within reasonable limits."

"That is not acceptable." She looked

around the table at the circle of smooth faces floating above perfectly pressed suits, crisp shirts, sober ties, patiently folded hands. *They're part of a culture that's been around for thousands of years; they can wait out anybody. But not me. Not today.* Her impatience had been growing; now it rose like a breaking wave, and crashed upon the conference table. "I cannot imagine that a company as experienced and skilled as yours would fail at quality control of yarn dyes. You would be out of business in a week if you could not guarantee colors. I came to Baoxiang because of your reputation for excellence, but if I have been mistaken, and we cannot work together, there are companies in Thailand and the Philippines and Malaysia that have expressed an interest in working with us. I would like to work in China because your workers take pride in what they do, and I admire many of your products, but I must be satisfied or I will go elsewhere."

Her heart was pounding. She had no authority to work with any manufacturers other than those on her list, much less travel to other countries. But her voice had been decisive, and the words had come out as easily as if she had held them in reserve all this time. *That is not acceptable.* Exactly what she should have said at her first meeting, only five days ago. But then she had felt helpless, and now, suddenly, she was confident, daring, almost reckless. It was as if, through Li, she had found a place in China: no longer an impotent outsider, but someone who could be a player in their negotiating gamesmanship.

Besides, she had seen the quick look between the production manager and the vice president when she had mentioned those other Asian countries, and she knew she had struck a sensitive chord.

"It would be unfortunate for us all if our transactions were not successful," said the production manager, speaking to Miranda past his assistant who had been doing the talking. "Certainly dye lots can be consistent; selecting them is one of the skills that have taken shape here under our scientific management system. Whatever you need, we can provide in a superior fashion to anyone else."

"And the price?" Miranda asked bluntly.

"We will keep it to twelve hundred yuan."

Her heart was racing again, this time with exhilaration. Done, she thought. Well done.

Excitement surged through her. It seemed she had been buoyed by excitement since arriving in China, but it had truly flowered only the day before, in Xi'an—so much had flowered in Xi'an—and now she was excited about everything. New foods. New ideas. China. A commission from Meiyun. Dinner at Li's house. Love.

Excitement tightened her muscles, heightened her senses. She was alert to her surroundings in new ways, poised with anticipation, ready for today and tomorrow, no longer afraid of being taken by surprise or overwhelmed. She tried to remember when she had felt like this: confident that whatever waited around the corner she could face, and grasp, and incorporate into her life.

Never. I have never felt this way.

Like my children, beginning a new adventure.

It will go more easily now, she thought, then wondered whether she meant this meeting at Baoxiang, or her work, or perhaps her whole life.

Three hours later, when the production manager said, "That is the last one," it was clear that the meeting, if nothing else, had indeed gone more easily, the pace picking up, negotiations moving rapidly through the remaining designs to an amiable conclusion in which they all had made compromises. A pity I can't use that threat all the time, she thought, gathering up her worksheets and sketch pad.

"Do you wish a taxi?" the production manager asked her as the room emptied. Miranda started to say yes, but suddenly she knew that she could not possibly sit any longer; she was churning with restlessness and elation and she had to move, to feel her body stretch and come alive after six hours at a conference table.

"I'll walk," she said.

"To your hotel? The Palace?" He was shocked. "It is much too far."

"Is it?" She had no idea how far it was, but the farther the better: she needed space, movement, air.

"At least six kilometers."

Kilometers. How many miles was that? I should have learned this in school, she thought, but it had never seemed important. She nodded, as if six kilometers were an easy stroll, quickly made the rounds of the executives with proper goodbyes, then tucked her folder of papers and sketch pad into her briefcase and left the building, coming into late-afternoon sunlight with a sigh of relief. *Like being let out of school.* She laughed aloud, suddenly so piercingly happy she could not contain it.

Unfolding her map, she tried to memorize it, then she moved in the general direction of Wangfujing, keeping pace with the crowds, glancing at shopwindows, at the traffic, at faces. After a few blocks it occurred to her that not once had she thought of herself as one American surrounded by hundreds, thousands, of Chinese. She was simply one person walking amid shoppers and homeward-bound workers like herself. *They're just people. They don't look different anymore. How amazing that is.*

At an intersection, she stopped to study her map again and a small crowd gathered. "What is it you look for?" a young girl asked in careful English. "Perhaps we may be of help."

Miranda had wanted to do it herself, but

when she looked at the faces around her, another circle of faces but this time curious and friendly, she could not shut them out. "Wangfujing," she said. "The Palace Hotel." She pointed to her right. "I think I should go this way."

Some of the faces nodded, but then a discussion began, with pointing fingers and animated disagreements. Miranda waited, understanding nothing. Finally the young girl said, "There are two ways. Perhaps you would like us to accompany you."

"No! No, thank you," she added, not wanting to seem rude. She was confused by friendliness and generosity, having decided that China had only their opposites, and she was not sure how friendly she should be. "I like to go slowly, to see everything. To learn about the city."

They beamed. "You are impressed with Beijing."

"Yes. Very much." And when she walked on, after saying thank you and goodbye— "Xi-xi, Zaijian"—which pleased everyone, including herself, she did find the city impressive. More than impressive: beautiful. Beijing lay under a golden light that transformed the polluted air, gilded the garbage along the curbs, brightened apartment windows, turned cracks in the sidewalk to soft shadows. Miranda wondered at that light, but it fit so well with her own excitement and piercing joy that she accepted it, walking as easily as if she were at home. She no longer felt she was choking in the dense air; she barely noticed the peeling doorways or the garish neon signs hanging overhead, crowding against each other in a jumble of color; she was engulfed by the screeching, rumbling, chattering, clanging, honking street noises but none of them distracted her from her thoughts or dimmed her happiness.

She walked down one street and then another, smiling at a young boy on the back of his father's bicycle, bundles of leeks slung across his lap. She watched an elderly man doing his exercises, stretching, squatting, touching his toes, while smoke trailed lazily from the cigarette in his mouth. In the next block, she bought a roasted sweet potato from a vendor, and peeled and ate it as she walked. Beneath the blackened skin, the flesh was deep orange, meltingly soft, pungent, steaming, and she nibbled at the edges, too impatient to wait until it cooled. The sweet roasted smell was all around her as others ate their own, and it mingled with diesel fumes, soot, wafting odors of garbage, and the acrid smoke of Chinese cigarettes. Miranda breathed it in and did not frown.

In fact, she smiled, and others smiled back. And as she walked and walked, now and then checking her map, crossing at intersections where uniformed police on raised circular platforms tried vainly to create order, her stride grew longer. She enjoyed being part of the mass of people, part of their pulsing life and purposeful thrust toward home.

All of us going home, she thought. Wanting companionship and love. And dinner. And she knew that that was something Li had done for her: where once she had seen only the differences between people, now she saw how much alike they were. And because of that her world had expanded, and was still expanding, becoming enormous, varied, exciting, *real*. Thank you, she said silently, to Li, to China, even to herself, for being able to learn. She smiled at that. *Thanking myself. How very odd.* And at that moment she began to recognize buildings and shop windows and a cluster of stunted trees that told her where she was: Wangfujing was one block away, and she was almost home.

Not home. A hotel.

But it felt like coming home: the recognizable terrain of Wangfujing, the turn onto Goldfish Lane, dominated by the familiar white and red facade and broad doors of the Palace Hotel, the greeting from the concierge—"Ah, Mrs. Graham, welcome back"—the efficient formality of the clerk who handed her a fax from Talia, even the amiable grins of the white porcelain horses, almost life-size, that flanked the great white stairway rising to the mezzanine. She had been there only a few days, but as she walked through the lobby to the elevator, she moved with the ease of someone who knew exactly where she belonged.

Her room waited, neatly made up, exactly as she had left it the night before last, to go to Xi'an. Only two nights ago! How could so much have happened in such a short time?

And how much time is left?

A calendar lay on the desk in the window. Three more days.

Three? Only three?

Impossible. I have too much to do. I can't possibly finish in three days. How ridiculous, to plan such a short trip. I'll call Talia and tell her—

Talia. There had been a fax from her. She found it on the small table beside the door, where she had dropped it, with her briefcase and purse, when she came in.

"Miranda, we've arranged for you to meet with Tang Po, the director of Nantong Woolen Mill. They're in Jiangsu Province, but he's coming to Beijing to see you. Nantong makes blankets (cotton, silk, cashmere) and they want to expand into new areas; all details about the company at the bottom of this page. He'll call you at your hotel; spend a couple of days with him to see what you come up with. Sorry to keep you in China longer than you'd planned—"

Two more days. Two more days in China.

"—but this should be worth it; it sounds like a good company. You know we're counting on you, so stick it out a little longer. Love, Talia. P.S. Have you gotten the hang of chopsticks yet?"

Yes, and tonight a cleaver.

She laughed, and whirled about the room. *Two extra days. Thank you, Talia. Thank you, Mr. Tang. Two more days with Li. And working with Meiyun.*

She telephoned Meiyun in Xi'an. "Thank you for the commission; it's very exciting. I have three designs I like."

"I knew you would find it interesting." Meiyun's voice brought back her silk-hung dressing room and her smile when she met Miranda's eyes in the mirror, and Miranda thought, I love her.

"Who wants the cape?" she asked.

"An actress. Not a great one, but a popular one; she is receiving the Magnolia award for best actress in a television film at the Shanghai Television Festival and wishes to look dramatic and different."

"In one of your dresses?"

"It is almost certain. She tries to be indifferent, but she is obsessed with fashion and she cannot hide it. The cape is to go with a long gold dress with thin black straps and a black satin hem, close-fitting, highly dramatic, perfect for her figure. She does wear clothes well, and it will be a pleasure to dress her if I can tolerate her self-centeredness. She comes from a poor background and is clawing her way to the top and she thinks she does not have time for pleasant behavior. It is too bad, but there it is. So. I am coming to Beijing in three days with dresses for her to try, and she will try the cape with the gold dress. Will you be there?"

"Yes, oh, how wonderful. But, do you always do this? Make deliveries?"

"Never. But I wanted to see you, and Yuan Li also. The actress—her name is Wu Yi, by the way—thinks I am coming because I am hungry for her to be a client. And that is fine; it makes her happy to think that and happy clients are the best, of course. Now tell me about your designs."

Miranda described them briefly, then said, "I have one more, my favorite, but it's very different and perhaps too difficult. I've drawn it, but—"

"Tell me." And when Miranda did, Meiyun said, "Yes, that one. It is perfect for the dress."

"But to have it made in three days . . ."

"Two days. I have arranged it, leaving a third day for them to correct any mistakes. You will fax me all your designs even though I know which one I want; still, it is good to see them all with the dress. Whichever I choose, you will see it in four days. In fact, you will see it on Wu Yi. I would like you to come with me to the fitting. Will you do that?"

"Yes, I'd like that. What day will you be here?" They talked about dates and times, and then Miranda, acting with a boldness that she would wonder at later, said, "Will you have dinner with us that night?"

"Us," echoed Meiyun. Miranda flushed, but said nothing, and after a moment, Meiyun said casually, "That would be pleasant."

When they hung up, Miranda called the concierge and gave his messenger her drawings to be faxed to Xi'an. She turned on her bathwater, then sat for a moment, gazing through the window at the crowds walking through shadows and late-afternoon sunlight on the street below, and the yellowish-gray sky above. It might be filled with pollution, she thought, but it was also filled with possibilities. A whole world of possibilities. Beginning tonight, with Li. Being at home, with Li.

Home. I should call home, she thought. She went to the telephone, driven by an odd sense of urgency. And then, as before, she thought of the time difference and knew she could not do it. Well, then, I'll write, she thought. She had written postcards to all of them every day, but now she pulled out a stack she had bought the day before and wrote rapidly, filling the small blank squares with descriptions and anecdotes. Then to Adam and Lisa, she wrote, "Maybe I'll bring you here and we'll stay for a while; you could go to school here, and make friends you'd never meet at home, and learn about another country firsthand, instead of through books or television or movies. We could rent a house with different buildings connected by courtyards . . . that would be so much fun."

She stamped the postcards and tucked them into her purse. She could have given them to the concierge, but she did not. I'll mail them myself, she thought; as soon as I get a chance.

Then, at last, she shed her business suit and stepped into the deep tub, sinking into hot water perfumed with bubbles of lotus flower. Steam rose to the ceiling, an iridescent mist that swirled over gold faucets, the green marble walls and floor, and a porcelain sculpture of a royal lady standing in a niche beside the tub. Miranda lay back beneath mounds of tiny bubbles, gazing at the long-robed lady, breathing in lotus flowers and the elusive scent of yellow roses from a tall spray in a cinnamon-colored vase beside her.

The water caressed her with the same rhythmic waves as Li's caresses as he brought them both to the crest of desire, and her back arched and she closed her eyes, feeling him slide inside her, every touch and movement recalled by the swirls of water rippling across her breasts, her throat, her thighs. She lay there, breathing deeply, her eyes closed. The only sound was the faint bursting of the tiny bubbles around her, and an odd little hum that it took her a moment to recognize as coming from inside her: a hum of desire and excitement, and contentment, as well.

You know we're counting on you, so stick it out a little longer.

"Oh, yes, Talia," she murmured into the steamy silence. "I can do that."

For dinner she wore the blouse Meiyun had chosen for her. She had brought it with her from Xi'an, along with the blue dress and the jacket. "On your store account," Meiyun had said. And when Miranda had objected that she had no such account, Meiyun had replied, "You have, in my head and my heart. I will send a bill to your hotel and you will pay me when you can."

And now she was coming to Beijing, with a cape designed by Miranda Graham to pair with a dress designed by Ye Meiyun. It was almost dizzying, how quickly things were happening. Once, change had been something that happened to other people; now it was part of her life. And not frightening, as she would have thought; in fact, it was wonderful.

The blouse was burgundy-red silk with pearl buttons and full sleeves that fastened at the wrists with tiny gold monkeys. I hope he has an apron, Miranda thought, and turned in front of the mirror as she stepped into the skirt that was part of her black suit. It should be black cashmere, she thought, or black silk: narrow and ankle-length. A little monkey embroidered below the waist, just in front of the left hipbone. Maybe swinging from a branch with leaves and fruit . . . a few seed pearls for the fruit. Black suede shoes. A small velvet purse with a gold chain and a monkey for a clasp. Gold, with seed pearls.

Swiftly, she drew a sketch, and made notes. *I wish I could wear it tonight.*

But Li, not knowing what she was not wearing, admired what she was. In the lobby, he briefly took both her hands in his. "Beautiful. You are so beautiful. And glowing. That wonderful red . . ." His hands tightened, then they both pulled back, and he took from her arm Meiyun's black jacket with black embroidery. "Let me help you."

His hands curved over her shoulders as she slipped into the jacket and for a fraction of a second she leaned back against him. *If I'm glowing, it isn't because of the red blouse.* They walked to his car, parked under the overhang at the entrance. *He'll know that when I take it off.* A shiver ran through her and, though they were not touching, Li felt it. "Are you cold? It seems like such a mild evening."

"It is. I'm not cold."

He drove into narrow Goldfish Lane, merging with the traffic. Briefly, he turned and touched her cheek. Horns blared as the car swerved slightly. "Damn. I want to hold you, but this takes all my attention."

Miranda laughed. "Shall I do it? Hold you while you—"

"No!" He grinned. "Think of the headlines: 'American designer kills Chinese engineer and self by fondling in traffic.'"

They laughed together. "Where are we?" Miranda asked.

"Beichizi Street."

"There's a stream running alongside us."

"A moat. It surrounds the Forbidden City. Eight hundred buildings, nine thousand rooms, courtyards, gardens, terraces . . . a city inside our city. We'll go there soon; you'll be impressed."

"Some people on the street today asked me if I was impressed with Beijing."

"And?"

"I said I was. I am. It's a wonderful city. But I think it seems even more wonderful because I'm so happy."

Li drew a breath. "You always surprise me. You're so completely open."

"Not completely."

He glanced at her. "You mean you're keeping something from me? May I know it?"

"I'm not sure. You'll think I'm not ladylike."

"What does that mean . . . ladylike?"

"Repressed."

"Well, I already do not think you are repressed. At least, not recently. So what is this unladylike thing?"

"I was thinking about taking off this blouse, later on, and then you'd know it's not the reason my face is glowing."

He took the corner too sharply, and Miranda was flung against him. "I'm sorry," he said. "The picture came to me of you taking off your blouse. And of me helping you with it, the silk in my fingers, and the silk of your skin . . ."

There was a pause. "Are we really going to cook dinner?" Miranda asked.

He caressed the back of her neck. "At some time during this whole night that we have ahead of us, we will cook dinner."

She gripped her hands in her lap to contain the ripples of desire that spread through her like quicksilver, heavy and hot. This is new, she thought, as she had in Xi'an. I haven't known this before. I like it.

She looked through her window as they passed Beihai Park, with its huge serpentine lake, where they had had dinner their first night together. "How many miles is six kilometers?" she asked.

"Three point six. They don't teach the metric system in your schools?"

"Of course they do! They teach everything! I just never—" She fell silent, the hot desire that suffused her stabbed by sharp annoyance. "It never seemed important," she said, her voice subdued. "How do you calculate it?"

"Multiply by point six. I did not mean to criticize your schools; I know they are very fine."

"Some of them," she said honestly, annoyance gone, desire and happiness swelling again. She sat back, gazing at the city, focusing on nothing and everything. She looked at the sidewalks, flickeringly visible through streams of bicyclists, and her glance slid over scenes that were becoming familiar: groups of men squatting in circles to play chess or checkers, with other men standing above them, smoking, criticizing, gossiping; outdoor barbers bending over clients who leaned back in folding chairs, eyes blissfully shut, huge towels draped over chest and neck; men and women in dark business suits talking on cellular phones, dodging bicyclists as they crossed the street. By now, the sky was almost dark and the people had dimmed to silhouettes drifting in and out of dim lights. Miranda felt that Li's car had become a small dark capsule skimming ghostly streets to an unknown destination.

"This is my neighborhood," Li said, and as they turned the corner Miranda saw the street sign that said Xisi Bei. "And here is my house."

Li's house. *An unknown destination? Maybe . . . maybe, after all, I don't belong here. I don't know. I don't know.*

Suddenly gripped by panic, she sat rigidly while he parked the car off the street, beside a high wall, and came around to open her door.

She felt his swift glance at her face and wondered how she looked— fearful? reluctant? repressed?—but he thought it was something else. "If you're worried about anyone watching, I can point them out to you, about a block away. They will stay there all night, cold and disappointed, and we will have our privacy and never think of them."

He held out his hand, and Miranda stepped out beside him. "This is one of my favorite neighborhoods," he said casually. They walked to a gate in the high wall. "One of the few districts in Beijing where the old courtyard houses have been left alone. That is, left for some of us to renovate. It is much more Chinese to me than other districts that are a mongrel of modern and—"

"What?" Miranda stopped short, then laughed. "Hybrid. Isn't that what you mean? A combination, a mishmash, a tossed salad—"

"*Tossed salad?*"

"It's just another way of saying the same thing."

"I like it; it is far more colorful than hybrid. What is a mongrel?"

"A mutt. A dog of mixed, and usually uncertain, parentage."

"Ah. Almost as good as tossed salad."

They were inside the courtyard now,

relaxed and laughing, but as Li locked the gate behind them, desire rushed back, exploding within Miranda, driving everything else out, so that, almost blindly, she turned into Li's arms, into his embrace. Their lips met, their mouths opened, their arms curved and clung until the heat inside them merged, and melted the space between their bodies. Li turned, his arm tightly around Miranda's shoulders, and they moved in step to a door at their left. Miranda had a swift, dizzy impression of a brick house, a small dimly lit room, a deep bamboo couch with a tumbled array of silk tasseled pillows. And then she and Li were lying on the couch, and all the longings of that endless day rose and swelled, engulfing them in heat and silence, the silk pillows like surging waves lifting them, buoying them, slippery against their glistening skin, their silken touch on Miranda's breasts and thighs like an echo of the sensual hardness of Li's hands and the insistence of his mouth that brought a cry to her lips, and brought him inside her, immersed in her, clasped by her, so tightly that once again the space between them melted, and they were one.

When they were still, they lay for a long time, wrapped together, while their breathing slowed and their skin cooled, and when their eyes opened they met in a smile. "Never has a day crawled like this one," Li murmured. "I thought of you, I pictured you and heard your voice and felt your touch but I could not touch you, I could not even go to you. I *wanted* and *wanted* and it built up inside me and I thought I would explode."

"Yes." Miranda touched his face, his eyebrows, the ridge of his nose; she traced the thin lines of his lips again and again, as if memorizing them with her fingers. She felt she could not touch him enough. "I had to sit in a meeting and talk about money and heather and tweed."

"Heather and tweed?"

"Yarns. And all I wanted was to be with you; I was thinking of you all the time. But, still . . ."

"Ah. Not quite *all* the time. And in between? What happened?"

"I was different. I wasn't afraid anymore."

"So you were tough?"

She laughed slightly. "For me."

"And you got what you wanted."

"I did. I think I was as surprised as they

were. If they were; it was hard to tell." She paused. "Did you get what you wanted when you talked to Sheng?"

He smiled. "I am not sure parents ever get what they want when they talk to their children. But we made a beginning and I learned that he is not anxious for me to leave, in fact, he is afraid I might, afraid that I will abandon him. It is a strange fear for a man of thirty-five, but as I told you Sheng has much growing up to do.

He fell silent, then smiled ruefully at Miranda. "Why are we talking about our children when we are in bed together?" He drew her to him. "I love you. I cannot imagine a time when I did not love you. I love your face and your voice and your wonderful smile, with so much joy in it, and your very serious frown, and your hands touching me, and I feel they always have been there and always will be—"

Miranda kissed him, her hands framing his face, feeling the rapid pulse in his temple; she kissed him and their tongues met with their own silent words as their bodies shifted, stirring the silk cushions, the silken tassels brushing their skin with the shivery stroke of feathers.

She had thought their fever had been tempered, but they came together with the same fierce hunger as before, the same explosive longing they had fought all day, Miranda curving above Li and settling onto him, his hands at her waist, his mouth on her breasts; Li tracing Miranda's body with his mouth, kissing, tasting the contours and small hollows and hardness of bone beneath skin, down and down, until, raising her hips with his hands, he drank, as from a golden bowl; Miranda drawing Li into her mouth, into her throat, the softness of her tongue coiling around his hardness, her breasts crushed against his thighs, his hands in her hair, on her breasts, until, open and hungering, she slid upward along his body and they turned within the tumble of silk pillows, like swimmers arching through surging waves, and he lay on her and the molten darkness inside her drew him deep and deeper, and then exploded with light.

Night had fallen when they stirred again, and Li reached out to turn on a lamp. In its amber light, Miranda saw the small, square room clearly for the first time. Within pale walls, its only furniture was the chaise on which they lay, the lamp and table beside them, and a square black chest with dozens of tiny drawers embossed with Chinese characters in gold. "How beautiful," Miranda said. "What is it?"

"An apothecary chest, each drawer for a different herb."

"And do you keep herbs in it, in case you get sick?"

"Oh, I am too modern for that. I keep my herbs in the refrigerator."

"For sickness?"

"Some of them. Shall I show you?"

"Yes. And everything else. Your whole house." She stretched, raising her arms above her head, pointing her toes, arching her back. They had the whole night: time for everything. They were alone and secluded, they were in Li's house, and the rest of the world was at bay and invisible and, for the moment, did not even seem real. She stretched again, luxuriating in the smooth taut length of her muscles; she felt young and clean, strong, whole, protected, invincible. "What room is this?"

"A reception room. You would call it an entry hall, I think, but here it takes up all of the first house."

"The first house? How many are there?"

"Seven." He plucked Miranda's silk blouse from the jumble of their clothes on the floor and gently shook it out. "Not a good way to treat such a fine blouse, but it seems to have survived."

"A few wrinkles would be a small price to pay," Miranda murmured and Li chuckled as they dressed quickly and left the room. The courtyard was dark, lit only by the rectangle of light from the doorway of the reception room.

"In the old days there would have been kerosene lamps," Li said, "but I am too modern for that, too." He flicked a switch and wall sconces spread a pale yellow wash over the small brick courtyard, casting long snaking shadows from the outspread branches of a linden tree. The tree was on the far side of the courtyard, beside a door into a long, flat-roofed building. Li opened the door. "The kitchen. We'll come back here after our tour."

Miranda had a swift impression of wooden counters, woks balancing on wok rings over gas burners, cleavers lined up in flat baskets, and shelves of pure white dishes, and then they were through the kitchen and standing before a high, formal gate of green wood panels in a carved doorway. Beyond it lay a tiny courtyard with small buildings on either side—"servants' quarters," Li said—and then another wall with double doors set at an angle from the gate they had just come through. Li opened them. "We never build doors in a straight line," he said casually. "That would allow any evil spirits that might get in to flow straight into the heart of the house. There is a spirit screen in the first court-yard for the same purpose: to keep evil spirits out when the front gate is opened."

Miranda glanced at him with a smile, thinking he was relating an amusing super-stition, but his face was serious, his voice matter-of-fact. He took her hand and helped her step over the high wooden threshold into the third and largest court-yard where, once again, he turned on wall sconces. Miranda drew a long breath. "How lovely." The courtyard was framed by three houses, one straight ahead and smaller ones to left and right. To one side was an earthenware tub with a rose lotus floating in its center; on a long low step stretching the length of the main house were oleanders and pomegranates in earthen pots; before the two side houses were fig trees in broad tubs. "I wish I still had figs," Li said. "Their flavor is sweet and perfect. But it is past their time. Now we have chrysanthemums."

They were everywhere, in large carved pots and small plain ones, huge flowers in russets and golds and parchment yellow-whites. Nestled among the pots were stone benches and two stone pedestals, one holding a statue of a dragon, the other a bronze turtle, its head raised high. "The turtle of longevity," Li murmured. "And chrysanthemums are the flower of immortality. We stack the odds in our favor. Here is the main house."

It was brick, rectangular, with a long row of windows on either side of the doorway, its roof pagoda-like, with turned-up corners and small figures marching up the ridge line of each corner. The large main room, flanked by a study and a bedroom, was divided into living and dining areas by pale oriental rugs and groupings of deeply carved furniture polished to a high gloss, with cushions of peasants' cotton, old brocade, and embroidered silk. But what drew

Miranda's eye was a solitary sculpture against a brightly lit wall. Standing on a plain wooden table, it looked like a distorted tree trunk, two or three feet high, gnarled and knotted, with random openings through which the light shone. "Like a dream," she murmured. "A tree in a strange dream."

Li followed her look. "A scholar's rock."

She gazed at the twists and whorls of the stone sculpture. Now it did not seem distorted or gnarled, but graceful, its long slightly curved shape like two embracing dancers, its gleaming surface almost alive. There was something magical about it; it was as if the magic of the hours she and Li were together had found visible form. "Scholar's rock," she repeated. "What an odd name. It doesn't look like a rock; it's too alive, too fluid. As if it sprang from the earth and awakened to the sun."

"That's almost exactly right," Li said. "It comes from the earth, from the bottom of Lake Tai, and represents the forces of nature in the universe, and, rather mystically, is supposed to mirror the turns and twists of our thoughts. Scholars use them as objects of contemplation, hoping to understand the universe." He smiled. "Pretentious, but they believe it. This one is from the Ming Dynasty."

"When was that?"

"The 1300s to about the middle of the 1600s. A dark time in many ways, with wars and corruption, but also a time when great beauty was created."

"And do you contemplate your scholar's rock to understand the universe?"

"To understand myself. And to become serene in times of unhappiness." He kissed her lightly. "Right now, I cannot remember what unhappiness is like. Perhaps it is a myth. Unhappiness? There is no such thing."

"No, how could there be?" She kissed him and her arms gathered in the hard bones of his shoulders and the muscles of his arms. "I love you," she said. "I love you." The sound of her voice saying the words made her startlingly happy.

Li held her close and caressed the back of her neck, the shape of her head, the curve of her cheek. Then he put a few inches between them, and kissed her lightly. "Shall we make our dinner?" And Miranda understood that he was saying that there would be time for talk of love, and so much else, in this whole night that was theirs, and that they could stretch it out, savoring each moment, instead of cramming it into one or two overburdened hours. So they turned and walked back through the courtyard, past the turtle of longevity and the chrysanthemums of immortality, past the floating rose lotus and the bending fig trees, into the kitchen.

And there they cooked together, standing side by side at the long wooden counter scarred with thousands of knife cuts and deep gouges from cleavers. With Li giving directions, they chopped and diced, sliced and stirred, shredded pork and chicken. They poured rice wine, sugar, soy sauce and sesame oil into small measuring cups, and stirred it with chopsticks. They ground spices with a mortar and pestle, boiled noodles, and swirled hot peanut oil up the sides of two woks, working in harmony, concentrating or talking in low voices, until, at last, they sat at a small round table at one end of the kitchen, set with a white cloth and white dishes. "If my housekeeper were here she would serve us in the main house," said Li, "but rather than carry everything—"

"I like it here," Miranda said. And, in fact, the warm, steamy room with its dark woods, blue and white tiles, burnished woks hanging from large hooks, and colorful array of foods keeping warm on low burners gave her the same feelings she had had on the silk-pillowed bamboo couch where they had made love: young and clean, strong, whole, protected, invincible.

They ate slowly, leisurely, sliced pork with tiger sauce, *chiang-bo* duck, chili-pepper chicken with mushroom-smothered bean curd, stir-fried spinach, simmered radish balls, red-cooked spicy beef noodles, hot and sour soup, all washed down with quantities of Tsing-tao beer. It was almost midnight when Li said, regretfully, "We have no dessert."

"Or room for any," Miranda said. "I don't believe this. Could you really eat dessert?"

"Only a modest portion." He grinned. "To have something to go with our tea. Wait, we do have something." He took from the refrigerator a plate and a bowl and set them before Miranda. "Sweet cashew porridge and steamed sponge cake. I'm sorry we have only a little of each, but they are left over from dinner with friends a few nights ago." He divided the pudding into two small bowls, and placed diamond-shaped pieces of cake on two tiny plates. "And tea," he added, filling their cups with pale green tea, its fragrance curling upward in tendrils of steam.

The pudding was crunchy with candied cashews, speckled with raisins, and Miranda ate it all. The sponge cake was bland and she toyed with it.

"You don't care for it," Li said. "But sometimes a quiet flavor is good after a vociferous meal."

Miranda laughed. "Probably. But I loved all those vociferous flavors, and I don't want to lose them. How did you learn to cook?"

"My mother and grandmother thought that a man should be self-sufficient in stormy times. The war with Japan, and then our civil war, convinced them they had to prepare me for upheavals and chaos. There is a poem I like, by the Irish poet, Yeats; his book was in my father's collection. 'Things fall apart; the center cannot hold; mere anarchy is loosed upon the world. . . .' The first time I read it I thought it was written about China. A terrifying poem, and cooking is a good thing to do when one is terrified; it turns one's thoughts to life instead of death."

They sat quietly, drinking their tea. The tick of a wall clock was the only sound. *Alone and secluded. Young, strong, whole, protected, invincible.* She had never felt this way, never known this happiness. This is where I belong, she thought.

"You belong here," Li said, his voice so low it was almost as if he were thinking aloud. "You fit so well in my kitchen, in my house. It is good to hear your footsteps in the silence of my rooms." He smiled. "And we cook well together, that is always a test."

Miranda was watching him, her mouth slightly open. How did he do that? Not often, but several times since they had met, he had given words to her thoughts, as if, somehow, though they walked through separate lives and separate worlds, he briefly fell in step with her, their paces locked in perfect rhythm, their eyes looking in the same direction, with the same feelings. As if he were inside her, looking out. That, too, was new, and disconcerting, because she liked it and knew she could come to depend upon it.

Li held out his hand. "I want us to walk from the kitchen to the main house, to my bedroom, and go to bed as if we lived here and this were an ordinary evening and we were in an ordinary routine."

Miranda gave a small smile. "I think no evening with you would ever be ordinary."

Hand in hand, they walked across the shadowy courtyard, through the spicy scent of chrysanthemums to the main house. The scholar's rock gleamed in solitary grandeur against its pale, silk-covered wall; the rest of the room was in near darkness touched faintly with gold, like a shadowy landscape beneath a rising moon. In the dim light, Li moved surely between couches and chairs, and into the bedroom, where a lighted lamp stood just inside the low doorway. In the wall opposite was a deep sleeping alcove framed in dark blue drapes fastened with slender half-circles of bronze. An amethyst glass lamp hung above the brocade-covered bed. The walls of the alcove were a shimmering silver, dancing with violet shadows from the lighted lamp.

Miranda and Li turned to each other, clung to each other. Li kissed her eyebrows, her closed eyes, the tip of her nose, her lips. "I love you," he said, and Miranda put her head back to look at him fully. "I love you," she said. "And want," he added with a faint smile. "And want," she echoed. "Oh, yes, I want you, always, always."

Desire built again, swelling, lifting them with a power they had no will or wish to contain, a hunger that seemed never to be satisfied, fired now by the sweet harmony of their hours in the kitchen, and the sweetness of the many hours that still lay ahead, holding off the day. They kissed, and kissed again, and sat on the edge of the bed, their hands finding buttons, belts, zippers, their rhythmic breathing the only sound in the hushed room.

"Not ordinary at all," Li murmured, and they lay together on the silky, yielding brocade.

Chapter 10

Li swiveled in his chair to look out the window at the skyscraper under construction across the street. It was someone else's job, so he could watch its progress with disinterest. They've installed a ventilator grill upside down, he thought idly. I suppose at some point they'll discover it. He tried to concentrate on the grill, and the to and fro of laborers on scaffoldings and finished floors, but he could not do it. Even with his eyes open and sitting upright in his chair, he could feel Miranda beneath him, feel the silkiness of her hair between his fingers, and her mouth, her beautiful mouth, like a butterfly, whispering, shussshhhing, fluttering along his skin, her fingers moving over him, trailing little streamers of heat, and her thighs parting, wide and wider, welcoming him, until he was inside her, deep inside her, and his whole world was warm, soft, clinging, caressing, dark.

I've got to get out of here, he thought. I have to move.

Instead, he called Miranda in her hotel room, where he had taken her on the way from his house to his office. "I'm glad you're still there," he said. "I miss you."

"I was just leaving for Xiujiang."

"Your third company. Soon you will be an expert."

"My last, except for Mr. Tang." He heard her voice tighten on those words. *My last.*

"I want to see you," he said, "and there are too many hours between now and tonight."

"Yes. Oh, I wish I didn't have to— Except, if I didn't have this work to do, I wouldn't be here at all. Li, I must go; I'll be late."

"Six o'clock tonight, is that all right?" And then he added what he had been thinking about but had not been sure he would say until this minute. "I would like to take you to my daughter's house for dinner."

There was a pause. "You've told her about me?"

"I told her I have a friend I would like her to meet. You do not mind?"

"I don't know. I suppose it's all right. It feels strange, somehow."

"Not to me." When she was silent, he said, "It is important to me and I think you will not be uncomfortable. Will you do this?"

"Yes," she said, so quickly he knew she was overcoming her reluctance only because he had asked it of her. "I'll see you tonight. I love you."

And there was one of the profound differences between Americans and Chinese, Li thought. In an office, on the telephone, she could say it, and he could not.

"Father," said Sheng from the doorway.

His thoughts cooled, settled. "Come in."

Sheng took the chair opposite Li and held out a folder. "The report on the meeting yesterday with the laborers."

"Good. That was quick. And you called the other companies?"

"There is a list, with the names of their presidents, and what they said. Four of them will be at the meeting this afternoon."

"Good, very good." He was skimming the pages. "This looks excellent. A thorough report. Thank you." He looked up and saw his son sitting straighter. How much he needs praise, he thought. But, then, so do we all. No one is ever exempt from that.

"One thing, though," Sheng said. "They all heard about the meeting yesterday. They said you seemed to sympathize with the workers instead of the other construction presidents."

"That is not true."

"They heard it from the presidents who were here, and they said they won't be here tomorrow unless you take a hard line and don't give the workers anything."

"It is too late for a hard line. We have to deal with labor because we can do absolutely nothing without them, and the more satisfied they are, the better their work will be."

"You're the only one who thinks that way."

"Then I'm the only one who understands that this is one of the changes we must deal with today, and if we don't do it now there will be strikes, perhaps even violence. You don't believe this?"

"I don't know."

"Then follow my lead. I expect you to support me."

"They think you're a subversive!" Sheng blurted out.

Li sighed. "They'll find out soon enough that I am not subversive; only right. Was there something else you wished to talk to me about?"

"Yes, I need to leave early this afternoon. Right after the meeting."

Li looked at him thoughtfully. "How long do you think you can manage your two different lives when each one demands your full energy and attention?"

Sheng frowned. "Have I not given you my full time and attention?"

"Well, clearly today will not be a full day. Mostly your attention has been satisfactory, but I am looking to the future. Since you seem to be interested in becoming president of All-China Construction someday, I am wondering how you will master the skills and knowledge you will need when you spend so much time mastering other skills and other know-ledge."

Sheng's face became sullen. "If something happened to you, I could take over now. I know enough—"

"No," Li said gently, "you do not. You know a great deal; you could oversee the construction of a building, and I am glad to see that, but there is so much more to running a company, requiring knowledge of people, in which you still are deficient; patience, in which you are sadly deficient; the ability to compromise, which I have not seen in you at all; and skill in wending your way through our bureaucracies without losing your independence or alienating your suppliers or making enemies along the way, and I think you are a long way from that, as well."

"You don't seem to have done so well, since you're under surveillance."

"Well. That is another issue. I thought we had settled that."

Sheng shook his head, a stubborn little boy. "You're endangering all of us. Me, the company, yourself. Everything."

"Has someone told you that?"

"No! Why would I talk to anyone about

this? It is shameful and dangerous. I keep such things to myself."

How well my son lies, Li thought. His face bland, his words honey-smooth. Parents take pride in their children's accomplishments; shall I take pride in this, that Sheng lies well?

A wave of boredom washed over him. Why am I wasting my time on this pipsqueak? Pipsqueak. Not even a pip of a squeak. And yet a few minutes ago he gave me a good report and I admired it. But now all I want is to be alone, to think about Miranda. To prepare for the meeting this afternoon. To think about Miranda. To do my work quickly and well so that I may tonight be with Miranda.

He stood. "I will see you at the meeting this afternoon. Please telephone the four presidents and remind them of the time; I am sure the workers need no reminders. And I have a list of companies in Shanghai and Guangzhou; please call their presidents, too, and ask them if they can participate in a conference call tomorrow morning. Eight o'clock, if that is convenient."

Sheng nodded. "And I will be leaving today right after the meeting."

"Yes, we settled that."

Sheng hesitated. He felt he was being pushed out by his father, and that was not right: they should be equals. He glanced at the list of names. A secretary could do this. He looked up. "Couldn't—?"

"No, absolutely not, a secretary could not do this." Li's voice was impatient. "We are trying to establish a common front for dealing with worker demands that will change the entire construction industry and certainly increase our costs. Do you think those presidents will talk about these matters with a secretary? I am asking you to call them because you are an executive of this company, someone with whom they will feel comfortable sharing ideas."

Well. That put a better light on it. Except, Sheng admitted to himself, I should have understood that right away. "I'll do my best," he said, and left the office trying to concentrate on his father's confidence in him, and forget his shame at missing such an obvious point.

Knowledge of people, in which you still are deficient.

He made the telephone calls to Shanghai and Guangzhou, and because those

words rankled—*deficient, sadly deficient*—
he was careful with each sentence, careful
with the sound of his voice (warm but businesslike, cooperative but firm), careful to
make no promises that he or his father
could not keep. And every president he
called said he would participate in a conference call and work with Li and Sheng to
solve the problem, which was becoming
nationwide, of troublemakers demanding
decent housing.

It was a proud moment: a job well done.
His father would be pleased. When the
telephone rang, he reached for it still in the
glow of achievement.

"Two of our people," said Pan Chao, "at
least two that we know about, will follow
their leaders and walk out, if it comes to
that. I have replaced them. But we need
the names of all the leaders."

"I gave you names after yesterday's
meeting." Sheng's glow had vanished.

"You gave us three names. There must
be more. This is moving around the country; I heard of trouble in Shanghai and
Wuhan today."

"And Guangzhou," said Sheng. "We
can't stop it; it's too big."

"Of course it can be stopped; this is not the first time laborers in China have threatened strikes. The government will deal with it; the question is, how quickly. With the American president coming in two weeks, there is no way they will allow strikes or other disruptions. It will end very quickly, I am sure of that."

I sympathize with them; their housing is wretched.

Sheng heard the echo of his father's words the day before. Which side was his father on?

"But meanwhile we must replace anyone who is an agitator or a sympathizer. For now we have a full crew to handle our next shipment, but for our shipments to other companies we must know who will be on the job, not out on the street yelling slogans, or arrested for subversive activities. When can you get us more names?"

"There is a meeting this afternoon. I'll get as many as I can."

"Bring them when we get together later. We rely on you, Sheng. If we act promptly, this will not harm us; we will find people willing to work for us and the government will stamp out the others."

I sympathize with them; their housing is wretched.

Sheng shook his head. His father could not be foolish enough to defend them. They were ignorant laborers who came from the countryside, a whole village at a time, to work on construction projects; they slept in cardboard hovels or wooden lean-tos, and ate scraps, because whatever they earned here was more than they would ever earn at home. If his father gave them any sympathy, then he and Sheng were on different sides. Sheng had a business to protect. So did his father, if he would only see it that way.

"Now, something else," said Chao. "I need to make some telephone calls from a place that can't be traced to me. I'd like to use your office tonight, after everyone leaves. You do have a key to the building, and the offices?"

"Yes, of course. Anytime you want." This was a little odd, Sheng thought. Of course everyone knew that telephones were routinely tapped in China, mail and packages opened, messenger deliveries intercepted, so it was necessary now and then, especially with a business as complex and risky as theirs, to look for privacy. But there were many places Chao could go to make a private telephone call. He had never asked Sheng before. Does he want to spy on me? Sheng wondered. No, it's nothing; just an ordinary request. I'll think about it, though. I don't like things I don't understand.

"Bring me your key, then," Chao said, "or an extra one, if you have it. What time can you get away from your father?"

"I can get away *from the office* as soon as the meeting is over. I should be at Dung Chan by four-thirty."

He looked in his desk drawer for another set of keys, and found them pushed to the back. He stuffed them in his pocket, then turned his thoughts to more important things: his meeting that afternoon with his father and construction company presidents and labor representatives, and a later one at Dung Chan, the company he and his partners had formed as an umbrella for their various businesses. And tonight, Wu Yi. She had told him, on his third call, that she would cancel an engagement for him. And so, tonight, Wu Yi.

She'll fizzle, like fireworks.

I know, Sheng thought. But until then . . .

"Are you ready?" His father was standing in the doorway. "I thought we might go down to the conference room together."

"Oh. Yes." He gathered up his notes. "All five presidents will be ready for the conference call tomorrow. I had to make it eight-thirty to get all of them."

"Fine. Excellent." Once again, Li put his arm around Sheng's shoulders as they walked down the corridor. "You will of course be part of it; I want your ideas as we go along, and then it will be good to discuss it later."

He was trying to make up for his earlier boredom with his son, which, of course, Sheng knew nothing about. How irrational we are with our children, Li thought. It is perhaps the only constant in our relationships with them. Except for love. We cannot forget that.

At the meeting, he was mostly silent, listening. The others were here at his invitation; therefore it was incumbent on him to hear them fully, and not to contradict or cut them off. But he was troubled. The laborers' representatives were adamant, the construction presidents rigid, and with so much stiffness in the room the idea of bending to compromise seemed an impossibility. They would have to talk in smaller groups, where there would be less posturing. And waiting for the government to act.

Li knew it was past the time for the government to act by itself. China was moving too quickly, and the people would grab power if it were not granted to them.

The people would grab power? Others would call him mad for suggesting such a thing. But he knew it could happen, and even if it took years, in the meantime the country would simmer, ready to boil, undermining the structure they had to create in order to prosper and make the Chinese people happy.

The only question was, when change did come, would Li's company be in the forefront, or helplessly swept away by it?

One or the other, he thought. I hope I can help us be in front. I owe it to everyone who depends on me.

As soon as the meeting ended, with promises that there would be another next week, and no strike until then, Sheng left, but not without making proper farewells, which pleased Li. And when he went to his office, he realized, with a shock, that for the entire meeting, he had not thought of Miranda at all.

But now he let himself think of her, and of meeting her in the lobby of the Palace Hotel at six o'clock, and saying what he had been unable to say on the telephone.

"I love you," he said as soon as he slid shut the partition behind the driver. But Miranda had seen his quick look behind them, and she was drawing back.

She looked through the rear window of the car. "I never see anyone. I believe you that someone is there, but I never see him. Or her. Is it ever a her?"

"Sometimes." We will always have to deal with this, Li thought, and he was angry, furiously angry that his government would not allow him to love simply and quietly, without distractions.

"Him or her or them," said Miranda, facing the front again. "Don't they ever quit? They must suspect something very real, they must be ready to *do* something, or they wouldn't still be following us."

Li took her hand. "Listen to me. Sometimes people are followed for years, and nothing is done. It is one of the ways a government controls its people."

"Through fear."

"Yes, it is an old story in most of the world. And we get used to it—"

"Lulled. You forget how awful it is that someone would violate your privacy *all the time,* and when you've convinced yourself it's nothing, no different from a rainstorm, they *pounce.*"

He smiled faintly. "Not always. And not, I am sure, on us. You still do not believe me in this?"

"I want to."

"That should be enough. Miranda, I am not asking you to forget that someone is there; I am not asking you to shrug it off as normal. For you it can never be normal, I understand that. But what is far more important is that no one knows what we say to each other and what we do in private. So if you cannot forget it, I ask you to ignore it. It will not hurt you or me or us, and so it is annoying, possibly unpleasant, but not important enough to distract us from each other."

He held her hand more tightly. "I love you. I want to kiss you and hold you and make love to you, and all I can do is hold your hand here on the seat between us, very discreetly, so that my driver and the crowds around us see only two respectable people traveling to the great unknown."

He could see Miranda sink into it and knew that once again she would go along with him. "I thought we were going to your daughter's house," she said with a smile.

"An unknown place to you. But I promise that you will find it pleasant." He surveyed the tortuous crawl of traffic. "This is going to be a slow ride. So . . ." He took a small flat package from his jacket pocket and gave it to Miranda. "For your birthday."

"My birthday is in February."

"An early birthday present. Or late, from your last one. Will you open it?"

She took it from him, wonderingly. "I bought *you* a present. How strange this is. I was going to give it to you tonight."

"Then I will look forward to that. And it is not so strange, you know. We each want to give, because we are grateful."

"Grateful," she murmured. "Oh, yes." She untied the gold ribbon and opened the box. Nestled between two layers of cotton padding was a jade bracelet, a seamless circle of pale green, the palest green, almost silver in its translucence. Miranda picked it up and it was lustrous in her hand. "How wonderful. I've never seen anything like it." She slipped it over her hand and it hung on her slender wrist. "It's like moonlight, cool and shimmering and so clear . . ." She held out her wrist, turning it. "Thank you, Li. It's the most beautiful bracelet in the world, more beautiful than anything I own."

"Then it is right for you, because of the beauty you have brought into my life." They smiled briefly at each other, afraid of what their faces might show if they looked too long and too longingly. "This was a mistake," Li said. "We should have gone to my house first. Only to my house. Shall I cancel our dinner?"

"No." She smiled mischievously. "You made your bed; now you'll lie in it."

He chuckled. "The wrong bed." Their hands met again and held tightly while the driver wove through clogged traffic, eventually coming to a quieter part of town and stopping at a modern brick townhouse identical to those up and down both sides of the street.

Li felt Miranda tense beside him. "It will be all right; she is really quite civilized."

"Oh, everyone here is. But I want—"

"Warmth. I know. And she is capable of that, but it takes time."

"But you once told me you don't like the lives your children lead."

"That was not really fair to Shuiying. Sheng would say she and her husband are small-time; I would say they are corrupt but not as skillfully corrupt as Sheng. Corrupt enough to get along today, I suppose. I think you will like Shuiying. And her daughter is perfect."

"Spoken like a grandfather."

"Ah, but in this case it is the truth."

She laughed. Her tension had eased and she looked at the house before them with calm interest. Like all the others on the street, it was tall and narrow and resembled a child's drawing: windows upstairs and down on each side of a bright-red front door, two bushes flanking the front step, a peaked roof, a single chimney. But the house had something none of its neighbors had: along one side of the cherry-red door were Chinese characters, painted in gold.

"What do they say?" Miranda asked.

" 'The heart in full blossom.' It is a wish

for happiness. It says that when hearts unfold, like flowers opening to sunlight, beauty and joy will come to all the world."

"What a lovely wish. How does it sound in Chinese?" Li read it aloud, and Miranda echoed it, trying to sound like him. "I can't make it slither around the way you do; I'd have to practice it. But it's lovely in any language."

"My daughter is a poet, at least part-time." Li lifted the door knocker and let it fall. "Mostly she is a computer programmer. And her daughter, five years old— Ah, Shuiying." He embraced the woman who opened the door. "As I promised, I have brought a friend. Miranda Graham, Yuan Shuiying."

He watched them appraise each other as they shook hands, and as they sat in two armchairs in the reception room, he wondered what they thought of each other: his daughter, small, slender, dark, very beautiful, and Miranda, the same height and slenderness, but fair, not nearly as beautiful as Shuiying, yet so dear to him that he saw in her a rare loveliness all her own.

"Tea, father," said Shuiying formally, in

crisp English, and with that he recognized what he should have seen from the first moment: his daughter was stiff and wary, as correct and cold as the Western furnishings in her house, arranged with precision, not a rumpled cushion to be seen. And Miranda was clearly uncomfortable, sitting very straight, studying the room with little glances so as not to seem rude, watching Shuiying's meticulous movements as she poured green *longjing* tea into three small cups. Li took his cup and sat opposite the two of them, framing them together in his sight. "Miranda," Shuiying said coolly, "please tell me, how do you like Beijing?"

"I like it very much. More and more, as I get to know it. The city seems to unfold, like the poem on your front door."

Shuiying bowed her head and Li wondered if Miranda understood that that meant she was pleased. "And how do you like our food?"

"Oh, it is so good. And so new to me. Our Chinese food is nothing like yours."

"Chinese people who leave home are no longer truly Chinese. Where have you eaten?"

Miranda named the restaurants. "And

breakfast with Li's friends on the street one morning—"

"On the street?" Shuiying frowned at her father. "That is not a place for visitors. What will Miranda think of us? We have such fine restaurants."

"The food was excellent," Miranda said, "and what else is important?"

Shuiying contemplated her. "You have studied Chinese food?"

"No, but every meal has been an education."

A smile flickered on Shuiying's lips. "And my father says you are here to work."

"Yes, another education." Miranda smiled slightly. "At first it was difficult, but now the people seem friendlier, even anxious to work with us. I find that very refreshing."

Shuiying met her father's eye and laughed softly. "Refreshing. Yes, I can imagine that it would be. And is your work successful, then?"

"Yes. Very. I think we will do a great deal of work in China."

"Where are you staying?" Shuiying asked, and when Miranda sighed Li thought perhaps the interrogation was going on too long. But she answered easily, "The Palace Hotel. It is very beautiful and very comfortable. And I met Yuan Li at the airport, if you are wondering, when he helped me battle your crowds and get a taxi. He was very kind."

Shuiying was momentarily silenced. She leveled a long look at the circle of jade on Miranda's wrist. "Have you visited other cities in China?"

"Xi'an. That was very exciting."

"And where did you stay there?"

"The Xi'an Garden Hotel."

"Somewhat out of town, surely. Why did you choose it?"

"She did not," said Li when Miranda hesitated. "I took Miranda to Xi'an, and I chose the hotel. We both stayed there."

"I admired the warriors," Miranda said quickly. "They're so solid, as if the past has taken physical form and become part of the present instead of fading away."

"That is nicely put." Li heard the approval in Shuiying's voice. Miranda was sitting back now, drinking her tea and talking more easily, though still pinned down by his daughter's watchful gaze. "And did you watch *tai chi* in the morning? It is done all over Xi'an."

"No. I would have liked to have seen that. I've seen photographs, and a movie once. It looked so graceful, I thought it would be lovely to learn it. Someday, perhaps, I'll find someone to teach me."

"I can show you now." Li's eyebrows rose in surprise. This was not like Shuiying. Was she doing it to help Miranda or to show her up? He watched Miranda walk with Shuiying to the center of the room. "The movements flow from one to the other," Shuiying said, "but very slowly." In slow motion, she raised one bent leg and turned on one foot, so gradually it almost seemed she was not moving at all, then lifted one hand, palm out, and, inch by inch, pushed it outward, as if pressing something away from her. Then, slowly, so slowly, she raised that arm straight up, and, still on one foot, turned again and slowly brought her arm down in a wide arc, and then, in the same slow motion, lowered her leg to the floor. She turned to Miranda. "Now, do it as I do."

As she repeated the movements, Miranda followed her, watching intently, frowning as she fought to control her quivering muscles in the discipline demanded by each deliberate movement up, out, around, down.

Watching the two of them, so beautiful in their dreamlike grace, Li felt something inside him crack and weep. He imagined them as friends, close friends, mingling their different worlds, learning from each other in so many ways, laughing together, sharing secrets, and that image of a family, of their family, was a shimmering mirage beckoning to him in his longing.

I love you, he said silently to both of them, yet he knew he would never be as close to his daughter as he would like, and a future with Miranda was all shadows and uncertainty. Still, as he watched the dancing women, he felt himself reach out to them as a thirsty man would move toward a shining mirage: reaching for a beauty so clear it was as if all that he had dreamed had truly come to pass.

"Would you like to do it one more time?" Shuiying asked, and Li knew that this was indeed a test; few people were able to complete more than one *tai chi* routine the first time.

"Yes, I'd like that." Li saw the rigid line of Miranda's neck, and the way she clenched and unclenched her fist, and a rush of love filled him. But, oh, how sore she will be tomorrow, he thought. She has no idea how hard her muscles are working. Or she does, but she is determined to show Shuiying . . . what? That she is as good as she? Or that she is good enough for Shuiying's father?

The two women repeated the movements, and when they were finished Miranda almost collapsed into her chair. "That's the hardest exercise I've ever done," she said to Shuiying. "I admire you; you do it so beautifully. How strong you are, to make it look mystical, not like exercise at all."

Shuiying smiled, more warmly than at any time since Miranda's arrival. "It takes many years. You are excellent for a beginner; you should continue to practice. Of course these are only a few of the hundreds of movements, increasing in difficulty. But many of them you could do." She refilled their teacups. "Dinner will be ready soon. Zemin will not be here; he has business in Guangzhou. My husband," she added, to Miranda. "He is a tour operator and does not make much money, but he has other activities and they are very profitable. How much money do you make as a designer?"

Miranda's face flushed with confusion and embarrassment, and Li came to her rescue. "Americans do not talk about money, Shuiying."

"Why not? It is part of everything." She turned to Miranda. "If I asked how tall you are, or how big is your house, or how old are your children, would you tell me?"

Miranda frowned. "It isn't the same."

"What is the difference? Are you ashamed of how much money you make?"

Miranda's face hardened. "I'd like to make more, but that doesn't mean I'm ashamed of it. It has nothing to do with whether I'm a good person or not." She looked surprised, and Li realized that, in America, what she had said would be startling, since Americans seemed to equate character with income. Rich people never reveal their income because that might show they make less than richer people, and the richest people keep it a secret because it would seem they are bragging about how much better they are than everyone else, and people with small incomes refuse to reveal them because they cannot admit that they are less worthy than the rich and the richer and the richest. All of which is obviously absurd, he mused. Why don't they understand that?

Miranda broke into a low laugh. "How absurd." She drained her teacup and set it down firmly. "I earn forty thousand dollars a year, which is enough for me and my two children."

"Forty thousand— Three hundred twenty thousand yuan! You are a very wealthy woman!"

Once again Miranda looked embarrassed. "It may be a great deal of money in China, but in America it is . . ."

"Modest," Li said quietly.

"What do you earn?" Miranda asked with a boldness that surprised Li.

"Two thousand yuan a month. I will earn more next year."

Miranda's eyes widened. "Two hundred fifty dollars a month? But how can you live on that?"

"My husband earns three times as much. But of course it is not enough; it is never enough. We will earn much more in the future. You said you have children. Where is your husband?"

"He died many years ago. I could probably earn more if I went to New York, but my children are happy in the small town where we live, so I'm happy staying there."

"No one is happy making less money," Shuiying said firmly. "Money is good. Making more money is better. Being rich is best of all."

"But other things are important: close friends and family, and good schools, and living in a place you love."

"It is better to be rich. Money is the only thing that matters."

"How can you be a poet and think so much about money?"

"You do not believe that poets think about money? Poets have to eat, just like everyone else. It all comes down to money, and to get it you do whatever you need to do because without it nothing good happens."

"What does your husband do besides lead tours?" Miranda asked, clearly trying to change the subject.

"He is an official with business and government organizations, and a director of two private ones."

"What kind of organizations?" Miranda asked, and her innocence was so un-Chinese that Li longed to reach out and hold her, to smile into her clear eyes and experience, even if briefly, that ignorance of corruption that was like a state of grace forever denied the citizens of modern China, now that they had flung it from them with both hands.

"Many kinds; Zemin is very skillful. He is an official of a government agency—" The front door opened and a small girl ran in, stopping short when she saw Miranda. She saw Li and began to run to him, but changed course, going first to her mother to greet her and kiss her on the cheek. Then she ran to Li. "*Laoyeh!* Where have you been? You haven't come to see me for sooooo long!"

In Chinese, Li said, "Can you say that in English? This lady is from America. Her name is Miranda." Holding the child between his knees, he said, in English, "Miranda, this is my granddaughter, Chen Ming."

"*Ni hao,*" Miranda said.

A stream of Chinese burst from Ming.

"She wonders why I asked her to speak English," said Li, "when it is clear that you speak Chinese."

Miranda laughed. "Not when I get past hello and goodbye and thank you. Does she really speak English? At five?"

"I told you she is exceptional." He whispered to his granddaughter, and she turned to Miranda.

"How do you do," she said carefully. "Are you well? I hope you like China. It is bigger than America, and richer and more beautiful."

"Forgive her rudeness," Shuiying said. "At her age, they learn simple sentences and she does not truly understand what she is saying."

Miranda knelt before Ming and brushed back a strand of black hair that fell over the little girl's eyes. They smiled at each other, and Li saw Miranda close her eyes and knew she was thinking of her own children, missing them. "I hope you do think your country is the best in the world," she said to Ming. "You should be proud of China; it's your home."

"Oh," Shuiying said. "Americans do not usually talk like that."

"I just hope she understands that Americans feel the same way about their country. I hope no one teaches her that America is a bad place, or that we are her enemy."

"No one would teach her that."

Miranda's eyebrows rose, but she said nothing. She kissed Ming's cheek and returned to her chair. "She's a beautiful child."

Li spoke to Ming in Chinese, and Shuiying said, "Don't tell her that; it will spoil her."

"She should know that Miranda thinks she is beautiful. Now, I'm going to take Ming to the kitchen for something to eat."

"You spoil her all the time."

"I hope I am only making her happy. We'll be back in a few minutes."

From the kitchen, Li saw the edge of Miranda's chair, and her arm with the jade bracelet. He poured juice for Ming and as she chattered about her day at the children's school, he listened to the two women.

"—government agency," Shuiying said. "But he may stop that when his other companies begin to make more money."

"What kinds of companies?"

"One is a pharmaceutical company that makes medicines—"

Li's thoughts went to the thousands of Chinese who died every year from adulterated or fake drugs, and he wondered if Zemin were responsible for any of them. The Chinese people had a saying: "The butcher hangs a sheep's head in the window but he sells dog meat." Everyone knew it but no one did anything about it. *How dirty are my son-in-law's hands from all of that?*

"—and they also make Crest toothpaste and Chanel Number Five and Flex shampoo; they sell very well in China."

"You mean he's a director of American companies?"

"No, Chinese companies. Americans have nothing to do with it."

"But those are American products."

"In China, they are Chinese products. Why not? The Americans make huge profits from them; it does not hurt them if our people make money from them, too. Even if the Americans complain, the companies are quite safe because they are owned by the sons of high government officials and military officers. And the products are popular, so everyone is happy."

Li pictured Miranda trying to digest all this.

"And Zemin's other company manufactures TV satellite dishes. The factory is owned by men he knew when he was in the army, and they made him a director because he is shrewd in business. He gets a nice commission on each one he sells, and they sell excellently."

"You can have satellite dishes? And watch anything you want on television?"

"Why not? Oh, you think it is against the law. Well, officially it is, but since the military own the factories everyone looks the other way."

"It seems very strange. Your government violating its own beliefs . . ."

"It is money," Shuiying said, as if that explained everything, and perhaps, Li thought, it did.

Li and Ming returned to the reception room, and when Shuiying spoke to Ming in Chinese, the little girl ran off. "She will wash for dinner, and I must do some work in the kitchen. Forgive me, but I have no cook, you see. Soon I will, when Zemin becomes a partner in the satellite dish company."

"I'd like to help," said Miranda.

"Oh, no, a guest does not help. I will call you when I am ready."

"Please. In America we help each other. And I'd like to watch you make dinner; I could learn so much."

"Ah." Again Shuiying bowed her head in pleasure. "Well, then . . ."

Li watched them go through the dining room and into the kitchen, his gaze lingering on Miranda's fair hair. His love for her was so powerful at that moment that he thought he could not contain it, could not even fully understand it. Every part of my life is hers, he thought; she settles into it as if she belongs here. She does belong here. With me, wherever I am. And what am I going to do about that?

Are you going to America?

He could almost hear Sheng's voice blurt out the question in his office.

ARE YOU GOING TO AMERICA?

It was, after all, not an impossibility. All over the world, people moved from country to country, for one reason or another. Love was as good as any. Better than most.

"Laoyeh!" Ming peered around the corner of the doorway.

Li knelt, and she ran into his arms. "Aren't you supposed to be washing your hands?"

"They're very clean. I can't get them any cleaner. Will you read to me after dinner?"

"Yes."

"Oh, you are so good. And play a game, too?"

"We'll decide that when we see how late it is."

"You have to do twice as many things with me when you don't come so often."

"I'll do three times as many if it's not too late."

"What time is too late?"

He laughed and kissed her. "Let us see when dinner ends and then we will have some idea."

Ming nodded. "I told mama you would read to me and play many many games. She said you would be too busy with your friend. Miranda. She is very pretty, isn't she? She has such a nice smile. Now I have to go upstairs again, so when I come down mama will think I came straight to her." She burrowed her lips against Li's cheek. "You're such a good *laoyeh*," she said, and ran up the stairs.

How did she learn such wisdom? Li wondered. To know that Shuiying expects everyone to come to her first. Or perhaps that is not so much wisdom as self-preservation. How early we all have to learn self-preservation.

"Li, Shuiying wants to know—"

Miranda was coming in from the dining room and he met her halfway and roughly pulled her to him and kissed her. "I love you."

"Shuiying is in the other room! This is her house! What if she saw us?"

"She would be surprised."

"I think she'd be angry. She'd never invite me here again."

"Of course she would. She likes you. She did *tai chi* with you and I have never seen her do that with anyone. She'll invite you many times." Their eyes met, and Li knew that the only way Miranda would ever return to his daughter's home would be if she were staying in China. Living in China. With him.

Are you going to America?

It's not impossible. But neither is it impossible that Miranda would stay here.

Stay with me. Live with me. Be my—

"No, Li." Miranda took a step backward. She had seen it in his eyes. "I don't want to talk about that."

"Later," he said, his voice trembling with new thoughts, new possibilities. "We have to talk about it; we've known that for some time now." He moved away and picked up a carved ivory figure, turning it in his fingers to calm them. "What does Shuiying want to know?"

"Oh." Nervously she ran her fingers through her hair. "Whether you want cold and hot appetizers, or just hot. She says you don't like cold. I didn't know that. I think she's trying to show me that I don't really belong here because I don't know you as well as she does."

"You belong with me. She knows that, whatever she may be pretending. A long time ago I did not like cold appetizers; I've changed. Perhaps daughters don't like to think of their fathers changing. I would like both, and I will tell her so."

"No, I'll tell her. She says she doesn't like men in her kitchen."

Li stood still, his fingers following the contours of the ivory figure as he gazed at the doorway through which Miranda disappeared. *You belong with me. That is what we have to talk about. That is what we have to remember.*

But he put off talking about it, even later, after saying goodbye to Shuiying. She had not invited Miranda to come to dinner again; she had not even said she hoped they would meet again. "I didn't really think she would," Miranda said to Li as they drove to his house. "But I guess a little part of me thought she might." She paused. "And I wanted her to. I thought she liked me."

"She did. She simply does not know what to make of you. That will come. Give her time."

But we have no time.

Both of them thought it. Neither of them said it.

In his house, he locked the door and brought Miranda to him, holding her close, his lips against her hair. "I like coming home with you. I like thinking about coming home with you. You make my house warm and alive." He took her hand.

"I have a surprise in the bedroom. I hope you like it."

Miranda stopped in the doorway as she saw the new silk spread on the bed. "I do like it. Oh, I love it."

The spread was deep blue, almost black, embroidered in dragons and fantastic birds of gold that seemed to flicker beneath the hanging lamp. "It will be better with us on it," said Li. "I bought it for us. Together."

Their clothes slid to the floor; they lay on the bed, and Li kissed the small pulse in Miranda's throat. "Together, wherever we are. Where I can look for you and know I will find you, where I can say your name and know you will reply." His lips slid to her breasts, her stomach, the blond curls between her thighs. "I want you always, your body and your smile, your voice, the look in your eyes . . ."

His mouth parted her thighs, her hands were in his hair, and he tasted the honey of her, golden and sweet, and heard the quickness of her breath and his name on her lips, and then her body rose beneath his mouth and fell back, shuddering.

They stayed that way for a moment,

floating, drifting, without thought, a sweetness in the air curling over them, until, as if
awakening, Li moved along the smoothness of Miranda's body to lie full length
upon her, his body matching hers, curve
into curve, and he came into her with the
sureness and ease and endless gratitude
of someone coming home.

"I missed you all day," Miranda said
when they lay together, her head on his
shoulder, his hand slowly caressing the
outline of her face. "It was as if I could see
you and almost touch you, and everything
else didn't matter."

"Meishi," Li murmured.

"What?"

"That means, it doesn't matter. I said that
today, too, and I was very angry that anything was interfering with my thinking about
you. And now I have something for us." He
went to a cabinet and brought a bottle and
two slender glasses to the bed. "We have
never drunk champagne together and I
thought it was time."

They touched their glasses. "Taittinger,"
Miranda said, reading the label. "Amazing."

"Appropriate, I think." Leaning against
the silk-covered wall, they drank in an easy

silence, drifting again, images moving across their thoughts without context or urgency. Until Miranda said, "We forgot your present. I left it in the car. Would you get it? It's on the back seat."

"I'll be right back." He slipped on a silk robe and was gone only a few minutes before he returned with a shopping bag. But his absence had given Miranda a chance to think about what was outside, and as he came into the bedroom, she said, "Are they still there? Watching us?"

He hesitated, and she knew how easy it would be for him to lie. But he would not lie to her; she believed that. "Still there," he said. "Probably sleeping in their car. We are not exciting subjects."

"Is that all they do? Wait for someone to come in or out?"

Again there was a pause. "No, that is not all they do."

"What else, then?"

"Open my mail, tap my phone—"

"Your telephone?"

"Oh, yes, my phone is tapped." He said it so casually it took Miranda's breath away. "It happens frequently; we do not think about it. All it means is that we are a little more careful what we say. Miranda, I would like to open my present."

She stared at him, at his easy posture and calm face. How terrible to take these things for granted, she thought, and she pitied him, and then her love for him rushed through her, so overwhelming she thought it would wipe out everything else. "Yes," she said. "Please open it."

He kissed her lightly and sat on the edge of the bed, taking from the shopping bag a large flat box wrapped in blue silk. "Most unusual and beautiful," he murmured, untying its silk ribbon. "To wrap a gift in silk."

"For an unusual and beautiful man," Miranda said.

His hands stilled as gratitude and gladness swept through him. He wondered if he would ever take compliments from her for granted. No, impossible, he thought. I will always be grateful; I will always feel this joy that she makes me feel so special.

Always, he thought. How long is always?

"Are you going to open it?" Miranda asked.

"I was appreciating what you said about

me." He lifted the lid. Beneath layers of tissue paper lay a camel-colored cashmere blazer with leather buttons. He lifted it out, the fabric soft and yielding in his hands. "For me," he said, almost wonderingly. "So very fine. Nothing that I own is this excellent."

"Appropriate, I think," said Miranda.

He chuckled. "I like the sound of my words on your lips." He turned the jacket in his hands. "I have not seen anything like this in China."

"Your manufacturers send these abroad. It will have an Armani label in Europe and America."

He leaned over to kiss her. "What an amazing, wonderful gift. You remembered that I once told you I like cashmere."

"Even though you knew nothing about goats; of course I remember. And I wanted to give you something you couldn't buy for yourself."

"Now I will learn about goats. I would like to find the one that stood still to be shorn so that I could have this most wonderful jacket."

She smiled. "It took more than a hundred of them. You can thank them in spirit. Will you try it on?"

"Yes, what a good idea." He stood and put on the jacket, and Miranda laughed as he turned and posed before a full-length mirror and turned again, naked except for the blazer. "Note the perfect cut," he said in a fair imitation of Elsa Klensch on CNN. "Note the sheen, the soft glow of each fiber that only the most high-class goats can provide." He stretched out his arms, the jacket opening wide to give a full view of his lean body. "How it enhances the male figure, giving the impression of youth and vigor that every man longs for in his most salacious dreams."

"Wait," Miranda said, collapsed in laughter. "I can't get my breath."

He laughed with her, giddy with the freedom of nonsense and the power of such complete openness as he had never known.

"Champagne helps with breathing," he said, and refilled their glasses. He sat back, still wearing the jacket, and put his arm around Miranda. "Feel the softness," he murmured. "Sink into its rare warmth and cuddleness. Is there such a word?"

"If there isn't there should be." Miranda kissed him. "I love you. I love it when you're able to laugh."

"Because of you," he said.

Slowly they settled into quietness, talking a little, but mostly drifting again. Just *being,* Li thought. *Being together.*

When he put away the empty bottle and their glasses, Miranda lay back and Li bent to kiss her. But he held back, gazing at her. From beneath her body, gold-embroidered dragons leaped to right and left: heads, tails, outstretched wings, flaring mouths spewing flames, their outlines darkly burnished in the soft light of the hanging lamp. Birds soared among the dragons, poised to dive, with wide beaks and quivering plumage, their eyes devouring the sky, their talons curved to grasp the treasures of the earth. Against blue-black silk and gold threads, Miranda was like a long white flame, soft, radiant, magical.

"How glorious you are," he said, "with dragons and great birds flying all about you. As if you are deep inside all the fairy tales and legends ever told. As if plays would be written about you, and operas, and long, lyrical poems of love, lovely poems of love . . . and I am drunk with love."

Miranda smiled. "You are drunk with champagne."

"Ah, no, though it perhaps played a part in unlocking a reluctant tongue, too long denied a chance to run free, and dance, and fly, and kiss." He kissed her, slowly, then more deeply. "You are my love, my only love, and all my life I have been waiting for you, and for the rest of my life—"

He felt her muscles tighten, and knew that still she was not ready to talk of the future. And was he ready? What would he say? What would he offer, or ask?

"—for the rest of my life, I will drink champagne when I feel like saying 'I love you.' But for now we must talk about tomorrow. Can you leave work early? I have plans."

Miranda smiled sleepily; it was very late and the champagne filled her with warmth and languor. "You have plans for everything."

"Not for us," he said quietly. "Not yet." And then, more briskly, he said, "This is what I have thought of. Tomorrow I would like to take you to Dazhalan Market, and then we will have a special dinner to celebrate your first week in China. We must get there a little early, to see the Summer Palace first."

Your first week in China. Miranda looked at him, but barely saw him. *A week. How could so much have happened in one week? How could I have changed so much?*

And I have four days left.

"And if you can end your meetings early the next few days, we could go to Liulichang for antiques on Thursday, and on Friday the Xiushui Silk Market. And on Saturday the Forbidden City."

He's filling our days. And the nights take care of themselves. And on Sunday morning . . .

"Unless you think I am filling your days too full."

"No. Oh, no. But . . ."

"And there will be time for talking. Because of course we do not plan to sleep very much."

There will be time to sleep on the plane, she thought, and the thought kept her awake, sleepy as she was; she lay quietly beside Li, his warmth warming her as he slept in the way he had, on his back, hands folded on his chest, his breathing slow and even. When she finally slept, she was restless, waking, dozing, waking again to think of airplanes high above vast, indifferent oceans.

But the next morning, since they slept late, they had no time to think of anything but getting to work on time. Miranda showered first, and Li gazed at the long line of her back as she stood at the marble washstand, combing her hair. "What shall I wear to the Summer Palace?" she asked as they dressed, and Li said, "Something casual. Pants with the black jacket from Meiyun."

"I asked Meiyun to have dinner with us. How will that fit in with your sightseeing plans?"

"It will change them. She'll be here day after tomorrow?"

"Yes."

"She could go with us to Liulichang after dinner."

"I'll ask her when I talk to her today."

How easy this is, Li thought as he buttoned his shirt. We are as casual and comfortable as a married couple beginning a new day. *Comfortable. At ease. Familiar. In love.* He ached with unsaid words.

"Oh, how late it is," Miranda said, pulling on her suit jacket. "I can't have breakfast."

"A quick one; we have plenty of—" There was a knock on the door. "Why would they do that?" Li murmured. "They've worked for me long enough to know they are not to interrupt—"

"Father?" Sheng's voice came through the door. "I must talk to you."

Li's eyebrows rose in shock as Miranda shrank back. "What shall we do?" she asked.

"He has never done this," Li murmured. "Something must be terribly wrong. Or he is terribly frightened." He looked at Miranda as if he had just heard her. "We will invite him to join us for breakfast. We have done nothing wrong and we are not hiding. Are we?" He opened the door and Sheng strode in, his hair disheveled, his tie hanging loosely around his neck.

"I have to talk to you; something has happened—" He stopped, and stared at Miranda.

"You've met Miranda," Li said easily. Fear was rising in him, but he would not show it. "We were about to have breakfast; will you join us?"

"No. Father, I have to talk to you!"

"Li, I'll go on to work," Miranda said.

He hesitated, but he knew it was best. "My driver will take you. Please send him back for me. I'll call you later."

"Goodbye," she said to Sheng, briefly met Li's eyes, and left, walking through the courtyards almost blindly, shocked and afraid of all the things she could not name but, because of that, feared even more.

Li watched her through the open door until she was out of his sight. "Now," he said.

"Do you know what this is?" Sheng took from an inside pocket an envelope stuffed with papers. "Your letters to student dissidents. Your telephone lists. Your plans for disrupting the welcoming ceremony for the American president in Tiananmen Square." He began to shout. "How could you do this? First that woman, and now this! You're betraying all of us! You'll ruin all of us!"

"Wait." Li's heart was pounding. He took the envelope and pulled out a sheaf of typewritten papers. They were all signed in his handwriting. Stunned, he read them. "I never saw these before. They are not mine. I have no idea where they came from."

"Your desk! Where else would they come from?"

"Some other place." He looked steadily at his son. "They came from somewhere else before they arrived at my desk. They did not originate there." The room was silent as he read and reread the pages and his signature. It was not his style of writing but he had never written political agitation before, so one could say it might be his. But then he saw that something was wrong with the signature. It was close to his, but not exact; the strokes were tighter, more cramped, less sweeping than his. It was not totally different from his, but different enough for him to know.

He looked up. "How did you find these?"

"What?"

"You went into my desk. When?"

"This morning . . ."

"Do you do that often?"

"Of course not!"

"But this time you did."

"I was looking for something."

"Obviously. Looking for what?"

Sheng looked at the papers in Li's hand. "Why should I believe they aren't yours? They were in your desk, they're signed with your name, and I recognized your handwriting right away."

"Signatures can be forged, you know that. What were you looking for in my desk?"

"You don't know anything about what's in them? All those lists, names of students, telephone numbers, plans for disrupting the welcoming ceremonies?"

"Nothing. I've told you I have nothing to do with all this. Why are you in such a hurry to believe it?"

"They were in your desk! Signed by you! What am I supposed to believe?"

"That something is wrong about this whole thing. You know I have nothing to do with dissidents, and you should know me well enough to know I would never be part of making a scene with the American president."

"That woman knows dissidents. You told me she's being followed because of it. And she spends the night here! You're mixed up in something; the government knows it, or they wouldn't be following you. You told me she delivered a letter; you said—"

"I know what I said. It has no importance. She did not know what the implications were. She has nothing to do with any of this. *What were you looking for in my desk?*"

Sheng frowned. "I didn't know," he said at last. "I just thought there might be something there. I looked in mine, too."

"*Your* desk?" Agitated, angry, Li stood up. "You suspected someone in our company of framing one or both of us, is that right? And now it seems that someone *is* framing me. So you went to work early this morning to look in our desks, is that right? Is it?"

"Not quite." It was almost a whisper.

"Well what is wrong with it? Stop this childish game you are playing and tell me what is going on. Whom do you suspect in our company? And why?"

Sheng slumped in his chair. "Not in the company. Out of it. *Biao zi yang de,*" he swore ferociously. "I thought, when he wanted to use my telephone, and asked for the keys to the office, I thought it was a reasonable idea, he said he needed a place where his calls couldn't be traced, but the more I thought about it the more peculiar it seemed."

"You gave someone the keys to the office," Li said quietly, holding in his growing rage. "Who was it?"

"Pan Chao. He wanted to make some phone calls."

"There are telephones all over Beijing."

"I know. That's why I began to wonder about it. I thought maybe he wanted to check up on me."

"Or to plant something in my desk. Or yours. And then what? Report to the State Security Bureau that they should search my desk. But no one has. When did you give him the keys?"

"Yesterday afternoon; I saw him after our meeting with the construction presidents."

"When did he give them back?"

"He hasn't, yet. I didn't need them; I gave him a set I found in my desk."

"For the office," Li muttered. "But if he is serious, the office would not be enough." He looked around the room. "Nothing out of place. But he would be careful . . ."

"You think he came here?" Sheng asked. "Broke into your house? But you were home last night. You're always home."

"I was having dinner at Shuiying's last night."

"Tsao," Sheng exclaimed and they dashed from the living room into Li's study. They had to hunt for it, but they found the envelope buried in a file beneath rolls of blueprints and specifications. *"Tsao,"* Sheng said again despairingly, and slumped against the desk. Li stood a little apart, his fear cold within him.

"Why would anyone do this? If State Security had found these, I would have been doomed." *Added to my student newspaper, my friendship with Professor Ye, my closeness to Miranda, whom they already suspect, even the meetings with labor representatives that are being held at my instigation, in my office, with construction company presidents who think I am subversive. . . .* "Why?" he asked again. "Why does Chao want to have me arrested?"

Forcing the words out, Sheng said, "They might want you out of the way."

" 'They?' You mean both of your partners? What is it to them where I am?"

"They think I should be president of the company. They talk about it all the time. They think I would run it better."

"Why?"

Sheng winced. "We need younger people," he faltered. "Better able to understand China today, more flexible, more *part* of things."

"And you think that describes you?"

"Not . . . really. I thought about it last night. I don't think I can. I mean, I don't know enough."

"Yes, we talked about this before," Li said, but more gently this time. He felt great sorrow for his son, that he had to admit so much to a father he had always wanted to defeat. But he could not linger on that now. "What is it they want you to do with this company if you are president?"

Sheng shook his head, back and forth, back and forth. "I can't tell you."

"You'll damn well tell me, and right away!" He waited. "Did you hear me? Look at me! I'm talking to you! Who is it you're protecting, them or me?"

"I have to think!" Sheng shouted. "It's not so easy . . ."

"I don't give a damn whether it's easy or

not. Your friend has put my whole life at risk . . . I could lose everything—"

"He's not my friend." The words came out jerkily. "I thought he was, but . . ."

"Then why are you protecting him?"

Still slumped against the desk, Sheng bent over, holding his stomach. "*Tsao*," he said resignedly. "They don't really care if you're arrested, or go to America, or what; they just want you gone, so I can take over the company."

"And do what with it? Something I would not allow, is that it?"

"You see, they kept saying I would be a fine, modern president, and I thought they meant it—I wanted to believe they meant it—but I think they were really planning to use me. Last night . . ." He groaned. "Last night Wu Yi asked me a lot of questions about Chao and Enli, whether they admired me and if I thought they told me the truth. It was very strange: she never asks about my work and I said it was like a test and I asked her if I'd passed and she laughed. But she kept asking questions, and finally she said that when they talked about my being president of the company it sounded . . . *rehearsed.* And she's an actress, she knows these things, so I paid attention. You know?"

"Yes," Li said, sadness for his son filling him again. Wu Yi, running after the powerful and successful, questioning his son to see if he met the test. Yes, of course it was a test. Sheng had it right, without knowing it.

"She said she thought they weren't honest; she thought they were using me to get something, and she didn't like to see somebody close to her being used. You know, weak enough to be used. And I kept thinking about that, and what you'd said, that I'm not ready to take over the company, and you see me at work, but Chao and Enli don't, so why would they be so sure I could do it?"

"And then?" Li asked.

Sheng spread his hands, his head down. "We were in bed and she'd gone to sleep and I kept thinking, and . . . I started crying. A goddam *baby*." He shook his head. "It was terrible, so terrible . . . I couldn't stop; I kept thinking about you and how hard it must be for you to admit that I haven't learned what most men my age have learned, how to run a company, a legitimate company with a good reputation, and I thought, you don't enjoy criticizing me, but you do it because you know I'm not ready, no matter what they keep saying. And you're right; I know that. I haven't learned enough; I've been too busy plotting with Chao and Enli, and pretending I was powerful because they liked me. And then I remembered that I hadn't let them use All-China's warehouses . . ."

"For what?"

There was a long pause and it was almost as if Li could see him deciding to make the leap to the other side. Burning his bridges. Yes, we all have to do that, he thought, at one time or another. "We have contracts with factories," Sheng said, "to manufacture building components with foreign labels—American, European, Japanese, Israeli—and we have contractors who buy them from us instead of the ones their architects specify."

"At a much lower price," Li said, immediately seeing the whole scheme. "These are not structural components?"

Sheng shook his head.

"So no building will fall down because they're used, but everything inside will wear out faster."

Sheng looked at his father with admiration. "Yes."

"So you need a warehouse to store the faked goods, and your partners want ours."

"And our trucks, to ship them around the country. Nobody would question ours, you know, the company is so respectable . . ." He spread his hands. "So I figured that was why they wanted me to be president, and when I let myself say that it seemed that I'd lost everything: I didn't have partners, I didn't have a company, I had no way to get anywhere. And then I started crying, damn, it was hideous, and Wu Yi woke up and told me to stop and I couldn't, you know, I couldn't, I was shaking and crying and she started screaming at me to get out, that I wasn't the man she'd thought I was, that she didn't know what she'd ever seen in me . . ." He looked at Li with tired eyes. "She kicked me out and I was still crying—*tsao,* what a baby I was—and feeling alone, and lost . . ."

Li put his arms around his son and held him tightly, as if he were indeed a baby. Or a child. Wasn't that exactly what he had said to Miranda? *My son has much growing up to do.* Perhaps now, he had taken the first step. I love you, my son, Li thought, and if you want my help, I will give it to you, as much as I can.

Sheng pulled out of Li's embrace, but not harshly; he was still caught in his recollections. "And then I thought, if I don't go along with them what will they do to me? I've always known they would get rid of me any time I wasn't useful to them, but I would have stayed until I *had* to leave because I didn't know what else to do, but then I found these papers and *I couldn't do that to you!*"

The words were wrenched from him and Li saw how difficult the choice had been, between admitting his weakness in caring for his father, and a future at his partners' side that still beckoned, even knowing what he did.

The telephone rang, and Li snatched it up. "Mr. Yuan," his secretary said, "the Security people just left; they went through your desk and all your files; they would not let me call you. Will you be coming in today?"

"Yes. Did they take anything with them?"

"No, nothing."

"If you're sure of that, you may put things away."

As he hung up, Sheng said, "They were in the office."

"Yes. They'll be here soon. You must go."

"We have to hide these papers."

Li looked at the envelope in his hand. "Leave them on top of the desk," he said wryly. "Anything out in the open does not interest them."

"No, how can you make jokes about this?"

"Sometimes it is the only way to survive." Li met his son's frightened eyes. "All right, I won't joke about it. Sheng, I'm going to put these documents away and you will not see what I do. This is my secret and mine alone."

"Yes." Sheng nodded, accepting his father's protection without argument. "Thank you."

Li left him in the study and went to the living room. He rolled back three feet of the large rug near his scholar's rock, lifted a square of parquet, and tucked the envelope inside. When he had replaced the parquet and readjusted the rug, he stood in the doorway of his study. "Now go," he said to Sheng. "You must not be found here. You are too close to me; they would suspect you."

Sheng nodded. But his footsteps slowed as he reached the door, and he stood there, his back to Li. Finally a long sigh broke from him and Li saw him square his shoulders. He turned and walked back into the room. "They don't think I'm close to you. Why would they? What have I done to make anyone think I was close to you?"

Once again Li was filled with sadness. "Very little. Until now."

"Exactly." Sheng came to his father. "This is my fault, letting Chao and Enli make trouble for you, making them believe I'd go along with them. People shouldn't begin things if they don't think about where they might end up. I should have known where this was going when they started talking about using our company. But I didn't. It's what you said: I'm not ready for anything."

Li shook his head. "You must not blame yourself."

"Why not? I have a lot to straighten out in my head; maybe this is a way to start." A silence fell. It seemed to Li that his son leaned slightly toward him, as if to embrace him, as he had embraced Sheng the other day. But the moment passed. Someday, perhaps, Li thought; how many self-discoveries can I expect Sheng to absorb in one day?

Sheng stood before a mirror to comb his hair and knot his tie. He buttoned his suit jacket, straightened his collar. "We'll wait for them together," he said.

At that moment, Li admired his son more than ever before. "You still have not had breakfast," he said. "Shall we wait in the kitchen?"

Chapter 11

Miranda arrived at the Palace Hotel in time to change her suit and gather her sketches and notes for Tang Po. She kept looking at the telephone as she moved about the room, wanting to call Li, needing to hear his voice, to hear that the frightening moment when she had left his house had led to nothing; that whatever Sheng had had to say did not involve them and could be dealt with easily.

She did not really believe that. But she did not pick up the telephone. He knew how to reach her; he would call when he could.

Exactly on time, she greeted Tang Po in the hotel meeting room she had reserved for that day and the next. He was a small man with alabaster-smooth skin, a slightly pursed mouth, and an aristocratic air that took her aback.

"You see, Miss Miranda," he said in a reedy voice, "we wish to expand our line, to make Nantong Woolen Mill one of the finest, the very best, in China. But we will do this slowly, without haste, beginning with two, only two, products, and watch our sales performance, our success or failure in these new ventures."

Miranda smiled. Evidently Mr. Tang liked to say everything in two different ways. Well, that way he would never be misunderstood.

She spread her sketches on the table. "I have cashmere robes and throws," she said. "The robes are for men and women; I have some ideas for children's, as well. They may be different from others you have seen—"

"Different, yes." He was studying the sketches so closely his nose almost brushed the paper. "Theatrical," he said.

"Not all of them." She pointed to a red

and black check, and a blue and green plaid. "These are for country wear, rather than city."

He looked up and smiled slyly. "Not Chinese country. Paris country."

"For now," Miranda said, "but someday . . ."

"Ah, yes. So many people in China making money, getting rich, young people becoming Western, very modern; it seems strange to an old man like me, but for business it is good."

Young people like Sheng, Miranda thought as Tang Po went back to poring over the sketches. If everything is all right, they'd be at work.

"Would you excuse me?" she asked Mr. Tang. "A brief telephone call."

He waved his hand. "Yes, yes, I am happily occupied. Such fine designs."

But Li's secretary said he was not there. "If you would care to leave a message . . ." but Miranda said it was not necessary. She would call back.

"This robe, the embroidery," Tang Po said. "Perhaps each flower could have its name embroidered below it?"

"Yes, what a good idea." Once again,

Miranda shut out everything else. "Perhaps below some flowers and beside others."

He beamed. "Very elegant."

"It increases the cost," Miranda said. "Are the names written in one character, or more than one?"

"Some are more than one. It is all right. This will be our very expensive, top-price robe; it will show how reasonable, how moderate, the others are, and attract customers who think something is not good, not desirable, unless it costs a great deal, and also those who do not need to think of cost at all. There are many of those in the world, are there not?"

"A great many. You are very wise."

"And you are an excellent designer, a truly fine designer, and a lovely lady, and it is very good that I came to Beijing. Now let us discuss your designs."

They settled down to work. Miranda tried to keep herself from looking at the telephone until, an hour later, when Tang Po said, "Perhaps you should try to make your call again," she knew she had in fact looked at it more than once.

"Thank you," she said. "A moment only."

But once again Li was not there. Where

could he be? I can call him at home, she thought. Just to see if he's all right.

Oh, yes, my phone is tapped. That casual statement, no more dramatic than a comment on the weather. But it had chilled her, and she would never call him there; she would not let them eavesdrop on anything she and Li said to each other.

So she would not call him at home, and she had no idea where else he might be. I don't know him well enough, she thought, and, remembering their love-making, thought what a strange and topsy-turvy affair they were having.

"These robes for children," Tang Po said when she returned to her chair. "Very nice, yes, very nice. Perhaps matching ones for the parents?"

"Yes, there could be, for many of them. I thought of that, but I've had no time to make separate sketches." She took out her notes. "I thought of appliqués on pockets, collars, cuffs, sashes: animals for both children and adults; cartoon characters, probably just for children; stars and planets, cars, airplanes, ships and boats, flowers, probably just for girls and women. The list is really endless. I'd begin with three or four designs and if they sell well, expand to others. I also have another idea, which you might find interesting."

They bent over the sketches spread across the table. The next two hours passed quickly, and Miranda was able to hold off returning to the telephone. In fact, in spite of the knot of fear in her stomach, she enjoyed the time with Tang Po, because she liked him and he was excited about her new designs. She had not been sure he would approve them, but he had not rejected any of them, and even when he had his own suggestions, he deferred to her expertise. The perfect client, Miranda thought, grateful to him for making the time pass quickly.

At noon, he stood and nodded his head rapidly. "A productive morning, time well spent. I thank you, Miss Miranda. This afternoon we will look at your designs for throws. And now, may I invite you to lunch here, in the hotel?"

She was so tense she almost wept at his courtliness and kindness. "No, thank you, Mr. Tang, you are very kind, but I have other work I must do."

He bowed his head. "Then I will see you here at one o'clock."

Upstairs, in her room, Miranda called Li's office. "He was here, Mrs. Graham, but he has left," said the secretary. "He asked me to tell you that he will see you at four-thirty this afternoon and if that is not convenient you may tell me now."

"No, it's fine." Her heart was pounding. He's all right. Whatever happened this morning, he can still be with me. He'll see me at four-thirty. Four and a half hours from now. How can I wait that long?

Tang Po, with his kindness, made waiting easier. For two hours they talked about cashmere throws: fringed throws, throws with satin trim, throws with embroidery or woven designs or decorative button detail or appliqué, throws with pockets for books or reading glasses, throws that reversed to velvet or heavy satin, throws so fine they could double as shawls.

"You have done wonders with these," Tang Po said just before three o'clock. "The choices are narrower, less broad, than for robes."

Miranda laughed. "To put it mildly. Thank you. I'm sorry I have to leave early, but we can begin tomorrow at whatever time you like."

"Nine o'clock will be fine. I hope you have a pleasant evening."

"Yes. Thank you."

Upstairs again, she showered quickly and put on her silver-gray suit with the burgundy blouse from Meiyun. And my bracelet, she thought, slipping it on again; she wore it everywhere. And then it was time to be downstairs, waiting in the lobby, so he would see her when he arrived.

"My dear one," he said, not touching her but standing close, "I am so very glad to see you."

"Are you all right? What happened this morning?"

"Yes, we will discuss that. Come, my driver is waiting."

They made their way through the clusters of businessmen, and tourists greeting each other as if they were long-lost relatives. Miranda understood that now, from the times she heard English on the streets and in the restaurants of China: when travelers hear strangers speaking their own language, the strangers seem closer than all the foreigners surrounding them. But then she knew that she was closest of all to Li, and that the two of them were separate from the noisy crowd, like wayfarers sheltered in a cave, warm and dry while a deluge drums above.

So far, we have always been able to find shelter.

In Li's car, with the partition behind the driver tightly closed, she said, "Now tell me. I was so frightened."

He told her, briefly, minimizing the consequences to him if the documents had been found. "But they weren't; my dear friend Professor Ye had lived in my house for a year during the Cultural Revolution, after Meiyun had been sent away, and he had carved out a few hiding places for his most treasured books and papers."

"So you hid them. Are they still there?"

"Yes, until we decide what to do with them."

"But I don't understand. If Sheng's partners had been planning this, wouldn't he have known it?"

"It seems they do not take him into their confidence: one of his many recent discoveries. As for planning it, I think they took advantage of the fact that I am being followed. It made it easier to suggest that the

State Security Bureau search my office and my home."

"So it comes back to me. If it weren't for me, you wouldn't be followed, and the Security people wouldn't—"

"No, no, you must not blame yourself. They would have searched my house and office anyway, on a telephone tip; it is how they justify their existence. Security forces do this often and they know they will be disappointed a certain percentage of the time; they get many tips, usually from disgruntled employees, and many are exaggerated or completely made up."

"You mean, employees plant incriminating documents on their bosses, and then call the Security people?"

"Usually there are no documents; the accusation is enough. The search makes a terrible mess and some people feel that is satisfactory revenge for whatever wrongs they think they have suffered."

"Ugly," Miranda murmured. "Terrible and ugly."

"There is always ugliness in life; that is why we search for beauty. But Sheng and I can deal with this because it is not unfamiliar. And one good thing has come out of it: we are on the same side, mostly because he became frightened enough to come to me."

"Not only frightened. He cared about you."

"Yes, is that not astonishing? All this time, beneath his hostility there was something about caring. The communists could not wipe it out, and neither could the chase for money. Now here we are at Dazhalan, and I have put all this into a compartment and locked the door, and we will not think about it for the rest of the day and night."

"You can't mean that. You can't do that."

"I intend to try. There is nothing Sheng and I can do tonight. If there is nothing to do, I will not let it consume me. I told you: this is something we learn. It is like a chameleon putting on a new coat to deal with new conditions. I can take off the coat tomorrow; for today, I wear it, and so will you."

She studied the hard lines of his face that she knew so well by now: harder than usual, anger just below the surface, distraction in his eyes. But determined. He had made up his mind, and though it was clearly not as easy as he made it out to be, she would not make it harder by refusing to join him. If he wanted to lock his compartment, she would not force it open.

The driver had opened Miranda's door and they walked from the quiet of the car into the maelstrom of Dazhalan. From the description in her guidebook, Miranda had pictured something like an American shopping mall, and so she stared in disbelief as Li led her into the narrow *hutong,* no wider than an alley in an American city, so crowded that the shops could barely be seen. Everything was old, from the crumbling and potholed street to the faded brick buildings with sagging roofs, but the atmosphere was festive, with rock music blaring from invisible speakers and shoppers chattering non-stop as they bored their way into and out of the shops.

Miranda and Li, crushed together, made their way into some of the shops, and Miranda soon found herself shoving back with all her strength to have space to inspect everything from Mongolian hot pots to fur hats and cameras. Across the way, she caught a glimpse of a pickle shop so jammed with shoppers she decided it was not worth the effort to get closer, and, next to it, one that seemed to be a pharmacy. She pointed to it and Li nodded and they plunged into the crush to cross to the other side.

Standing in the doorway, Miranda gazed at glass display cases and shelves crammed with boxes, jars and plastic bags. At the back, in a tiny booth, a black-clad man perched on a high stool. His long gray hair was tied back with a piece of string and his eyes were magnified by thick lenses in horn-rimmed glasses. A long line of people waited to see him, some holding babies, others stooped over canes, a few reading newspapers or magazines.

"What are they waiting for?" she asked.

"He's a doctor," Li said. "Probably retired. This is the most famous traditional medicine shop in Beijing, and he is diagnosing medical problems and prescribing medicines that his patients can buy here."

"Without examining them first?"

"He would tell you that he has seen and heard everything in a lifetime of examinations, and in the wisdom of his years he can diagnose and prescribe without any more of them."

She looked at him. "Do you come here when you're sick?"

"Fortunately I do not get sick. But if I did, certainly I would come here. People speak highly of him and the line waiting to see him is far shorter than those in the hospital. Would you like to buy something? Ginseng root, ground tiger bone, fungus, deer antlers, dried sea horse, rhinoceros horn, dried slugs, snake wine, plus of course the obvious ones like hyacinth, angelica, loranthi, pubescentis, white paeonia, and a thousand or so others."

"You're making fun of me."

"Only a little. And with love. I am trying to tell you—"

"That you take this seriously? You really would go to him and swallow things like that?"

"I would," he said gently. She could barely hear him in the noise of the crowds and the blasts of rock music, but she knew that he thought her foolish for dismissing his kind of medicine so easily, and she tightened in annoyance. But she also was confused, because Li was not a fool or a superstitious peasant; he was an urban professional, educated, well-read, smart.

So how could he believe in this nonsense?

"It works, you know," he said. "Your
Western medicine is now discovering that.
China has had five thousand years to
refine the use of plants and animal parts,
and slowly your doctors are admitting that
we are right. They recently decided that
acupuncture is a useful technique. If they
had not been so quick to call us primitive
and stupid, you would have benefited from
it for decades."

"I never said you were primitive and stupid."

"Of course not. I don't hold you responsible for the arrogance of Western medicine."

"Arrogance! Do you have to tear down
everything that is part of my life?"

He looked startled. "I was not thinking of
it as yours."

"America!" she cried. "When I'm in
China, everything American is me!" She
put a hand to her mouth. "Why are we
quarreling?"

"Are we? Perhaps we are just having a
discussion." He was jostled by a customer,
and he made a gesture of frustration. "This

is no place to talk. We'll go somewhere else. Before we leave, would you like to buy something?"

"Yes. Aspirin."

"This shop does not carry any. A pharmacy nearby will have it; shall we go there?"

"No." She was ashamed. "I'm sorry; I didn't mean to ridicule . . . I mean, I understand that you all take it seriously. But it seems like hocus-pocus to me."

"Someday you may change your mind."

She started to argue, then let it go. "I would like to buy something," she said, thinking that Adam and Lisa might be amused by it. "Fungus. I'll buy some fungus."

"May I suggest something else? Ground tiger bone. It looks like a powder, but its name is far more exotic than fungus, and we will have them put a colorful label on it."

"Fine," she said, and then, "I'm sorry; I didn't mean to sound arrogant."

"You are not arrogant. You are my love." Waiting in line to pay for the ground tiger bone, his voice was very low. "You and I do not fit into categories. We are two people in love. We have nothing to do with countries

and governments or the crowds of Dazhalan or all the herbal medicines in the
world."

But they had everything to do with countries and governments, and Miranda knew
they both were thinking that as they left the
shop, the tiger bone in her purse, encased
in a small clear bag with a bright label covered with Chinese characters. They walked
the rest of the way through Dazhalan, past
a group of theaters, past stores with mannequins wearing silk and wool and poly-
ester suits—

"Li," Miranda said suddenly, "why are all
the mannequins Western? Even in billboards and magazine and newspaper ads,
they all look American. It's very odd."

"A sign of our inferior feelings." He
stopped beside a mannequin of a blond,
blue-eyed woman, tall and willowy, wearing a suit that was a copy of a Calvin Klein.
"Our people still believe that only Western
things are the newest style. If our mannequins were Chinese, the people would
think the clothes they wore were of poor
quality, or last year's style. That will change
someday, when we think we are truly as
good as anyone."

"How sad," Miranda said, as if she herself had not just thought that the Chinese were superstitious and gullible for believing in the potency of roots and herbs and bones and flowers.

"Shall we go?" Li asked. "We need some time to explore the Summer Palace before dinner."

They walked on until Miranda stopped at a shop window filled with jade. "Do we have time for me to buy something for Lisa and my mother?"

"We will make time."

The shop was no bigger than a closet, with flat trays crammed with hundreds of jade necklaces and bracelets. Miranda picked up a bracelet and turned it over and over, watched closely by a wizened man on a stool in the corner. "It doesn't look at all like mine. Is it really jade?"

"Less fine than yours, but still jade." Li picked up a necklace of dark green hearts. "And so is this. Do you think Lisa would like it?"

"Oh, yes. But—" She took it from him and turned it in her hands. "I'd like to buy her something that glows the way mine does. This one is pretty, but it's so flat."

"I think this is better for a young girl," Li said. "If we are given the rarest of treasures when we are young, what do we have to look forward to?"

Miranda gave him a long look. She glanced at her wrist. "This was an expensive bracelet, wasn't it?"

"No more than fine jade is worth. Now, if you think Lisa would like this one, I should determine what price you will pay for it."

"The price tag says five hundred yuan."

"Which is far too high and, in any event, means almost nothing, except to unwary tourists." In rapid Chinese he and the vendor bargained, their voices crossing and sliding, each of them looking astonished or shocked or insulted at each offer. At last Li turned to Miranda. "One hundred sixty yuan. About twenty dollars."

"*Twenty dollars?* It doesn't seem fair; how can he make a living?"

"He will still make a good profit. I told you: it is not a high-quality jade and labor is cheap in China."

"Then I'll take it."

"And for your mother . . ." Li ran his fingers lightly over several of the flat trays, and plucked from one of them a long necklace of pale pink, irregularly shaped stones. "Do not look as if you want this too much." He handed it to Miranda, and turned again to the vendor, to begin bargaining. At last he took the necklace from Miranda. "We do not want it," he said emphatically, and leaned over to put it back.

"But I do," Miranda objected. "It's very beautiful. I'm willing to pay more for it."

"And you will. But not what he stubbornly insists on." With his hand on her arm he turned her to walk away when the vendor's shrill voice came after them. Once again the bargaining began, and soon Li had his wallet out.

"No, I'll pay—" Miranda began.

"You'll pay me back," he said shortly, counting, and when the necklaces had been packed in small fabric-covered boxes, the lids fastened with a tiny piece of bone slipped through a silk loop, they did walk away. "Forgive me, but there is a time not to interrupt. Of course you will pay me; they are your gifts for your daughter and your mother. Your mother's necklace is sixty dollars. I thought that was fair; it is good jade."

"Thank you," Miranda said. "I have no idea how to bargain."

"The first rule, perhaps the only rule, is, never show that you want something. After that, it is simply a question of endurance."

Miranda was silent as they drove to the Summer Palace. Primitive medicine and sophisticated jade of many degrees of fineness. How did people adjust to swinging in such wide arcs between one extreme and the other? Unless they're not so extreme, and I just don't understand them, she thought.

The Summer Palace, once a royal park, was now a vast public preserve, lush with pavilions and palaces, menageries, gardens in the last stage of their fall splendor, and the huge expanse of Kunming Lake. Miranda and Li strolled through the gardens, talking of their childhoods.

"What was your favorite color?" Li asked.

"Blue. What was yours?"

"Green. Why did you like blue?"

"The sky was blue, and the sky was freedom and infinite possibilities. Why did you like green?"

"For growth and renewal and the mystery of unfolding promise. How much alike we are! And what were your favorite books? And dreams. Did you have wonderful dreams of what you would do when you grew up?"

"I dreamed I'd be a movie star." She stopped and looked around. "There's no one here. How incredible, in China. Where is everyone?"

"This is Suzhou Creek, not on tourist itineraries, so almost no one comes. I want to kiss you."

"Outside? In public?"

"The public is at the lake, and in any case we are hidden by bushes and trees." They kissed, holding each other as if for the first time, everything new: the fresh smell of gardens, the sound of the creek, the breeze brushing past them. How many things we haven't done, Miranda thought. Little things, like kissing outside, and big things like . . . kissing outside. Feeling free enough to kiss outside. Hundreds, millions of things not done. A lifetime of things not done.

Li's lips moved along Miranda's cheek, her closed eyes, her throat, her mouth. "How new this is, to kiss you in a park. I want to kiss you here and in other parks, and inside buildings, and everywhere; I want to drink you and eat you, take you into me and hold you there, part of me, forever and ever."

Footsteps clattered nearby, and they sprang apart. Miranda ran her hands through her hair. An elderly man with a child came around a bend, followed by another child and then a young couple, and Li murmured, "Never quite alone." They turned to walk on. "Did you say you wanted to be a movie star?"

"Oh, for about a month; I was always changing when I was young. What did you dream of?"

"Being a drummer in a jazz band. I thought there was nothing more American than that. But there was no jazz or jazz band in China then, so I decided to be a poet. I am not a good poet and never was, but it seemed safe to sit in a hidden corner and write about beautiful things, or even ugly things in a beautiful way."

"And did you?"

"Yes, but as I said, I was not a good poet, so eventually I decided to build. Tall, mighty buildings that would slice the sky and make people think how powerful I must be to create such things."

"But you told me you are not powerful."

"And I am not. I might want people to think I am, out of some kind of childish vanity, but in reality I know that in this society, at this time, I am powerless."

Instinctively, Miranda looked behind her. A few people strolled in small groups, a boy and girl chased a ball, a baby cried and was picked up. As usual, she saw no one watching them. "What a terrible feeling," she said.

"Only when you long for power, or need it. What most people want is to live quietly, to find love and friendship, to make enough money for a comfortable life, to have small successes that give pleasure and a sense of accomplishment. For that, all we need is to be left alone."

"But they don't leave you alone in China."

"When that happens we retreat into our shells and wait until a calmer time."

"Is that what you're going to do now? They're trying to frame you, and you're going to retreat into your shell?"

"There are many ways to survive in China; that is one of them."

"You didn't do it when it would have been safer to stop seeing me."

Li stopped walking. "No," he said slowly. "I did not do it then."

"I'm sorry," Miranda said quickly. "Please forgive me. I have no right to criticize you; I don't know anything about it."

"You know about courage." He was gazing past her, at a temple silhouetted against a fiery sunset. "Sometimes we forget about courage. We become tired and cautious and want only peace, which is perhaps a kind of death." He looked at Miranda. "But I found you and then I wanted life, with all its beauty and uncertainties and danger. And hope." He picked up a stone from the path and rolled it in his palm, then suddenly flung it into a row of bushes. "I did not want this! I have had my fill of turmoil and tragedy."

"I'm sorry," she said again, her words muted. "I should have kept quiet."

They walked in silence. "But you are right," Li said at last. "I might talk about crawling into a shell, I might even think that I want to, but it is too late: I turned my back on that when I stayed with you. I chose life, and now I must figure out how to live it."

"What does that mean?"

He was silent. Then: "This part does not concern you."

"Li, don't shut me out. I want to share this with you."

"Without knowing what I am talking about?"

"Yes."

"Well, then. There are ways I can take care of Sheng's partners so that they do not bother him or me again. If I play by their rules."

"What does that mean: play by their rules?"

"Do things that I know are wrong. Be a person I do not much like."

"But—"

"But sometimes it is necessary. Sometimes it is either that . . . or crawl into a shell."

"Will Sheng play by those rules?"

Li gave a small laugh. "They are the only ones he believes in. He would be happy to . . . how do you say it? Do his partners in. Punish them so that he can be free of them."

"Is that really what he wants?"

He gave her a quick look. "You understand so much. Yes, that is the problem. If he really wants to. I suppose, before I ask him to join me in doing his partners in, I should be sure of what he wants. I can do it myself, of course, and I will, if I must." He stopped, then chuckled. "It seems I have made up my mind to go ahead with this. You see, my Miranda, what being with you has done for me." He leaned toward her, to kiss her, but suddenly people were everywhere and they stepped back, away from each other, and without speaking turned to walk on. "Where were we?" Li said, trying for lightness. "Dreams. Weren't we talking about dreams? Yes, of course. You were telling me what you dreamed as a child."

"I don't know how you do this," Miranda said, almost angrily. "You can't really lock a compartment and convince yourself that nothing is there."

"Please," he said quietly, "talk to me about these new subjects. It makes life seem normal."

"Oh." She gave a small nod. "Well, when I was a child. Oh, I dreamed of so many things. Of being a writer and a carpenter and a ballerina and a designer. And of course a wife. We all assumed we'd be wives, my friends and I; that was not a dream, it was destiny. For the other dreams, my father said I wasn't beautiful enough to be a movie star, and publishing was too irrational for anyone to depend on it for a living, and he was sure I'd cut off a thumb or something if I became a carpenter, and I wasn't particularly graceful, so how could I be a ballerina? He did think I could be a designer, since I'd designed sets and costumes for high school plays, but he kept telling me that marriage was the safest. That way I'd always be taken care of."

"Yes, you said they were fearful people."

"Of most things," Miranda murmured, and thought again of how far she had come this week.

Li pulled her hand through his arm and they walked along the creek, through gardens that stretched away on all sides, until they came to a quiet grove of pines and turned onto the path that cut through it. "And what did you read? Books of love, like most girls?"

"Mysteries and westerns. I loved Zane Grey and—"

"Zane Grey! So did I! One of my father's boxes had many of his books. How wonderful, that we share so much! Do you remember . . ." He rattled off a list of characters who strode through Zane Grey's stories. "And the land! I could smell the sage and feel the wind across the prairie and hear hoofbeats and the shouts of cattlemen. Your West was my dream: it was freedom, anarchy, brutality, beauty. Everything a young boy wants. And then I found them, but not the way I wanted." He stopped beside a temple adorned with small statues of Buddha in carved niches, and said thoughtfully, "I have found anarchy and brutality in modern China; I have found freedom in my thoughts. I have found beauty with you. Beauty and love and freedom. Come, I want to show you something."

At the edge of the water stood a strange boat. "Marble," said Li, standing close to Miranda as tour groups walked past, behind guides lecturing and answering questions. "Restored, as was the entire Summer Palace, by the Empress Cixi with money meant for the Chinese navy. One of the many follies that make up Chinese history."

Miranda shook her head. "How can you be proud of your country when you say so many harsh things about it?"

"I still recognize its strengths and beauties; I know how great it can be. You do the same with your country."

"Americans aren't harsh about their country; they love it."

"They say that their government is greedy, wasteful, full of sex and campaign money scandals, that their senators and representatives are concerned only with getting re-elected. Americans want government to stay out of their lives. They think their government is no good."

"You keep making all these pronouncements but you don't understand anything about democracy. Americans criticize a lot of things, because they can. No one will have a secret trial or put them in jail for something they said. So they say whatever they feel like, and sometimes they exaggerate, to make a point."

"They don't really mean the government should stay out of their lives?"

"Some of them do, some of the time. They're happy to take government help after a flood or tornado, or when they want an airport or new highway, or more police. A lot of people are confused about what government should and shouldn't do, but at least they're debating it in public, instead of thinking about it inside a jail cell. Why can't you understand that? Just because we criticize America, doesn't mean we don't love it."

"Yes, exactly. Just as in China."

"But there's a difference," she said stubbornly. "You can't say these things out loud—"

"You have heard me say them."

"To me. In private. I'll bet if you called a meeting and made speeches attacking your government, you'd be in jail before you knew it."

"Give us time," he said, very quietly, and Miranda felt a stab of pain. Why did she have to attack China, when he had made it so clear that he cared deeply about it and hoped it would see better times?

That's why. Because he does care, and I don't want him to. I want him to say that America is better, a better place to live. I want him to want to live there.

And she knew then that she had been wanting that for some time, that it had crept into her thoughts, taken root and flowered, and now she could no longer ignore it.

The light faded, the tour groups returned to their buses, and still they stood, looking out over a darkening lake. "You see how much alike we are," Li said at last. "We both wanted to be writers, we loved Zane Grey, we found professions where we create things, we criticize our countries but still love them. And we both have American fathers."

Miranda burst out laughing. "That's certainly true."

"And now we will have dinner." He led her down a long corridor. "Here is our restaurant, Tingliguan, the Pavilion for Listening to Orioles."

"What a lovely name."

"And a lovely place. Come, we have a table."

They sat close together, at the water's edge, and chose their fish for dinner from a squirming, thrashing tank. "The Empress Cixi had one hundred dishes for each meal," Li said, "but we will have fewer."

She looked disappointed. "How many fewer?"

"Oh, say half as many. But if that is not enough, we will order more. Shall we choose together?"

They bent over the menu, Li translating and describing the dishes, Miranda recognizing some of the written characters and reading them with delight. They drank Yanjing beer and talked of childhood and school, work, parents, children, friends made and lost. And when dinner was finished and they left the pavilion where once emperors and empresses had listened to the songs of orioles, Miranda became aware of their dreamlike movements, so familiar, almost a routine. Once again, they left a restaurant, arms touching, and walked to Li's car. Once again, they drove to his house and parked by the gate in his wall. And once again they moved through courtyards to his bedroom, to his bed, where, once again, they made love and slept and woke to the sun to begin a new day that would belong to them because they would begin and end it in each other's arms.

It was so perfect that she hugged it to herself, cradling it in her thoughts. But it was not perfect, even as a dream.

Because there was no identifiable place in which it could be repeated again and again. There was no place in which she could imagine with certainty each new day truly belonging to them.

"My love, my love," Li murmured, sometime in the middle of the night, and Miranda could not tell if he were awake or asleep. "Always, always . . ." His arms tightened to bring her closer and they woke and he moved his hand along her body, bringing her to desire. She stretched beneath him, her arms above her head, her long neck arched. "Ah," he said with a quick brightening of his eyes, "now I have you." He clasped her two hands in his and pinned them to the pillow, he kissed her eyes, her mouth, the vulnerable line of her throat. "We are free of all bonds, except the one that holds us to each other. This one. This one that cannot be broken. I have you now, and I will never let you go."

"No, don't," she said. "Don't let me go. Ever."

He kissed her again, and, still imprisoning her hands, came into her, and when at last he released them, Miranda felt a quick stab of sorrow, as if something had been lost. But she held him to her as he lay upon her, and would not let him go until they began to fall asleep and then he slid down beside her and they lay locked together beneath the silk coverlet with its leaping dragons and soaring birds, and she breathed in the warmth of his skin, and felt his steady heartbeat answering hers, and her hands moved over him in long lingering strokes, beginning and ending in whispers, and so, in the soft darkness of his bed, they slept.

"Did you dream?" Li asked the next morning as they drank tea and ate sweet bean paste buns in his sunlit courtyard. "I dreamt I told you . . . no, it must have been real. Did I speak to you last night in my sleep?"

"Yes."

"Did I tell you I love you? And that you belong with me always?"

"Yes."

"I thought it was another part of my dream. Perhaps it was, and you were in it. Do you think I am dreaming you and soon I will wake up and find none of these days has been real? Or perhaps you are dreaming me. In which case everything is all right as long as we don't wake up." He looked beyond her, his face meditative, then shook his head. "No, it has its attractions, but I would rather be awake with you than dreaming. Shall I tell you what I dreamt? That you and I were on a sailboat, at the helm, and we passed an island with a magnificent fairy-tale castle. Smoke was coming from all the chimneys, so we knew that everyone was at home, all the princes and princesses and kings and queens and servants, and we decided to go there because we were sure they would let us in to share their wonders. What did you dream?"

"Oh, it was much more confused than yours. You and I were riding bicycles to the market, and then I was in a garment factory signing a hundred contracts, and then I was measuring a terra-cotta warrior because I wanted to make a cashmere sweater for it, and then I was in Beijing, walking in the Haidian district, and I got lost and knew I'd never get back to my hotel, and I was incredibly sad, and then you found me and we went on the marble boat and sailed away."

"Ah, we both dreamt of boats and sailing."

She smiled. "Among other things."

"So it is clear that we both are thinking of travel."

"Yes."

"But, alas, instead we go to work."

She smiled. "And are you still going to talk to Sheng about . . . whatever it is you're going to do?"

"I have not changed my mind, if that is what you mean. Yes, I will talk to Sheng, but I will go ahead on my own, if I must, because it seems I have committed myself, in my head. Now." He switched subjects again with the abruptness she had come to expect. "You remember that tonight we are going to Liulichang."

"And dinner with Meiyun. She left a message at the hotel yesterday, saying she would meet us there at five o'clock."

"Then we shall be there."

They kissed, and, like the couple in Miranda's dreamlike routine, like a man and woman who had found a place to be permanent and make each day theirs, they left the house and drove away, to spend a day in the city.

"You are less anxious today," said Tang Po in the conference room at the Palace

Hotel, and it was said so kindly that Miranda did not feel he was intruding on her privacy.

"Yes," she said. "Thank you for being so understanding."

"We all have troubles and disappoint- ments and losses," he said. "Sometimes they vanish, and sometimes not, and if not we find ways to adjust and make a life. A different life, perhaps, but not necessarily a worse one."

She carried those words with her when they parted at the end of the day, along with a contract from Tang Po that was far better than anything she had dreamed of. Good and bad, she thought. A contract that is everything I could hope for, and advice telling me to adjust if I don't get what I want.

Li. The two of us. Together.

But what if I don't want to adjust?

Chapter 12

Li arrived at the Palace Hotel to find Meiyun in a small booth in the bar, drinking vodka on ice. "You look happy," Meiyun said, almost accusingly, and he laughed.

"Do you think I shouldn't be?"

"I think you are risking a great deal. As I told Miranda in Xi'an."

"Did you? She did not tell me that."

"And does she tell you everything?"

"I don't know," he said, looking surprised at the idea. "I hope not."

"Well, then, why should she tell you this?"

"Because it was a warning."

Meiyun looked at him closely. "And have you not had many warnings, in your days together?"

"I love her," Li said quietly. "Next to that, the warnings fade."

"Oh, my dear." She reached across the table to take Li's hand. "The day before my husband took his life, he wrote me a letter, which I found when the authorities allowed me to go home. Among other things, he quoted a line from our favorite poem: 'The sun warms the dancing lake, but overhead the heron casts a shadow that warns of cold below.' Dear Li, to ignore the warnings is to drown in the cold."

"Or to fly with the heron upward, into the warmth."

A quick frown passed over her face. "You are going with her, to America?"

"I did not say that."

"Then I am an old woman who hears but does not understand."

He smiled faintly. "You are far younger than most, and you understand everything." He gazed at his hands, folded on the table. "So few days. Things move too quickly, sweeping us along . . ." He looked at Meiyun. "I think about going to America with Miranda. I think about asking her to stay here with me. Would you approve of either one?"

"It is not for me—"

"I am asking you."

She sighed. "What can I say? Some people uproot themselves and are happy, or at least satisfied, while others long always for home; they are always strangers." She leveled a look at him. "Love is not enough."

Li winced, remembering a conversation with Miranda. "I called Miranda a romantic for saying that it ought to be."

"And here she is." Li turned to see Miranda walking toward them.

"Meiyun," Miranda said and with American openness spread her arms wide. To Li's amazement, Meiyun did the same, and the two women embraced like old friends. Men would not do this, Li thought, certainly not at only a second meeting, certainly not across cultural and geographical boundaries. How fortunate women are, that they can do it.

"Wonderful," Meiyun said, standing

back to admire Miranda in the blue dress with its deep collar. "The dress has improved since you first tried it on. No, how foolish of me. It is you who have changed. Happier. And more easy with yourself. You no longer slouch. Now the dress is truly yours. But come, I am impatient to show you this. Here, sit beside me." She took a box from the seat beside her. "Open it, open it, I cannot wait another moment."

"The cape," Miranda said. "It's really finished? I didn't believe you could do it." She opened the box and unfolded the pale gold tissue inside. "Oh," she breathed. "Yes, it's exactly as I imagined it."

Li leaned over the table to look and when Miranda simply sat, gazing at the folded cape, he plucked it from the box and held it up. "Beautiful," he said softly. "A beautiful design."

The cape was a cashmere fabric, lightweight and soft as silk, deep black lined in gold satin. Scattered about the blackness were the gold outlines of large, lush magnolias that had been laser-cut into the fabric so that the lining could shine through. A hood lay softly over the shoulders, the gold lining like a flower all its own. A single jet button was at the throat.

"Purity, simplicity," Meiyun said. "Nothing extraneous. But those flowers! They move with the cape: alive and truly sexy." She looked from Li to Miranda. "Would you not say?"

Miranda laughed. "I would, but I didn't think you would."

"Sex is the thread that holds all fashion together, you know that, Miranda. Stand up, please." She took the cape from Li and placed it on Miranda's shoulders, fastening the button and smoothing the fabric. She draped the hood lightly over Miranda's head, framing her face. "How lovely it looks on you. I am very sorry that it is going to someone else. You deserve it."

"It belongs on you," Li said, his look absorbing Miranda, drawing her deeply into him. He knew Meiyun was watching and it did not matter. I adore you, his look said, his look that lifted and consumed Miranda, and for a long moment they all were silenced by the power of his love.

"And who does get the cape?" Li asked. He had ordered champagne and he filled their glasses. "Someone we can admire?"

Meiyun smiled faintly. "Not very much. She is an actress of ordinary talent but great beauty. You may have seen her on television; her name is Wu Yi."

"A small world," Li murmured. "She is having an affair with my son."

"Sheng and Wu Yi?" Meiyun was surprised. "That means he is doing well. From what I have heard, Wu Yi does not look twice at men who are not successful."

"Yes, he worries about that." Li shrugged. "I cannot help him there; what father would be listened to, telling a son who is mad for a great beauty that he would be better off staying home with his wife and child?" He contemplated the cape, softly folded again in its box. "You must have made this very quickly."

"Meiyun has good people," said Miranda. "They had only three days, but they did it beautifully."

"It was the design," Li said. "People always do their best work when they are creating something brilliant and perfect."

They looked at each other. Meiyun turned her attention to her vodka while their eyes held, their hands clasped beneath the table. After a moment, she said, "You have come very far. You chose not to stop when you could. And now what will you do?"

"We're just being together," said Miranda. "We haven't talked about anything else."

"As if you will be in China indefinitely?"

"As if . . . we have time to think about it."

"And what is it you will think about?" There was a silence. "Come, you must be precise. This is not a time for fuzzy thinking. Shall I tell you the questions you should be asking?"

Miranda shook her head. "We know them. I'd rather not talk about this now. I thought you and I would talk about working together."

"Ah. To help your thinking. To have all the pieces of the puzzle in front of you before you begin to put them together. Very sensible. Well, then, of course we can work together, my dear. You have brilliant designs locked inside you, and you need a place to set them free. My shop can give you that. I am not as excellent a designer as you, but if we are clever we could make our reputation all through America and Europe, and in China, too, with women who have money; there are more of them every day. We would be very hot, as you would say. Women like Wu Yi, who are mad for fashion, have no nationality; they are the same all over the world, and they would pay top money, very top money, for designs with our label."

Miranda's eyes were bright. "Meiyun Miranda. What a good sound."

"I think Miranda Meiyun; it flows better. And a Western name in front would be more popular in China and perhaps everywhere else. So, now you have those pieces of the puzzle."

"Yes, but where would we work?"

"That is not for me to say."

"But we could be anywhere, couldn't we? With faxes and E-mail . . . it wouldn't really matter where we are."

"For most things that is true. Where would you like to be?"

"It's where I have to be," Miranda said after a moment. "My children, my family, my work are all in Boulder."

"And Li is here."

Miranda met Li's eyes. Their booth was a little island that had drawn into itself as the bar grew crowded and noisy. The three of them were leaning toward each other, to be heard, and their closeness made Li think of a family, leaning inward for support, until Meiyun's words made them draw a little apart. *Li is here.*

Li met Miranda's eyes and read her thoughts. *But he could be in Boulder.* "Yes," he murmured. "I could be." He knew they were slipping into this discussion because of Meiyun's prodding, but that was all right; without her, they might have put off talk of the future until the last minute, when it would be too late. Meiyun's unwavering gaze insisted on honesty, and forced reality into the artificial world they had created in these few intense days.

"I could be," he said again, still looking at Miranda. "I would have to make arrangements, and that would take some time, but I could be in Boulder, with you."

"Or not," Meiyun said flatly, forcing them to look at all possibilities.

The brightness faded from Miranda's eyes, and Li turned to Meiyun. "I could do it. Is there so much that keeps me here? These past few days . . ."

"What?" Meiyun demanded.

Li told her, beginning with his interrogation, the constant surveillance, the planting of documents in his office and home. "Of course it is not all the government—"

"But others took advantage of the government's interest in you. We know how often that happens. So. Now you want to get away from all this."

"Yes. And more. Begin again. Build something new."

"Can you?"

He looked at Miranda. "Yes."

Miranda let out her breath. "If you really mean it. . . . You do mean it, of course you do. Oh, Li, you'll love it; we'll live together in my house; it would be your house; you would make it yours."

Her words came faster, and Li realized how many times she must have said them to herself, longing to say them aloud. "There would be work for you. So much work. I know people who can help you get a green card and if we're . . . if we're . . ."

"Married," he said gently.

She flushed, and he saw Meiyun's look sharpen, and he realized that in all their talk and lovemaking neither of them had spoken of marriage. He watched Miranda think about all its implications, and he wondered if it would frighten her and she would change her mind. But instead she smiled. "If we're married, it would be easy for you to stay. And you would find work; start a new company, if you want; work with new architects—" She stopped. "I'm sorry, I get carried away when I'm excited."

Li touched her face, as if they were alone. But then Meiyun said, "It will take some time to make these plans. And right now, I am very hungry. I thought you had invited me to dinner."

Li would have resisted—*We're finally talking about this; leave us alone*—but then he thought perhaps she was right to make them pause. "We did," he said amiably. "And I have chosen a new restaurant, not far from here."

He walked between them down Wangfujing, smiling ruefully to himself at the picture they made: Yuan Li between two suspect women. Meiyun, the widow of a professor still considered subversive for his writings on representative democracy and pressure groups, and Miranda, courier of mail from an exiled dissident to mainland China. Whoever was following them tonight would think he had struck gold. But still nothing would happen. And that perhaps was the true horror of it, as he had said to Miranda: it was done to control a populace, to intimidate, to alarm, to wear down. The fact that there still were dissidents and a rising chorus of political discussion was a testament to the stubbornness and tenacity of the human spirit. Even in China. Perhaps especially in China.

"What will you do about Sheng's partners?" Meiyun asked at dinner. "They will try again, you know; people like that do not give up after one try."

"Why don't you frame *them?*" Miranda asked.

Li's eyebrows rose. "It is amazing how quickly China pervades the soul of a visitor. Perhaps you should stay here with me, my Miranda; already you think far more like a Chinese than I do as an American."

Miranda's chopsticks clattered to her plate. "You're not serious."

"But you have thought about it. Haven't

you? Staying with me? Working here with Meiyun?"

She concentrated on arranging her chopsticks on her plate, making them perfectly parallel. "When I was designing the cape, and that day I walked to my hotel, and when I worked with Yun Chen on designs, and with Tang Po, I did think about it. It seemed exciting, and possible. I even wrote postcards to Adam and Lisa, telling them I wanted to bring them here, that we would live here and learn all about China from the inside—"

"You wrote that?" Li's voice rose. "Then they will want to do it! Young people have itchy feet and eyes big with curiosity; they will say it is a great adventure and when they read that you want them to—"

"I didn't mail them."

There was a pause. "The postcards. You did not mail the postcards."

"No. I put stamps on them, and kept saying I'd do it later, but finally I knew that I never would. I couldn't, Li, not when I really thought about it. Because everywhere I go, whether I'm alone or with you, whatever I do, *I can't fit myself in.* I don't feel that I belong anywhere here. Except in your house, in your kitchen, in your bed. And as wonderful as that is, it isn't enough for a life. Or for my children's life."

"It takes time. And if you truly leave your old life behind, and we are together, you would *want* to belong. You would want it so much you would make it happen."

"And my children? What would be their motivation?"

"Adventure, excitement, all the things young people love. They would make friends—"

"They don't speak Chinese."

"Most schoolchildren here speak English, at least in the cities, and Adam and Lisa would learn Chinese quickly. For young people languages are not so hard. They would learn about China and teach their friends about America; they would grow up with understanding and wisdom, and they would have a wonderful time."

"You want us here," Miranda said after a moment. "Instead of coming to America."

"Yes."

"But you just said—"

"But *I* was asking a question," Meiyun interrupted, and they turned to her with surprise; they had forgotten she was there.

"About Sheng's partners. My hearing must be bad because I did not hear an answer."

"Miranda gave an answer," said Li. "She suggested I frame them."

"We," Miranda said quickly, "I'd want to help."

"And I," said Meiyun with a smile. "A small conspiracy to defeat a larger one. Have you any ideas?"

And this was what it came down to, Li thought. *Do things that I know are wrong. Be a person I do not much like. Sometimes it is either that . . . or crawl into a shell.*

"Ideas?" he said. "Of course; our government is filled with examples and role models. The problem is how to bring down Chao and Enli without dragging Sheng with them."

"Are you sure Sheng wants to do this?" Miranda asked.

"An excellent question," said Meiyun. "What if his feet get frozen?"

"Cold feet," Miranda said.

"Ah, for Sheng they might be frozen. What if this happens and he balks halfway through your plot? You would be exposed doing something illegal—I assume it would be illegal—and Sheng and his partners would go untouched. And you would be arrested, gone, which is just what the partners want."

"Sheng would have to agree at least to stand aside. He would not betray me. But I believe we will be together in this."

The waitress ladled portions of soup into their bowls. Li watched the graceful turn of her wrist; he glanced at the jade bracelet on Miranda's wrist and then at Meiyun's small hand holding her soup spoon, and suddenly he was filled with an extraordinary sense of well-being. Whatever turmoil awaited beyond the restaurant, however much tension and uncertainty lay like shadows over the future, with these two women he loved and admired, he felt content, and blessed.

An odd word for someone who has no religion. But that is what it feels like. Enriched by those who have come to me. Grateful. Blessed.

"What will you and Sheng do together?" Miranda asked and Li grimaced slightly at the balancing act they had to perform, like people everywhere, he imagined, to stay upright between serenity and crisis.

But with those thoughts of gratitude and

blessing, he had made a decision, and so he said, "I cannot tell you. I should not have said even this much. Sheng and I will not involve anyone else in this."

Miranda looked at him. "You told me you wouldn't shut me out."

"It is not shutting you out; it is protecting you from ugliness."

"I don't want to be protected! People have tried to protect me all my life, and all it did was make me feel helpless as soon as the scenery wasn't familiar. Li, please don't do this. Let me be part of it. Let me help you."

He put his hand on hers. "I'm sorry. I did not intend to sound like your parents. Well, but this is nothing like your home, and what could you do?"

"How do I know, when you won't even tell me what you're planning?"

"An impasse," said Meiyun. "Li, when you and Sheng have a plan, you certainly should tell us, and then we will know if we can help."

"I don't see that."

"But we are involved, already. We are close to you, and Miranda is under surveillance, and they have a file on me, and of course they know that we are together right now. You should tell us what you plan, because being half-involved is like being half a virgin: unsatisfactory, and besides an impossibility."

Li chuckled. He looked at Miranda, who nodded. "Well, when I have a plan, I will tell you," he said, "even though there will be nothing you can do."

"We will decide that together," said Meiyun.

Li gazed at her. "So stubborn. You always have been."

"It helps my character. And also my survival. Now, shall we go to Liulichang? As I recall, I was promised that for tonight, also."

With little subtlety, she had directed much of their evening, Li thought. But perhaps that was what they needed: to be pushed . . . somewhere.

"Yes, let's go," Miranda said. "I've heard it's wonderful. And I have so many presents to buy."

The three of them strolled through Liulichang with crowds of evening shoppers. The street was built to look like an ancient Chinese village, with shop windows crammed with antiques: porcelains, linens, furniture, ivory and jade figurines, chess sets, jewelry, painted fans. Not an inch was wasted: antiques filled the shelves, hung from hooks on walls and ceilings, tottered in stacks on floors and display cases.

"I feel so greedy," Miranda said. "I want everything, much more than I can afford."

"Then it is time for bargaining," said Li.

"I couldn't. I've never done it."

"You should learn how; it will always be of use to you."

"Not in Boulder Colorado."

"In China," he said abruptly, and led the way to a shop with sculptures and vases arrayed in its plate-glass window. "Which would you like?"

Miranda debated, then pointed to a translucent white jade figure of a woman standing beside a drooping willow tree.

"A fine piece," Li said. "Decide what you want to pay for it, then pretend that you are not terribly interested, but it might make a pair with one you have at home. When you bargain, do not offer a sum so low it demeans the owner, but low enough to show her that you do not take her first price seriously."

"Li, I told you, I have no idea how to do that."

"It will come to you. I think it is instinctive in all of us, this game-playing. It gives us a chance to win without dire consequences; that is the fun of it."

The shop was dim and it took a minute for Miranda's eyes to focus on the owner, small and hunched, with a thin face and gray hair in a tight bun at her neck. Her sweater had a hole in one sleeve and her skirt dragged on the floor. Her face was impassive. "May I help you?"

"We're just looking," Miranda said. She paced the tiny shop, six steps to the wall, six steps back. Finally she stopped at the window, picked up a vase and put it down, then another one, and finally the figure she wanted. "How much is this one?"

"One thousand yuan. Very fine, very old." She made a small bow. "You have excellent eye."

Miranda returned the figure to the shelf. She wanted it. She loved the timelessness of the pose, the aged luster of the white jade, the woman's meditative face. But Li was watching, and she put it back. "I'm afraid it's too much for my budget. I thought it might make a pair with one I have at home, but perhaps I'll find another one somewhere else."

"Another? There are none as old or as fine. Still, I can perhaps lower a little; I can sell to you for eight hundred."

Miranda shook her head regretfully. "I'm sorry. I can't pay more than two hundred."

The owner looked shocked. "Impossible! This so old, so fine . . . but perhaps I could lower to six hundred. No more, however; that is the best."

"I can't afford it," Miranda said. "That's seventy-five dollars. I might be able to manage three hundred . . ."

"No, no, too far. But if you truly cannot afford it, I can lower a little more." She folded her hands. "It is for me hard, too; I live with grandchildren because parents are dead, two little girls, one eleven years old has a problem with her heart, and doctors say she dies if she does not have hospital and medicines. But you are very pretty lady, and very nice, and you can have jade figure for four hundred fifty yuan."

"Fine," Miranda said abruptly. She pulled out the money and waited impatiently while the woman wrapped the figure in many layers of bubble wrap. Outside, she tucked it into her shopping bag. "I should have bought something for my parents, but I really didn't want to start all over again."

"You could have gotten it for two hundred," Li said. "You believed her about the grandchildren."

She stared at him. "There are no grandchildren?"

"Probably there are many. But I have shopped here before and she has many hardship stories; she tailors them to her customers and they are never the same."

"You don't think she has a sick granddaughter?"

"I doubt it. I have not heard her tell that story before."

"Well, thank goodness."

"You're happy about this? That she fooled you?"

"Of course I'm happy. Should I be sad that there isn't a child dying of heart disease?"

"Even if it means that the woman cheated you?"

"Out of what? A few dollars. And if there really is a sick granddaughter, then she needs the money. I can't believe you think it's fun to take advantage of poor people who are trying to make a living in their pathetic little shops."

"No one is taking advantage of them, and in fact it is a game. Bargaining is done all over the world; shop owners inflate their prices a few hundred percent to allow for it. Many of them are poor, it is true, but not because they bargain; that is simply a way of doing business. In fact, they usually win, especially with tourists. As she just did."

"Because I cared about her! I'd rather spend too much than be as cynical as you are!"

Meiyun put a hand on her arm. "It is not cynicism in Li, and it is not gullibility in you. You have different traditions in shopping and that is nothing to quarrel about."

"Were we quarreling?" Li asked. "I thought it was a cultural exchange."

They laughed, but Miranda said, "If you were in America you wouldn't shop that way."

"Ah, but if you were in China, you would. And you did so well; I was thinking again how quickly you adapt."

"And what about presents?" Meiyun asked, once again steering them in a new direction. "What interests you, Miranda?"

"Everything."

"But save something for tomorrow," said Li. "The Xiushui Silk Market is excellent for shopping."

"But first we visit Wu Yi, at nine," said Meiyun to Miranda. "You can do this?"

"For an hour. I have a meeting at ten-thirty."

"Then at eight-thirty I will pick you up at your hotel."

A silence fell. Miranda looked at her hands. Li frowned, contemplating his shoes. And then Meiyun understood. "You will not be at your hotel in the morning, is that correct?"

Miranda nodded.

"Ah." She gazed at them, began to say something, changed her mind, and said instead, "I will be at Li's house at eight-thirty. You will be ready?"

"Yes. Thank you."

Thank you for understanding, Li thought. Thank you for not chastising us for being foolish. Thank you for being our friend.

And late that night, after they had left Meiyun at her hotel, after they had walked into Li's house and made love, when they were holding each other in the slow drowsy minutes before falling asleep—*like other couples all over the world, like people who know what tomorrow will bring*—Miranda said, "Do you think she knew why I thanked her?"

"She knew," Li said. "She understands so much. She wants us to be happy."

"In China or America?"

He raised himself on his elbow. "Wherever we would be happy. Do you want to talk about this tonight?"

"No, I'm sorry; we're both too tired. And I think I'm afraid to. But tomorrow—"

"Tomorrow we will talk about it and not be afraid. And on Saturday, when we go to the Forbidden City"—*your last day in China; the last day for everything to be settled*—"we will talk about it some more."

"And decide—?" Her eyes were closing.

Li kissed her forehead, her lips. "And decide. I love you. Now sleep."

They woke late and had time only for tea before Meiyun arrived. "She is slightly hysterical," Meiyun said in the car, "so you should speak quietly and innocuously."

"I won't speak at all," Miranda said. "I'm tired and I don't feel very well. Don't people often get sick in Beijing? The pollution, or something?"

"This is not pollution, my dear. You are filled with tension because you have today and tomorrow before you leave and great decisions to make, and you would rather not make them."

"Not make them?"

"I think you would rather go on like this, the days spinning out one after the other, you and Li like children playing in a beautiful park that closes at sunset, but somehow sunset never comes. Or, you would rather that someone else make the decision for you."

"How wise you are. Would you tell me what you think I should do?"

"There would be no wisdom in that, only foolhardiness. This is only for you and Li, my dear, as you both know. And here we are at Wu Yi's apartment. Stay behind me so that she does not see you right away."

"But, you did tell her I was coming."

"Of course, but she is the kind of woman who is suspicious of other pretty women, so it would be best if she sees me first." She rang the bell, and stood in front of Miranda, which Miranda found amusing, since Meiyun was six inches shorter than she.

So, when the maid led them to the living room, it was Miranda whom Wu Yi looked at first. She dropped her gaze to Meiyun and said, in Chinese, "You brought them?"

Meiyun introduced Miranda, in English. "I wish to speak English today. I have brought dresses, and the cape. You will want to try them together."

Wu Yi took two garment bags from Miranda and disappeared into her bedroom. A few minutes later, Miranda and Meiyun heard a long "Yes, yes" float through the open door, and then Wu Yi returned.

She was stunningly beautiful: fully made up, her complexion pale and rosy, her eyes darkly outlined, her black hair gleaming. She had left the cape open, and her perfect figure shimmered in gold within the parentheses of black cashmere strewn with gold-outlined magnolias that danced and swirled as she moved.

"Magnificent," Meiyun said.

Wu Yi stood before a long mirror. She began to speak in Chinese, then caught Meiyun's gaze and switched to English. "I am very beautiful. And the dress and cape are good. Very good. But the price is too high. I am only an actress; I cannot afford such expenses. If you agree to reduce all your prices, I can make you famous and rich. I will buy first from you, always, you and . . . who did you say this person is?"

"Miranda Graham," said Meiyun.

"Graham. And that blouse she is wearing, with the little gold monkeys . . . where did she get it?"

"In my shop."

"You let your assistant wear your clothes?"

Meiyun looked at Miranda.

"We have a partnership," Miranda said evenly. "The label on our clothes, including the dress and cape you are wearing, is Miranda Meiyun. We have customers in China, Europe and America, and our prices reflect our art, the skill of our manufacturers, and the demand for our designs. The prices are the same all over the world. We do not discount for anyone."

Meiyun's eyebrows rose so high they almost disappeared. But then she began to smile, and her smile grew as broad as her eyebrows were high. "If you do not wish to pay for them," she said to Wu Yi, "we will take them back. I would be sorry, because you look truly magnificent, but—"

"You will not take them back." Wu Yi gazed at her image. It was clearly a struggle, but fashion won. "I will pay your price this time," she said to Meiyun's reflection. "Next time I may not."

Meiyun nodded gravely. "The dress needs a slight alteration in the length; I can have it adjusted this evening and returned to you tomorrow."

The telephone rang, and Wu Yi's maid appeared. "Miss Wu, it is Pan Chao calling. Will you talk to him?"

"No! I'm very busy! Tell him I will call him later."

"Pan Chao," said Meiyun thoughtfully, her back to Miranda so their eyes could not meet. "I have heard of him. A well-known businessman, I believe."

"President of his company," said Wu Yi.

"A special person?"

Wu Yi was contemplating her image in the mirror. Her gaze slid to Meiyun's reflection. "Why?"

"I only wondered. There are so few special men in the world; most are dull or weak. Or taken."

Wu Yi's lips almost smiled. "He is incredibly boring. But maybe not. I've talked to him a few times in his club, but we only went out for the first time last night. He is very successful." She shrugged. "You have lived a long time; you know what is important. Sweetness and niceness are not; even good sex is not. Money is. It makes life go."

Meiyun nodded. "You are very strong. Passing over others to find the person who will give you what you want is not always easy."

Briefly, the hard lines of Wu Yi's lovely face wavered. "Not easy," she repeated. Then, again, she shrugged. "It is how things are. I will buy the dress and the cape and I want to see everything you have for winter. Bring them next week."

"Ah, next week I cannot come to Beijing. I can send you photographs, or fax drawings to you, but the best way would be for you to come to Xi'an."

"Xi'an!"

"I will set aside an entire day for you. You can try everything, at your leisure, and we can make alterations in design or fabrics or fit as we go along. I will provide lunch. At the end of the day, you will have a winter wardrobe that is yours alone."

"But . . . in Xi'an!"

"That is where I live. That is where Miranda Meiyun designs are to be found."

Wu Yi gave a reflexive glance at Miranda, sitting quietly on a hassock. "I will let you know. You would give me an entire day? You would see no one else?"

"No one."

"Well. Leave your card with my maid." She nodded to Miranda, shook Meiyun's hand, and returned to her bedroom as the maid appeared to lead the way to the front door.

"I have not been paid," said Meiyun. "Please inform Miss Wu."

Scowling, Wu Yi reappeared. "Send me a bill."

Meiyun gently shook her head. "Miss Graham and I have delivered a dress and a cape designed and made especially for you. Payment is on delivery."

Their eyes locked for a long moment until Wu Yi strode to a desk and furiously wrote a check. "You have strange rules."

"They are my rules."

Outside, Miranda said, "Do you think Sheng told her anything that she could pass on to Pan Chao?"

"I have no idea. We must ask Sheng."

"Oh." She shrank. "I can't. He doesn't like me."

"How do you know?"

There was a pause. "He was cold when we met one day. Rude, in fact. He didn't like it that I was with Li."

"Well, perhaps that is understandable. I would imagine it is easily corrected." In the car she had hired for the day Meiyun took out her cellular phone, and called Li. "It seems that Wu Yi has somehow fastened herself to Pan Chao."

"What? How?"

"We don't know that. I imagine she shifts

from one useful man to another as easily as a driver shifts gears. The problem is, if Sheng has told her anything about turning against his partners—"

"Yes, I'll ask him. He's out of the office; I'll have to track him down. Will I see you tonight?"

"I'm flying back in two hours. Unless you need me."

"I don't think so. Is Miranda with you?"

"Here she is." She gave the telephone to Miranda, and turned away to look at the passing scene.

"I have to find Sheng," Li said. "May I call you later? We may have to skip the silk market if I don't find him soon."

Repeating Meiyun's words to herself— *understandable, easily corrected*—Miranda closed her eyes and plunged. "Why don't you ask him to come home for dinner tonight? We could cook together and it would be a quiet place for you to talk."

Home, Li thought. Home. But he did not say it aloud. What he did say was, "You are an extraordinary woman. Do you really want to do this?"

"The two of you need some quiet time, and maybe Sheng won't hate me so much if we're together for an evening."

"Extraordinary," Li murmured again. "Thank you; I will ask him. He doesn't hate you, you know; he doesn't know you. But it would please me very much if he did." *Because if you stay, if you marry me and bring your children to live with us, we will have a most interesting family.*

When he hung up, he read again the list he had been making. A list of crimes, he reflected. A list I should not be able to make. A list that tells how much I am a part of this system, even though I often feel like an outsider.

He telephoned the sites where they had buildings under construction, but Sheng was not at any of them. He thought of calling Sheng's other office, but he would not take the chance of Chao or Enli answering the phone. He had nothing to say to either of them, and if he hung up, they might become alarmed.

That was the danger, anyway. They would become alarmed and furious if Chao learned that Sheng had turned against them. Would Sheng have confided that to Wu Yi? He might have. And Wu Yi, protecting her new protector, would pass on the story without a qualm.

So, they had to act today, before Chao and Enli found a more foolproof way to incriminate Li and, this time, Sheng as well.

Too restless to sit still, he left the office and roamed the city. He visited his construction sites and observed others; he bought a roasted sweet potato and ate it as he walked. *Miranda loves these; Adam and Lisa will, too.* He gazed at scarves in a shop window—*We may have to give up the silk market tonight*—and went in to buy one for Miranda, three feet square, heavy, sensuous silk covered with an abstract painting of birds and flowers in deep pinks and browns and gold. *A scarf for winter; winters are so cold in Beijing.*

When he returned to the office, he found Sheng in the conference room, looking at blueprints spread out on the long table. "I've been looking for you; where were you?"

"At the Great Wall." Sheng's face was sheepish.

"The Wall? It's jammed with tourists this time of year."

"Fifteen minutes of walking and you leave them all behind. I go there to think. It's so crazy, you know, this huge wall snaking over the mountains, wide enough for horses and armies, and you walk on it all by yourself, and you can't believe anybody was stupid enough to think it would keep out invaders. And then you think how stupid most people are, anyway, and you are, too, I mean I am, stupid, stupid, stupid." He stood up. "I went to the office last night, dawn, really, and took out some files. The important ones."

"Will they look to see what is gone?"

"I don't think so. Not right away, anyway."

"Wu Yi is now seeing Pan Chao."

Sheng's head snapped back. "She wouldn't. How do you know?"

"She told someone. What does she know about your relationship with Chao and Enli?"

Sheng stared at him through puffy eyes. "I called her last night," he said finally. "I thought, after she had time to think about us, she might have changed her mind." He saw Li shake his head slightly. "She might have!" he cried. Then he added sadly, "If she had been someone else. But she isn't, you told me that."

"You already knew it."

Sheng shrugged.

"What did you say when you called her?" Li asked.

"At first she wouldn't talk to me, so I had to tell her maid I had some plans to talk to her about, and when she came to the telephone, the only plan I had was to get out of Dung Chan and just do construction, so I told her that." He shrugged again. "She was not impressed."

"You told her you were getting out."

"Well, how could I know she'd be talking to Pan Chao?"

"If not Pan Chao, someone else. People talk to people and soon everyone knows everything. Did you tell her anything else?"

"No. Only that I was getting out."

"More than enough. Well, we have very little time; the two of them will clean out your office as soon as Wu Yi talks to Chao. So now we must put this together. Come, hurry."

"Where are we going?"

"Home. Miranda and I want you to have dinner with us. We will talk there."

Sheng collapsed into his chair. "*Miranda and I—?*"

"We can talk in the car. I told you; I want to leave. Now."

"You are not in enough trouble already? Now it is *Miranda and I?* What do you think you are doing?"

"I hope I am making a life that will be good for all of us. Sheng, I will not wait."

"All of us," Sheng muttered, but he followed his father out of the conference room, to his office where Li stuffed papers into a briefcase, and then to the car. "I will drive tonight," Li told his driver, and when they had pulled away from the curb, he said to Sheng, "First we pick up Miranda at her hotel. You will be polite to her. I am not asking you to like her, not right away, but I am saying that she deserves courtesy."

"Are you going to America with her?"

"I do not know what will happen. I want to take care of your partners and then perhaps I will have time to think about it."

"You've thought about it already."

"I will not talk about it tonight."

"I just want to know if—"

"I said I would not talk about it. Is that clear or must I find another way to say it?"

"I need you here." The words sounded strangled, but Li was sure he had heard correctly.

"We will work everything out," he said quietly. They drove in silence, until they turned into Wangfujing. "One more thing," he said as they approached the Palace Hotel. "We will speak English tonight."

Sheng nodded. As they stopped in front of the hotel, and saw Miranda waiting, he stepped from the car, shook hands with her, saying "Good evening," in perfect English, and sat in back, so that she could sit with Li.

Li and Miranda looked at each other, awkward with the strangeness of his son in the car. "I'm glad to see you," Li said, speaking with his eyes on the traffic. "Did you finish your work today?"

"All but the signing of the contracts, tomorrow morning. Everyone was very friendly."

"And warm?"

She laughed, and Li thought, Well, so

we have started out with a private joke. That will tell Sheng a great deal.

"And did that take all day?" he asked.

"No, we finished at three. I went to the silk market and had a wonderful time. What a marvelous place that is! I found presents for everyone. You would have been proud of me: I actually did some bargaining and it worked."

"I am always proud of you. Did you buy a gift for yourself?"

"No, I ran out of time, but it didn't matter because I was having so much fun buying for everyone else."

"Well, if you will look in my briefcase, there is a flat box, black with silver writing."

Miranda looked at him in surprise. He knew it was mostly because he was making Sheng a witness to their closeness, and, trapped in gridlock at an intersection near Beihai Park, he turned to smile at her, telling her without words that he loved her. Her answering smile was a little uncertain, as she felt him drawing her ever more deeply into his life, further from her own.

As she opened the box, Sheng leaned forward, no longer pretending that he could not hear or see what went on in the front seat. He let out a small grunt of admiration when he saw the scarf. Miranda held it up, running the heavy silk through her fingers, letting it fall against her jade bracelet. "How lovely it is. I saw some of these at the market but they're so large and—" She bit off the last word.

"More expensive than some of the others," Li said casually, and then the traffic began to move, and he drove on.

Miranda folded the scarf diagonally and put it around her shoulders, knotting it loosely in front. Its autumn colors were bright against the deep burgundy of her blouse; the jade bracelet floated above it like a pale moon. "A painting," Miranda murmured. "Thank you. You bring me so much beauty."

"As you do me." They fell silent, Li concentrating on the traffic and gripping the steering wheel to contain a growing exhilaration. They were together in his car, the three of them, such a perfect picture of a family that it made its own reality, and consumed him. Whatever else they had to deal with, this feeling, so like the one he had had with his daughter and granddaughter, was enough, for the moment, to give him hope.

At home, he was aware of Sheng's sharp eyes watching Miranda move about with easy familiarity, hanging her jacket behind a screen, setting her briefcase on a bench in the reception room, leading the way to the kitchen. Li waited for him to make some comment, but he said nothing, and Li admired his control. *He will not do anything to cause trouble. He is worried, and he needs me.*

"Would you tell me about your son?" Miranda asked Sheng as they worked in the kitchen. The three of them were at the long wooden counter, cutting, chopping, slicing, stirring. They had rolled up their sleeves. They wore white aprons.

"He is very smart," Sheng said, trying to cut celery slices on an angle; a kitchen was foreign territory to him. "Extraordinary for his age."

Miranda, making paper-thin slices of pork tenderloin, smiled. "Is he reading now?"

Sheng talked at length, and the more easily he talked the more clumsy were his slices. But Miranda and Li, with one quick shared glance, said nothing. Sheng was having a fine time; what could be more important than that?

"And he likes to sit in my lap and have me read to him," Sheng said, concluding a long list of Rongji's admirable qualities. "Some people say I should insist that he read by himself, but—"

"Nonsense, you should read to him," said Miranda. "He has a lifetime to read by himself; right now it is something you can share: a way of showing love."

Sheng's eyes rested on her fully for the first time. "You really think that?"

"Anything you do together is good. A boy needs a father; he needs strength to lean against, and trust and reassurance to carry inside him as he grows up and faces difficult decisions."

Sheng's face was brooding. "And where is your children's father?"

"He died many years ago."

"So they grew up with no father. Are they angry about that?"

"Angry? At whom?"

"At him. For leaving them."

"They were at first; they were very young. But when they understood that he had no choice, they were sad, but not angry."

Sheng swept the celery slices onto a plate, retrieved those that had fallen to the floor, then began to slice green onions. "What is your house like?"

Miranda answered his questions, and Li listened, organizing the cooking until everything was finished and they sat at the table at the end of the kitchen.

"This is nice," Sheng said. "I never cook, you know, but I liked it."

"We enjoy it," Li said, which, he knew, revealed as much of his relationship with Miranda as anything else. He sat at the table and served pea shoots with shiitake mushrooms. "We must talk about Chao and Enli."

"Would you like me to leave?" Miranda asked.

"No, why would you?" asked Sheng.

Li felt a shock of surprise and pleasure, but he said only, "Yes, I promised Miranda that she would know what we plan. But we can't plan anything unless you've definitely decided that you're finished with your partners. Are you? Or have you thought that perhaps you'll stay with them, after all?"

"Stay—? No, how can I? I would have to betray you, and I won't do that. Besides, they don't trust me anymore; they think I'm not good for anything except times when they can use me, and that isn't . . . that isn't a partnership."

"There are others who have more confidence in you," Li said, and he saw Sheng's shoulders straighten. Yes, he thought, give him high expectations to live up to, and he'll do it. "Well, then, I have some ideas about ways to trap Chao and Enli, and keep you clear of them, but first I need—"

"Is this room bugged?" Sheng asked suddenly.

Miranda turned pale, looking around the kitchen as if seeing it for the first time.

"No," said Li. "I had it checked two days ago."

"Checked?" Miranda echoed.

"It seemed like a good idea. Of course the phone is tapped," he said casually to Sheng.

"Of course. And your mail?"

"Opened and read; I'm sure they find it boring. Now, I need some information. Who rents the offices you use for . . . what is your company's name?"

"Dung Chan. And Pan Chao rents them."

"Good. And where does he do his banking?"

"The Beijing Bank."

"In his own name?"

"No, under Dung Chan."

"And Meng Enli?"

"I don't know which bank he uses. And his name isn't on the office rental. Chao did almost everything."

"Well, if we get Chao with a big enough net, it may trap Enli, too. Now, this is what you must do. You still have a key to your office?"

"Yes. Unless they've had the locks changed."

"That is why we must hurry. They will. So, tonight you will go to Pan Chao's office and leave copies of the documents he planted in my office and here at home."

"But your name is in them, and your signature."

"I made copies today, replacing my name with his wherever it appeared. Now you will forge his signature; you've seen it often enough, and of course you have letters, documents signed by him."

"Yes, of course, but—"

"And when you have signed them all, spread them loosely at the back of one of his desk drawers. The letter calling for a demonstration during the American president's visit should be on top. Make sure that deposit slips from the Beijing Bank are also there. You can do that?"

Sheng's eyes were wide. "This is not like you, to think of these things. To *do* them."

"This is the way my generation runs to keep up with yours. I am not proud of it. You can do it?"

"Yes, I'll go there about two or two-thirty. No one will be there."

"Good. Now we need some other people. Miranda, you will help with this?"

Her eyes were somber, and he wanted to reach out to her, to tell her that he was not like this, that he was doing something he had never done before and wished he did not have to do, now or ever.

"What can I do?" she asked.

Oh, I love you, he thought. I love you. And, after all, I cannot involve you in this. I thought I could, but I cannot.

"In fact, there is nothing," he said, "because you do not speak Chinese. We need people to leave messages on Dung

Chan's answering machine. Meiyun will do it, and three other friends, none of them in Beijing."

"Saying what?" asked Sheng.

"Mostly hints. References to demonstrating, printing leaflets, the American president's visit, locations, mainly Tiananmen Square, where the welcoming ceremony will be held, the Great Wall, which every head of state visits, and the Forbidden City; it will surely be on the list. All the messages should sound as if people are checking in with the head of an organization. I will write those."

Sheng was looking at his father with admiration. "You are very good. And I will call the State Security Bureau first thing tomorrow and advise them to search Dung Chan's offices and listen to the telephone messages."

"Can you disguise your voice when you call? They will tape it."

"I know how to do that. And should I tell them about the Beijing Bank?"

"No, it will be enough that they find the deposit slips in Chao's desk."

"Does anyone search my hotel room?" Miranda asked.

Li frowned. "Why?"

"I just wondered. All this talk of bugging and opening mail . . ."

"Of course they do," said Sheng, "since you delivered—" He caught his father's warning look. "Or maybe not. No, probably not. They wouldn't want an incident so close to your president's visit."

This time Li did reach across the table and take her hand. "What are you thinking about? You are not planning something—?"

Her eyes were wide and innocent. "You told me there was nothing I could do, because I don't speak Chinese."

"And you believe that?"

"I believe that not speaking Chinese would be a great hindrance to me in many, many ways."

"That is another subject," Li said angrily. "We will talk about that later. You cannot use this as a way of deciding . . . anything."

Miranda laid her hand along his face. It did not matter that Sheng was there, or that Li was capable of doing things she would not have believed, or that tomorrow was filled with unknowns. All that mattered was that she loved him and that tomorrow was also her last day in China, and in that way, too, was filled with many unknowns.

Li kissed her palm, holding it to his lips. His thoughts moved ahead to the time when they would be alone, when they would go to bed and wake together and eat breakfast, and plan a visit to the Forbidden City, like an untroubled couple. But though he repeated it a dozen times, ten dozen times, they were not an untroubled couple, and he could not make it so by pretending it.

Do you think I am dreaming you and soon I will wake up and find none of these days has been real? Or perhaps you are dreaming me. In which case everything is all right as long as we don't wake up.

Chapter 13

Sheng parked his car a block away from the low building near the airport, and walked down the middle of the dark road to the door that led to Dung Chan's offices. In the blackness, he felt his way along the corridor to Pan Chao's office, sidling along the walls and around two filing cabinets and a work table, to the desk, angled in the far corner. A clock ticked; there was no other sound.

Finding the metal handle, he pulled open the middle drawer, cringing at the noise. He cleared a space at the back, behind notepads, a pencil sharpener, scattered paper clips, a pack of cigarettes and a lighter, and shoved in the documents he had signed with Chao's signature. He added a stack of Beijing Bank deposit slips, then slowly slid the drawer shut, shrinking again at the sound it made.

All this had taken less than two minutes. Good, he thought; easy. And then the telephone rang.

He froze. No one made phone calls at two in the morning. He stared in the direction of the telephone, hearing it but not seeing it, and then the answering machine clicked on and he heard Pan Chao's voice telling the caller to leave a message.

"Pan Chao, we have thirty-six for Tiananmen at eight-thirty." A woman's voice Sheng did not recognize. "Behind the Great Hall of the People, as you ordered, to appear when the president arrives. We are trying to get fifty, as you requested; it is very difficult." The caller hung up.

Sheng felt a long shiver of excitement. One of his father's friends. They had begun.

He felt his way along the walls, reversing his earlier movements to the doorway, and into the corridor. He had just reached his own office when all the lights went on.

Blinded, Sheng flung an arm across his eyes. "What the hell—!" His heart was thumping. He peered through half-closed eyes at a stranger in the doorway from the parking lot. "Who the hell are you?"

The stranger strode toward him. "I'm the watchman. You'd better tell me who *you* are."

"We don't have a watchman!"

"How do you know? Pan Chao hired me to—"

"When? When did he hire you?"

"This afternoon." He gripped Sheng's arm. "Come on."

"This is my office!" Sheng cried.

The man squinted at him. "You're lying. Pan Chao said there are only two people here, him and Meng Enli."

Sheng's stomach clutched. Already he had become a nothing. "He meant full time. I have another office in the city." He jerked his arm free and drew himself up. "Now get out of my office, or I'll call the police."

"Police," the man said scornfully. "I work here; I'll stay as long as I want." But his gaze wavered past Sheng, to his office. "What's your name?"

"Yuan Sheng." He had seen that wavering glance, and he was beginning to feel better. "I am partner with Chao and Enli, and I am telling you to get out of here! Now!"

"I heard the telephone. It's my job to investigate."

"And you see that everything is fine."

"I should call Chao."

"Yes, wake him up; he will be so angry that you are calling to say his partner is in his own office that he will fire you. There is the telephone, call him!"

Once again the man looked into Sheng's office, at a box on the floor addressed to Yuan Sheng. "I guess I don't have to." He backed away, to the door to the parking lot. "Are you staying until he comes in?"

"It depends. I forgot what time he said he would be here."

"Six o'clock. He and Enli. He said they had a lot to do."

Sheng nearly fell over. He had been planning to call the State Security Bureau at seven. "I can't stay, but I'll be back at six," he said, proud of the smooth way the lies slid from his lips. He walked into his office. "Be sure to close the door on your way out."

He stood with his back to the corridor. When he heard the outside door close, he dashed back, to make sure the man was gone, then returned to his desk and reached for the telephone. *Can't wait until seven; have to do it now.* He began to dial, then stopped. *They can trace the call. It has to be someplace else.*

Racing now, he took a quick look through his desk and removed a few papers, stuffed his CD player into an old briefcase, and slipped his favorite fountain pen into his pocket. A silver-framed photo of Wu Yi smiled professionally at him. He weighed it in his hand, then tossed it in the waste basket. No, he should leave nothing personal. He retrieved it and put it in the briefcase, to throw away at home, then turned off the lights, shut the door of his office, and walked out of Dung Chan for good.

Outside, the man was not to be seen. Sheng forced himself to walk normally and look straight ahead so that no one would think he looked furtive. Carrying the heavy briefcase, he walked the block to his car and drove a mile, until he found a call box. *Don't look around; don't look suspicious.* Inside the box, he dialed the general number of the State Security Bureau and listened to it ring. *Somebody has to be there; they never close.*

After twenty rings, a man answered. Sheng pitched his voice to a higher register with a Chongking accent, and rattled off the name Dung Chan and the address of the building. He repeated it more distinctly, to give the person on the other end time to write it down, then said, "Counterrevolutionary activities; trouble when the U.S. president arrives."

"Your name—?" But Sheng had hung up. His heart pounding, afraid to look around to see if anyone were watching, he strode to his car, and started the engine. No wait, he thought, I should call father. He'll want to know that everything is all right.

But he imagined Li in bed with Miranda, the two of them curled up together, and a stab of jealousy pierced him, and fear.

What is he going to do about her? He looks at her as if there is no one else in the world for him.

He drove away, toward the center of the city. Ten minutes later, headlights blinded him. A car was approaching, at high speed: the only other car on the road at that time of night. Sheng slowed to look back as it passed him, going toward Dung Chan. Unmarked, but they always were. State Security, he thought; what else could it be? He had used the most potent words—Counterrevolutionary. Trouble. U.S. president—and here they were.

How speedily they responded! One could be proud of one's government for that. Father should know this, Sheng thought again. But he knew he would not call; he could not bear to hear Li's sleep-filled voice coming from their tangled bed. Tomorrow, he thought. I'll tell him then.

And for what remained of this night, where would he go? Not his father's house, not Wu Yi's apartment, that was closed to him forever. He had nowhere to go but home, where his wife and son would be asleep, accustomed to his being gone most nights. But they would be glad to see him in the morning; they always were. Sheng found that a surprisingly comforting thought. I will go home, he thought, and be there for them when they wake up in the morning.

In the morning, Li drove Miranda to the Palace Hotel before breakfast, so that she could pack before her meeting. Methodically, she emptied the closet, the desk and bureau drawers, and the bathroom countertop and shelves, becoming so depressed by their bare anonymity that she could not prevent other thoughts from breaking through: her last day in China, checking out of the hotel, signing the final contracts, packing the gifts she had bought, packing the jade lady and a pair of carved wooden chopsticks she had bought at Liulichang for herself, packing the blouse and dress and jacket from Meiyun, packing, packing, packing.

But it will be all right, because Li will come to America. Not tomorrow, I know that's unrealistic; but soon. As soon as he can.

How did she know that? I know it, she thought stubbornly. I know it.

She packed her books, adding to them one Li had taken from his shelves their first night in his house. It was a collection of thirteenth-century poems translated into English and she had had no chance to read it, but now she saw a small gold clip on one of the pages. It marked a short poem, with Li's handwriting above it: "For Miranda."

> Do you not see
> That you and I
> Are as the branches of one tree?
> With your rejoicing
> Comes my laughter;
> With your sadness,
> Start my tears.
> Love,
> Could life be otherwise
> With you and me?

Tears sprang to her eyes. That's how I know it, she thought. Because he marked this for me. Because life could not be otherwise for us: the branches of one tree. She tucked the book in her briefcase. And so of course he will come to live with me.

Come live with me and be my love, and we will all the pleasures prove . . . That was from another poem, an English one she had learned in high school. I'll buy it for Li when I get home, she thought, and send it to him, for the time we're apart, before he comes to Boulder.

She slipped shoes into shoe bags, hung suits in her garment bag, folded the blue dress in layers of tissue, and began to do the same with the blouse. *No, I'll wear it. Today with Li and tomorrow on the—* Her thoughts faltered; they could not fasten on the word "plane." *I'll wear it today and tomorrow.* She packed an overnight bag with the things she would take to Li's house that night, squeezed everything else into her suitcase and garment bag, and set them in the vestibule for the doorman to put in Li's car when he came for her.

Once more, the room was an ordinary hotel room waiting for the next traveler. I'll miss it, Miranda thought, even though I haven't been here very much. She opened drawers to make sure she had emptied them, then came to the desk in the window, empty except for the telephone and the hotel's message pad and pen.

Does anyone search my hotel room?

Of course, since you delivered—

A letter, Miranda thought. Sheng thinks my room is searched because I delivered a letter. Probably Li does, too, though he didn't say so, and stopped Sheng from saying it, I suppose to protect me from being frightened.

But I'm not frightened. I'm leaving tomorrow; there's nothing they can do to me.

But I could do something for Li and Sheng. Leave some notes here for the Security people to find. Pan Chao's name, the date of the president's visit, Tiananmen Square. That would help cook his goose. Oh, I have to tell that one to Li. I wonder if he knows it. *Cook his goose.* She smiled. *Chinese style.* Excitement ran through her, the excitement of conspiracy and action. *No wonder people get a kick out of this.*

But as soon as she began to write, her excitement cooled. She could not do it. She might indeed help cook Pan Chao's goose, but it would make her even more suspect than before, and that would spill over to Li. He would be in danger, yet again, because of her.

She put down the pen. Li had been right.

There was nothing she could do for him. *Except love him and be here for him.*

And even that she could not do. Not after tomorrow morning, when she boarded a plane for America.

Unless she stayed in China.

But there was no time to go over it again; it was time for her meeting.

Around the conference table, everyone was friendly, with smiles and nods of agreement. The meeting felt strangely valedictory to Miranda, with the same bittersweet feelings she remembered from high school and college graduations: she wanted to stay, she had mastered the survival tactics and had come to enjoy it, but she had no choice but to move on.

She shook hands, saying goodbye and wishing them well in Chinese, and the executives said goodbye in English, adding formally, "We hope you have so good trip home and that you come back to Beijing." It was all so congenial that she had difficulty remembering her anger and feelings of isolation at her first meeting, less than two weeks ago.

"They've gotten nicer," she said to Li when they met for lunch. "I couldn't have changed that much, so it must be that they have."

He chuckled. "All the leading garment manufacturers in Beijing were magically transformed in just ten days. Remarkable."

"It was magic," Miranda said. Then, more slowly, she repeated it. "Magic. All of it. A magical time."

"It will always be magic, with us." Li's hand brushed hers as they simultaneously reached toward the bubbling Mongolian hot pot before them. The pot sat on a circle of flame in the center of the table and with their chopsticks Li and Miranda took slices of raw chicken and beef, beady-eyed shrimp, and vegetables from a large platter and submerged them in the boiling broth, fishing them out when they were cooked and dipping them in different sauces before eating them. The soup, by then fully flavored, would close the meal.

Miranda found a piece of cooked chicken in the clear bubbling liquid and neatly removed it with her chopsticks. It's really so simple, she thought; like a lot of new things that were daunting only yesterday. Like getting along with Sheng. "Have you talked to Sheng this morning?" she asked.

"Yes, very early. He had to be more speedy than he had planned."

"But he did put the papers in Chao's desk?"

"Yes, and the bank deposit slips. And he telephoned the State Security Bureau. He thinks he saw a Security car headed for the office as he was driving away, so it is likely that the offices have been searched by now."

"And then?"

"If I were they, I would be at the Beijing Bank, waiting for Chao to make some transaction under the name Dung Chan. That would be the end of him."

"Cook his goose," Miranda said with a smile.

"Cook—? Oh, I like that. Cook his goose. But why goose? Why not duck or chicken or pigeon or even buffalo?"

"I don't know. It dates back to street ballads of the eighteen hundreds, but why they chose goose is a mystery."

"Like love. A mystery. Why it begins, why it grows, why it endures." He took her hand.

"Miranda, don't go back. Stay with me. We cannot lose this mystery, this magic; we cannot let it go. Please stay with me; we can make a life here, a good life; Lisa and Adam will be happy; we will be happy. Please . . ."

"Li, I can't talk about it; this isn't a good place."

"No place is good for you. Do we need Meiyun with us before we can talk about it? We keep putting it off; we run from it as if it frightens us. All right, it frightens us, but what will we say tomorrow when I take you to the airport and we have no more time to talk?" He gave her a long look. "Or is that what you want? That we hide and hide until time runs out and then you will not have to decide anything because it will have been decided for you, and you will go home even if you do not want to—"

"I do want to." She looked around, as if trying to find a way out. Yet she loved being there with him, she loved Li and everything that they did together. But— "I do want to go home; how can I say that I don't? To give up my whole life—"

"But isn't that what you want me to do?"

"Yes," Miranda said after a moment,

"because it's better to live in America than in China. Everybody knows that."

Li was silent. In a moment, they returned to the business of cooking and eating, until Li said, "Do you want to go to the Forbidden City?" as if that plan had not already been made, and Miranda, tense and unhappy, nodded. Why not, she thought. One more day of seeing Beijing before I leave it.

One more day of being with Li before I leave him.

But that was not a thought she could hold on to.

He'll come home with me. I know he will. He has to.

The Forbidden City had been home to emperors and empresses and almost twenty thousand administrators, staff people, favorites, and hangers-on. "An unreal place," Li said, "where people pretended they were inviolable: safe from the outside world. Just like us. Pretending."

Miranda nodded. It was true; everything was simple and wonderful when they shut out countries and governments and political systems: when it was just the two of them and the little space they shared. But the world keeps intervening, she thought. Such an inconsiderate world.

They walked in silence along a maze of corridors, through brick houses opening into courtyards and gardens crouching behind high walls that shut out China, America, the world. "There is nothing like this in America," Miranda said. "We've never had a time when the government walled itself off from the people."

Li put his hands on her shoulders and turned her to him. They were alone in a corner of a high-walled courtyard, where papery leaves from crab and plum trees skittered across the broad stones and early October flowers drooped on frail stems. They were alone, most visitors having been frightened off by the forbidding clouds, dark and lowering, heavy with threatened rain. "We have nothing to do with history," he said. "We have nothing to do with governments or political systems. There is just the two of us and what we can build together."

"But you just said that was pretending." She looked at him with such sadness that he felt he could not bear it. "We have everything to do with governments and political systems, and with history. It's what we are, and we can't change it."

A gust of cold wind cut across the courtyard, and Miranda shivered. Li put his arm around her. "We've been outside too long; we need to be warm."

"I don't want to go to a restaurant."

"No. We'll go home."

"Oh. Yes." She settled into the curve of his arm, melting into it in the way that always made him feel he would take on the world to protect her. "Yes," she said again, and then added in a voice so low he barely heard her, "We've seen enough of China."

They did not speak on the drive to Li's house. The clouds seemed even heavier; the air was gunmetal gray. How bleak everything is, Li thought: people bundled in dark jackets, heads bent against the wind; dirty streets lined with flat facades looking blank and hostile with no sunlight to soften them. He drove slowly, looking for something to point out that would lift the gloom, but he found nothing beautiful or beckoning, none of the excitement and vitality and promise that he knew were there. Why would she want to live here, he thought, when she has blue skies and mountains just outside her front door?

He was glad to get home and shut the door on the despondent gloom. They walked together into the serene elegance of the main house, warm and golden from many lamps and the glowing wall where the scholar's rock stood, a symbol of wisdom and eternity. I need them both, Li thought; I have never needed them as much as now.

In the center of the room, they held each other, and then there was a knock at the door and they sprang apart. "Sheng," Li murmured. "I hope." He went to the door.

"I couldn't use the telephone," Sheng said. "They would be listening."

"Of course."

Sheng gave a small bow to Miranda. "I hope you are well."

She smiled at his formality. "Yes. Thank you."

"What happened?" Li asked.

"They've arrested Chao."

"Very fast. Where was it?"

"At the bank. They cleaned out the offices, mine, too, but I hadn't left anything interesting, and then they waited for Chao at the bank. He made a withdrawal this afternoon and they stopped him and took him away."

"How do you know this?"

"I was there, watching. And I've talked to a friend in the State Security Bureau. He said they asked him about a demonstration when the U.S. president is here, and people calling him to check on the time—I heard one of the calls, you know, when I was there; a woman's voice; it sounded very good. Chao denied everything, but he could not explain the calls, or how the papers got into his desk."

"Did he try to blame you?"

There was a pause. "I wasn't going to tell you. A watchman came in while I was there; I never thought of a watchman. Chao didn't tell me he'd hired him. He told Chao I'd been there, so Chao told Security I planted the documents. Of course he recognized them since he was the one who made them in the first place, but how could he defend himself by saying that? It must be driving him crazy. It would be funny, except . . . it isn't, because . . ." He sat down, his hands between his knees. "He'll find a way, you know; somehow he'll find a way to shift the blame to me, even though right now nobody believes him about my planting them. But I've been a part of Dung Chan from the beginning, even though they didn't tell me everything; I've been involved with all the business deals, the piracy . . ."

Miranda and Li exchanged a look. "I wasn't sure of the piracy," Li said.

"It was so profitable, so *easy;* even when things went wrong I could fix them. But that's just it: *I* fixed them. When Chao tells Security to check with the people in Beihai, they'll find out."

"Why would Chao tell them?" Li asked. "If the piracy was a Dung Chan enterprise, why would he dig himself deeper into a hole? Even if he did, why would anyone in Beihai—I assume you mean people like the mayor and the chief of police—admit to being on your payroll?"

Sheng scowled. "I don't know."

"They have every reason not to. As for Dung Chan itself, you said you cleaned out your desk?"

Sheng nodded.

"And the documents you planted mention no one but Pan Chao, and have his signature. And the telephone messages all refer to him by name. It's true that you are part-owner of the nightclubs, but that is legal, and in fact encouraged; you would be commended for that. For everything else, you were a flunky at Dung Chan, an errand boy; you knew nothing and participated in nothing."

"That's not true! For two years I was a *partner* in—"

"Sheng," Miranda said quietly, "your father is saving your neck. Pay attention and don't argue with him."

He stared at her. "Oh." His face changed as the realization sank in. "*Gao shi,*" he swore. "To have that story get out, to have to pretend it's true . . ."

"It probably will not get out," said Li. "Chao isn't big news; neither are the stories around him. He will be imprisoned for a few years, and possibly Enli, too, and few people will notice, and then he will be free to begin again, and I am sure he will. But by then you will be so busy at All-China Construction you won't have time to notice."

Sheng thought about it. "But, still, they'll take me in for questioning. I've never been interrogated; I've always been on the other side, you know . . . safe."

"You're still safe," Li said. "Think of a good reason for being in your office when the watchman saw you, and don't change it. They'll ask you a hundred times why you were there; you must give the same answer, the same way, a hundred times. It will be unpleasant but not fatal."

"They'll put me under surveillance."

"One can live with that."

"I thought there was something wrong with people who were, that they were guilty of something, or too stupid to do things right."

"It's like being sent away during the Cultural Revolution," Li said quietly.

Sheng's face flooded with embarrassment.

"You were a child," Miranda said. "Children think grownups are all-powerful, so they can't understand that when bad things happen to them, it might not be their fault."

Frowning, Sheng looked at her as if trying to see beyond her words.

"It wasn't your fault, or your father's," Miranda said. "It was a terrible time that made everything seem wrong. Whatever you said or thought didn't fit anywhere because your whole world was off balance."

He was staring at her. "How do you know all that?"

"Li told me about it."

"Told you."

"I know it's not the same as being here, living through it, but still I can try to understand it. I want to understand what you all went through."

Sheng nodded. After a moment, he held out his hand. "Thank you for saying what you did, for trying to make me feel better."

"I hope it helped."

"Someday, when I can think about it some more, it will."

Their hands clasped and stayed that way for a long moment.

"I must go home," Sheng said, embarrassment in his face again. "I need to warn Peng Jia and Rongji that Security will come for me."

Peng Jia and Rongji, Li thought. Sheng's family. I hope it lasts. I hope I will have my own.

"You did well," he said to his son. "I'm proud of you."

"No, I am proud of you," said Sheng. "I did not think you would do anything like this."

"I hope never again. I'll see you tomorrow; I'll be at the office by noon."

"Goodbye," Sheng said to Miranda. "Perhaps we will see each other again."

"I leave tomorrow," Miranda said. "I hope all goes well with you."

Sheng looked at his father, but learned nothing from his face. He and Miranda shook hands again, quickly, and then he was gone.

"You'll be friends now," Miranda said into the silence. "I'm glad."

Li pulled her to him and kissed her. They held each other and he ached with the wishes clamoring within him. *I wish she would say that she cannot leave, she cannot imagine living anywhere without me, she wants the success she can find here more quickly than in America, she wants to become the person she has always dreamed of being. I wish, I wish, I wish.*

But she had said she wanted to go home.

In the kitchen, he made tea and took it to the living room. He turned on still more lamps and they curled up at opposite ends of a deep couch, facing each other, and when Miranda stretched out, Li took her feet onto his lap, running his hands over the silky nylon, feeling each fine bone and the deep curve of her arch. Desire filled him as he held those slender feet, and he closed his eyes, fighting against reaching for her, fighting the memory of skin on skin and the smooth wet passage she opened to him. Not now, he thought. For now, they had to talk. He opened his eyes. "Are you warmer now?"

"Yes, this is so lovely."

"Then stay here. This is your home, yours and your children's. We will make a life here, together. We can do it, Miranda, I have thought so much about it. You can work with Meiyun, perhaps with others whom you have met here; we will find tutors for Adam and Lisa until they can go to school . . ." His voice trailed away as the enormity of it swept over him.

"You see," Miranda said.

"No. I mean, of course it will be difficult, all of us will have problems to solve, but you and I will be together and everything else shrinks next to that. Dearest Miranda, we have love, we have laughter, we have joy in life and the life we can make, we have dreams. They are good, those dreams, they are about the best we are and the best we can be if we are together, nurturing each other, supporting, sharing. . . . Sharing. The most beautiful word. How can we brush our dreams away and say we do not want them?"

"I do want them. You know I do."

"There is plenty of room: the building off the bedroom would be your office and studio, and Adam and Lisa will have their own rooms in the building off the living room. They can furnish them with whatever they want, with television and VCR's and explosion boxes—that does not sound right."

"Boom boxes. Li, I don't think—"

"And we will have a large family," he said, refusing to stop his flight. "You have made Sheng admire you and like you, and Shuiying, too; we will be a real family. And you and I will be together, and at the end of each day we will talk about our work, we will cook together or go to little restaurants, we will talk about the books we are reading, we will share our thoughts, we will listen to music and watch television and when something reminds us of something we did together, our eyes will meet and we will understand without speaking. My God, can you let us lose all of that when we have only tasted it, without giving us a chance to make it grow and fill our lives?"

He leaned forward, holding her feet tightly to his chest. "Miranda, I love you. Everything inside me stretches out to you. I want to give you all that I have so that you never again worry about money, and have the freedom to do the work you want to do. I want you to feel loved and protected. . . . You were the one who said it, remember? You wanted a love that flowed, there would be a flow, you said, without words, of giving and receiving, of understanding, of laughing and crying together, of being astonished together at the wonders of the world. We found that, we have it together, I want that for you: that you know you are wanted and needed and you will never be alone or lonely again. I want you to be happy."

In the golden lamplight, Li saw tears make glistening tracks on Miranda's cheeks, and she did not raise her hand to wipe them away.

"There is nothing I would not do," he said quietly, "to make you happy."

She raised her head higher. "Then come with me to America."

Her hands were clasped tightly and she held them beneath her chin, her body taut with intensity. "I want you to love what I have, what I've known all my life. I want you to share it with me. I like that word, too, Li, but sharing isn't tied to a place, it's tied to *us*. I want to share everything with you, but we have to think of other things, too, all the things that make life easy or hard or pleasant or unpleasant. If you come with me, you'll live in freedom. You'd like that, wouldn't you? Doesn't everyone?"

"Yes. Everyone does." He looked at his hands, holding Miranda's slender feet. All the sirens are singing to me, he thought. Luring me to places of dreams and visions. And I want to go. I want this woman, and the life she is offering me. I cannot imagine saying goodbye to her, living without her. I cannot imagine awakening in the morning and reaching out to find emptiness, or looking across a dinner table at emptiness, or walking through the city and turning to share a thought and finding emptiness.

This love came to me so unexpectedly, so late, so wondrously. I do not think I could bear the end of it.

"Li," Miranda said softly, and he looked up. She was leaning forward, reaching a hand to him, and they moved together, shifting their positions until they were almost touching. She took his hands in hers and kissed them. "I love you, I love you. I was so sure I'd never find someone to love, someone I wanted to live with, and I can't think about losing you; it hurts too much. I can't imagine saying goodbye to you; I can't imagine not being with you every day, eating and sleeping and sight-seeing and talking. We always have so much to talk about; we need a lifetime to talk about everything and to learn all we can about each other. Don't you feel that way? How can we let it end?"

I can't, I can't, he thought. She is the whole world to me.

He pulled her to him and kissed her, driving his tongue into her mouth. He stood, drawing her up with him, and in the bedroom they undressed each other with mindless urgency, frantic to be together, to be inside each other, to clutch and stroke and hold as tightly as arms and legs and mouths could hold, to take and give and have, and let the maelstrom of a passion they were sure of, the one thing they were absolutely sure of, sweep away the words that could not be resolved. Not yet.

When they were quiet again, they heard rain drumming on the roof, and they lay together, Li's head on Miranda's breast, breathing in unison, and, above their breathing, wind and rain. Li listened to the rain with a kind of wonder. "Everything goes on. Whatever we do, there will be seasons and births and deaths; trees and plants will grow, and birds will sing, and storms will sweep around the earth in a great circle, touching everyone. How unimportant we are."

"No, not true." Her voice was warm and slow. "Small, maybe, when you look at the whole world, but we're very important. And love is important. How do you know the seasons would still be there, and rain and snow and birds, without it?"

He smiled at her serious look. "I don't know. But I would like to think that they would not be." He ran his fingers across her forehead and down the bridge of her nose. "Such a lovely small nose. Do you know, Americans are called Big Nose in China, but yours is small, smaller even than mine. So perhaps I am the foreigner, not you."

"Maybe you are. Maybe you don't really belong here at all. You said yourself once that you wished you could leave it all behind."

"But I also said that that would be running away, and that was something I do not do."

"It wouldn't be running away if you came with me. It would be moving to a new life." She kissed him, a long, slow, searching kiss that aroused him and made him feel that he was dissolving into her, and she into him, that there was no more separation, no boundary or space between them, no cleft for a wedge to pry or a wall to rise. He felt a leap of exultation, because he had never known such unity, the dream of every human being, lonely in a lonely world, and he lay on her and her legs spread wide to bring him in, then clasped him and pulled him into her, so smoothly, so easily, their separate outlines vanishing, that Li knew their unity had taken pure form: *We are one person: one body, one heart, one consciousness. The branches of one tree. And nothing can tear us apart.*

They made love with a new kind of joy: they rolled on the bed like children, laughing and breathless, Miranda on top of Li or stretched out beneath him, the two of them on their sides facing each other, lips clinging, legs entwined. They knelt and crouched and swayed and curled together back to front, like half moons nestled one into the other, drinking in each other's pleasure, feeling gratefulness and love enhanced, doubled, reflected, endlessly renewed.

Through the long evening, and into the night, while rain drummed on the roof, settling now and then into a soft patter before rising with renewed fury, they made love, exploring and searching, as if, Li thought some time after midnight, they were building a store of memories, a catalogue of whatever was new to them, so that they could refer to it later and recapture this night, every moment of it, even in an empty bed—

"No," he said aloud.

Miranda, drowsy beside him, opened her eyes. "What is it? What won't you do?"

"I won't lose you. I won't sleep in an empty bed or face empty days and weeks, an empty life; I can't live that way. I'll go with you to America, I'll do whatever you want, whatever we must do, but I won't let you go."

"Oh." Her eyes were wide. "You really will? This will really happen? Oh, Li . . ." She kissed him, again and again. "We'll be together; oh, how wonderful, *wonderful* . . ." She sat up. "I feel so *light,* as if nothing could keep me down, ever again. I can't believe this . . . it's so incredibly wonderful . . . I can't *wait. . . .* Oh. How long will it take? I haven't the faintest idea what we have to do. Can you just buy a ticket and come with me tomorrow? No, it's after midnight, isn't it? Today. Can you come home with me today? You have a passport, don't you?"

"Yes, but it is not enough; I need a visa." He propped up fringed pillows and they sat back beneath the heavy coverlet, holding hands. "It is not simple to get into your country. Your government is afraid that if the doors were opened, millions of Chinese would flood America, needing to be taken care of."

"But you're a professional; you can support yourself. And you'd be married to me."

"That is not enough."

"It has to be!"

"There are other ways." They were practical and brisk, now, as if planning a business deal. Li smiled. *A joint venture.* "My company could send me to America to inspect construction sites, learn new techniques. That is done all the time. Or I could join a professional group touring the U.S., or a delegation of scientists. Something like that. Either way, it would be easy to get a temporary visa."

"Temporary? How temporary?"

"Usually about a month. But then if we married, I would simply stay."

"Then it's all right! Oh, but how long does that take?"

"To get a visa? A few weeks."

"That's too long."

"Isn't that how long it took to get yours from the Chinese embassy in Washington?"

"Yes, but I wasn't in a hurry. This is different. I don't want to wait. And something could happen, your government could decide to crack down on engineers or something, and you couldn't get out at all. Li, there must be some other way."

"There is, but it is not easy. We could get married here, in China. I know someone who did it and it was difficult but not impossible. I believe he could help me arrange it. If we were married, I might be able to get a visa more quickly, and then we would leave together."

"Oh, let's do that. I'd rather be married here anyway."

"And have it finished, do you mean? So even if your family objects, it would be too late."

"No, no, that's not what I meant; I only thought it would be so much simpler . . ." She frowned. "It would just be simpler," she repeated firmly. "How long would it take? I think I could stay for a few more days if we could do it soon."

"We probably could arrange a marriage in three or four days. But getting a visa after that would still take at least two weeks. Nothing in China involving paperwork gets done quickly."

"I can't stay that long." She looked at him closely. "You've researched this. Or does everyone know it?"

"Most of us know most of it. But, yes, I did some research."

"You didn't tell me."

"We were not talking about this; we were avoiding it. And I could not be sure that we would get this far."

She kissed him. "This far and much farther. A lifetime farther." Her eyes were bright. "I can't believe it: you're coming with me! We'll be together, we don't have to say goodbye . . . oh, Li, I love you, I can't wait for us to live together—"

"What will your children think?"

"They'll be surprised and then they'll love you. They'll teach you American slang and they'll spout Chinese phrases at school and impress their friends. And you'll love them, Li, they're so bright and loving and funny."

"I would love them because they are yours, even if they were not all those things. And your parents? What will they think?"

"They'll be surprised."

"An understatement, surely."

She smiled. "They'll be astonished."

"And unhappy. Angry. Furious. They will think you have brought the enemy into your life. They will think I have hypnotized you, to get you to do this in such a short time. They will be sure I do not love you, that I am using you to get to America. They will not speak to me and they will cut you out of their will."

"No. Good heavens, how dramatic. You're right: they'll be unhappy; they won't understand it, but they love me and they don't want to lose me or the children, so they'll spend time with us, and after a while they'll love you, too."

"They will never love me."

"Well, that's probably true. But they'll respect you when they see that I'm happy; they might even like you if they let themselves."

"And change their minds about the great devil communism?"

"No, I'm sure they won't. But you're not a communist."

"I was."

"They won't understand that, but they'll explain it away by saying you were too young to know what you were doing."

They laughed, and Li thought yet again how wonderfully close they were. Molded by totally different cultures, they were more harmonious than he was with many Chinese friends, even women he had slept with and cared for. *Still, her parents will be a problem. Her father, especially.*

"You're worried about them," Miranda said. "Especially my father. It will be all right, Li, I promise. I know them. They've got lots of stock ideas about the world, but what they truly care about is family, and when they see how happy the four of us are, they'll find a way to make that fit with their other ideas. I don't know how they'll do it, but they will, because they need to feel sure of everything, and if my life doesn't match what they've always believed, they'll make up stories to make it match. To make their world orderly."

"That is a harsh picture you paint."

"No, just honest. I love them, but I understand them. They're good people; they're just afraid of anything they don't understand. But they'll try to understand you because they won't have any choice. Oh, you know, we could build you an office in my house, our house, and ask my father to help. He built an addition on his house so he'll recognize how good you are, and if you listen to his suggestions—you don't have to take them; just listen—he'll be a happy man. Communism is small potatoes to my father next to construction."

"Small potatoes?"

"Inconsequential. You're going to need a car, too and my father knows every dealer in town. What kind do you like?"

"I don't know. There are not many choices in China."

"There are in America. You'll have to get used to that." She kissed him again. "I feel so excited. As if I'm a little girl again, pushing away the days to my birthday."

"All the days will be birthdays," Li said, keeping sudden doubts out of his voice. "For all of us." He looked at his watch. "One o'clock. Can you call your family? You can tell them you're staying awhile longer, even if we don't know exactly how long."

She calculated the time. "It's ten in the morning there, on Saturday; Lisa has a ceramics class and Adam will be at soccer, with my parents watching. I'll call in a couple of hours; they should be home by then. But I can't stay here too long, Li; Talia expects me to report on the trip."

"Then you will go first, and I will follow as soon as possible. As long as we are married, it will be all right."

"You said three or four days. Couldn't we do it sooner?"

"I'll know tomorrow, when I talk to my friend. How calmly and coolly we are talking about marriage."

"Yes, it's very strange. As if we're discussing a business deal." She smiled. "A joint venture."

He kissed her. "Would you like some dinner?"

"Yes. What shall we make?"

"Whatever takes as many ingredients as possible. I'll have to start cleaning out my cupboards." He felt an odd sinking within him. *Cleaning out my cupboards. Because I am leaving my house forever.*

"What will you do with your house?" Miranda asked.

"Rent it, perhaps. No, probably sell it. A friend can do that for me. These courtyard houses are hard to find; it should be easy to sell."

An unexpected silence fell between them. Wearing his silk robes, they went to the kitchen and made dinner without speaking, the only sound the rhythmic chopping and scraping of cleavers and the hiss of stir-fry. Li put some music on so the silence would not seem oppressive as they ate. They talked sporadically as they cleaned up and returned to the living room, and then, exhausted, holding each other, they slept on the deep velvet couch until Li sat up with a start and looked at his watch. Three o'clock in the morning. The rain still fell, a steady drumming, the only sound in the stillness of his house.

He lay back, holding Miranda close. Her body curved to his, even in sleep, and she murmured, "I love you," without waking. Li listened to her steady breathing. *I feel so excited. As if I'm a little girl again, pushing away the days to my birthday.* He tested himself for excitement. What was wrong with him that he was not excited? Everything he had dreamed of was coming together—his father's country, his imagined home, a new life, and Miranda, a love of wonder and exultation—as if a sorcerer had invoked magic words, and made it appear solid, within his reach. Then why did it waver in his mind like a mirage, evaporating into the sky?

He tried to picture the landscape he had dreamed of for most of his life. He pictured himself and Miranda coming out of her house, crossing the wooden bridge over the small stream running through her front yard, walking down the long street with its leafy parkway sloping all the way to the center of Boulder Colorado. He pictured them in her kitchen, her dining room, her bedroom, laughing, making love, holding each other through the night until the skies brightened and made visible the mountains nearby. He could picture that, and excitement flickered within him. *There we are, at home, making our own life, and everything about it is good.*

He pictured himself on construction sites: American union workers in hard hats, American supervisors, American techniques, and Yuan Li working on buildings in Colorado, not in Beijing and Shanghai and Hangzhou, where everything was familiar, which rules to follow and which to break with impunity, which people to trust and which to bribe, the very fabric of each working day.

He pictured himself in someone else's company, working with strangers instead of with the contractors and suppliers with whom he met once a month, at dinner, to compare techniques, solve problems, trade stories, deal with emerging labor problems, and share new ways to outwit the bureaucracy: contractors who, like himself, were changing the skylines of his country.

He pictured himself halfway around the world from Sheng and Shuiying, whom he loved and who suddenly were drawing close to him, and from his granddaughter Ming, whom he adored, and his grandson Rongji who now, it seemed would become more a part of his life.

He pictured himself in America, surrounded by newspapers and magazines in English, street signs and shop windows in English, television and movies in English, the talk on streets and buses and trains, in conversations at work, in dinner parties at private homes, all, all in the flat monotone of English, the very air American, not Chinese.

He willed himself to see America as the fulfillment of all his dreams, the realization of all that he had ever said was essential for his happiness, and for the first time he understood that there were too many dreams for any one landscape to be large enough, or fertile enough, to sustain and nurture all of them.

But, still, as Miranda stirred in his arms, he willed himself again to see her country as his, the place where he would settle and be complete. And what he saw was Yuan Li, trying to merge with the American landscape, skimming the surface of America, putting down roots in Miranda's house but nowhere else. Yuan Li, torn from the fabric of China.

And he knew he could not do it.

My love, my love, he thought, his face buried in Miranda's hair. I don't know if I can tell you this. But I cannot tell you anything else.

He took a long breath and kissed her eyes and lips, and she woke, looking into his eyes. "I fell asleep. Is it morning?"

"A little after three o'clock."

"Oh, I have to call my mother."

"Not yet. Wait."

"Why? It's lunch time there; the best time."

"Not yet," Li said again. He tried to say more, to find some words to move them forward to what he had to say, but no words came. Miranda's eyes searched his, and he saw their clear look become puzzlement, then slow comprehension, and then wild dismay.

"You've changed your mind! Li? You're not coming with me?"

"My love, I cannot—"

"Don't say it!" She pulled away, back and back, until she was at the other end of the couch, her eyes wide and bright with tears. She tried to stand up, but the tangles of her robe held her fast and she fought to straighten them, pulling them from under her, fumbling with the sleeves and the sash until she cried, "Oh, I can't do this!" and she began to sob.

Li thought his heart would break. He gently straightened her robe, closing it around her and tying the sash, then put his arms around her and held her. She looked up, tendrils of wet hair clinging to her cheeks. "Why?"

"Because I cannot turn my back on everything, any more than you can. Come, sit with me. I will explain, if I can." She curled up beside him in the deep cushions, her head on his chest. She was shivering. "You're cold; I'll turn up the heat."

"I'm not cold. I'm afraid."

He held her close. She seemed smaller and more fragile than in the passionate hours they had shared these past days, when she had met him with a ferocity that equaled his, and his arms encircled her now as if to ward off anything that might crush that fragility. And how could he do that when they were thousands of miles apart?

"I can't," he murmured, the words breaking from him, and he did not know what he meant: protect her, leave her, stay with her.

"What did you say?"

He rested his cheek on her head. "All the things that make me what I am are here. My family, my work, my country. I cannot cut them out of me as if they are separate pieces that fall away and leave me unchanged, because I would not be whole without them. I thought they did not matter, or at least not enough, but they do matter; they are the forces that shape me and drive me. Especially now, when I am beginning to rediscover my family, and

China, too. So much is happening now, the changes in the economy, in the government—"

"Your government! What do you care about your government?" She sat up angrily. "You use your government as a role model for criminal acts! Oh, I'm sorry, I'm sorry; I know you did those things to save yourself, and Sheng; I know you're not proud of them, but that's the point. Your government makes you do things you don't believe in."

"Sometimes. But change is everywhere, now. People call this the Beijing Autumn because—"

"I know why." Miranda was frowning, remembering. "Sima Ting, the Chinese woman I met in Boulder, talked about that. And . . . other things."

"What other things?"

Slowly, wishing she had not begun this, Miranda said, "She said I couldn't understand her longing for home because I *was* home. She said her bones were Chinese and they hurt when they weren't touching the ground in China. That she could never truly become an American any more than I truly could become a Chinese. But, Li, others do it! Millions of people all over the world move to new countries, and are happy there and never want to go back."

"Some can do it," he agreed. "And some cannot. Miranda, there are so many reasons. . . . How can I leave Sheng? My father left me; can I do the same to my son?"

"You were a child! He's a grown man!"

"There are many kinds of need. Age may change them but it does not wipe them out. And Shuiying will need help when her husband gets into trouble, and whom can she turn to? I promised myself once that I would not abandon either of them as my father did me. And people in my company depend on me. And there are other things I have to do . . ."

"Like what? March in Tiananmen Square?"

"I don't know. Whatever seems the right thing to do."

"Nothing is the right thing in China!" Her hands twisted in her lap and once again tears were in her eyes. "You'll be arrested and spend years in jail and how will that help your family and your work and your country? You'd be better off in America, with me!"

"Possibly. But it seems to me that I would be a hollow man in America—"

"Even with me?"

"Even with you, because I would have torn this life out of myself." He took Miranda's hand between his. "It is not only Sheng and Shuiying. I would like to see Ming grow up, and Rongji; I like being a grandfather, you know; and perhaps I could make their lives easier in what will be difficult times. Isn't that what all grandparents hope to do?"

Miranda was silent. She cannot answer that, Li thought sadly. How can she tell me I am wrong to stay with my family?

"All our dreams," she murmured. "None of them strong enough—"

"They are," Li insisted. "Listen to me. They are strong enough, but why must there be only one way to reach them? Stay with me, Miranda. Everything that we can build in America we can build here."

They sat, looking away from each other, while the rain swelled to a deluge. The skies are weeping for us, Li thought, as we are weeping inside. *With your rejoicing comes my laughter; with your sadness, start my tears. Do you not see that you and I are as the branches of one tree?* Yes, oh yes, we are, he thought, but perhaps it is not enough.

A shudder tore through Miranda's body. "I can't. I can't live here. I can't imagine bringing my children to a country where you get used to being followed, *you accept it.* There's someone outside now, isn't there? Waiting for us. And we both know it and we hardly think about it; it's so normal. Your phones are tapped, your rooms are bugged, your mail is opened, and you accept it all. And you do things you hate, illegal things that aren't like you at all, because that's the way the system works. I can't imagine living that way. I can't imagine bringing up my children in a country that takes all that for granted." She paused, then slowly shook her head. "I thought it didn't matter where we lived; all I wanted was to be with you. But I can't picture myself living in China; I can't see myself leaving America. I'm too used to freedom, Li. I'm too used to having a government that protects its people instead of attacking them, and people who aren't afraid to criticize it often and loudly and passionately. And I like having friends and family and familiar places nearby, and customs I understand and a language that embraces me instead of pushing me away. America is complicated and there are a lot of things about it I'd like to change, but it's my home and it's where I belong. I don't belong here, Li. You would fit in, in the United States, far better than I would fit in here."

"That is probably true."

"But it isn't enough."

"No."

He went to the kitchen and when he returned with a pot of tea and two cups, she was sitting as he had left her, curled up on the couch, enfolded in his robe, her gaze far away. Li filled the cups and handed one to her. "Oh, it is so good," she said, sipping it. "I wonder if I can find Dragon Well tea in Boulder."

"I'll send you as much as you want."

"No, I think we shouldn't write or call, or send packages—" Silent tears ran down her cheeks, and she let them, looking straight ahead, her wet face shining in the light.

I cannot do this, Li thought. I cannot let this happen. And it is up to me, because she is right; everything would be easier in America. All I have to do is say I will come with her.

He opened his mouth to say the words, but they did not come, and he knew then that they never would. Where, only the afternoon before, there had been no space between their bodies, no room for a wedge to pry or a wall to rise, now there was an ocean, and eternity.

Miranda looked at her watch. "Four o'clock." Her voice was dull and flat. "What time should we leave for the airport?"

He let out his breath, tears stinging his eyes. "Seven-thirty."

She nodded. "I'll get ready."

Too early, he started to say; we have hours. We could be holding each other, making love, giving ourselves more to remember and keep in our hearts for all the time ahead. But he held back the words. What they had to do now, for these few hours, was get used to the idea that she would leave and he would stay and all the dreams would shatter.

Miranda stood, and as she walked past

him toward the bedroom she rested her hand on his head. For a long moment they were very still: Li sitting on the couch, all his being focused on the light touch of her hand; Miranda standing beside him, her fingers alive with awareness of his body, his breath, his heart. And then she went on, into the bedroom. She let the robe drop to the floor and stepped into the shower, standing with her head back as the hot water sluiced her body. Washing away China, she thought, and began to cry, tears and water streaming down her face.

She dressed in the burgundy blouse with the gold monkeys, the scarf and bracelet Li had given her, and the black jacket from Meiyun's shop. *Cross-cultural.* She could see Meiyun's smile as she said it. But I'm not, Miranda thought. I wish I were, but I'm not, and neither is Li. Did we know that, when we began? Probably not. But it wouldn't have mattered if we had. I would not have missed these ten days for anything.

In the living room, Li was standing beside his scholar's rock, his back to her. "Are you looking for wisdom?" she asked.

"We have none, you and I; we're foolish people, agonizing over something as small as a love affair, an infinitesimal speck in the universe."

He turned. "You said we were important. Small but important. You said love is important."

"I was wrong. The world will go its own indifferent way, and never pause to notice that we're on opposite sides of it." She came closer and saw that his face was streaked with tears. "Oh, Li, my darling, don't cry, I can't bear it." She put her arms around him and they held each other, faces buried in each other. "My love, my love," Miranda murmured. "I know we're foolish, small and foolish, but it is so hard; it hurts so much . . ."

Li led Miranda to the couch, and began to talk. He talked to push away thought and to hold back time. He talked to keep back his tears, and hers. He talked to fill the silence that he knew would be the only thing left in this room when she was gone. "I want to tell you a Chinese legend about a cowherd and a weaving maiden. Every July there is a festival in their honor. This is the story.

"The Emperor of Heaven had a beautiful daughter, excellent at weaving. One day she descended to earth and fell deeply in love with a herdsman, and married him. But the Queen Mother commanded her to return home, and she obeyed and flew off to the sky. The herdsman attempted to follow, but before he could reach her, the Queen Mother took a golden hairpin from her hair and with it drew a great river between them. We call it the Milky Way. The weaving maiden now sits on one side of the river, and the herdsman sits on the other side. The two lovers are allowed to meet only once a year, on the seventh night of the seventh moon. At that time, flocks of magpies fly close together to form a bridge so the maiden can cross the river and be reunited with her husband."

He took her hand. "So the universe is not too big for lovers. There are so many like us that this story was born. Wherever we are, and for always, our love will be a bridge between us, and I will cross it in my thoughts every day, and so will you, and we will meet in the middle and embrace and be together, as we have dreamed."

She smiled wryly. "I can think of lots of better ways to embrace and be together."

"Well, yes, so can I, but we cannot seem to manage them."

"We could, if—" Her restless gaze wandered the room, stopping at a small sculpture of a tiny butterfly in pale blue jade fluttering on a spray of white jade chrysanthemums. She picked it up. "Butterflies and chrysanthemums: longevity and everlasting love."

"Yes. You remembered."

"I will remember everything of this trip. You've filled your home with symbols of longevity and eternity, but you won't give us more than ten days."

"Neither will you," he said quietly.

She nodded, and reached out to replace the sculpture. "Take it with you," Li said.

"Oh, may I? I like it so much."

"I wish I could give you everything in this room. What else would you like?"

"You won't give me the scholar's rock," she said smiling.

"No, my love, that must stay here. But you may come back any time, whenever you are in China, to visit it."

"I will never come back to China."

So final, he thought. Such awful finality. "Not even to work with Meiyun?"

"We'll find other ways; she comes to New York and Chicago; I could meet her there."

"And what else will you do, when you go back?"

"I'm not sure; there are a few things . . ." Her gaze dropped to the sculpture in her hand. "I wish I could give you something as special."

"Ah, but you can." He laid his hand on her hair, lacing his fingers through the short curls, still damp from her shower. "It is foolish and old fashioned—I thought it only happened in books—but still . . ."

"Oh." A small smile lit her face. "Yes, if I can ask the same of you. I'll have to buy a locket."

"So will I."

He took a small scissors from his desk, and gently cut a strand of Miranda's hair. Then he bent his head and she did the same with his. She closed her hand over the brown strands, remembering the feel of his hair in her fingers while his tongue probed the deepest parts of her, and the glints of light in it as he bent to take her breast in his mouth; and Li held the fair, silky curls in his palm, holding with them the scent of her, the smooth clinging of her skin against his, her mouth opening to meet his, her smile and her laughter, and the lilt of her voice when she was happy.

"A locket," he murmured. "A gold one, just for this."

He kissed Miranda and said, "I must get ready," and quickly went to his bedroom, to his shower, to get past this moment. He stood for a long time beneath the hot water, not thinking, not dreaming, soaking up the heat, then put on a white shirt and brown slacks and the cashmere jacket she had given him. When he came back, she said, "How handsome you look."

"It is the jacket."

"It is the man inside the jacket. The wonderful man inside the jacket."

He drew a long breath. "Tell me what you will do when you get home."

"Oh, there are a lot of things. Some people at the University have been asking me to teach classes in textiles and design; I never thought I was good enough, but now I would like to do it. And I'm going to tell Talia I want to hire a new group of young people, and be in charge of it, to design a different line from anything we've done. And I'll work with Meiyun; I have so many ideas for . . ."

She was turning the butterfly around and around in her fingers, and Li watched the changing expressions on her face: from bleakness to anticipation.

"Do you remember the birds in their cages?" he asked. "When they were brought outside for fresh air, you said—"

"That they were happy, and the men, too, being free."

"Yes, but also you said that all of us live in cages of one kind or another. And now you have escaped from yours."

He watched her struggle with it: the possibilities of a new kind of life now that she was no longer locked in by old fears, but at the same time her concern that if she showed it, he would be hurt.

And it did hurt, but he would not let her see that. From now on, she must only look ahead.

"You and Meiyun will make a powerful team. Soon I will see your designs on CNN, with Elsa Klensch so excited about the newest name in fashion."

"Thank you," Miranda said. "That is the most wonderful thing you could do for me. Not only that you made me stronger—"

"No, no, you became stronger by yourself. You have conquered China."

Through the tears still streaking her cheeks, Miranda burst out laughing. "China is blithely unaware of it."

"Well, then, you conquered your terror, of China and so much else."

"With you. I couldn't have done it without you."

"And now you can do anything."

"Except be with you."

He clenched his fist, waiting for the pain to subside. "I meant at home, finding new adventures. You can expand your life, even at home, if you have courage and trust in yourself." He chuckled, hiding the pain that gnawed him with each word that sent her farther into a future where he could not follow. "You will make Boulder Colorado an exciting place."

She touched his face. "You are the best person I know, the best person in the world. To give me so much."

"I gave you what you have given me. The discovery that I can love, more deeply than I ever imagined. And that you and I could become part of each other, and that it will never disappear."

Miranda gave a small smile. "I hope Tang Po was right."

"In what?" Li asked.

She closed her eyes, remembering. "He said we all have disappointments and losses, and sometimes they vanish, and sometimes not. And then he said, 'If not, we find ways to adjust and make a life. A different life, perhaps, but not necessarily a worse one.' "

"Very different," Li murmured. "That may be wise, but right now it seems bleak."

After a moment, Miranda said, "And what will you do for this different life, tomorrow and all the days after that?"

"I don't know. There are many choices. Imagine: choices in China. Somehow, I will help China change. Whatever that takes; however I may be useful. Sheng knows more about the inner workings of the government than I do; perhaps he will have suggestions." He was silent, gazing beyond Miranda, beyond the protecting walls of his house and thinking of a life of action and attempted change in China. It

was not a pleasant prospect. But how can I
be fearful, when Miranda has conquered
China?

"You'll find someone to love," Miranda
said suddenly. "Someone to share all the
things you care about."

"No."

"You shouldn't live alone, Li. You have so
much to give someone."

"That someone is you."

"But not forever."

"Why not? How many times do we find
love in one lifetime?"

There was a long silence, and then she
rose and went to the window. "The rain has
stopped. And the sky seems a little
brighter."

"It is no longer weeping for us?"

She smiled. "No. There is a time to stop
weeping."

He looked at his watch. "We must leave
soon. No, wait, wait. I have no picture of
you. In all these days, we never. . . . Wait, I
must have a picture." Taking a camera from
a nearby chest, he began to circle her, the
shutter clicking again and again, while she
gave herself to his film, to his eyes, to him.
"You have a certain smile; all your own," he

said. "You did not have it when you arrived, but now it is so much of what you are, I will see it before me all my life."

She took from her purse the small camera she had used for souvenir photos throughout her trip. "Only four left," she murmured, and took more time than he had, planning her few shots while he stood in place, trying to imagine his photograph in her home, perhaps in a silver frame, perhaps in her bedroom or in the sunroom where she worked, perhaps in her wallet. In all the places where he would have hers. Wherever his eye might light in the course of a day or night.

When she was finished, she said, "Now we should go," and Li nodded. He would have suggested breakfast, another half hour of talking, but she was right: it was time for them to go.

He took her overnight bag to the car, and when she did not follow, he went back and found her standing still, wrapped in the hush of the living room, breathing in the faint scent of sandalwood, memorizing the furniture, the art, the whorls of the scholar's rock, the soft palette of the rugs. He saw it all, with her, and thought, It will never look this way again because I will not be seeing it through her eyes.

At the airport, while his driver carried her luggage inside, Li and Miranda walked to the ticket line. It was not a line, but a swarming crowd of Chinese tourists and Li looked at them with bitterness. The throng shoved and elbowed and thrust forward and, almost absently, Miranda shoved back, moving forward as if parting the waves. She looked at him and they began to laugh.

"But I couldn't do it if my knight in shining armor hadn't come to my rescue, that first night," she said, and their hands touched, and Li wanted her so wildly that he had to fight to keep his hands to himself, his body still, his face bland. There was a roaring in his ears; he wanted to pick her up and run from that place, run for hours, for days, until they found shelter, where they would be alone, and safe.

But suddenly it was time to board the plane, and they faced each other at the gate, in the midst of another milling crowd. "I love you," Li said.

Miranda laid her hand along his face and kissed him, and he held her and they kissed as if they had indeed found a space that was theirs alone, a space that was not China, or anywhere else. "I love you, Li," said Miranda. "I love you, and I will come to you on our bridge, I promise."

"I promise," he echoed, and their hands touched, clinging, one last time, and then she turned to go. She gave her ticket to the gate attendant, and beneath the noises of the crowd she thought she heard Li's voice, she was sure she heard Li's voice. "Be happy, my love. Be happy in your home." She turned to see him, but all she saw were crowds, Chinese crowds; he had been swallowed up by them, and she could not see him at all.

"Miss, you must get on," urged the attendant, and Miranda walked into the dark passage that led to the plane, and when they rose from the ground and banked to turn toward the ocean, and America, she did not look at the city falling away beneath her; she closed her eyes and saw Li's face, his eyes on hers, telling her he loved her, and his smile.

Glossary and Pronunciation of Chinese Terms

Yuan Li	Yuan Lee
Yuan Sheng	Yuan Shung
Yuan Shuiying	Yuan Shway-ying
Ye Meiyun	Yee May-yeu win
Pan Chao	Pan Chow
Meng Enli	Mung En-li
Feng Zhiwen	Fung Jer-wen
Beihai	Bay-hi
Xisi Bei	Suh-see Bay
Xiujiang	Shee-oojee-ahng
Xiushui Silk Market	Shee-oo-shway
Liulichang	Lee-ooleechong
Empress Cixi	Tse-shee

Biao zi yang de	Bee-ow dzu yong doh
gao shi	(shit) gow shur
gou zaizi	(mutts/bastards) goo-dzeye-zuh
za zhong	(bastards)
guanxi	(connections) guan-shee
lao tian	(good God) lao tee-an
meishi	may shur
youtiao	yootee-ow
zai-jiang	(goodbye) dzeye-jee-en
ni hao	(hello/good day) nee-how
xi-xi	(thank you) shee-eh shee-eh